THERE'S
NO
COMING
BACK *from*
THIS

THERE'S NO COMING BACK from THIS

A Novel

ANN GARVIN

LAKE UNION
PUBLISHING

Text copyright © 2023 by Ann Garvin
All rights reserved.

Published by Lake Union Publishing, Seattle

www.apub.com

Amazon, the Amazon logo, and Lake Union Publishing are trademarks of Amazon.com, Inc., or its affiliates.

ISBN-13: 9781542033596 (paperback)
ISBN-13: 9781542033589 (digital)

Cover design and illustration by Kimberly Glyder
Cover image: © Nisian Hughes / Getty

Printed in the United States of America

For Julie Ann and Meghan Erin

To be nobody-but-yourself—in a world which is doing its best, night and day, to make you everybody but yourself—means to fight the hardest battle which any human being can fight and never stop fighting.

—*e. e. cummings*

She kept her cards so close even she couldn't see them.

—*"Dear McCracken," Bug Hunter*

CHAPTER ONE

TEAM LIVELY

I half jogged, half walked to catch up with my seventeen-year-old daughter in Chicago's O'Hare Airport, giving myself a pep talk. *You are good at pivoting. You are the pivot. Be the pivot.* I dodged a drug-sniffing dog who lifted his head as I slid by. For all I knew, my nervous energy could be detected, and I'd be labeled as a threat to national security. If I was detained and strip-searched, my ungroomed body hair alone would trigger alarms. No one would be the same after that—and that was the last thing in the world I wanted. The very last thing.

If I kept my anxiety in check, my secrets stowed, Robyn would spend her summer unaware of the mess I'd made of our lives. By the time she returned for college, I'd have a solid plan for the IRS debts, our house back in our name, and money for her to start college. The only evidence of a struggle would be a few gray hairs on my head, which I could dye.

"Robyn, did you weigh your luggage? It costs a ton if it goes over fifty pounds."

"It's at forty-eight," she said over her shoulder. "I was careful."

Of course she'd checked. We were cautious people who didn't like surprises.

It was May, and Robyn had graduated valedictorian along with sixteen other valedictorians—don't get me started. And on graduation day she'd been brimming with confidence and possibility. Today, though, she looked young and vulnerable. When a neighbor recommended her for a nanny position in the Big Apple, the job sounded like the perfect summer experience before starting nursing school in the fall. Now, faced with the unknowns of a big city, a new family, and three solid months away from home, she was like a cat skidding on a slick floor toward a swimming pool.

"It's normal to be nervous about change," I said, tucking a strand of her silky hair behind her ear.

"I'm going to miss everything," she said, her brown eyes wide.

Robyn didn't realize how true that statement was. She'd miss IRS calls where I'd use my high-pitched stress voice begging for dispensation, pleas to the mortgage lender for a loan deferment, and the final gasps of our family business finally being kicked to the curb. She'd miss witnessing her mother trying again and again to get in touch with the accountant who'd pocketed all our money and applying for jobs that wouldn't make a dent in the debt in time for anything.

I needed to focus on what my daughter was really saying—we weren't talking about me here. She'd miss tubing with her friends for the hundredth time, sitting in basements giggling and flirting with the same boys she'd gone to grade school with. High school was over and adulthood was on the way, and I knew she felt that loss, as I did.

"You'll miss some things, but all your buddies have a job. Nobody is as free as you imagine." Her best friends were going to be camp counselors, lifeguards, waitresses at resorts, and Robyn would have her own experience away from her mother's failings.

"I could help you put the business online," she said. "If I stayed I'd have more time to pack for school. Maybe work in a nursing home instead of going so far away." Robyn's face flushed. "I'll miss you so much, Mom."

"I'll be right here when you return. Everything will be the same as when you left." And there it was, two simple sentences uttered as if they weren't a vow. Two promises I knew I'd do everything in my power to keep.

The irony on which my future hung, at least my future as a person who didn't live in federal prison, was this. I'd hired an accountant to help during Robyn's busy final years of high school. I'd agreed to chair committees, host dinners, be a present, helpful mother. I knew that Dawna Klump, CPA, wanted a wine fridge and a trip to Turks and Caicos, but what I didn't know was that she refused to pay my taxes and pocketed that cash to get them. Now, the IRS had unceremoniously drained my every bank account, and Robyn's college accounts, to pay federal business and property taxes. On top of all of that, the university bursar's office needed a down payment to hold my daughter's place in nursing school, and state business and property tax liens were sure to come.

Robyn glanced at me uncertainly; maybe she felt my energy dip. So I beamed support and said, "Go on, honey. Step up to the counter," and I watched her move to check in. A large man with an enormous set of Louis Vuitton luggage stepped in front of her, and I suppressed a violent urge to haul him back by the collar.

"It's okay, honey. Just let him go ahead. You're next," I said and gestured her forward.

Getting Robyn in the air was the only thing that kept me from calling any and all hotlines and hyperventilating. I knew I'd have trouble fixing our finances with her watching and wondering how I'd let everything fall apart. I couldn't bear that she might experience all the insecurity I'd had as a child.

While Robyn hefted her luggage onto the scale and handed the Delta agent her ID, I surreptitiously breathed into the neck of my shirt like it was a paper bag.

"Forty-eight pounds!" Robyn said with a thumbs-up.

I blew an overly juicy raspberry of relief, wiped my mouth, and smiled.

A woman pushing a luggage cart trundled past me, suitcases piled high, clutching the hand of a small child. That mother would appreciate my secrets, my desire to protect my child from hardship. She might even understand how it all came unraveled. Or at least, how I became the last person to know that my life had burned to the ground.

Last week I'd squeezed in a haircut, and when I tried to pay with my debit card, the woman with the purple hair and a stud in her forehead said, "Insufficient funds," as if she'd seen it all before and was exhausted by the hustlers and cheats of the world. I fished out cash, paid, and in my car called the bank. After hitting a punishing online menu of options, I prematurely spoke to a recording, another recording, and finally a person. "Says here that the US Treasury drained your account."

"Why would they do that?"

"Well, I suspect it was back taxes. That's how they roll. I've seen it before. Not much, though."

"You have? They can take everything?"

"Do you do your own taxes? Does your husband do them? Ask him about—"

"There's no husband! What year is this?" I said so loudly, the person on the phone said, "Ma'am. Please."

"I think Dawna Klump should pay," I said.

But it was like my dad said to me all my life: "Money talks. Nobody cares what you think." I'd argued with him once, saying, "If Mom were here, she'd care." I was nine years old, and she'd dropped me off at school and left our lives for good.

"If she cared, she would have stayed," he'd said, and yanked a brush through my tangled hair until I yelped.

Sweating, dry mouthed, and shaking in the car, I'd called the IRS number and croaked out a question, and the catastrophic answer hit me sideways. "We sent a notice that your accounts would be garnished. You didn't respond. You have considerable back taxes."

"No I don't," I said, certain that I didn't.

And the person on the end of the line said, "Indeed you do," as if we were doing a Rat Pack song and dance. I called my best friend, Chelsea, and gulp-cried so unintelligibly into the phone she picked me up in the parking lot at All in the Family Hair Care.

I'd tried explaining to the IRS, mortgage lender, and university in a barely concealed, low-key panic that my business had failed. "No one needed in-person coupons when there was no in-person shopping," I'd said. The business limped along; I'd let the accountant go but not soon enough. "Not soon enough, I tell you!"

"Robyn!" I called across the terminal, not alarmingly so, not a 911 call, no, just loud enough to alert her that she was standing in the first-class line. "Rob. Grab a name tag for your carry-on," I said, using her nickname to soften the parental summons. She nodded, filled out the tag, and looped it onto her backpack. My heart clutched at how much she'd grown, how much she had to learn.

I'd use every James Bond tool in my long and storied career of being a woman to get us back on track, for her. This was the *as God is my witness, fist shaking to the heavens* thought I had seconds before a massive people mover swerved in my direction.

The driver didn't zig while I zagged. I knew he saw me—we'd made eye contact at a crucial moment and he did not zig.

"No! Oh no," I said and dropped my hot venti latte, taking the full hit of the dark liquid on my overly optimistic white jeans. "Excuse me!" I shouted as the vehicle scooted away. "Sorry, sorry, sorry!" I said to travelers giving me a wide berth, as if I hadn't watched where I was going. I'd been pigeon-toed growing up; it cleared up as I matured but reappeared in times of stress and fatigue. Believe me when I say I watch where I'm going.

"Oh, Mom. Yuck." Robyn sighed, footsteps away. "It's okay. I know you're stressed."

"What? No I'm not. I mean I'll miss you, but you'll be home soon."

"Maybe I shouldn't do this."

"No!" I said but not too loudly. "I'm not losing it. I just didn't see that thing coming." I pulled a small microfiber towel from my bag and patted my legs. "See. All good."

"Are you sure? Do you need to smell my hair?" she teased. I loved to sniff her signature scent. We joked it was my aromatherapy. Calmed me in an instant—not this time, unless her hair smelled like a horse tranquilizer.

"No. Yes. But later I'll go into your room and smell your pillow."

"Weirdo," Robyn said, watching me, a sweet-and-sour look on her face. "Remember when I was little and made you promise to be my roommate in college?"

I knew what she was doing. Pulling attention from the coffee mess. We were a team, she and I. Robyn and Poppy Lively. Team Lively.

"I'm sure you still want me as your roomie. At the end of the summer, we'll buy matching shower caddies and pajamas. For sure, the dorm will let me move in."

"I don't think the college will mind. You're nice," she said, and picked up the empty cup and tossed it flawlessly in the trash.

"Nothing but hoop," I said, using Quidditch humor for a little nostalgic nudge, nudge.

Robyn had that wistful look kids get in their eyes before they go off on their first adventure: *Didn't we have fun, you and I?*

And we did. I'd made sure of it. When my girl wanted a Quidditch team slash *Harry Potter* book club in fifth grade, I created the reading schedule, found a field, made the brooms, and called the other mothers—who did the same for their kids. I was there for the plays, sports, dances, and fundraisers that sent goats to families in Zambia. I always said yes.

"You want to go to the bathroom and clean up, Mom? Then you can walk me to security."

"I can wait," I said. "You have the *emergency only* credit card, right?"

She nodded, half listening, checking her phone like every kid her age.

"What should you use it for?" I asked. I'd learned from the multiple conversations I'd had with Amy from IRS customer service that our credit cards were not frozen, but she warned me that using them made everything worse. "Interest and all," she'd said conversationally.

"Manicures?" Robyn glanced at me slyly. "Just kidding. Safety or starvation," she said.

Good. Robyn saw this as just another mother-daughter moment, not a harbinger of future jail time. There were jokes to be tossed, fun to be had.

"Here's a little cash," I said to show her that while I was not one hundred percent myself, cash money was not the problem—even though it was the only problem.

"No, Mom. I don't need it." She turned slightly away.

"What's gotten into you? Put it separate from your card. So if you lose one, you'll have the other."

The tip of her nose reddened, and she tucked the money into a side pocket, studied me, and I kissed her on her smooth forehead.

"Don't go soft on me, sweetie. Off you go."

I watched her find the boarding pass on her phone, remembering how, as a toddler, she'd pretend our square digital kitchen timer was a cell phone.

For a moment the pinch of that memory, of missing her, took over. In a matter of months she'd be home, attending college down the road, coming home for her favorite lasagna, semester breaks, bringing her friends with her, and I would be there for her as always. It would be fine. But that couldn't happen if there wasn't a home to come home to. If I had to sell it right away.

We moved in the stream of colorful people toward the security line. Before entering, Robyn shouldered her carry-on bag.

"I guess this is it," she said, a tremor in her voice.

We hugged, and I spoke in her ear: "You are Robyn Lively. Your name is your cheerleader."

She kissed me quickly and turned. "I'll text you when I land," she said, and cleared her throat.

I watched my girl walk away, her dark-black, shoulder-length hair ironed flat—so different from my wavy pixie cut. Someone bumped my shoulder and a child hit my shin with a pink carry-on, but I wasn't taking my eyes off Robyn until she was entirely out of sight. When I saw she didn't need one more glance from me, I turned toward the bathrooms like a starter gun had gone off.

I found the restroom, got in line behind several women. My nerves jangled with energy to burn—I needed to start some kind of fix. While I waited I scanned the terminal hall, newsstands, and coffee shops to keep myself from obsessing, and that was when I saw the man I always thought of as the one that got away. The past love I returned to, if only in my mind, time and time again. I can tell you one thing for sure—my fantasies did not include wearing stained pants, tearful from empty nesting, and in debt without a plan.

I thought about hiding in the bathroom, but shoving my way past all those full bladders was a scene I couldn't afford. He was close enough to see me but far enough for me to get away if I pretended to—and that was the exact moment we made eye contact.

CHAPTER TWO
STAY TRUE TO YOUR SHELF

You had to hand it to the Universe. It lies in wait and the second you get a little comfy in life, maybe even a little judgy about another parent feeding their child deep-fried chicken tenders, your kid will refuse to eat anything but McDonald's chicken nuggets, then go on to name their favorite stuffed bear Chicken Nugget. Most likely before the toddler can say your name clearly.

This is nothing compared to what the Universe has in store when you're feeling beaten, like the worst that can happen has occurred. That's when it really piles it on. Makes you confront all the big questions you had in your life. Like, why did you ask for help? Why did you capitulate when Dawna pushed to do the taxes? What is prison like? Why was my heart acting like a greyhound having spotted a rabbit at the mere sight of this old boyfriend?

There he stood in the Starbucks line, maybe a hundred feet away. A pushpin of my youth and life choices in the form of a six-foot-three, handsome-as-ever man. Three was his name. A nickname. He was the third Herman Blatterman in a family of Blattermans, and nobody in the twenty-first century wanted to be called Herman Blatterman. Sixteen years ago, when we met, he introduced himself to me as Three, and forever Three he was.

Before he saw me, his gaze had been on the barista, clarifying his order. The young woman pulled into his magnetism. My unruly body joined the fun and warmed without my permission. Didn't it realize I had to keep my overactive imagination and reactions for saving our lives? My body was acting like Three was the Caribbean sun warming everything within a hundred-foot radius.

Or I was having a hot flash, because that was also possible. My unruly hormones blasting their last shot across the bow, Hail Mary, *yoo-hoo you're still a woman* callout.

"Thank you," he said, and put a bagel in the man-bag he carried across his wide chest.

His robust voice opened muscle memories in pleasure centers that had been on life support for a long time. I remembered what it felt like to have Three's loving attention focused on me. How cold the world felt when he pulled it away.

He was ten years younger when we met. Meaning he was twenty-three to my thirty-three. I knew he had a whole life to live, but I couldn't resist his charm. "You have the keys to me," he'd say with a convincing gaze. The kind of gaze I'd always wanted, the way my father had looked at my mother before things went south.

Our year together had been a whirlwind of Three fitting me in between his classes and friends. Me filling the rest of the time running the business and being a mother to a one-year-old. It was thrilling to be desired, words of love whispered in my ear, when my days were routinely spent on mothering and spreadsheets. I'd cook dinner on nights he was free; we'd make love while his clothes tumbled in my dryer. He'd be gone in the morning before Robyn stirred in her crib, the orange juice container empty in the fridge—a reminder, a love note left behind.

I cringed at my younger self remembering it. Love, in the moment, is a smoke screen to differences, age, stage, or anything else.

When we made eye contact across the terminal hall, there was a questioning look on his face, a head tilt. A woman in a one-piece yellow terry-cloth jumpsuit and sandals walked between us and he didn't look away.

He took a step forward and said, "Can I help you?"

That's when I realized he didn't see me, Poppy Lively, long-lost love. Older, sure, but more beautiful because of time and the road of life. Nope.

He didn't recognize me. I was just a strange, disorganized adult woman with a brown stain on her pants, staring at him. Foolish girl, I'd cut my hair short. Become a fifty-year-old lady. I stood frozen like an aging deer having heard the snap of a branch, hoping the buck wouldn't recognize me. I could slip away mortified, the wreck that had become my life not discussed.

Realization dawned on him at the same time as he tried to cover up his confusion. "Oh my . . . it's you. Poppy?"

With as much dignity as I could muster, I walked toward him and said, "Is that you, Three?" As if I also had only just made the connection.

"Yes, it's me!" he said.

The warm rush I felt had to be Pavlovian, reminding me of laughter, conversation, connection, and sex. Good sex. The kind I replayed with a battery-powered device in hand on nights when Robyn was at a sleepover.

"Should we talk about what's happening with your pants?" he said, walking toward me.

"My pants don't even want to talk about my pants, so no." So easy. It had always been so effortless with him.

Again that smile. A T-shirt under a beautifully shaped blazer, soft nubuck driving moccasins, no socks, his ankles on display. It looked like he'd found the money he always knew he'd have. He made it and bought the things he wanted, as he did in college, but maybe now without the credit card debt.

In his gaze, I felt seen—not as the dreary Poppy with her mortgage in arrears but what was inside of me, a good person, flawed, yes, but trying so hard. It was as if he were a mirror that reflected admiration back and there was no looking away.

I gave him a quick hug. He smelled the same, like cedar and smoke, like man and boy, like all those years ago.

"I smell like pie," I said stupidly.

We stared at each other. I mentally searched for appropriate small talk, since I didn't have any small topics in my life right then.

"I have some time before my flight. Do you have a few minutes to catch up?" Three said, looking closely at me.

If I were a quick excuse maker, I would have said, *No. One hundred percent no. I have a colonoscopy,* or some other get-out-of-conversation-free excuse. But I am someone who says yes against her will because I don't know how to say *no, this is the worst time of my life, and I don't want to spill my guts and be that tragic girl whose life recently hit the skids.*

Instead, the appropriate human inside of me, the game girl, smiled that ever-ready smile.

"I'd love to," I said, and my heart went beat, beat, beat like the ticking on a time bomb in the middle of the airport with no security in sight.

He touched my elbow, steered me to the bar, and said, "You never were much of a drinker, but I think champagne is in order. Tell me everything."

I rarely, if ever, drank. He remembered. When you were the only parent on call, you couldn't be impaired. You had to be fully ready for emergencies. Not out on a date drinking tequila with a man from a dating app or swilling wine in a tub somewhere.

Three smiled at the woman bartender, and I could swear her pupils dilated with attraction. The college-aged girl poured him a glass and said, "And for your mom," and handed me my glass.

He didn't even look at her when he kissed me lightly on the lips as if he were French, worldly, not from Wisconsin. My lips woke up remembering his, ready for more if it was being offered.

"Cheers," he said, and lifted his flute.

"Just one drink," I said, and took a long gulp of champagne, then sneezed like a rookie from the bubbles. "You talk first."

I watched him as he spoke, I didn't want to miss a micro-expression on a face that seemed to flutter between his younger and older selves. I tried not to fix my hair self-consciously or adjust my posture for the most flattering position while he talked about leaving Wisconsin for Los Angeles. I took a sip from my empty glass, and Three gestured for a refill, ignoring my flimsy "No," and I drank.

While he talked about his progression from acting in commercials to films, I surreptitiously checked my teeth for lunch remains and sipped on. When he outlined the move from producing stage plays to indie films, I tried to hide the stain on my pants with a cocktail napkin, pictured his life amid the bright sun and stars of Hollywood. Wondered if kissing, really kissing, him would feel the same now that he was famous, and with that thought, I knew I was if not drunk, then solidly tipsy.

"I've talked enough. Please tell me about your life," he said. The way he spoke and looked at me had me almost convinced I wasn't a shambles—I was amazing.

With my third glass of champagne nearly empty, I spectacularly underachieved by telling him Robyn was very smart. Following up with a stunner of a story about her starring role as one of the fifteen children in her elementary school's production of *The King and I*. Sue me—I was trying to relate with a theater story. I didn't stream shows like so many people did. Seriously, who had the time?

I couldn't bear to tell him that my father's coupon mailer business with the head-shakingly obvious name Coupons By Mail had been my entire career résumé. That I'd kept the business going all these years. That I'd hired Dawna Klump as Robyn's extracurriculars increased so I could be there for her like the other mothers. That Dawna and the money were gone.

Three's clear brown eyes locked onto mine, and I wondered if he felt the same familiarity I did, the rewind of the clock, the ticked-back calendar days to our youth. I didn't want to catalog my mistakes, confirm he had been right to leave us, that we were a mess. Admit to being manipulated by Dawna and her overbearing, seemingly helpful ways. *Don't you trust me? Go be Mom and Dad to Robyn.* That I let her ruin us. Not just let her. Hired her.

"Really, Poppy. Tell me what's been going on with you. It's fine to hear about your daughter, but what about you?" And he touched the top of my hand, one finger, a soft brush, an age-old gesture. "You've always been astonishing. Raising a daughter by yourself. Running a business. No one like you," he said, and I wanted to say something like, *"Right?"* A weak agreement but seriously, right?

By then the champagne, more than I'd drunk in years, sloshed in my near-empty stomach. I blinked that slow blink you do when you've had just enough alcohol to relax the muscles of your eyeballs but not enough for your body to go limp and pour you off the barstool. Here was this man who sincerely wanted to catch up. Who knew me. Could listen in context and realize how hard I'd worked. I put my champagne glass on the bar with a tinny tap and looked directly into his soft brown eyes.

"Things are not so great for Poppy Lively lately," I said, using the third-person point of view, which had uncomfortable echoes of my mother off her meds. A little girl waddled in front of her father on a pink furry backpack leash, and I straightened on the barstool.

I tried a last-second non sequitur hoping to distract him. "Kids are like tiny hostages. At the whim of their parents." I could hear the boozy pacing, the sibilant *s*'s in my words.

I felt his eyes on me; he wasn't going to let me off the hook.

"Okay, here's what you movie people call the sizzle reel." I cleared my throat with gravitas. "No job, big debt, possibly prison." I put my hand to my mouth as if telling a secret. "Unhomed," I said with my eyes going theatrically wide. I lost track for a second. "You are very pretty." I touched his nose. "Boop."

Alarmed, Three leaned forward. "Poppy."

"Here." I picked up my empty champagne glass, touching it to his. "I got it. Nice lady, hard worker, tax man cameth," I said, holding a finger in the air for emphasis. I waved that thought away. "Nobody would watch that show." I wiped my hair from my forehead. "Hang on. I've got it." I licked my lips and met Three's worried gaze.

"Poppy. I . . ." Three said in a soft voice that might undo the knot of mixed emotions deep within my tear ducts.

I held up my hand and said, "I wrecked things . . ."

Before I could finish, he said, "Poppy, I have to go catch my flight."

"Right," I said. "I'd go too if I were you. I'm fine. Having a day." And I swallowed lumps of humiliation for trusting Dawna. Shame for what my dad would say. Disgrace at my lack of foresight and selfishness. And the worst of it, Robyn deferring college—something I had to do years ago and vowed that she would not ever be forced to do.

"No, that's not it. My flight is boarding."

I lifted my eyes and held his gaze. He looked like he was doing math in that big, luscious brain of his. "Give me your phone number. I could use some help with something." His troubled gaze passed, and he looked certain.

"It's okay, Three. I'm fine."

"Oh, come on," he chided, smiling. "I bought the drinks. You owe me."

Somehow even that tiny joking request felt too much. I started to say no when he said, "You can be too proud, you know," with a mischievous grin.

That had me wondering. Pride? Had pride gotten me into this financial predicament?

I hauled a pen from my canvas book bag with the words STAY TRUE TO YOUR SHELF (all caps) printed on the side and wrote my number on a dry cocktail napkin—instantly becoming a barfly from a 1970s movie.

Three pocketed it, stood, and said, "If I had the time, I'd get you home. Under no circumstances should you drive." He kissed me on my head, and I nodded. "I may have a job for you. It just opened. It pays well. I'll text you," he said.

A job. I'd been searching, having to talk about my demoralizing situation during interviews. The hope of a job. It filled my throat along with this unasked question: *Is that the only reason you wanted my number?* Which, good God, woman, don't you have enough going on?

Before turning he said, "You've always had the keys to me," and held my gaze one, two, two and a half whole seconds. Enough time for my stomach to tell my pelvis something was going on down in the engine room.

The bartender appeared and filled a glass of ice water, set it near me. Instead of saying thanks, I said, "I'm not his mom."

The bartender, unfazed, said, "You know you have something on your pants."

CHAPTER THREE

BUST A CAP IN YOU

The floor-to-ceiling windows of the airport had an *anything is possible* feeling, and I wanted to march over and smear something sticky on them. That way, at least there would be truth in advertising. Sure, things are possible, but no road in life is as obstacle-free as the runway outside those shiny panes of glass. Instead, drunk, I took a nap on a padded bench under those tall, broad windows like someone with a long layover killing time before jetting off to their next adventure.

I woke, foggy headed but sober, my pants stiff with dried coffee, and able to drive the two and a half hours to Madison, Wisconsin. I found my car and drove through the knotted ribbons of highway away from the airport. While the landscape changed from city to farmland, I relived the hope that there really was a job, as Three had said. The mere suggestion a vote of confidence, a lifeline.

On the long, straight stretch of highway between Illinois and Wisconsin, I ran the numbers in my head for the hundredth time. Three years of back taxes on the business and one year of property taxes. I considered how much money I needed. It wasn't that much, in the world of millionaires and rocket ships to space, but for me, it was devastating. The house would be sold, no college for Robyn, find a job to pay the IRS, and live how? Where? Those were the top-tier worries—there was no money for damage deposits, car payments, or health insurance, and if I so much as got an infected hangnail, I would die of a flesh-eating bacteria camping in the neighbor's backyard. A wildly specific daymare that had me clenching my teeth as I passed fields of green alfalfa and greedy corn reaching for next month's sun. I needed a lucrative job yesterday.

I brushed my fingers across my lips thinking of Three. He'd grown up and somehow remained the same utterly engaging man I remembered. When he left all those years ago, for a paid internship in California, I didn't ask him to stay. I'd told myself it was because it wouldn't be fair—he was so young. Needed to experience life. In truth, I couldn't have handled his rejection if I suggested he stick around, so I let him off the hook first. Despite our pillow talk of making a family, Robyn and I being perfect for him, I knew it was a fantasy.

It was possible that I'd let myself fall in love partially because I knew he would leave, though I hoped he wouldn't. I wasn't caught off guard with the leaving like I'd been when my mother left and Robyn's father disappeared before learning he would become a father. At least with Three, I'd had the memory of his goodbye, infused with lovey eyes and ultimately bad timing—a vague *if only we met at a different time* whispered between us.

I blinked hard at the landscape ahead. If he had a job, and if it paid well, as he said, I could stop googling how to make a shelter out of moving boxes and cling wrap.

I dialed Amy the Tax Person, as I'd come to call her. She'd given me her number out of pity and time management. "You sound like my mom. Call me, but don't tell anybody I gave you my number. And I have to hang up after one hour. Boundaries are important to me."

When she picked up, I said, "Amy, if I get a job, will all of the money I make go straight to the IRS or do I get to keep any?"

"Yeah. It goes to your plan, of course. The IRS won't wait."

"How do I live?"

"I don't want to be mean, but we've been over this. The US Treasury doesn't care. Once you don't respond to their warnings—"

"Dawna Klump didn't respond!" I said, but Amy knew. She even knew that Dawna wore floral tops with faux silver studs on the shoulder seams because she thought it was edgy fashion. Amy knew everything, ergo the hour time limit for our calls. "So even if I get a really good position, I can't pay my daughter's tuition with it?"

"Well . . ." she said. "Like I'm home right now and you're a very frantic friend calling in general about tax stuff. Right?"

"Yes, this is between two pals who would be eating avocado toast together if we could."

"If you direct-deposit your paycheck into a friend's account, the IRS won't really know. So theoretically"—she enunciated every syllable—"you could pay tuition from your friend's account. Otherwise, the IRS is the Honey Badger—they don't care. They want their money, and they will tack on interest and penalties while you wait."

"Penalties," I repeated.

"And interest. This one guy sold his kidney but then he died. Nobody could find the kidney, and his daughter had to pay his debt, so that didn't work out very well."

I pressed where I believed one of my kidneys lived, wondered, irrationally, if a person had two for financial reasons.

"Amy, I can't sell my kidney," I said, stunned.

"No, you shouldn't. But here's a fun fact. If you can stay hidden for seven years, the IRS forgives your debt."

For one hot minute I considered how that might work. If Robyn and I went on the lam, I'd have to tell her everything. Admit to my failure to thrive, to care for her, to keep her future sacred. And how would we pay for that lam? With my mint-condition collection of number two pencils and coffee mugs?

"One more thing. You have up to six months to sell your house. Don't wait."

This was a fire hose of information, and I was having trouble catching my breath. I stared at a simple red barn in the distance, my thoughts a gnat cloud trying to recover from a champagne bender. It didn't matter how many times I tried to problem solve this; the IRS was gravity, and you can't fight gravity.

I said goodbye before I overstayed my welcome. I needed Amy's goodwill. I needed her to answer the phone when I called. The good news was this: if I made some money, put it in Chelsea's account, I'd suffer but my kid's life could go on. Her future would not be handicapped by me.

I couldn't bear to drive straight to my silent house, the only anchor Robyn and I had ever known. I needed my best friend. She was the person who knew enough details of my finances to help me make sense of things and ease back into going home.

At Chelsea's front door, my friend greeted me with a white allergy pill and a glass of water in her outstretched hand. Two elderly pugs from the same litter and one of her cats snuffled to my side.

"You don't look so great," Chelsea said.

"I know, I spilled coffee all over my pants."

"No. You have something on your face. What is that?"

I looked in the hall mirror, and the letters FLEH were smudged in black on my cheek. "Oh, I took a nap on my book bag. The S didn't make it, or it would be FLEHS. See." I held up my bag, the printing faded slightly, the ink of SHELF having transferred backward onto my cheek. I rubbed the letters off my face.

Chelsea was a nurse practitioner, a natural caregiver, and gestured for me to swallow the pill and water. "Have you been drinking?"

"Day drinking. It's a brand-new-era me, my friend," I said.

"Okay. Well, enough of that. I have a new legal pad. Let's solve some finance problems."

"I'm exhausted, Chels. I just said goodbye to Robyn, and I talked to Amy again."

"Stop talking to Tax Amy. Call legal aid; maybe you qualify for something. We can run scenarios. What are the police doing about Dawna? Have they found where she's holed up?"

This conversation had a very caffeinated feeling to it, and I longed for gentle Supportive Chelsea, not Kick-This-Problem-in-the-Ass Chelsea. Both Chelseas were my best friend, but in times of extreme stress like this, Kick Chelsea was a lot to handle. She had fantastic ideas, but often she wasn't great at reading the room—and my room, me, was maxed out.

"I've called the cops so often they answer the phone, 'Hi, Poppy, still looking.' The IRS's payment plan is suffocating, the Realtor is taking photos of the house to sell, the lawyer is filing documents and told me the best thing I can do is find profitable work. Today."

I knew she was trying to help, to be the good friend, the trouble-shooter, but her legal pad was making my neck itch. No matter what I'd say, she'd counter with a solution.

"You could move in with me and Brad. Hold on." She picked up her phone and texted. "Let's see what Google says about assets and unpaid property tax."

Her fiancé aside, I would not be moving in with Chelsea. I put my hand over her phone. "Google says the house has to go." My friend knew talk of selling our home would have me crying again. She knew what it took to get it after my father died. How it had been our refuge for decades.

My phone rang. "Ugh, this is that IRS agent who keeps leaving me messages." I hit "Ignore." "I can't talk to that person. Not today."

Chelsea shot me a worried glance.

I'd met Chelsea in the emergency room at a local hospital on Halloween ten years before. She took Robyn, bloody from a costume mishap, back for X-rays. Robyn had created a living portrait of Dumbledore from a flat bicycle box. Once she'd climbed inside, the arm holes were restrictive and one raised-sidewalk crack did the night in. She caught her toe but not herself and pitched forward like a tree felled by an axe.

I hadn't saved her because I was making eyes at a single dad whose son was dressed as a velociraptor. I was complimenting the empty paper towel tubing arms when Robyn hit the sidewalk with her tiny nose. That's when I knew dating was out—you had to keep your eye on the ball, or your kid's nose, or it *was* a 911 call. Single was safer.

Chelsea was on duty and did not judge me when I laughed with hysterical relief after we learned Robyn's nose wasn't fractured. She had cuddled my daughter and complimented her on her wizarding ways, and forever after Robyn wanted to be a nurse. "Mom," she'd say. "If I can make one person feel like Chelsea made me feel, I want to do that job."

Chelsea gave Robyn a *Harry Potter* cauldron coffee mug for her last birthday, and I'd watched my daughter pack it in her luggage that morning.

"Okay. We can start after you take a shower, another nap. Or tomorrow, I guess. But no more drinks for you. Spreadsheets are your coping mechanisms, not drinking in the daytime alone."

"I wasn't alone." I handed the empty water glass back and licked my lips. "I couldn't drive right away, so that's why I napped."

My phone buzzed and the worry nodule in my brain said, *Uh-oh.* I hoped it wasn't Robyn texting me something like, *I'm at the airport. I didn't get on the plane. Come get me.*

It wasn't Robyn. The text was from Three. I glanced at Chelsea, and she read my face.

"What? Who is it?"

"It's him. From the airport. Three."

Three: This is Three. So great to see you. Really great.

"Your Three?" she said with a frown. Chelsea had heard all about the epic love story, my broken heart at the time, how I romanticized him. How that one past relationship brought on a ruthless melancholy after watching *The Way We Were* yet again. *He was my Hubbell,* I'd blubber, clutching my one glass of chardonnay.

Chelsea took my elbow and moved me into the living room. The dogs followed, panting as if they didn't want to miss a detail in this retelling. "What's he like now? Still fly by night?"

"Fly by night? Is that how I described him to you?"

"Kind of, you know. He wasn't super dependable."

"He was a kid. Now he's older." Then I added, "Dreamy." My eyes were glued to my phone.

Three: I'm a producer for a film and we have a position suddenly in Wardrobe. You'd have to get to LA by Monday. At Universal studios.

I glanced at Chelsea, eyes wide. "This is the job. He told me he might have a job and he does!"

Chelsea read the message, eyed my face, kept her frown in place.

"It's in LA. Los Angeles," I said as if my friend might not know how the second-largest city in America is abbreviated.

"Yeah. I got that."

I texted back.

Poppy: What's the salary?

Three: 2.5K a week. Might be more because schedule is tight. Long days.

I did the math. I'd applied for so many positions in the last couple of weeks, but without corporate experience, no one wanted the mailer coupon gal, especially when everything was online now. I wasn't unemployable, but nowhere would I make 2.5K a week starting next week.

Three: Can you sew?

Poppy: Yes. I sew.

"You don't sew. I sew. You hot glue and tape things," said Chelsea.

I hit the microphone and spoke into my phone. "I'm a really good sewer."

"Seamstress," said Chelsea, and my phone picked up her voice and typed the correction.

I put my hand over her mouth and smiled the warmest smile I had in my arsenal of smiles—she was my best friend. I moved my hand, and Chelsea licked her thumb and cleaned my face.

Three: It would help me so much. You're perfect for this.

I wanted to know why he thought I was perfect for this. I'd be good at any job, I knew that, but I wanted to hear his words. See it in his eyes again. See if despite seeing me at such a low point, he knew I was capable, the old me.

Then he sent a kiss emoji. My tummy gasped.

Three: Hang on, let me check on a few things.

"He sent a kiss emoji," I said, and I felt like a dry kitchen sponge that had been parched for weeks and someone, Three, had plunged it slash me into the perfect warm water–filled bathtub. "That's flirty, right? I think he's flirting." I knew I wasn't still drunk, but I felt high with the idea that a partial solution could be so close at hand.

"Is he married?" Chelsea said.

"He wasn't wearing a ring. He didn't mention a wife or kids."

"It would be an important detail to understand if his text was flirty or not." Chelsea gave me the side-eye.

"Me wondering if a behavior is flirty feels the same as me trying to understand Bitcoin. I haven't flirted or been flirted with for sixteen years," I said, walking the flirty topic back.

"Untrue. That dad at the bake sale. He flirted."

"I'd had too much coffee that day. Who knows if he was flirting or just in love with my lemon ricotta cookies?"

"Brad would leave me for those cookies."

"So here's another buzzkill in a week of buzzkills. Three didn't recognize me. I look . . . you know. Different. Old."

One of Chelsea's cats wound herself around my ankle and another was perched on the side table and kept trying to get my attention by patting my arm. "Why do your cats like me so much?"

"Because you're allergic. They are the ultimate anxious avoidant boyfriend. You move away and they get closer. Try to pet one and they'll . . ."—and here my friend affected the most ridiculous Irish accent—"take your bleedin' hand off, they will."

I knew we were joking, but I could feel Chelsea's doubt underneath this light but heavy conversation.

"That's why I can't live with you. Brad, the animals, *and* your accents." I dropped my bag and said, "I gotta sit." I plunked myself on the couch, and Chelsea took the chair across from me.

Three: Three maybe five months. Details to evolve. Staying here on set. Would this help you?

Poppy: It would, yes.

"I'd be staying on set. No living costs," I said.

"Do you think this is for real? Wasn't Three kind of haphazard when he was younger?"

A radio wave of impatience zipped through me. I wanted clarity and support. I needed this lifeline and wanted Chelsea to be hopeful.

"Yeah. Three was disorganized. Sixteen years ago."

He'd shared a house with five undergraduate guys who stood on a cutting board in the shower to keep their feet off the bottom of a tub that hadn't been scrubbed in a year. We saw each other in a bubble; he came to the house. He was big, adorable, like a long-limbed puppy, charging through life.

"You think he's different now?" Chelsea scratched one of the dogs behind his ears as she watched my face.

"He's a producer in Hollywood now," I said on the way to the bathroom to throw some cold water on my face. To cool off the urgency I felt to make a point to Chelsea. This job was an opportunity even if I hadn't examined every crack and crevice. People who hadn't grown up with chaos didn't understand you couldn't reject any possibilities to restore stability. Those people had spouses, parents, safety nets. I turned on the faucet, let the water run on my pulse points.

One time, just before the end, Three borrowed my car for errands and was gone for two days. I couldn't reach him. I was frantic but also needed my car. He was always good for this kind of mystery move. He returned finally with a box of my favorite candy on the front seat like that was equal dispensation for disappearing. I remembered saying to him, *Grand theft auto is not paid for with a box of Dots in any court in the land.*

He laughed and wrapped angry-me into him. For the first time, when we made love that night, I predicted almost down to the week when he would leave. He was restless. Wanted more than I could provide. Now here he was, offering me a job. Taking care of details. Being the adult I knew he would be. Successful, responsible, dynamic.

I patted my wet, cool hands on my face, wiped it dry with the hand towel, emerged from the bathroom safe house.

"Poppy, I only want the best for you," Chelsea said. "If this job is it, I'm all for it. It just seems really fast."

Three: It would be great to have you here, I'll need your social security number, and a few other details. I'll text you all the info.

Poppy: Hang on. Checking something.

"He's not a stranger; he knew me when. Get your legal pad," I said.

She'd been doodling question marks in the margins of a blank page. Chelsea was born ready for any pro-and-con analysis.

"Pro. No more waiting for interviews. Job offer. Real money. Start date," I said.

"Con," Chelsea said. "It's far away. Can we trust Three? No experience in the job."

"Pro," I said, my palms sweating. "Job from old friend."

"Con. How will you justify this to Robyn without telling her about . . ." Here she paused, looking for a sensitive way to say *this catastrophe.*

"Pro. Will tell Robyn I'm going to California for business. Meanwhile, I won't have to work at Target while interviewing for a graphic artist job that they ultimately fill internally. I won't have to obsessively go over the calculations that without fail come up red. I won't stagger over to Dawna Klump's house and scream murderous obscenities after drinking a White Claw that I stole from your fridge because I can't afford my own. I can put off confessing to Robyn that her dreams of going to nursing school are over, for I don't know how long."

I said all this in one breath, inhaled deeply, and kept going. "I won't have to go home every night to my empty house missing Robyn with my dad's voice echoing from the Sheetrock." I affected his vocal fry: "'Not so easy being the only parent now, is it?'" As if that had been my fault and he hadn't driven my mother out with his toxicity. "And why is that? Because there will be more than likely no home to go to."

Building that argument had highlighted a future so bleak, so like my past, that my head said, *This is not our first rodeo*, and my heart said, *I'm breaking; please help*. I took Chelsea's hand.

"But going to LA. Keeping this secret. Is this what you want?" Chelsea said.

"Who cares what I want?"

"I do, honey." Chelsea took a moment, then lifted her phone and opened a map app. "It says it will take one day and four hours to get there. Twenty-eight hours. If you drive eight hours a day, it will take you three and a half days."

"I'd have to leave Thursday," I said.

"Probably." She wrote and circled *empty house* on her yellow pad. Doodled a roof on the words.

I stopped her hand. Turned the legal pad over.

"You can stay here tonight," Chelsea said. "If you don't feel like going home. We could tell Robyn about what's happening together."

"No." I shook my head. "I want her to have a fun and carefree summer with those kids. I don't want her worrying about family finances. My dad was always talking about money. How spendy my mom was. How little cash we had. I want her to keep her dreams clean and clear from worry."

"How will you—" she started.

I didn't let her finish. "Whatever you're thinking, I don't know. I'll figure it out. I always do. I know this is fast. Life moves on, and the trick is to not let it leave you behind."

Three: You there?

Poppy: I'm In.

I heard Chelsea exhale.

Three: Catch a flight, you're going to LA. What's your email? Few things to tie up here. Details over the next few days. Okay? We'll need your social security number.

Poppy: Sounds good.

Three: You trust me?

Poppy: Of course.

"I'll drive my van," I said, leaving that off the text. "I can't afford a plane ticket, and I'll need my car. You can visit," I said, flying a little too close to the sun with thoughts of the future.

"And you'll come back home soonish," Chelsea said, a hesitant cheerleader unsure if her team was winning with this impulsive decision. She moved next to me on the couch, and the pug brothers repositioned, taking over the warm cushion she'd just vacated.

"Selling the house gets us started on the payback plan, making real money, gets Robyn to college."

"The way you always talked about Three. Sometimes it reminds me of the way you talk about your dad—"

I interrupted her. "My dad? He is the farthest thing from my dad. I mean my dad didn't give me the time of day unless he wanted me to do something. When Three is around, you are the only person in the room."

"Ahhh, yeah. I can see that." My old friend, with her blue eyes and blonde lashes, her sincere, caring face. The one I knew patients saw as she helped them through any number of painful and embarrassing procedures. How lucky they were to have her. How lucky was I to have her hardworking friendship? Even if it was overwhelming at times. I lifted my phone.

Poppy: I don't even know how to begin to thank you.

Three: We'll think of something.

And like ice dancers doing an old, practiced routine, Chelsea swiveled her head, eyes wide as if we'd skated over an obstacle, each of us labeling it differently.

Then I talked to her about sending my paychecks to her bank so that Robyn might become a nurse.

CHAPTER FOUR

SEWING, HOLLYWOOD,

BANKRUPTCY, AND THERAPY

When you're a single mom with one child, your house becomes more than the place where your bed is—the structure that holds your pot holders, washing machine, and winter boots. It is a member of the family. If you grew up in it, purchased it after your father lost it to the bank and not for the reasons he told you, you think of it as the quiet best friend you rescued. Once you strip the wallpaper and discover your mother's handwriting on the wall, you promise not to abandon the few memories you have of her for a tax crime you didn't commit—knowing full well this would be impossible.

That is why Chelsea treaded unusually carefully with her problem-solving words where my Dutch Colonial was concerned. That's why she mentioned it only peripherally with an option to move in with her.

I stepped through the threshold, noting the gap between the door frame and the floor. I knew I needed to plug that space or the mice would continue to take refuge in the basement in the fall. I'd tell the Realtor to tell the new owners, and a brick of dread landed in my stomach.

I ran fingertips across the wall so the house could read my thoughts through my touch.

If there is a way to save you, I will do it again. We will come back. I will restore the life we have. Had.

Unable to sit, I looked for an email from a Realtor I'd found. My daughter's face appeared on my home screen, and I held the phone up.

"Hi, Mom," she said, and I knew from her voice she was tired and homesick, but I'd let her tell me how she was feeling. I'd listen.

"Hi, love. How are things? Can you talk?"

"Mom. Check out this apartment." She flipped her phone, and I saw an all-white bedroom, an enormous tufted headboard, an ornate gold floor-to-ceiling mirror on the wall, and what looked like a gleaming ceramic egret in the corner.

"It's so fancy. Are you feeling better? Less unsure?" I said, impressed and happy to see that the family had made good on the promise of a lovely bedroom for Robyn.

"So much better. The kids are as cute in person as when we FaceTimed." She sighed. Looked past me. "Are you sleeping in my room tonight?"

"Maybe," I said with a sideways smile.

Before there was FaceTime or Zoom, the idea of seeing someone's face wherever they were in the world seemed like the most luxurious thing. That was before I had kids. Before I understood it was just an e-tease. One that left you wanting so much more. I craved to cup her face, kiss her soft cheek, and until technology included that feature, well, the Apple and Google geeks needed to get back to work.

"Can we go into my room?"

"Sure. Let's go." I climbed the stairs to her bedroom while she chatted about her flight and meeting the family. I nudged the door open, and the flood of peace I felt seeing the owl lamp by the bed, the bear she named Chicken Nugget on her pillow, had to be better than any anxiety drug available on the market.

"I miss my room. Isn't that dumb?" Before I could reply she said, "Go over to Nana's wall."

My mother, who was mostly unknown and unknowable to both of us, had her own spot in my daughter's room. After she'd left, my father rarely addressed her absence and never in a kind way. I knew he made up his own realities. I didn't press him. I needed him. As a child I watched him at the few parenting events he attended. Handsome enough to captivate the mothers, spinning his tales of vulnerability. I came to mistrust his version of the truth. For this reason, it felt like a challenge to see my mom differently than he did.

Robyn and I peeled and scraped the green-and-blue bunny wallpaper when my daughter wanted something more befittingly cool for her twelve-year-old self. There had been a loose corner of the old paper, right by the window with the view of the neighbor's yard, and we'd left it attached to the wall. Lifting it revealed a message my mother had written to the house or whoever found it. In her loose script I'd come to know from the scraps of grocery lists and other notes I'd found over the years, my mother had written, *I am mine, Gemini Lively.* After we found it, so much shifted in my mind about my mother. It helped fill in the blanks about a woman who felt she was losing herself.

I pointed the phone to that spot now, raised the paper, and saw Robyn's handwriting penciled under my mother's, her grandmother's, declaration. *We are the Livelys —Robyn Lively.*

"Oh," I said. "Sweetie, I love this."

"Sign your name. Use the pencil on the windowsill."

"Okay, I will," I said and put my phone down. Underneath my mother's and daughter's names I wrote mine. I picked up the phone and showed Robyn. It was a solid action, like re-signing loan papers from when I reclaimed the place after almost losing it. Or in this case, signing over the papers to the bank, leaving a tiny personal stamp of ownership.

"I wanted to, you know, add our names—like a family tree," she said, watching me for my reaction.

A loud squawk of static sounded from somewhere, and Robyn jumped. "That's the kids. They use this old intercom. It drives their mom crazy. I gotta go. They should be asleep."

I wanted to hold on to this moment, but there was no speed limit for life, no brakes at all.

"Wait. One quick thing. I'm running the numbers on the business. Seeing if I should take it online or try something new. I got a job offer. Out of town. California."

"I gotta go, Mom. Can you tell me about it later?"

"Definitely. But I might take it. Just to ease things up."

That caught her attention, and she said, "Ease what things? In California?"

The intercom screeched and Robyn peered at me, and I smiled my all-good, forever-your-girl smile and said, "You'd better go. Love you. Have fun!"

And she signed off. The quiet that followed, the paper covering our words, the streetlight illuminating a grape juice stain on the carpet by Robyn's bed had me in its grip.

I wanted this house for Robyn and me to come back to. The IRS or the bank would have to drag me out of this house screaming Dawna Klump's name like a *Harry Potter* Howler. I'd swipe Dawna's wine fridge and set it on fire in her driveway before losing this house. Liquid resolve slid through me and turned to steel. As it must have done for my mother when she claimed herself and wrote her name on the wall and left.

Big talk from someone whose mother never returned and who was currently without options. Big talk.

Instead of crawling into Robyn's bed and breathing in her scent like a high schooler huffs whippets, I began packing. *Only essentials,* I told myself as I hauled my empty luggage up from the basement. I grabbed a pile of underwear and dumped them into my suitcase.

The day my mother dropped me off for my first day of fourth grade, on the sidewalk in front of George Washington Elementary School, she'd squeezed my chin, her mood ring glinting in the sun, and said,

"Promise me you'll never take a man's last name. Like I didn't take your dad's name. If you feel yourself slipping away, you only need to sign Poppy Lively." She let go of my face and, with a flourish, wrote my full name in the air as if holding a lit sparkler. "You will be reminded of your spirit! Of course, I'm talking about if you get married—which is a terrible decision for women." She said this last phrase looking past me, as if speaking to an imaginary studio audience.

"Did you take your meds today?" I said in the way my father did when my mother broke the fourth wall as if onstage and performing for fans.

"Meds, schmeds, give 'em to the feds," she said as she always did.

I answered as my father had, many times before this fateful day. "Better living through Big Pharma, Gem. You need 'em."

The ritual of these sentences was like our little family's secret hand-shake—when Gemini spoke to invisible people, we talked pharmacology. And usually, that's all it took. Gemini swallowed her meds and remembered to pack my lunch, do the laundry, and pick me up from the curb after school.

I wondered what crucial detail I'd missed during those last moments we were together. I was distracted by my pants. They were an inch too short, and there was a rat's nest of hair at the base of my neck that I couldn't brush out. I was afraid the other kids would see these things, know what it meant, that my mom wasn't like their moms. Helpful, present, tuned in. In the end, I didn't ask for more information. I was afraid of the answer.

If my mother had a wilder-than-usual look in her eye, I didn't see it. "Don't ever give your Lively away. I kept my name for a reason," she'd said. When she threw me a dry-eyed smooch over her shoulder, I was tugging my pants to hide my ankles. I didn't realize that would be the last air-kiss I would ever get from my mom. I never specifically asked my dad why my mom left. I worried he'd say I was too needy or hard. His mood dictated what he represented as the truth.

When I went to bed the night my mom left, I found a note under my pillow. *You are yours, Poppy Lively. I'm not me. I love you.* I cried for days, weeks, months, and years and finally her memory faded, the wound scabbed over. In college, I'd taken an abnormal psychology class and the professor said, "Mental illness isn't personal, it's illness." Going on to say, "You wouldn't take another person's diabetes as a slight against you, would you?" I carry that quote in my wallet to this day.

Once Robyn and I found the wall, it helped me feel empathy for the woman losing her grip while trying to hang on. It was my father I held accountable. His ways were harder to understand. This house was the last tenuous thread to my mother's love, the evidence to my dead father that I'd saved our way of living all by myself. And I'd continue to try my hardest to hang on to it.

———

I spent the next two days making bold moves. I sold a few things on Facebook Marketplace so I would have a fist of cash that would get me across the country.

My dad would say, *You have to spend money to make money,* even though I would learn that he spent money without making it and that was how we lost the family home the first time. It had been news to me that he was the extravagant one, not my mother like he claimed. I'd heard the phrase *unreliable narrator* and recognized my father in the definition.

I told the neighbors that I was going to be gone, handed them a spare key for emergencies, and forwarded my mail to Chelsea. I didn't eat much over these days. I couldn't stomach the idea. On my laptop in a leap of faith that I don't think faith deserved, I put Robyn's university down payment on a credit card. I was already a criminal in the government's mind. Chase Bank might as well be pissed too.

On Thursday morning, with my car packed I waited for Chelsea outside her apartment, eager for the mood-stabilizing effects of Iowa and Nebraska while simultaneously dreading and eager to leave town.

Poppy: I'm here.

I couldn't go inside, see her cats, and start my trip itching my way across south central Wisconsin. There was no way I wanted to say goodbye to the pug brothers, so I stayed outside. When Chelsea walked toward me holding snacks for the road, I bit the inside of my cheek for stability. I had made a decision to go, and I couldn't handle the slightest blink of questioning my sanity.

"You have the key to my place. Don't take the dutch oven when you water my plants. Or take it. You deserve it. Take whatever you want. Take it all."

"I'm not taking anything. Your car looks like an Escher painting. Or like someone shoved it over. Do you know where everything is?"

I followed her gaze. The answer was no, I had no idea where anything was in the jumbled back of my van. I had boxes of photo albums of Robyn, two jumbo pieces of luggage—one with shoes, the other, clothes that were fine for the Midwest but Los Angeles would surely sneer. A small fire safe with legal papers was shoved against Robyn's Quidditch broom, and there was a tower of blankets and pillows for car sleeping. Tucked everywhere were keepsakes, shampoo and lotion bottles, and enough Tylenol and allergy meds to kill someone.

"Sort of. I had trouble leaving things behind. I'll organize it on the road. I took a lot of files. I don't know. Just in case there is something in them I missed."

"Is that your sewing machine?"

"Is that dumb? Yeah, they'll have their own. Here. You take it." I tugged the old Singer out and put it on her front stoop.

"I have a bunch of things for you to do to pass the time on the road. I'll text it to you. I've collated a list of podcasts about sewing, Hollywood, bankruptcy, and therapy."

"So this is a study abroad program. Will there be tests?"

"There is an amazing YouTube series on pelvic floor strengthening for truckers," and with that she motioned for me to take a sip from the water bottle she'd given me. Hydration was almost a religion with her.

"Thank you for all this," I said, my lip twitching.

"Wait, Poppy. Los Angeles is a huge city. What if you get out there and . . . I don't know . . . you meet nefarious characters and you disappear?"

"You and Netflix need to take a break. Wicked characters do not lie in wait for fifty-year-old women to drive into town in a ten-year-old Toyota Sienna van. What would they do to me? Ask me for my recipe for lasagna and make me set the table? Nobody wants me."

I said that last sentence offhandedly. And I meant it that way. A comment at the end of a thought, like punctuation. Or as if I were in a debate and needed a zinger to close the argument. It was Chelsea's reaction, her immediate concerned expression, that had me reviewing my words.

"You know what I mean," I said. "I'm broke. I've got nothing to steal. I'm not young, beautiful, and innocent."

"What should I tell Robyn if she calls me?"

"She knows a little about me leaving. I'll drop bits of info as things develop. I'll keep you posted. Don't you dare give me that pursed-lip disapproving look. There are things you don't have to tell your kids about. They don't have to know your vibrator's name, that you have a huge crush on the mailman, or the balance in your bank accounts. In fact, I would add that it's appropriate to treat them like children and not little adults."

"Did you google Psychology Today?"

"Yes. I can weaponize Google too."

"Don't run out of gas," Chelsea said. "I don't want you on the side of the road somewhere in the desert. Those big rigs could sidle up next to you and . . ."

"Whoa, don't waste this idea on me. Put it in a note and I'll pitch it to Three after I start my job where I measure the inseam of Brad Pitt and his old pal George Clooney. By the way, I drove by Dawna Klump's house. The woman has two stone lions the size of second graders on the front porch of her 1970s ranch. I probably own those. Get Brad's truck, would you, and pick them up in the night."

"You vant I should keel her?" she said in a terrible Russian accent.

"If you can find her, yes." I hugged my friend, opened the car door, and that felt like a commitment. "I'll text Three when I get on the highway. Something breezy like, 'On my way!' He'll send the details and I'll tell you everything."

"Okay. Good plan," Chelsea said. I saw her upper lip thin in the way it does before her tears appear.

I pointed at her. "Don't. I'm leaving. Come visit. Goodbye." I put the car in gear. I drove past the stores on Monroe Street away from the lakes and parks of Madison, Wisconsin. Past the ice cream stand where Robyn licked her way through hundreds of cherry chocolate chip ice cream cones.

At the traffic light where Robyn and I used to cross the street on the way to a library or school, I waited for a family—mother, father, and child hustling across with a red flag on a bamboo stick to stop cars. I watched until someone honked their horn at me to get moving.

I opened the driver's side window, felt the air rush in and help me move through this scenery—the warm air keeping my eyes dry. I've had a recurring dream throughout my life. The way I felt right now had me remembering it. I'd be on a ladder, high in the air, on the side of a building and the steeper I climbed, the more it felt like I was falling backward unable to see the ground.

CHAPTER FIVE

BEYOND THE RAINBOW

As I drove toward LA, the mile markers increasing, I'd get the sensation of that falling dream while I was wide awake, my foot on the gas. In those moments I'd sync my headphones and listen to my daughter's Spotify playlist. It was the best distraction I had, and I spent a lot of time rewinding rap songs to figure out what in the world they were saying about their dicks. It was very grounding.

A few hours into the drive, I voice texted Three.

Poppy: On my way!

Three: ☺ Contract Coming

That tiny message offered a surprising amount of security, mostly because of what he didn't text. *Don't come. No job. Have a good life.*

When Three sent a contract that I e-signed on my phone, the falling-ladder feeling dulled a bit.

Poppy: If I do well is there a possibility of more work?

If I could keep putting money into Chelsea's account to pay for schooling, Robyn would come home, go directly to school on an uninterrupted timeline. I wouldn't be there, in our home making her friends lasagna, but I wouldn't be in prison either.

Three: Definitely. It's like a slice of home is coming my way.

Sigh. I drank from my water bottle, my mouth chronically, stressfully dry ever since Dawna Klump disappeared. It was time to drop some info Robyn's way. Not a full avalanche, just a snowball or two.

Poppy: Lots to tell you. But, I decided to go to California. There's an opportunity. Just while you're gone. I'll tell you more soon.

Robyn: With the kids now.

Poppy: It's in Los Angeles.

Robyn: ok. Talk later.

Which I understood to mean, maybe we will, maybe we won't; it all depended on her nanny family.

Next I'd tell her about the job and eventually about the Realtor with our house keys, the staging that would happen while I was gone.

There was no worse torture for me than sitting with my thoughts about my failings for miles and miles. All I worked for gone, because I'd thought I needed help. I drove through the nights, pulling over to nap when I felt my eyelids droop. I listened to Chelsea's sewing podcasts with names like *Sewing Out Loud, Sew & Tell,* and *Stitch Please!* As I got closer to California, I started the Hollywood podcasts. I learned everything there was to know about Elizabeth Taylor and Richard Burton's tumultuous love affair and the abominable way MGM treated Judy Garland. I sang "Somewhere Over the Rainbow" along with Judy. At the final verse, the big finish—"If happy little bluebirds fly beyond the rainbow, why, oh why can't I?"—I ended on a big crescendo, the acoustics in my van excellent. Then I cried for little Judy, me, and my raggedy van motoring away from my life.

By Las Vegas, with no more texts from Three with instructions about where to drive, live, or how to show up, I refused to allow myself to second-, third-, and fourth-guess this decision. He'd sent a contract. All would be well. I had faith.

While filling the gas tank, I browsed a Los Angeles real estate site and did a double take at how much a one-bedroom, studio, then a bachelor apartment cost in Los Angeles. Month-to-months were outrageous, and I was grateful not to have to budget for this. I worried about the van's fluid levels, and one gas station attendant in the middle of the desert measured the tread on the tires with a penny and said, "Not good."

To which I replied, "Nope." Following up with, "Just kidding, thank you."

Wednesday night, I reached Los Angeles. The reputation of epic traffic made good, and Teslas, BMWs, Porsches, and rusty pickup trucks whipped past me. My van felt like a floating couch in the middle of an expensive car dealership and still no directions from Three. I'd called twice, and it had gone to voice mail with the message, "Probably in meetings. Glad you called. I will get back to you."

I did a little self-talk to calm myself. "Good for you for trusting again. Courageous Poppy, leaping to an opportunity," I said, flinching as horns blared while I exited the highway or merged into traffic. "Stupid you for not confirming more; you are too trusting." I was my best and worst friend in uncertain times. My phone buzzed.

Three: Hi!!! Be at the Studio at 6:30 AM tomorrow. They have your name. You'll get a drive on pass. Go to Soundstage 37 on the Universal lot. Find the wardrobe trailer. Check in with Wanda Merinchowski. Costume Designer. You're a must hire.

Oh my God, the relief.

Poppy: Yes. Ok. Got it. Good. Perfect. Roger. What's a must hire?

Three: They must hire you because you know me.

Poppy: Do they know I don't have any experience?

Three: Must hires never do. All newbies. I'll take care of union. So exciting!!!

A location popped onto my screen. Universal Studios.

Poppy: Will you be there?

Three: Yes. Maybe. Can't wait You'll be so close.

If my emotions were a tuning fork, the words *exciting* and *close* struck them with a rubber mallet. Zing!

He texted as if he were running into surgery and someone was bleeding out. Or as if he were breathless from making deals with rainmakers who could not be kept waiting. He'd always been like that, catching a bus or wave or moment—grasping, living—and it was thrilling then and now. It was so long ago, hard to even recall that time—there is an amnesia that comes when caring for an infant while living and loving. The time is blurred, the memories unspecific, but I recalled the excitement, fatigue, joy, love, and abundance.

As I drove, I became ever more aware of the bubble I lived in. I'd never seen a person covered by a huge blue IKEA bag sleeping on a mattress in a median before. I slowed, and angry drivers made it clear that this was not something people slowed for. In Wisconsin, if a person was found lying on the side of the road, 911 was called. People stopped.

I watched the traffic barrel past, and that's when I saw the encampment under the overpass. A jumble of tents, boxes, tarps of all shapes and sizes, and people clustered along the sidewalk. I knew now how this happened to people—you live, take out a second mortgage on your home to get through a pandemic, hire a criminal with too much eyeliner and an old perm. You trust that person, google what a kidney does and how much it's worth.

This job was a survival move. I'd do it and set things right, even if the math was wonky. A woman on a broken bike caught my eye. She wasn't my mother or me or Robyn, but she could have been, or we could be her. I shuddered and turned the air vent off, finding it already closed.

I'd planned to sleep in my car the night before showing up to work, but the tent city depressed me so much I found a motel that in Iowa or rural Wisconsin would be considered mom-and-pop but in LA felt very estranged alcoholic uncle named Larry. It was cheap but another expense on my credit card that the piper would have to pay. The place appeared fine on the outside, but once I'd bumped my luggage into the room and caught the scent of mold and something like burned hair, I paused.

Chelsea would create an entire kidnapping story with one glance at the battered molding where the dead bolt wobbled into place. I considered examining the mattress for bedbugs but instead took the shower curtain and spread it on the bed and congratulated myself for my resourcefulness. I had a blow-up airline pillow and a lightweight puffy coat that could be used as a bathrobe or a blanket and easily tossed in the wash. No way would Robyn's *Blue's Clues* nubby blanket cross this threshold.

I calculated the time zones between New York City and Los Angeles. It was after 10:00 p.m. on the East Coast and Robyn might still be awake.

Poppy: Hi lovie. How's life in the big city?

Robyn: MOM. It's amazing. They just moved me into my own apartment downstairs from theirs. It's GORGEOUS. The twins are ADORABLE. Hayden already told me she loved me. Hollis hit me with her stuffed dog, but Lizzie said that means she likes me. The mom is super glamorous. We're going to the Hamptons on Friday. They have like 3 houses.

Poppy: YAY!

Such good news. Robyn was busy, happy, and out of town. I could focus on what was ahead without worry. My little Robyn's egg was settled and unaware. I turned, and the shower curtain rolled with me, the plastic rubbing loudly against the printed polyester bedspread. I had the random thought that if someone came in and knifed me, it would be a tidy crime scene.

I closed my eyes and saw the unhomed woman on the street again, and the fragility of peace, the shallow curb before the fall, filled me with indecision. I tried breathing like a yogi, but who was I kidding. I tried to examine my anxiety as if it were an item at the grocery cart. To read its label: a negative feeling that you don't need. Put that package back on the shelf and breathe.

Eventually, all that shopping and respiration wore me out, and I fell into a restless sleep. My inner guru rolled her eyes.

CHAPTER SIX
YOU GOT BONES

The next morning, I threw the thin bath mat into the tub so I didn't get any unseen microbes on my feet and cleaned up. In the aged mirror I said, "Stop wallowing."

Which was *not* the affirmation of this generation, but I came from the bootstrap, get your head out of your ass generation. Push those nerves down, ask for nothing, get to work were our anthems. I'd watched a video over Robyn's shoulder once, where a gray-haired man with nail polish said, "You are enough," and I laughed.

"Mom. You are," my daughter insisted.

"Yes, we are," I said with fake enthusiasm, thinking, *How can everyone be enough?* That doesn't even work statistically with normal curves and all. I was happy for Robyn, though. She was enough for me.

My mood improved as soon as I exited the motel room. My hair dried quickly in the California desert breeze while I followed the GPS to the back entrance of the Universal Studios campus. To my left stood several concrete-block buildings without windows. Through the eyes of a Wisconsinite, they looked like a great place to take cover after hearing the blast of a tornado siren.

The security kiosk sat just inside the gates. As I lowered the window, a uniformed woman said, "This isn't the park entrance, and it doesn't open until ten a.m."

I frowned.

"Also, the *Jaws* attraction is being repaired."

"I'm Lively. Poppy Lively. I'm to report to Studio 37." I held my phone up with an open text from Three as proof that I was in the right place.

She narrowed her eyes a fraction and pointed to the MUGGLES ON BOARD decal stuck to my side window, the Sorting Hat perched jauntily on the capital *M*.

"You can see my confusion."

"I have a Quidditch broom in the back if you want it." If I'd remembered the nerdy sticker was there, I would have scraped it off.

"ID, please," she said and held out her hand.

"I don't have one yet. They told me—"

"Driver's license," she interrupted.

"Of course!" I said, embarrassed. "Yes, I do have that kind of ID." She peered at me, lining up my driver's license photo with my face. "It's not a great photo. They told me not to smile. I'd just had my hair cut and you know how right after a cut your hair looks so weird. I didn't get a chance to fix it." I stopped talking, closed my eyes, and said, "I am here for a job in costumes."

She gave me the once-over and shook her head. "It's wardrobe. They gonna eat you alive, lady."

"They are?" I felt as if I were Robyn's age without the arrogant confidence of a teenager. I looked beyond the immediate buildings, the white-and-silver rectangular trailers, and spotted the spires of a castle and said, "Is that where they filmed *Harry Potter*?"

She clucked her tongue and pointed to a parking lot. "No. Do yourself a favor and don't ask anyone that question. Park your car there. Studio 37 is over there. Take what you need for the day. Tools, phone charger, whatever. You won't have time to go back to your car." The woman handed me a square of blue printed paper. "Put this in your window. Find the wardrobe trailer. It's a fifth wheel with clothes everywhere. Keep your head low."

"Luckily that is my motto," I said, but she'd already turned away to read something on her phone. That wasn't my motto, though. Mine was: Be likable. Ask for nothing.

I crept toward a square building with the NBC peacock high up on the side and above that the words EDITH HEAD. My nerves did a hop and skip. This was real. I'd heard about Edith Head on the podcasts I'd listened to. She was a costume designer with a huge number of Academy Awards, and all of a sudden my lack of fashion knowledge and inability to nail the tension on a sewing machine crashed together and dinged my confidence.

I snapped a photo of the Edith Head building and sent it to Chelsea.

Chelsea: Remember. You ran a business for years, raised a great kid. You wrote a grant for the High School Theater department.

Poppy: Ok. Please tell me stuff about your life.

Chelsea: The movie business is make believe. Make believe you belong. Brad got his hair cut.

Sweating in the morning heat, I walked, backtracked, and turned, asking directions from anyone who appeared even the least bit more official than I did. Which was everyone. Some spoke English, some didn't seem to, or they ignored me. Finally, a scruffy-haired man in a golf cart pulled up next to me and said, "Did you get separated from your tour bus?"

"Oh, no. Thank you. I'm looking for Studio 37."

"Get in," he said, and with my STAY TRUE TO YOUR SHELF canvas bag egging me on, I sat in the passenger seat. We drove around the corner; it couldn't have been fifty feet when he pointed at an enormous cement building with the number 37 on the side.

"Oh, this old thing?" I said, trying for a joke, but the driver didn't respond. Nearby I found an enormous white-and-silver fifth wheel with no windows and clothing hanging from unseen rails just as the guard had said.

I knocked on the side, peered in. "Hello?" I took the four grated silver steps into the trailer. All the way at the back was a woman seated behind a desk and another one, leaning in and speaking. I waited for them to notice me, but when they didn't look up, I said, "Hello. Hi. Excuse me." Items of clothing hung from high and low racks on each side of the long trailer. Shoes cluttered the floor in baskets, and there were boxes labeled with names. Hairy. Sweetie. Allen. Jeffery.

Face-to-face with this entirely unfamiliar environment had me at the kind of disadvantage that often brought out my insecurities. The enormity of entering this trailer and knowing nothing and no one—I had a real impulse to back out slowly before anyone noticed me.

The two women stopped and peered at me, like two foxes caught in the wild, unafraid but wary.

"I'm Poppy Lively."

"That is not your real name," said one of them. She wore a black tool belt around her waist, and glasses hung from a colorful beaded string around her neck.

"It is, actually. My mother was a hippie." I stopped myself from explaining too much as I had at security and got to business: "Are you Wanda Merinchowski?"

The second woman, who also had reading glasses perched on her nose, looked between me and possibly–Wanda Merinchowski.

"Are you our must hire?" the first woman said.

"Yes," I said, recognizing the term. I held up my phone as if it were some kind of official paperwork and said, "I was told to come here by six thirty. Ask for Wanda Merinchowski. I'm to start work today in the costum . . . wardrobe department."

"She's our must hire?" the second woman said to the first.

"Is something wrong?" I noticed a quiver in my hand, put my phone in my pocket, kept my hands out of sight.

"You can't be someone's niece," said the second woman.

"Or girlfriend. Are you someone's sister? Mother-in-law?"

"I don't understand. What are we talking about?" I said.

If I were being honest, I was feeling irritated. These women were my age, and they were roasting me. And for what reason? I was here to do a job. But then I imagined what they saw. An unqualified person foisted into their career space. They knew nothing about me and had no idea how capable I was. Or what a loser I was. Either way, to make this work here, I needed everyone to like me. I needed this job, and I could do it.

"Where do I start?" I said, hoping they didn't say *go get a sewing machine and make a dress.*

"I'm Wanda. I'm the designer. This is Muriel. She's my wardrobe supervisor. Whatever she says goes. Where's your kit?" Wanda asked.

"My kit? I wasn't told . . ."

"She's never done this before," said Wanda. Then the fun they were having at my expense evaporated. "Seriously. How did you get this job?"

I gathered enough from the situation to not admit that I was Three's old girlfriend. I wasn't going to give them any more ammunition for their disdain. "One of the producers sent me."

"Are you their aunt or something?" Wanda said.

"She's no older than you," said Muriel, surveying the length of me. "You're not from around here. You sound like Frances McDormand in *Fargo.*"

"Wisconsin. I'm from the Midwest."

Both women said, "Ahhhh," simultaneously, like it all added up.

"Where should we put her?" Muriel said.

Wanda laughed and said, "No you don't. That's all you. I'm not taking any responsibility for this one."

"She'll blend in," Muriel said. At first I thought that was a compliment, but after a moment's thought I realized she meant I'd be unnoticeable. I was unremarkable. I touched my face. Wished I would have taken a little more time with my makeup or clothes choice. But to be fair, these women weren't stylish at all. They didn't live up to my expectations either. Their lips looked normal size and not like the inflated lips of aging starlets I'd seen on the red carpet in *People* magazine at my dentist. Wanda's forehead moved, and Muriel had on a pair of old Nikes and no traces of makeup on her face. In fact, while we were talking, she pulled some no-name colorless lip balm from her tool belt and rubbed it on her lips.

"We'll start her as a runner. Or put her on the dogs. Continuity. Set up, work with the trainers."

"Dogs? Is that a nickname for something? Key grip or whatever?" The Hollywood podcasts spoke endlessly about the key grip.

Wanda blinked, and Muriel put on another layer of lip balm. They both looked as if I'd said something in a language they didn't understand and were taking their time to translate.

"Do you call dogs something other than dogs in Wisconsin?"

"I . . . no. Dogs are dogs in the Midwest. Is there a dog in this movie?"

"Dogs. This is a doggie rom-com. Did you not know that?"

I sneezed. And sneezed again. It was as if the mere mention of animals alerted my sinuses of soon-to-be-coming allergens. "A doggie rom-com?" I rubbed my nose and eyes, immediately watering with the thought of being around dogs and their fur all day, every day. It was cats that caused me most of the problem. Only some dogs were difficult, so I'd be fine, I told myself.

"They're remaking all the Nora Ephron movies but with dogs." Muriel glanced at Wanda, who seemed tired of the entire interaction. She waved her hand over her head like brushing away a gnat. "*When Hairy Met Sweetie* and *You Got Bones*."

That's when it occurred to me I should have listened to current Hollywood stories instead of the golden ages. The women eyed me— they had to have seen this before, rookies coming with glamour in their eyes and ending up with dog dander up their nose. I needed to rally.

"Wow, it *seams* like I'm going to *needle* all the help I can get," I said, putting the emphasis on the key puns and finishing with an awkwardly placed, "LOL." I felt my face heat up as, once again, my stress-joking did not hit its mark.

"Okay, Fargo," Muriel said. "Probably never make that joke again, okay?"

CHAPTER SEVEN
UNDERPROMISE, OVERDELIVER

Muriel signaled for me to move out of the trailer ahead of her, and I hustled through the racks of clothing onto the asphalt. She wore a headset around her neck and held a large three-ring binder under her arm. Muriel pointed and gave instructions the moment she cleared the trailer's steps. The enormity of the buildings, the expanse of grounds, the hustle of workers, so utterly removed from my home office with just the one chair. I don't know what I was expecting, but I needed a map, something to hold to get my bearings.

"We're in base camp and just left the main wardrobe trailer. Wanda is in and out and not always on set. I'm the supervisor. You report to me. You'll get a call sheet at night. Our call times are on the back, and on the front is the scene numbers and descriptions of what is being shot that day. We work from these sheets. If your name is on the sheet, you still have a job."

"They might take me off the sheet without telling me? Then I'm fired?" I'd listened to a podcast on Judy Garland being fired from *Valley of the Dolls* and wondered if they'd just erased her. I could not be erased. "How do you *not* get erased?" I said.

"Whatever time your call is the next day, you will not be late."

She halted, and I skidded to a stop inches from her. Muriel made unflinching eye contact with me and said, "Call time is the time you start working in the morning." I nodded bobblehead-style and she strode off. "Supplies are all over the trailer. Get to know where everything is in there. You'll need a portable kit that you wear all the time. A large fanny pack works well. A cross-body if you'd rather."

I tucked my canvas bag out of the way. Robyn had given it to me when she was in fifth grade—an elementary school kid's birthday gift—and suddenly I was overwhelmed and embarrassed. This was no place for mommy gifts and missing my daughter. This was not about catching up; it was about thinking ahead. I should have known I'd need sewing supplies.

I wondered what to put in a kit and if I could afford supplies. I didn't want to ask questions and make my ignorance known. Sweat dripped from the creeping heat of the day, and I was barely in control of my nervous system.

In the short time I'd been on the lot, many more people had appeared, walking with certainty. I felt as I had at my first waitressing job in high school, anxious to keep up but confused by the terminology. Muriel's directions were peppered with baffling vocabulary.

"Keep your call sheet with you at all times, take notes, keep them until wrap. I'll give you a headset to wear so I can always find you. In your kit, you should have"—she lifted her fingers and counted off—"double-sided tape, alcohol swabs, scissors, more safety pins than you'd ever think you will need, a Sharpie, a Tide stick. Labels, sewing kit, lint brush, nipple covers, binder clips."

I dug into my book bag, found a Sharpie, took notes on my hand. Here she stopped, glanced at my palm, shook her head as if to say, *Okay, that's new.* Then she looked me in the eye. "No wandering off. No hooking . . ." She narrowed her eyes at me. "I was going to say no hooking up on the job with the grips or actors. But . . ." Here she stopped.

One look at me and she'd decided I was not hook-up material. Which . . . okay. Fine. But I had hooked up in my day. I once made out so energetically with a sous chef in the walk-in freezer as a waitress in college that we knocked a whole tray of fried chicken onto the floor. *A whole tray*, my mind emphasized. But the impulse to speak didn't reach my tongue, because this memory had been ages ago. I wrote "Hook Up" on my thumb and put a slash through it so she knew I'd gotten the point.

Once Robyn was born, having been ghosted by my mother and then by Robyn's biological father, I got the message. People did not stick around. You had to be ready for it. Not get too attached unless you made them in your belly.

No matter how many times I'd called or texted Liam on that impossible Motorola phone of mine to tell him that I was pregnant, I couldn't get him to answer. Finally, after I literally camped out in my old Toyota in front of his place, his roommate knocked on the window and said, "Liam went to Spain."

"Without me?" I'd said pathetically and obviously.

"He told me to tell you to go to France, if you want to go on vacation."

Which was a puzzle, because I'd told Liam I wanted to go where he was going. That my ability to speak French would help in Europe.

Amid the confusion and despair of another abandonment, I felt relief. The other shoe had dropped, and I could take control of our lives—I was thirty-three at the time, going to be a mother, and didn't have to factor in another parent. I created a life for my daughter where she would not be left behind. She'd never wonder where I'd gone as she waited on shifting ground for a parent's return. From then on, we kept our numbers low, along with our expectations.

Then there was Three. I recognized his brand of wonderment. It was so like my father's energy when he was in a sales meeting or talking to the mothers of my friends. Although my father's could be turned off and on depending on what he wanted from you. He'd woo mothers into helping us bake for fundraisers and forget he'd done it when they dropped the cookies off. That was where Three and my father diverged.

My dad could be brutal, dismissive, especially with me. Three had never been that.

After Three, I hadn't met anyone with his glimmer. And, if that was absent, if there wasn't that bubbling, undefinable chemistry, why bother? Robyn's father wasn't Three. In fact, he would at times find me irritating to be around. Said I was too agreeable when I didn't care what restaurant we went to and talked about a vacation destination. I never understood how that could be an annoying thing. I shook my head. Strange to be thinking about all of this right now with Muriel huffing it up the hot asphalt while speaking to someone in her headphone. She turned.

"I need to know where you are at all times," Muriel said. "Get a notebook for continuity documentation. See this?" She pointed at a rolling rack with a shelf on the bottom near the side of a trailer. "This is a set rack. Don't move the set rack unless I personally tell you to move the set rack."

I nodded, but she had resumed her tour and didn't see my enthusiasm. I occasionally said "Okay" or "Got it," because even though nothing was okay and I knew very little, I wanted her to know I was still physically following her.

Eyes wide, taking in the trucks, rolling clothing hangers, equipment, wires, and props, I marveled at what felt like a city. People moved out of the way of golf carts, some individuals themselves were given a wide berth, and others were barely noted. Those that hauled extension cords and lights walked carefully and without comment.

Why had Three said I'd be perfect for this job? He didn't know how quiet my life had become. How small. What had he seen in me that said, *Perfect for chaos and unknown*? This down-on-her-luck lady was just right.

"The actors' trailers are over there. Keys are in the wardrobe trailer or with security. If I ask you to, you'll need to set costumes in there for the day after they've been prepped."

A man with a Yankees ball cap called out, "Hey, Muriel," and waved. "Does she need a ride to the tour bus?"

"No. Thanks!" she said in a cheerful tone. Not the tone she was using with me.

"Why does everyone think I've lost the tour bus?"

She ignored my question and continued.

"That's the Honey Wagon over there, if you have to go to the bathroom." Muriel pointed to a long semitruck with silver stairs and doors. I'd never seen anything like it; it looked like a motel on wheels.

"The AD confirms the scenes on the call sheet. We will get you a list of all the costumes and changes for everyone in the script for the day. Starting today. That includes socks, underwear, jewelry. Everything you wear in the real world, they wear in the movie world, and continuity is king around here."

"Continuity?"

"Everything must be exactly the same in consecutive scenes. If a top button is done or undone, it has to be that way during reshoots too. If sleeves are rolled, it stays that way before and after lunch, after a bathroom break, anytime. It's our job to make sure everything is the same for filming. Keep notes. Sharp eyes. Full attention."

"Keep notes. Sharp eyes. Full attention," I said, nodding.

"The team is steaming the clothing, writing notes, setting first costume change in the actor's room. Just for the one day, do you hear me? Do not think you're saving time by putting the next day's clothes into place. Nod that you understand."

I nodded and I could hear her speaking, but full comprehension was a bridge too far. I worked to hide my partial understanding, knowing I'd figure it out with practice and observation.

"Then we take a nondeductible breakfast. We give color cover for stand-ins and lighting."

Deducting breakfast, that's a laugh. I wished I could stop calculating hours, days, pay against my debts—taxes, tuition, mortgage. The constant mathing was distracting and had me feeling that my engine was revving and my tires were stuck.

When I thought of costumes for a movie, which I never did in my life before driving cross-country for this job, it never occurred to me that the process was so involved. If you'd asked me, I probably would have said that actors take their costumes home and come dressed to film every day.

We weren't far from the parking lot where my car sat in front of the big square Edith Head costume department. Muriel jogged up the concrete steps, past a bunch of old-fashioned streetlights, two velvet couches, and several ornate birdcages. Her arm shot out and pointed. "Props."

Without pause I followed Muriel through the large doors and down a hall, and we stopped in front of a woman in shorts and a T-shirt. She handed us three pairs of identical brown loafers. "Thanks," Muriel said and looked me in the eye. "Poppy, this is one of the women who may occasionally supply much of what you need."

We nodded at each other—I with the full sunny smile of the Midwest Hello and the young woman behind the counter with a nonplussed head tilt.

"We have our own cages for the show, and that is where I'll send you to collect items. When you work with actors, you must make sure they have everything they need. Help getting dressed. A clasp on a necklace, tricky buttons, a necktie. If you deliver a costume for a dog, you will hand the costumes to the trainer but don't trust them to get the clothing on right. Trust no one. Except me. And Wanda. If something needs adjusting, or tacked, or stitched or cleaned, that is your job. Then we go to set for rehearsal. After rehearsal they go straight to filming. We strive to never hear 'hold camera' because of wardrobe."

"Got it," I said. The urgency in Muriel's voice required acknowledgment, if not honesty. I'd stay up reading all night if I had to, and get it I would.

"If there is a break, do not let the dog or an actor out of your sight. No one can mess up their look, take off an earring, or pee on their outfit. A shooting day could take eight hours or twenty hours, and you are on the entire time. If you have to go to the bathroom or eat something . . . well, try not to, except during lunch break. We all eat together. Or not. It's catered. Do you have any allergies?"

I almost said, *Yes. Cats, some dogs.* But I got ahold of myself in time to say, "No. I can eat anything except bologna, because gross." Which I didn't mean to say. I wanted to contribute something.

"Nobody eats bologna in California."

We maneuvered the steps and back into the fresh air. My mouth was dry, and I imagined Muriel had to be parched, but she didn't stop.

"If we don't have something we need or an article of clothing gets wrecked, we might send you to the costume shop or shopping." Here Muriel stopped, looked at my jeans and running shoes. I'd worn a plain white T-shirt, and since the morning was cool, I'd thrown on a white collared button-down shirt. "Maybe we won't send you shopping. White gets filthy around here. You could be a trailer runner except"— she tilted her head—"I feel like you'll get lost. I'm going to give you a partner. Any questions?"

I wanted to ask something that showed her I was a capable person, one who realized the complexity and importance of this job. But, like the one phone call you might get in jail, I didn't want to squander my question. I did a quick calculation—should I go for respect and comprehension and say, *No. No questions.* Or should I get information on something critical, a word that rolled off her tongue that was clearly important?

"Let's see if I have this right." I held up my hand and counted off on my fingers. "Call sheet. Steam. Dry cleaning. Set first costumes only. Eat. Lighting. Dress actors. Rehearsal. Film. Continuity. Wear a colored shirt? No mistakes."

Muriel put on the brakes and looked at me. "That's right," she said and seemed to focus in on me.

I stopped myself from saying, *I'm not a dope, I'm new*. Then I remembered trusting Dawna Klump and thought, *I'm not always a dope*.

My father used to say, *Underpromise, overdeliver, Poppy. Your name is already making promises it can't keep. Be a pleasant surprise, not a disappointment*. The subtext was that I was a walking, talking letdown, and I pushed against that my whole life and became über capable.

"Do you need to use the bathroom before we get to it?"

I didn't, but I excused myself anyway so that I could text Chelsea. I sprinted up the steps to one of the Honey Wagon bathrooms. Inside I sent a quick SOS text.

Poppy: I'm feeling really overwhelmed.

Like a boss waiting by her phone, Chelsea texted me immediately back.

Chelsea: Look. You got your kid dressed every day. You sewed on buttons. It's fine.

Chelsea: I'll do some googling for things that might be helpful and text you. The pug bros are on a diet.

Getting more information through my phone from Chelsea thousands of miles away didn't feel calming, but I didn't want to offend my supportive friend, so I texted YES!

Poppy: This movie is a Doggie Rom Com.

Chelsea: Cute!!! Have you seen Three?

Poppy: No. Gotta go.

I emerged from the Honey Wagon, tense because I didn't see Muriel right away. I spotted her, standing near the doors of Studio 37, far enough away that I'd be royally sweaty once I got to her. Halfway there a golf cart pulled up next to me and I scowled. "Do not ask me if I need a ride back to my bus."

"Poppy?" It was Three with a boyish grin on his face.

I wound up for a big greeting, maybe a hug. I was so gushingly grateful for a familiar face, so thrilled to see his smile, his warm eyes.

The expression on his face stopped me. He put a covert finger to his lips and said under his breath, "Better nobody knows we have history on the first day. Better for you, if you know what I mean."

I nodded quickly. "I think I do." I couldn't help feeling a twinge of disappointment in my chest. I hadn't expected a make-out session, but I thought, I don't know, something more. A tiny treat tossed my way, an inside joke that touched on our history. The way he was making our lives work right now.

"I gotta go. Just wanted to see that you were settled in."

"Wait—who do I see about lodging?"

"Lodging?"

"When we talked you said something about staying here. At Universal?"

He blinked, paused. "Oh. Poppy, we're filming on set and on the back lot. That's what I meant about staying here." The way he'd said my name, as if I were cute and maybe a little Midwest dumb. He was being sweet, but I hated the origin of that kindness was that I somehow didn't know something other people knew. That I was not impressing the person I needed to impress for a myriad of reasons.

"Of course," I said, laughing at myself before he did. "I knew that. I was surprised when you said that before. I was just checking to make sure I had it right," I lied. Ugh, back to the Murder Hotel. How would I pay? The credit card was meant for emergencies only, and I'd purposefully put a credit limit on it. What if Robyn had an emergency and couldn't get help because of charges from that disgusting hotel?

I hated more than anything to be unprepared. Unaware. As a child I missed everything without a mother to show me the way. From how to use a tampon to how babies were made to how often to shower. I was always feeling stupid and hiding my questions. I'd started my period at school and, in shock, told one of the mothers who helped out the school nurse that I might be dying. I saw her suppress laughter; then her face filled with pity and finally there was this condescending conversation that started with the word *pudendum*.

"All good, then. Let's get together. I'll text you." He accelerated an inch. Stopped, made eye contact, and said, "You look great. Just great."

And off he drove in the opposite direction. I'd text him later, I promised myself. I'd ask if he knew of a cheap place or someone who needed a roommate. The fourth-grade girl who had survived without her mother for years and years whispered, *No you won't. You know very well what happens when you ask for things—nothing good. Isn't this job enough? Geez, Poppy. Figure it out.*

CHAPTER EIGHT
OH, FOR SEWING OUT LOUD

My old bra would not support a jog to Muriel's side, so I racewalked, afraid that moving faster would look as if I'd stolen one of the dogs and shoved it under my shirt. If I didn't look as desperate as I felt, maybe I could hint around about where new people might find an affordable place to stay. When I got to her side, she looked equal parts curious and suspicious. She'd seen me talking to Three, or at least to a person in a golf cart.

I gestured to the general area I'd come from. "Why are people asking if I need to find my tour bus?" Maybe she'd buy that Three had been one of those people. I did not want special treatment, just basic needs.

"You read differently than the typical employee. Let's walk." We strode between buildings with gigantic sliding barn doors that must have weighed tons. "Most must hires on a movie set for the first day come all glammed up. They hear costume designer, and they think black capes and red lipstick. You're dressed like you're going grocery shopping at Ralphs."

"I don't think I'm dressed any differently than you." Muriel wore a pair of light jeans and a T-shirt. I gauged her to be somewhere between forty and sixty, that ubiquitous age for a woman that teens considered ancient and homogenous.

"Right. But . . ." Muriel was quiet. She lifted her earpiece, set it back on her shoulder, and said, "You have a very midwestern way about you. No offense."

"Is it offensive to be from the Midwest?" I knew Wisconsin wasn't considered the hub of US style, but come on. I wondered how that might affect my likability here, my continued employment.

"Don't you know if you're not from California or New York, you're not from anywhere anyone can find on the map." Muriel said this as if she was aware this point of view was the height of snobbery, so I wasn't offended. I was curious. I'd been in the Midwest, around my tight circle of people, for so long, I hadn't seen myself through outside eyes. I wondered what else they saw that categorized me. Subtle things I wore like skin but they saw as a label or a truth.

Muriel steered me around a corner, and I saw a city street with brownstones, sidewalks, and awnings over the windows. "I'm showing you this area because eventually we'll shoot outside over here."

I wanted to memorize the pathways we walked so I wouldn't get lost, but there was so much to process, and I was distracted by the idea that I was a walking Midwest cartoon of a woman. It didn't matter how far you'd come in the world of competency; women were always judged by their outward appearance.

I thought of my too short jeans from elementary school, my lunches of whatever was left in the fridge from a take-out meal with my dad. How I shopped at charity stores for both of us, hanging shirts in his closet to not embarrass him. He'd wear those shirts to an occasional school event and receive a compliment from a mother who he'd charmed. Make up some fancified story of where he'd gotten it.

It had been years since I'd resurrected those old memories of him, unsettling as it was for me to review those insecure years. Why now? I wondered. What was it about this place that brought my father to mind?

Static from Muriel's headset pulled her attention. "They need me back at the trailer." She peered at me and said, "You smile all the way up to your eyes. Like you don't have anything to hide."

"I don't," I said, happy to hear I was successful at hiding my over-loaded senses and fear of failure. My time urgency, and my current practice of calculating bill payment options between breaths. My mind returning to my debt was like finding a rough spot on a tooth and not being able to keep your tongue away from it. I'd keep all of this in check so I didn't get erased for something stupid like not looking the part. Because I knew while I didn't look like I fit, I could do this job. I could do whatever was asked of me, despite setbacks. I would sleep in my van if I had to. I'd keep my mouth shut and do what it takes.

Muriel considered my expression. "Here, on a movie set, people are concealing a lot. In fact, that's what costumers do. We don't just put fabric on people. We hide the actor in clothing and shine focus on the character. We are masters at it in this business." She turned and I followed as she jetted toward the trailer.

We approached a young woman at the door of the main wardrobe trailer, nose in her phone, the same posture Robyn often assumed by default. Muriel slowed and said, "Poppy, I'd like you to meet Emilie. Emilie, this is Poppy. She's new today. Replacing Kristi."

"Kristi's really gone," Emilie said. "So stupid."

"We'll talk about it later," said Muriel.

I tried to gauge Emilie's age. Her smooth skin had a childlike blush high on her cheeks. She had straight chestnut-colored hair and what I called a kitten nose. A small beauty-button that tied her features together with symmetry. The girl smirked at me while I beamed my *let's be friends* grin, because I couldn't help myself when I felt disliked or insecure.

"Emilie, I'd like you to show Poppy around the costume shop. Make sure she knows who to see when we need something ASAP. Explain meals, who to submit receipts to if we send you two shopping, and she needs a kit."

Emilie surveyed me from the tip of my dirty New Balance shoes to the top of my short, sensible hair. I smoothed my bangs and pushed a fringe of hair behind my right ear. A mannerism left over from a longer hairstyle that Robyn had called a mom cut. This girl's appraisal wasn't a positive one; it had an air of assessment that said, *No way am I hanging around with this oldie,* even while knowing she would be forced to.

Emilie gave me a false smile, and I saw what Muriel was saying about the eyes. I wondered what this veritable girl, this young woman could be hiding. She had to be about Robyn's age. With that thought, I had the urge to text my daughter. To FaceTime and see if her smile filled her eyes; that she, alone in New York, wasn't feeling like I was. Out of place.

The silence between us stretched. It was as if Emilie was trying to work something out, waiting for information, a prioritization of the duties Muriel had listed.

"Today is an observation day, Poppy. Get your bearings. Be ready to run your butt off tomorrow," said Muriel.

"Why don't we start by getting me a kit?" I said to be helpful. As if I'd pushed a start button, Emilie moved back in the direction of the Edith Head building. I pumped my arms to keep up and at Emilie's shoulder I said, "So how long have you been working here?"

"From the beginning," she said. I think my daughter would have called that a low-key flex. A subtle way of saying *I was here first.*

She stuck her phone into her back pocket, where it pushed tightly against the fabric of her jean shorts. Emilie wore a pair of cutoff shorts that showed off the kind of legs you could only be born with. Long, lean, with a tight hamstring at the back of her thigh that I associated with gifted sprinters.

"You're a must hire," she said to me. Not a question.

"Yes, I am."

"Everybody hates a must hire."

"I gathered that," I said.

"Yeah, must hires don't have any experience. And they get in the way more often than not. They know nothing about costumes." And here she gave me a faster rendition of her earlier assessment. With a frown.

"You're not a must hire, I take it."

"No, I am. But now that you're here people will focus on you, being the new person on the set." Then she half turned, flashed a grin, and added a courteous, "So thank you. Also, don't make friends. They don't last."

"Is that what happened to Kristi?"

There was a hardly noticeable hitch in her step.

"Nah. She f'ed up," Emilie said.

"How badly do you have to mess up to get fired?"

We moved up the stairs of the costume shop, walked through a metal door and into the hallway.

"Not that badly," Emilie said. "You can't take a costume off set to wear it or show off or whatever. I guess that's what she did. I never saw it, though. Anyway, they don't fire you. Your name just disappears from the call sheets."

"So I hear." While ghosting was a newish dating term and conjured with it all my baffling feelings of loss without explanation, I was a single mother because of that practice. After getting over the abandonment, which I admit was miserable, I'd benefited greatly because I got Robyn out of the deal. I got to focus on my pregnancy without someone else's desires to factor in, because that was the crux of me. If others wanted something, I didn't know how to say no. Fewer people around me, fewer requests to fill, more Robyn time. Look, I'm old enough to know that you can get over your mother leaving, but you can still be damaged. Maybe I'd work on that when I returned home.

Here, though, an Irish goodbye could not happen. Every night, wherever I slept was going to be a death march to morning while I checked my email to make sure I hadn't been erased.

We walked around rolling racks of clothes, buckets of shoes, and baskets of accessories. It was like the largest thrift shop anyone could ever imagine. I wanted to stop. Read the manila tags hanging from every single garment. Imagine who had worn them once or who would wear them in the future. How they kept them all straight.

"Wow," I said. "So many clothes. How does anyone find anything?"

"It's all cataloged and sorted. It looks messy but it's not. Don't even think about borrowing something. It's tempting." It was as if Emilie was reminding herself not to walk away with any of the costumes that were the property of Universal Studios. "Who made them hire you?" Emilie said, and I had the feeling this wasn't the off-handed question she wanted me to think it was. She knew.

"One of the producers is an old friend."

We turned a corner and a woman with two enamel sticks protruding from a high, messy bun pulled shirts out of a laundry basket and put them on hangers. An industrial-size steamer emitted a hiss, and the woman I'd met before greeted Emilie.

Emilie narrowed her eyes at me. It was clear she was processing how I'd come to be here. I couldn't tell if she knew who Three was or not.

"This is, what's your name again? Polka-Dot?" Emilie said, not even trying to hide that she'd forgotten. Or apologize. Or be the slightest bit cordial.

"Poppy."

"Oh yeah. Weird," said Emilie. "She's our new must hire." She lifted one perfect eyebrow in a way that said, *Damn, don't you hate a must hire. Ugh.*

The woman behind the desk didn't play along. Instead, she said, "We've met."

Emilie had her phone out again texting someone.

"I'm here for a kit?" I said.

"Oh yeah," Emilie said. "That's what we're here for. Is Kristi's kit here? Give it to her."

The woman reached under the counter and pulled out a clear plastic fanny pack similar to Emilie's cross-body bag.

"Just until I get my own," I said. I clipped the bag around my middle, settling the bulk of it on my hip bones. "Oh, for sewing out loud," I said and then wanted to immediately die. Robyn and I liked silly puns. But the woman behind the desk, she looked pained.

"Sewing Tourette's," I said with a grimace.

Emilie acknowledged nothing and moved away as if she'd been pushed.

"I think I'm supposed to get to know the costume shop while we're here."

"Can you take her?" Emilie said.

"Am I supposed to take her?"

Emilie shrugged.

"Maybe you could give me an idea of the layout, direct me to where I pick up a headset," I said.

"Thanks, see ya," Emilie said and disappeared the way we'd come.

"That's the director's niece," the woman said.

"Ah," I said. "Good to know."

It was a quick, overwhelming tour where much hand waving and pointing occurred. I was handed off to another woman who left me with an older man with a thick accent who made shoes. I was a hot potato nobody wanted to be left holding at the end of the hour. When I remarked on a large wooden bin of gold shoes, the shoe man gestured, inviting me to touch them, examine them close up. I touched a pair of worn gold dancing shoes in a size six. So dainty, and I envisioned someone from *A Chorus Line* dancing across a stage. I turned to share this thought, but I was alone.

In my actual life, I'd always had a place to be. Home at work. Picking up and dropping off Robyn at sports or school until she could drive herself. When I volunteered at the food pantry, people greeted me as if I were a long-lost friend. When a chaperone was needed for a dance or field trip, they called Poppy Lively because I was helpful and liked.

It took a few wrong turns, past the sheer dresses from the 1930s and through an entire aisle of Chinese armor, to get outside and go back to the wardrobe trailer.

Back in the sunshine, I blinked and congratulated myself when I found the wardrobe trailer and Muriel.

"Good. You're back. I need you to steam these garments. Have you used a steamer before?"

"Yes," I said. "It's fairly straightforward. Just don't give me your taxes."

Muriel tried to compute that and shook her head. I wondered how many people she had to orient a year. "Emilie said you wanted to stay in the costume shop."

I didn't know how to respond. I wanted to be where I was supposed to be. I didn't want to contradict Emilie, but my wants weren't the priority. "I thought . . ."

"It's fine. Just let me know where you are. Always." I felt like a disobedient child, as if I'd wandered off.

"Here's your headset, and a set of keys for very late nights or early mornings. Emilie picked up a croissant for you, and a map of the grounds."

"She did? That was so nice of her. Gosh," I said, taking the microphone from her.

"Gosh," Muriel repeated in a slightly mocking tone. "She didn't do it to be nice. I asked her to do it."

"If I burn myself on the steamer, you can hear me say, 'Holy cow that's hot.'"

"Do not burn yourself on the steamer," she said, all business. "If you hurt yourself, the paperwork is never-ending. You're not in the union yet."

A voice in Muriel's headset pulled her attention before she could reassign me to an injury-free zone. I clipped my own headset in place. I'd worked backstage during Robyn's summer production of *The King and I*, an overly ambitious musical for a bunch of Norwegian kids who couldn't sing. My job was to make sure the king's children got onstage on cue, and not a single kid was injured under my care. I'd store that story away for the next time Muriel questioned my abilities.

My phone buzzed. Chelsea. How are the living digs?

If I didn't want that woman flying to my side, I needed a better answer than *I'm staying at the Murder Hotel.* I had to text Three.

Poppy: Hey, Three. Love the job. Muriel's amazing. I know how super busy you are. Hate to ask this but, do you know anyone who needs a roommate?

Before I could press send, little Poppy Lively from the curb outside her elementary school said, *Maybe wait until you are on more solid footing.*

Instead, I texted Chelsea, an avoidance move I'd learned from Robyn.

Poppy: Steaming clothes. Brb.

CHAPTER NINE

NAPPING CAMP

Inside the wardrobe trailer, there were rows of wrinkled clothing that needed smoothing. Shirts and pants, dresses and sweaters in adult and children's sizes, all for the dogs. There were tags to affix, items to be stored, and an organizational system to learn. I steamed, hung, and folded clothing while silently watching the roles of everyone coming into and going out of the trailer.

It was a marvel to do just this one thing. When you're the only parent, you are the yeoman of the land. There is no one but you to drop off a forgotten lunch while a living is earned, the lawn is mowed, the driveway shoveled. If your daughter needs seven trips to the dermatologist because her acne meds require it, you are driving, scheduling the next six appointments, and penning a grocery list while listening to your kid talk about AP biology.

I'd met Dawna Klump during the hairiest times in our pre–high school graduation lives. Our basement had flooded, Robyn needed to be fitted for a new mouth guard, and Dawna was seated next to me during a long and boring school board meeting. We were in a breakout group together, and I was looking for the name of a good dentist. She had a commanding way about her, and after listening to me talk about orthodontia she'd said, "A good mother knows something has to give.

I have several clients. I could take over your books." When she took charge of the taxes without asking that first year, I was grateful. I didn't see her as a controlling person at the time.

The steam sputtered and stopped about the same time as I ran out of clothes. I set to work on a tangle of jewelry that littered the desk beneath what I recognized as a hanging plastic makeup organizer. I'd finished unknotting the necklaces, bracelets, and earrings and placed each into Velcro'd plastic envelopes that hung from a peg on the wall. I moved on to fill the dry-cleaner bags and to sort the shoes that littered the floor. Emilie wandered in with her usual careless attitude.

I left briefly to use the Honey Wagon and when I returned unnoticed, I heard Wanda complimenting Emilie in that obvious way parents do when working to encourage repeat behavior from their child. "The trailer looks terrific. Nicely done."

Emilie took in the praise without a single guilty glance my way. I thought about making it clear that the tidy trailer was my work. I didn't know much about the business, but I assumed a director's niece trumped a producer's ancient girlfriend in the moviemaking hierarchy and said nothing.

"I didn't do the jewelry," Emilie said. "That new one did. PopPop or whatever." Which was both true and insulting, but instead of clarifying and appearing petty right off the bat, I backed out of the door and saw Muriel listening as well and watching me. The look on her face said, *Holy cow, watch yourself.*

Moments later, through my headset, I heard, "That's a wrap." There was a flurry of movement, as if the crew had been holding their breath and exhaled all at once. People streamed out of the stage doors, the crew rolled cameras and rewound cords, and extras stayed out of the way. I followed other costume staff as they hustled to collect clothing from actors and get it back to the trailer. I kept quiet and found my shoulders aching from carrying hangers and clothing in and out and up onto racks, hooks, and rails.

More chatter: "Early call tomorrow. Dogs on set. Roy, camera B repair cover." Wanda had human resources papers for me to sign. Emilie was surprisingly helpful, telling me, "Go return the C-stand to the grips. You don't want to piss off a grip."

If Emilie was more like Robyn, I'd have made a grip or gaffer pun. It wouldn't have to be a good one to get my daughter to smile—but Emilie was a tougher crowd.

One by one people said, "Good night," and I saw the truly obvious. No one stayed on set. Everyone went home for the night, waited for their call sheet, returned the next morning, and stood where they were needed. I didn't feel like joking now; in fact, my mood had dropped like a math-bowl champion on a chin-up bar. I wasn't without options, I cheered myself on. I had my car—nothing to brag about, but it was only until I could figure things out.

Moments later, alone in the wardrobe trailer, Muriel looked surprised to see me as she found her own purse and fished out her car keys. "Emilie went home. I told her to tell you that you could go too. To make sure we had your email."

"I stayed because I know how much I have to learn," I lied. Look, insisting on every niggling detail, being righteously correct about who did what, was beneath me, and terrible politics. Emilie was a kid; I was an adult. I wasn't going to whine about *he said, she said* stuff the first day on the job. I'd been my own boss for so many years, I knew how to talk to vendors, negotiate, be, if not tough, at least stern. Here I had no authority, and I wasn't about to compete in any way, make enemies, jeopardize my job.

"You don't get overtime," Muriel said.

I tried an Emilie shrug. "I just put a load in the washer. I'll transfer it to the dryer, then head out." I wrote my email on a scrap of paper and handed it to Muriel.

"We're missing the hero's necklace. The pearls with the charm. We need it for all reshoots. Have you seen it? Emilie said you organized the jewelry."

"I did that, yes. I know the necklace you're talking about. It's tagged in the organizer."

"No it's not. It's missing," Muriel said with her back to me, walking away. "If it isn't found it will cost a fortune to reshoot with something else."

The implication was clear: I saw the necklace last, it was my responsibility. This was the kind of thing people got erased for, and they'd be looking for a new must hire if I didn't find it.

"It's not missing. I saw the pearls. I'll find it. Don't erase me from the call sheet, Muriel!" Her name came out sounding like a parrot's squawk. She held her hand up, and I pushed my lips together.

"While you wait for the washer, see if you can locate it," said Muriel, and took off.

I'd find that necklace. It would be fine. I'd walk into that trailer like I did when Robyn lost things in plain sight and hold the one-of-a-kind necklace in my hands in victory and relief.

The sun had set and the battery on my phone indicated I'd lose power soon. I assumed I'd have to move my car for security reasons, and I had a kick-ass flashlight in the glove compartment. I'd search for that necklace in every crack and crevice of that trailer and possibly find Emilie's number and call her.

The last of the crew rushed toward the parking lot. I wanted to call out, *Good work today, Tom.* Or, *Thanks, Wanda, I learned a lot.* Or, *Three—I'm so grateful for this job. Can we get something to eat?* But I was an unseen, unknown person who wasn't integral to getting anyone home.

I unlocked the van and hit my shin with the edge of the door as it opened. Strange. It was lower than usual. That's when I saw the flat tire. "No. No. Noooo," I said under my breath. I had to find that necklace, not unload the entire van, find a spare tire, try to change it in front of all of Hollywood. Did I even have the tools deep in the bowels of the van to do the job?

The necklace came first. I hurried to the security kiosk where I had received my drive-on pass and said to the person inside, "Hey, I'm having a little car trouble. Is my van okay in the lot if, say, I have to leave it here overnight?"

The woman didn't look at me when she said, "If you put your pass in the window, you'll be fine."

The woman waved two men with security uniforms through the gates. While it seemed okay to leave my unoccupied car in place, I doubted sleeping undiscovered was an option—there was a definite uptick in security personnel as the movie crew left.

I put my most capable expression on my face and walked with purpose to the wardrobe trailer. I didn't want to involve Chelsea; she'd worry about me, but she was my rock, my support, and I needed her. Inside, I called her.

"What's up?" Chelsea said, ready for anything but sounding tired. It was late in Wisconsin.

"Workers don't stay on set, Chels. My van has a flat. And there's a necklace missing and I have to find it in the wardrobe trailer or . . ." I swallowed. "They'll make me pay for it and fire me. I don't have any place to sleep."

"Where are you now?"

"Searching in the wardrobe trailer. It's like a big camper. Like ground zero for the show costumes."

"Call Three. This is his fault. Tell him you need a place to sleep tonight."

"I can't, Chelsea. I should have asked more questions. This is on me. And I can't ask for more. It's so embarrassing. I . . ."

"Take a breath. We are going to reframe this. Tonight you have to find this necklace, and that's what you're doing. If you need a nap while you do it, take a nap. You aren't doing anything other than resting between looking."

"I'm not sleeping. I'm resting."

"That's right. If anyone comes, tell them to leave you alone; you are working late. Do it the way you yelled at me when I came too early for my surprise party. Say, 'Get out!' Like you did to me."

"Okay. That sounds good. Really good. I'll call you when I find it." And we said goodbye and I got down to business.

I rummaged like a meticulous raccoon, starting with the plastic hanging bag. When no pearls materialized, I became the girl I was in college. The one with all the colored highlighters and folders—the big desk calendar and multicolored Post-it Notes. Systematically, I shook out and refolded all the washed items, checking pockets and shoes. I switched my flashlight on and peered behind the washer and dryer, between bench cushions, and in every last corner of the trailer. I slid baskets out, checked drawers, and threw piles of dust bunnies away. I felt inside each shoe for a second time as I relined them up, sorted and tidied drawers, and wiped the surfaces. No necklace.

I'd seen it. Held it in my hands. Where had I put it? I searched every taped piece of paper above Wanda's desk, went through folders for Emilie's number. The top of my head felt like it might lift off in irritation, and my feet, like the hands on a clock, were pointing toward fatigue. I needed to get some sleep, wake with a clear mind, and think this through.

For our family vacations, the rare outings we took, we would go on what my dad called vacations for the frugal minded. We'd drive to a wooded area, not a campground, and we'd forge a trail in the woods. We had tents and mosquito netting. A propane stove and dishes. He talked about how people had gone soft, spending money on things that made them softer. My mother rolled her eyes at his pronouncements, but I was happy to be together.

Years later, after moving back in with my dad, I saw that he was not at all above spending money extravagantly. He'd emptied his accounts buying oddly specific items of comfort. Cashmere underwear, chamomile tea from Germany, and two freezers full of Wagyu beef. I'd sold it all online, except for the underwear. He lived above his means and told stories where you had no idea if there was any truth to them. He was a charmer to the neighborhood women, a warmth and focus I rarely felt from him.

Once on one of our excursions, my dad came upon someone's cabin and amid a downpour got us inside. "They won't know we were here." We slept on the floor, never touching anything in the place. I pretended we were survivors on the Oregon Trail and making do with little was an adventure. My mother cuddled me; I remembered her breath on my cheek, her body tucked around mine.

I'd think of tonight like napping camp.

It was dark when I walked back to my car and rummaged in the multiple bags on the back seat. I stuffed everything I'd need for a sleepover into my canvas bag, including the airline pillow and my versatile car napping coat.

I had to keep moving. If someone was watching me, I would not lead them straight to the wardrobe trailer to find me balancing on a bench trying to sleep. Instead, I strode into the back lot, walking quickly as if I had someplace to be and I knew where that someplace was. I passed the *Psycho* house, a huge crashed airplane set, and through a western saloon facade next to a train station. I didn't dare slow or try any of the doorknobs. I was sure any minute someone would stop me, haul me back to the Universal lost tourist collection room.

I ducked behind a pillar or tree if I heard a motor. I felt like I was in my own movie, an urgent woman, frantic, reckless, doubling back, staying in shadows, trying for a balance between *I belong here* and *don't look at me*. There was no glamour here, just a woman working for the greater good against insurmountable odds, like usual. With that thought, a kind of battle fatigue washed over me and I slowed and returned to the wardrobe trailer.

Before I put my key into the lock, I stopped and surveyed where I'd come. With no one in sight, I opened the door and pushed inside. A small night-light illuminated the space enough for me to find an outlet, plug in my phone. I listened hard for anything that might be near the trailer—footsteps, security, the police shouting through a bullhorn, *Come out with your hands up.*

Quiet.

Shakily, I put my hand on the cool wall. I was going to sleep in this trailer. I was an old hand at accepting circumstances for what they were. *You get what you get and you don't throw a fit,* my dad used to say. And so I adapted.

To wear out my nervous system, I cleaned the microwave and small fridge, throwing out old food and tossing sour half-and-half. Two shirt buttons and a shirt lay on the counter. I would do a quick repair before trying to shut my eyes for the night. I moved to a bench wide enough to sleep on and unzipped my clear plastic fanny pack.

My phone buzzed. A text from Chelsea.

Chelsea: Find it?

Poppy: Not yet.

Chelsea: You'll find it. My patient lived but she barfed on my shoe.

I found the sandwich I hadn't eaten from lunch and, suddenly starving, devoured it in a few bites. I finished it off with a few scoops of someone's peanut butter and grabbed one of the thousands of always available water bottles.

I heard the distinct sound of a motorized vehicle coming to a stop right next to where I sat. Whoever was outside the trailer was very near. I held my breath, my heart bumping up, up, up into my throat. Okay, this was not comfortable.

The motor dropped into an idle, and I heard a grunt as someone dismounted and walked the length of the trailer. I shut the light off on my phone. I heard footsteps on the metal stairs—one, two, three, four. The doorknob turned, rattled, and stopped. After an exhale that I imagined the person outside could feel on his cheek, the cart drove off.

My phone buzzed.

Three: How was the day?

I'd lived so long without the attention of men, I was surprised by my heart's skipping response to one now. It felt high schoolish and a bit thrilling. One of the many reasons I didn't date was a mediocre attraction to most men I met. I never felt the pull I'd felt with Three. He was my gold standard.

Three had this look that said, *I want to know everything about you, even though I see you.* And wasn't this job evidence of his deep knowing? That I could be taken out of my comfort zone and put in foreign territory, and I wouldn't embarrass him.

Poppy: A lot to learn. Fun.

Three: I like your hair short.

Poppy: Thanks. You look the same. Exactly.

Three: You're too kind. When can I see you?

My poor cardiovascular system was getting the equivalent of a spin class workout today. My thumbs poised and became instantly tremulous over the keyboard. So much to consider. Was this a friendly request? A professional one? A—gasp—romantic one? If this were sixteen years ago, it would be a request to come to my bed, in the apartment I shared with my infant daughter, quietly snoring in her room.

Poppy: You're the boss . . .

I liked this jaunty response. It could be considered flirty, friendly, or professional. It was one thing to be confident in your ability to get things done; it was quite another where men were concerned. Besides, he was busy, important. It wasn't for me to ask for a date around my availability. I wanted him to think of me as easygoing, game, amiable.

Three: I'll come find you soon. 😉

I was puzzling out this winky face when the three dots emerged indicating Three was typing.

Three: Is this job going to help your financial situation?

Poppy: You have no idea.

Three: Good. Lots of opportunities here. We can talk about others.

I waited for more. A possible date when we might go out. A time. When nothing more came, I knew why. I'd seen firsthand the speed and focus of this work. Three in particular seemed like he lived his life on a luge sled bombing from one thing to another without pausing.

I'd sew on the buttons, settle my heart. I pointed my phone light into my kit and found a needle and thread next to a folded slip of paper. I opened it and read the words printed in blue pen inside.

The button is in Emilie's kit. Call me when you find it, K, followed by nine numbers and the last either a 4 or a 9—dashed off quickly and stowed. I peered at the note.

Was this note from Kristi? Maybe she meant to leave it with Wanda? Maybe this was a kind of message in a bottle? To whom it may concern . . .

One day on a movie set and I was like Chelsea, creating stories where there was probably nothing. I replaced the note in the kit, rested my head against the wall. I closed my eyes and tried not to see the eyes of the woman outside the homeless encampment.

CHAPTER TEN

KEVIN

When the alarm went off on my phone, I was already up and reading emails and texts sent in the middle of the night from Robyn. It was Tuesday morning, and my eyes were gritty and my hips hurt from the bench.

Robyn: The kids take lessons at the Joffrey Ballet. It's famous mom. How's California?

If she knew where I'd spent the night, she'd be horrified, ask too many questions before I had enough answers, and turn the focus on me instead of on herself. I'd have to explain that the IRS needed the house.

My daughter hadn't been alive when my father died and I learned our family home would be taken over by the bank. Once I had a spreadsheet of my father's debts, I deferred college and went to work. I took over the coupon business, scaled it, updated the designs. It hadn't occurred to me to let it go, get an apartment. What if my mom came looking for me? Where would she look?

I was older than Robyn, still wanting a mother even knowing she wouldn't return. That all I had of her was the house. Robyn didn't know what it felt like to lose the only place you remembered being held by your mother. And, if I had it my way, she never would.

I continued to read her texts.

Robyn: Lizzie, the mom, is trying to get pregnant again. Said they'll need a live-in nanny for the year not just the summer.

It was 8:00 a.m. in New York, so I replied.

Poppy: Did you tell her you got into Nursing School. Early admission?

When I graduated from high school, I lived in the family home, renting out bedrooms to college students to make an extra buck. I kept coupons flowing all over Wisconsin and finally, at twenty-eight, I went to college part-time. I didn't have much in common with the appropriately aged freshman class. It wasn't the typical college BFF bonding experience that I wanted for my only child.

Robyn: She knows. Said she wasn't surprised. I'm a little homesick today. Excited for nursing school in the fall.

Poppy: Me too.

This emotional spinning wheel of fortune was normal for parenting a kid who was almost a grown-up. Excitement, melancholy, wonder, fear could be packaged in one sentence and forgotten the next hour. The trick was to listen, support, and do no problem-solving until a solid problem was defined. Emotions were not to be solved.

Robyn: I gotta go. Love you.

That was it—dump and run. I was satisfied that she wasn't texting me *Mom, I hate it here.* Or some other come-get-me plea like she had at gymnastics camp in eighth grade. I would not be able to leave here and get her or reassure her that all was fine. Nothing was fine.

I clicked on an email from HR. Please complete these employment forms, review your work schedule, termination conditions, employee responsibilities, compensation, and benefits. I scanned the compensation document and read the pay. Yesterday I figured I'd made $400 minus taxes (ugh, taxes were like an intruding parent at every turn). Today I'd make another $400. I'd keep at it and would have her first semester of tuition by the September 15 drop-dead date. She'd start school on time, and that was the thread I held on to.

It was time to solve the necklace mystery, and I'd call AAA road service. I wrote a to-do list on one of Muriel's Post-it Notes, and my sweaty hand slipped down to the tip of the pencil twice. I needed a shower and a cup of coffee but probably would get neither. I also had to pee. I eyed the stainless-steel sink. No, it had not come to that quite yet. I eased open the outer door, clipped my clear plastic kit around my waist along with my hastily handwritten ID name tag, and moved to the Honey Wagon, praying that at least one of the bathrooms was unlocked.

I smelled the cigarette smoke before I heard the voice say, "Aren't you the early bird."

An older man in a uniform stood a few steps away. He was shaped like the avocado pit I often tried to sprout in a glass on my windowsill. Big belly, toothpick arms and legs.

"You startled me!" I said.

"Is that right?" he said, sounding suspicious. Keys hung from the man's belt, and he wore a blue short-sleeve shirt with the word UNIVERSAL over a logo and a number. He was an official something, his skin sun damaged, his fingers thick and used to hard work.

I tried a conspiratorial grin, held my hand over my mouth like I was spilling a secret. "Not really. It's my second day. Trying to make a good impression." I felt my blood racing through my system like a fire truck races to extinguish a flame.

"You're not from here." He took a drag on his cigarette. Lifted his chin and released the smoke like an old-time television gumshoe.

"No."

Ugh. I was going to get fired for sleeping on the premises. For acting like I belonged here even though I didn't.

"I'm a must hire. Everybody hates a must hire." As I said it, I looked at his black shoes. Not as an actor might who was trying to look shameful. But as myself, embarrassed to be the odd girl out even after all these years. I was back in elementary school explaining why my mom didn't come to help in the classroom, why my clothes didn't fit. And I knew just what to do—turn on the likability. I'd smile big, crank up my sense of humor, and listen carefully.

"My sister lives in Milwaukee. You got that same nasal twang," he said, and my brain switched from *game over* to *game on.*

"Then you know better than anyone it's pronounced Muh-wok-key. The *l* is silent."

When he laughed, he exhaled the smoke in a burst and his belly, tight against his shirt, lifted and lowered.

"You got that right. Muh-wok-key. The best beer in the country."

"Drink Wisconsibly," I said, repeating the name of a pub that had unofficially branded the state as the place where nobody drinks responsibly.

"I lost a night or two at taverns visiting my baby sister. You Wisconsinites really know how to party."

"We sure do," I said, remembering the lightweight champagne nap I'd taken at the airport less than a week earlier.

"What brings you out this way?"

I saw the value of this conversation, an on-set friend with keys, but holy cow, I had to get into that bathroom.

"I got a kid. Needs to go to college. This is a great job." I accentuated my Wisconsin accent, rounding out the consonants and drawing out the vowels. "Hey, can I get into the bathroom? Too much coffee, ya know?"

"You betcha," he said in his own flawless Midwest imitation. He pulled his keys forward, moved up the steps, finished his cigarette, and unlocked one of the bathroom doors—he'd done this a thousand times before.

"You're the best," I said, and traded places with him on the stairs.

Before I shut the door, my bladder already unclenching at the sight of the toilet, he said, "Don't let 'em get you down. Not everybody hates a must hire. Just the jealous ones. You be you, Muh-wok-key." He cocked his head, trying to read my handmade name tag. "Puppy?"

"It's Poppy. My *o*'s always look like *u*'s. I have to go get the official one with the picture, but there never seems to be time."

"Days move fast around here."

He gave me a two-finger salute, and I repeated, "You're the best."

When I sat on the toilet, I shuddered at the close call of discovery. The man might have been friendly, but if he knew I'd spent the night on set . . . Security guards, Teamsters, or the movie mafia, whatever he was, were not known for breaking the rules.

———

Back in the trailer, I clipped my headset on, made sure the space showed no signs of my vagabond existence, and decided to search for the food area. Look for coffee. I'd walked only a short distance when I saw the door of one of the trailers open hesitantly and Emilie emerge. The girl had the same posture I had when sneaking around—shoulders rolled forward, furtive glances right and left. I stood out of her sight line. As any mother would surely notice, Emilie was in the same clothes as the day before.

I glimpsed the flash of a hand, and Emilie moved backward, as if caught. She turned her body and hugged someone. I took a step behind a truck to watch this young woman, so like and unlike my daughter and myself. I wondered if there was a man in that trailer. If she was breaking the no hook-up rule. For a second Emilie and Robyn conflated in my mind and I wanted to warn her, remind her of the rules.

Emilie was a must hire, but not like I was. She descended from those in charge. She had resources I didn't have. If she had the necklace, was playing some kind of game, hazing me, I had to be smart about it. I needed an ally, not another daughter.

I waited until she was out of sight, turned, took two steps, and encountered a pale-faced angular woman around seventy, possibly eighty by way of Botox and filler. She stepped directly in front of me clutching the oddest-looking creature in her arms and seemed simultaneously annoyed and thrilled to see me.

"You," she said, peering at the plastic tag around my neck. "Good. Wardrobe. Here's Kevin the Dog. He needs his outfit for today's shoot.

I can't be carrying him around all day." With that she off-loaded a diminutive black-and-gray furry bundle into my arms. Unprotesting and scruffy, his tongue hung from his mouth as if he'd taken a drink of water and forgot to retract it. "You tell James that the next time he needs a stand-in he's going to pay top dollar."

"James?"

"Green? The director? I'm his mother-in-law." The woman touched one lock of hair on her forehead with her middle finger and moved it to the side, as if she were opening a thick velvet stage curtain for all to view the wonders behind it. "James has my phone number. Obviously. Kevin must have his organic yogurt today. You're in charge of him." She looked over the top of a pair of thick black-rimmed glasses. "And you are . . . ?"

"Poppy Lively."

"That's not your name."

"It is." I tried to pull my name tag forward as proof, but Kevin's dry tongue appeared stuck to the lanyard.

"Never mind. It's Hollywood. Be who you want to be." She waved her hand in the air, effectively brushing us out of her sight. The last thing she said before swanning away was, "Kevin's depressed. The divorce is killing him." She disappeared more purposefully than my most certain walk, and I did not protest. How could I?

The chatter in the headset meant I was needed, and Kevin the Dog looked at me like, *Now what?*

"You're a scruffy little thing," I said. I let him sniff my hand before I tried to help him put his tongue back into his mouth. It went in and flopped back out. It looked as if a red pimento were stuck on his chin.

My lack of coffee was not helping me troubleshoot the situation, and I was about to take another stab at locating my morning cup of wake-up juice when Muriel found me.

"Good God, you got Kevin." Muriel scanned the area and said, "I should have warned you. Damn, that woman is wily. We'll get you a sling. He's yours for the day. Don't even think of handing him off; that woman will skin you alive."

I worked to get my head around what Muriel was saying. Was I to keep this dog, on my body, all day?

"What's the matter?" Muriel missed nothing, and I was certain a hesitation was a demerit.

"Where do I get the sling? And does he have a costume? And I haven't found the necklace but I will."

"No, he's not in the movie. The mother-in-law is confused." Muriel pointed to the Edith Head building like a Viking pointing to enemy troops on the horizon. "Go now. Report back. Big day. So many dogs. You're delivering costumes to trainers. Get a map."

"Got it." I turned and headed in the direction of the costume building.

"Who cleaned the microwave?"

"Emilie," I said, wanting to throw her off the trail that I'd had time and access to clean something so unrelated to costumes. It also showed how bad I was at sabotage. Giving Emilie credit for a good thing. I inwardly rolled my eyes at myself.

Muriel said, "Doubtful."

CHAPTER ELEVEN
WE'RE GOOD HERE

"I hate to tell you this, but people who get Kevin handed to them don't usually make it around here," said a woman behind the counter at the costume shop. She was new to me, and I appreciated her candor but didn't welcome the information.

"They don't make it?"

"Don't look so horrified. I'm sure you'll make it," she said, backing off. "It's hard to deflect the mother-in-law because she really comes at you, but Kevin's a rookie mistake. When Cruella comes a knockin' you gotta start walkin'."

"I did not get briefed on the mother-in-law. And as a rookie, I doubt I could run in the other direction and keep my job."

"Yeah, it's a tricky balance. Here," she said, and reached for Kevin while I tried to wind the elastic cloth covered in cartoon giraffes around me. I was sweating with nerves and exertion by the time I got the weave even close to right. The first two times I tried, there was no place for Kevin, but my cinched waist looked positively Edwardian. On the third try, Muriel's voice in my ear calling costumers to the trailer, I created a pocket for a dog the size of a small-size shower scrubby. I scratched my nose and tried to detect if this itch was an allergy thing.

The woman wedged Kevin in and said, "Just act like you don't even know he's attached to you, like you could do this all day. All year, even. First chance you get, hand him off to another newbie."

"Can I do that?"

"I've been here five years, but I got Kevin on my first day and got rid of him on day two."

"Hey, there's an important necklace missing from the costume trailer. Is it possible it was returned here accidentally?"

"A necklace is missing?" Her expression said something I couldn't interpret. I waited. "Things disappear at times," she said.

"Yeah, but like, I have to find it. Or I'll be out before they fire me for Kevin." I swallowed a dry lump in my throat.

She dropped her eyes, untangled a snarl of tags used for labeling costumes, pulled a Sharpie from behind her ear. "Ask Emilie," she said.

I checked the time. I had to get going. Day two was already picking up speed, and I didn't want to get yelled at for appearing like I wanted to hang around the costume shop.

With Kevin's head beneath my mouth and nose, I knew I should swallow an allergy pill just in case he was the kind of dog that was like a cat—the kind that made me itch. A full-body rash plus this rat's nest of a dog surely was the wrong kind of attention.

Inside the trailer, Muriel handed assignments to the same fleet of people I'd seen yesterday but had not been introduced to. While I tried to catch up, I found my canvas bag near a new dry-cleaning pile. I bent sideways, scrounged for my meds, my body remembering how to move with a baby-size mammal attached. I swallowed the pharmaceutical, which, despite its teensy size, stuck to the back of my throat. I coughed surreptitiously, cleared my throat twice, and gulped no less than twenty-five times until Emilie looked at me with an annoyed expression that rivaled Robyn's worst *I mean, come on. The drama.* I pictured the pill clinging to a tonsil as my uvula tried to shake it loose.

"Something's in my throat," I said, and Emilie stepped away from me.

One by one, the dressers with costumes in hand moved out of the trailer to place their items in dressing rooms and the stars' trailers. Muriel handed me a collection of clothing on hangers.

"Everything you need is on this manila tag," she said. "Knock on the door. If the actor is there, hand the costume over, ask if they have questions or need help. Stay if they need you. If no one is in the trailer, which should be the case because it's early, hang the costume on the hook and come back here. I'd show you myself, but we're short two staff today." I must have looked unsure because she said, "This is not rocket science. *My* job is rocket science but with egos instead of propellant. Tread carefully."

I'd have said something if I wasn't still working to get the pill in my throat to slide the rest of the way down.

"What's the matter?"

"Water," I croaked.

"You're allowed to drink, you know. Also, can you work on your poker face? You always look like you either want to cry or panic. I get you midwesterners are transparent and all, but here on the movie set, we try to look as unruffled as possible."

"Good note," I rasped.

Muriel shouted to the back of the trailer, "Water bottle," and someone pitched one in a perfect arc directly into her outstretched hand.

"Drink it and get going." An indecipherable mumble in the headset pulled Muriel to the back of the trailer.

I swallowed big gulps until Kevin wriggled. I let him lick water from the cap and zipped the half-empty bottle into my plastic kit that was basically a seat for Kevin's tiny bum. "Let's go. You're a dresser now, Kevin. Be cool."

Emilie sidled up to me and, completely ignoring the obvious canine strapped to my chest, said, "Who do you have?" Easy as you please, she traded her hangers for mine. "You look like you're on the struggle bus today. Take mine. They're easier than yours."

"Seriously?" I said, suspicious while knowing I needed her on my side. I faked some naive gratitude. "Awww, Emilie, that is so nice."

The girl said, in true mean girl fashion, "Try not to cry, Mom."

"Robyn," I said. "'Mom' is not an insult."

"Who's Robyn?" said Emilie.

"My daughter. Sorry," I stuttered. "Have you seen that important necklace? We need to find it," I said.

"Yeah, you do," she said without looking at me.

"You know this place better than I do. Have any ideas?"

"Nope," she said, and walked away with my hangers.

Bratty. That's what the mothers in my hometown would have called Emilie. I had to respect her ballsy confidence even as it ratcheted my angst ever higher.

Outside in the sunshine, it was even more active than yesterday. I held the clothes hangers so as not to let anything touch the ground. At the bank of actors' trailers, their numbers displayed, it was easy to find the one I needed. I marched up the stairs and knocked on the door, expecting it to be empty.

"Come in," said a male voice from within.

Kevin snuggled into the sling so only an ear showed at the top of one of the yellow giraffes.

I turned the knob, pulled the door open, and said, "I have a costume for you," which I wasn't sure was the right thing to say. I sounded like a pizza delivery person, or Uber Eats. I stepped inside the trailer and couldn't help but notice the bougie interior. It had the making of an expensive, narrow hotel room. Thrillingly nicer than the motel I'd slept in the first night. "It's impressive in here," I said.

A man sat at a table sipping coffee with paper tucked under his chin and reading something on his phone. He wiped his mustache with a cloth napkin and straightened his glasses.

I looked around for an obvious hook to hang up what appeared to be a blue suit. He put his coffee cup on the counter and said, "Anywhere is fine. I'll get dressed now."

"I'm sorry. I'm new to this. I'm not sure how I'm needed."

"You can practice with me. I've done this a few times." His smile said something I couldn't read. A humble brag? Or maybe he didn't know much more than I did.

"Okay. Thanks." Finally, I hung the costume on a hook on a wall.

"I see you're the keeper of Kevin today."

"It's a hazing for the new girl."

"How new are you?"

I wondered if it was an insult for him to be given the novice, the must hire, the clueless help. "I usually work in the trailer. We're short today." I concentrated on pulling the thin dry-cleaning bag off the shoulders of the costume. I quickly unbuttoned the white shirt, held it steady to help the man dress. "Do you need me to help you? Or am I supposed to leave? I asked Kevin on the way over. He doesn't know either."

"Give me a hand with the shirt and jacket. I have a stiff shoulder."

With Kevin between us, watching carefully, I helped the man out of his robe. He wore a white T-shirt and sweatpants, and first one arm, then the other, he shrugged into his shirt. I buttoned it as I used to do for Robyn when she was a little girl. Stopped. Looked at him to see if this was what he expected. He lifted his chin as a kind of permission to proceed. The beginnings of a caffeine withdrawal headache started brewing between my eyes.

At the buttons mid-chest, I saw a very small smile on his lips beneath a large '70s mustache. I stopped, stepped back, and said, "I guess you can do that," and I warmed with embarrassment again. "Sorry. I really don't know what I'm doing. But I'll get better."

"Do you watch a lot of movies?" Here he looked at my name tag and said, "Poppy?"

Kevin and I turned to get the suit coat, to give the man a modicum of privacy as he ran his fingers up the shirt buttons, and I said, "Not really. I'm woefully behind in the culture, as my seventeen-year-old likes to remind me."

"The culture is time consuming." He finished the top button and said, "What do you do in your spare time?"

My head was beginning to throb even as my sinuses dried out. I squeezed my eyes shut. "Spare time? I have a daughter. Just graduated. Not much free time. So many end of year dinners. Planning for college. Doing the mom thing." The button on the suit coat stuck, and I wasn't on top of my nervous chatter like I should have been. The button came loose, and I turned, held up the jacket for him to slip on. He was quiet. Too quiet.

I bit my tongue so I wouldn't apologize or make a stupid joke like I so often did when I was nervous. Kevin gave me a little pimento lick on my arm, the only thing he could reach, as if to say, *You're doing great, sweetie.*

"Go on," the man said.

"No. Sorry. I . . . I missed my coffee this morning. I have a raging headache, and if I wasn't talking so much, I'd be more helpful."

"It's fine. It only takes a minute to get dressed. Let me get you a cup of coffee."

"No. Nope. I'm certain that is one hundred percent against the rules."

Ignoring my protests, he poured coffee into a Universal Studios mug and handed it to me. He touched my hand, pointed to the remnants of the Sharpie there from the day before.

"What's this?"

"Sometimes I take notes on my hand. Muriel talks fast. This was a reminder to not hook up with people on set." My mouth watered at the rich coffee scent. I took a sip. "So don't get any ideas," I said. Placebo or no, the headache clouds parted, and I instantly felt better. I closed my eyes, took another long sip, and swallowed. "Not that you would. Ha. As if." And there was my stupid joke. "Sorry."

Kevin yawned, finishing with a whine as if to remind me where I was. I hazarded a gaze at the man and saw an unoffended smile. I did not follow up. I put the coffee cup on the counter and he dropped his sweats. He wore green plaid cotton boxer shorts and was in the midst of pulling on the suit pants. I looked everywhere possible except at the zipper as he fastened it.

"Crap," he said. "The pants are tight. I had one too many thin mints these past two weeks."

"I can help with that." I reached around Kevin, whose baseball-size butt was resting squarely on top of the plastic kit around my hips. I unzipped the pack and plunged my hand in, rooting around for a hair tie. When I found it, I said, "If you loop this through the buttonhole you can get a little leeway."

"Have at it," he said, holding his shirt out of the way.

Maybe I should have hesitated. I imagine Emilie would have or someone who wasn't a mother. But I'd dressed Robyn, helped kids into snowsuits, out of wet pants, back into dry ones many times over. I had not buttoned or unbuttoned a man's pants in a sexual way for quite some time, so it honestly didn't feel inappropriate. On some level I expected this—I was *dressing* actors; that was the job. I threaded, looped, and wound the piece of elastic, giving the man a little extra space in the top button. "How's that?"

"You guys in wardrobe know all the tricks," he said, exhaling.

"You'd know how to do this too if you'd been pregnant and grew into a kettledrum in under a month." I straightened and touched Kevin, like he was a baby. It felt natural to have something to do with my hands. "Emilie was right. You are easy."

"Emilie. Emilie the director's niece said I was easy?"

"Not easy. Easier. She traded with me and took someone that was harder, I guess." I hesitated. "More difficult. To dress? She was trying to be helpful. Because I'm new. Ish. Newish." The look on his face had lost warmth, and my ever-present fear of screwing up shot through me. "I don't know who she meant. I don't know anyone. I was grateful."

He made a little sound in his throat. The kind of sound that you wouldn't want directed at you. A tone of disapproval and a hint of dislike. If I had to describe it later, I'd have said that the air in the room frosted over.

"Thank you so much for the coffee. Unless you still need me, I'm off."

"We're good here," he said.

And on the way out the door, I thought, there's no way we were good here. No way.

CHAPTER TWELVE
BELOW THE LINE

At the bottom of the actor's trailer steps I stopped, oriented myself. Thought about what I'd said that had created that icy moment. I'd called the man easier. How could that have been an insult? Was *easy* an insult for men as it was for women back in the day when sex was taboo? Now, it meant weak, or maybe Hollywood actors wanted to be known as divas.

I consulted Kevin, who had something in his mouth. "Kevin, what do you have?" I pulled the fabric free, and he let out a throaty warning.

"Listen, mister, we're on this ride-along together. Give me that."

It was a pair of men's boxer briefs. The trim kind that fit snugly around a leg. "What the heck? Are you trying to get me fired?"

As silently as possible I climbed the few stairs to return the underwear and apologize. I was about to knock when I heard the man's voice.

". . . a problem I shouldn't have to deal with." There was another mumble, and I heard the word, "When?"

With great care, I hung the boxers on the doorknob and backed away. When I hit the asphalt, I jogged in the direction of the costume trailer, Kevin's head knocking between my breasts. My headache replaced with the words *a problem* reverberating in my mind. Was he talking about me? Was I being paranoid?

The next few hours I explicitly followed directions, worked hard to make everyone happy—something I was excellent at, having had years and years of practice. Waited to get yelled at for being a "problem."

Kevin and I rolled lint brushes over shirts, pants, and dogs—anything that looked wrongfully furry. I ran errands, picked up lunch, snacks, beverages for the women in the trailer, and delivered coffee when people got sleepy. I examined faces, tried to read the room, see where I stood in the pecking order, but these people were impassive.

In high school, working for tips as a waitress at a family restaurant where the owners and siblings communicated by hollering at each other and the staff, I coped by being hyperefficient and keeping a sharp eye out for each member of the family's bugaboos. Eunice couldn't stand an untidy waitress stand. Karl, her brother, fumed if tables weren't bused instantly. I never got used to being yelled at, never developed the thick skin the other waitresses seemed to have. I'd be lying if I said I didn't feel just like that now. Like a high school kid being bossed around by erratic people in charge. But I had something they didn't—I knew how to please while observing, predicting needs, and putting my desires for eating and peeing aside. There was power in this behavior and I knew it.

Not Emilie, though. She had a different kind of internal force that was so foreign to me. She was angry about something and didn't care who knew it. She was the anti-pleaser. As I was on the way to the costume shop to get some Velcro for a dog's necktie, Emilie appeared seemingly out of nowhere. The girl took a stand in front of me and looked like she wanted to get into a shoving war.

"What is your problem?" she said to me. I couldn't help but notice how stunningly pretty she was.

Instinctively I shielded Kevin from this very angry California girl. "My problem?"

"You tattled and they took me off delivering costumes. Now I'm stuck steaming and cleaning the microwave. The microwave!"

"Tattle on you? For what?"

"If you didn't want to trade costumes, you should have said no. I thought you'd be crazy to meet the star of this dumb movie. But okay. Next time, we don't know each other. In fact, just stay away from me. I don't need another mother. I have a shitty mom already."

Then she stamped her foot and showed her age. And dammit if I didn't laugh. I hadn't seen this kind of tantrum since Robyn was maybe in sixth grade. I'd washed her favorite red shirt with her mint-green pants, and I thought my daughter would never speak to me again.

Emilie looked older than Robyn, but if she was, it was only by a year. She stalked off, flipping her middle finger at me, which I kind of admired, honestly. When I was her age, the waitress at the restaurant, I never would have flipped off anyone.

"Emilie," I said. "I'm sorry. I laugh when I'm nervous." I pictured that girl running straight to the director and telling him to get rid of me. Or finding Muriel and saying, *If she doesn't go, I go.* Like Elizabeth Taylor in that podcast where she tried to get Richard Burton's costar fired. "I'm not laughing at you. I'm a wreck." If she heard me, she didn't let on.

I noticed I was swaying with Kevin, like you do when you hold a baby. Back and forth, easy does it. Self-soothing while I rocked.

"She's cold, Kevin. Cold as ice." I had a strange feeling that someone had witnessed a teenager bitching me out while I cradled a dog baby. I inhaled and turned.

Wanda stood at the door of the trailer, had her eyes shielded as if she were searching the horizon for a storm and instead saw a grown woman being told off by someone she could have given birth to. In the other direction and closer to the set was the man I'd dressed earlier. He glanced in my direction and wore the suit I put him in. And, finally, the man I now in my head called the Teamster standing next to the Honey Wagon called out, "Causing trouble, Muh-wok-key?"

"No," I shouted back. "No trouble."

The man threw his head back as if I'd said something so hilarious he could barely stand it.

I still had to get the Velcro from the costume department, and I decided, until someone with real authority gave me the bird, I would keep working. I knew where some of the sewing notions were stored inside the costume department, and I grabbed some sticky Velcro when one of the women that worked in the racks showed up. She emerged from one of the adjacent rooms holding a bunch of tags and a handful of Sharpie markers.

"Can I ask you a question?" I said.

"Sure. Shoot."

"Who is starring in this production? With all the dogs."

"Bosco is the head dog. You know, he was in that movie about the dog who saved his master from the alien invasion. He's got his own chair on set."

"No, what person is the big star?"

This woman, joining everyone I'd spoken to over the last two days, gave me a look that said, *Come on. The program. Get with it.*

"Allen Carol. He's got all that facial hair, so you can hardly tell it's him. But yeah. I met him the other day. All those Academy Awards and still so nice."

My mouth dropped open. Even I, the movie Luddite that I was, knew him. He was shorter and chubbier than the few times I'd seen him on television.

"He's very particular. Has a lot of pull. He's widely known as respectful to the below-the-line people."

"Below the line?"

"It's a budget term." Jenna held her hand up. "Directors, writers, producers, actors are up here. The rest of the crew are the itemized underneath. It separates production costs from the big-timers to us little guys . . . the crew, et cetera."

"That sounds like steerage on a cruise ship. The downstairs help," I said.

She shrugged. "It's always been this way. We're replaceable," she said in an offhanded way. From what I'd witnessed so far, if even one shoe got misplaced the show would not go on. Interesting that the people who kept the movie on budget were the ones relegated to and described as beneath the others.

"Last movie I worked on the star got half of the crew fired for leaking a video of him screaming at the best boy."

"Not the best boy!" I said as a joke—as if who would ever fire the bestest boy of all the boys.

"I know, right?" she said, missing my attempt at being funny. "No one is entirely safe."

"A problem I shouldn't have," he'd said. Allen the superstar on set, the man with the pull, had pegged me as a problem. And what does someone do with a problem? They solve it. With an eraser on a call sheet. Was I being deleted as I talked about this class system right now? Was I on the *Titanic*—running into an iceberg of rainmakers on top, peons below?

"I don't mind telling you, this place is going to give me nervous shingles. The suspense of possibly getting fired is exhausting."

"You get used to it," she said.

No. I knew I would never get used to shifting ground. That was the trade-off about being good at change. Although you might adapt, you could never let your guard down.

"One more question: Do you know of a cheap place to stay around here? I'm still working on housing, you know?"

"Do I ever. There's nothing cheap. You have to stay with a bunch of roommates in a closet to start. Or under the freeway." She laughed at her joke, and I tried to join along, emitting a nervous giggle that sounded like a horse's whinny.

CHAPTER THIRTEEN

WE CAN AFFORD THIS PLACE

After the conversation about not making it in the costume shop, I was on high alert in the wardrobe trailer. I worked saying the words *necklace* and *lodging* to myself, like a prayer or a worry stone.

The job was fast-paced, but after the "That's a wrap!" call from the director, I saw that the crew went into overdrive and wanted to get home. "Move it," Emilie said to me under her breath when I bent to retrieve a costume that had slid off a hanger and onto the floor. Staying clear of Emilie all day long was near impossible.

The actors undressed and dumped their costumes in heaps like little kids who needn't worry about the next day. Craft service cleaned up the food, trainers cleared dog poop. And Emilie? Well, she sighed, sneered, and hissed at me. I seemed to be everywhere she wanted to be. She was far more pleasant to others, if a little slow to hustle.

"Can you not?" she said when I stopped to refill the water in the steamer and my elbow impeded her progress.

"Where is your grandma? I need to give back Kevin," I said.

"You don't give him back. She finds you or she doesn't," Emilie said.

I felt my mouth drop open. Kevin repositioned in the sling as if he knew to make himself small.

With the scorn that came with youth and privilege, Emilie said, "Think of it as job security. As long as you're holding Kev, you're still here."

If I had been her mother, I'd pull her out of the trailer and talk about her attitude. If I were her boss, I'd sit her someplace, give her all the buttons that fell off all the shirts, and tell her not to move until she had every last one reattached.

But authority was not something I had in the costume trailer. What I had was a gamey-smelling dog attached to my torso, no knowledge of the industry that I was working in, and literally no place to go after the gaffers shut off the lights and the key grip stopped gripping. I stretched my neck, stiff with anxiety. Patted Kevin, thinking Emilie had a point.

I was not ready to admit to Three or least of all Muriel that I was destitute. Judge me if you want, but I admired Muriel and I needed this job. Admitting that you've lost everything might bring empathy, but it also brought difficult questions. If you were sleeping when a tornado hit your house, the people on Twitter would blame you for living in a place where tornados can hit your house. If your accountant stole your money, everyone in your book club would agree that you should have been paying better attention. The blame ball, in the game of life, rolled downhill and, as often as not, hit the victim. It was human nature, and I was sure Muriel or Three would not be immune to questioning my abilities.

"That dog smells," Emilie said, so close and in my ear that I started.

"Yeah, and so do I," I said in the worst comeback made in the history of mean girl clapbacks. Robyn would be disgusted with me. "Any sight of the necklace? It was here in the trailer when I tidied up."

"They get super pissed when things go missing," she said, and stopped long enough to give me a look that I could not decipher.

"What?"

"People sell things from movie sets. Make big money."

That never occurred to me. I swiveled my gaze around the others in the trailer, dropped my voice. "You think someone took it to sell it?"

When she didn't respond, I stared at her. Emilie eyed me back unblinking, as if we were playing a game of chicken. The first to break lost. "I don't know. Maybe." She said it like a challenge, as if she were taking her earrings off for a bar fight.

"You think I have it. That I'm going to do what? Put it on Facebook Marketplace?"

It was both irritating and demoralizing to spar with this pint-size dictator without a single earned wrinkle on her brow, but it was also fascinating. Her self-confidence was off the charts. What had her parents done to raise a girl who broadcast the attitude, *First me, then everything else*?

"Nobody knows where you came from," and that was it. She left the trailer and I stood there, mouth open like a carp gasping for air on a beach. To hide my discomfort and collect my thoughts, I sorted the pile of dirty costumes into two piles, one for dry cleaning and the other the washing machine.

There was something to learn from Emilie. She did not take whatever was given to her. She pushed, wriggled, and scowled and somehow didn't care who didn't like her. It made me incredibly uncomfortable watching her stand her ground.

A memory, one of the few I had of a conversation between my mother and father. My mother said she didn't want to teach our Sunday school class anymore. My father had said, "Who cares what you want. They need a teacher. You're the teacher."

"You do it. You're so good at telling people what to do," my mother said.

"Gemini," my father said in a lovely, caring tone, "did you take your meds?"

My mom didn't answer him as she moved away. She didn't hear him respond, but I did. I never forgot it: "Always so much trouble. Who would want her around?" he said.

I shook my head to clear it. All these odd recollections since I'd left Wisconsin, as if California unaccountably reminded me of home. In truth, while I admired Emilie, I saw the eye rolls, the exchanged glances behind the girl's back. Even when she did her job well.

I imagined the experienced staff covertly sharing looks whenever I asked a question, hesitated, or misunderstood what was needed.

Muriel appeared. "Bring these items to the cages," she said, and handed me several shirts on hangers. "Then you can go home."

"Muriel, I've searched everywhere for the necklace. I've asked Emilie, talked to a woman up in Edith Head. I can't think where it went after I put the jewelry away."

"Let's hope it turns up. It will be an expensive commission or reshoot with another piece."

"I'll keep my eyes open. I have a friend who prays to Saint Anthony whenever she loses something—she swears by it."

"That's adorable," Muriel said, and patted my hand. "Sure, ask her to pray for us." Her tone had the *oh, you cute midwesterners* quality to it.

"I was joking," I said to her. I felt dizzy with relief, hated her patronizing tone, and needed some air so that I wouldn't react. I unclipped my kit and dropped it onto the floor of the wardrobe trailer with a muffled thump. Kevin fell an inch, his butt no longer supported. I moved across the warm asphalt to the Edith Head building to deliver the clothing.

A new woman I hadn't seen before took the hangers. "Almost done down there?" she said.

"I think so. There's only a couple of us left. You heading out soon?"

"Yes. This is the last of it."

That's when I realized my keys to the trailer were in the kit. If Muriel left and pulled the door closed, I'd be locked out.

I shot out the door and hit the ground in seconds. Kevin grunted and I cradled his head. I could see the costume trailer by the set, the door closed for the night, the lights off. "Son of a . . ." I whispered as

I hit the silver stairs and grasped the smooth door handle. Locked. Of course it was.

This must have been how Sisyphus felt at the top of the mountain watching his boulder barrel to the bottom. I wanted to scream. Literally screech, *You idiot!* How could I have been so careless? What was wrong with me? I leaned against the locked door and wished more than anything I could cry to let off steam, but I was far too frustrated and only cried when I didn't want to.

My phone buzzed and without looking I answered with an irate, "Hello."

"Is this Dawna Klump?" Hearing that woman's name raked fury through me.

"No, it's not. This is Poppy Lively. Who am I speaking to?"

A man pushing a cart with the top of a large suspension bridge on it stopped to see who was getting chewed out. I turned my body away from him.

"This is the Internal Revenue Service. I understand the specifics of your particular case. Have you been in touch with Dawna Klump?"

"No. I can't find her. I've been to her house. Called her a million times. But I'll tell you this, if I ever get ahold of her . . ."

"I'm going to stop you right there, Ms. Lively. Before you veer into dangerous territory."

I closed my lips tight and let the words *I'll kill her* collect behind my front teeth.

"I'd like to talk to you about her access to your accounts and if you have paperwork—employment forms, records of salary and payment. I also need your last five years of taxes and mortgage statements."

"Is she saying I didn't pay her?" I blurted out that sentence with such force Kevin ducked. I had that feeling you get while upside down on a rickety state fair ride. You want to get off so badly because you want to survive.

"You seem upset. Is this a bad time?" he said.

"Every second of every day is a bad time," I said, not exaggerating.

"I'm sorry, but I believe we are victims on the same side in this case."

I sputtered, "Victim. The IRS? Give me a . . . Who is this?"

"My name is Brian Babbage. Like Cabbage. I'm the forensic auditor assigned to this case. Please forward me the paperwork as soon as possible."

"Are you recalculating? Am I going to owe more? Because, Mr. Cabbage, there is no more."

"Babbage. Like Cabbage," he said. "I'm not at liberty to say. I will be sending you an email. If you can attach the documents I've requested, that would be very helpful."

I could not manage more information. The vegetables. The casual recalculation reference. I wanted to shove this man off the phone. Punch Dawna Klump. Kick her stinkin' garage door in. Evoke some passive-aggressive revenge like send second-rate delivery pizzas to her daily so she dies of heart disease. But I couldn't afford it. I was doing my utter best to take responsibility. If there was going to be more due, a surprise number, *just kidding you owe this now*, I would have to stay here for as many jobs as I could get. I needed people to like me, and it wasn't going well.

"Are you there, Ms. Lively? Do you have the documentation?"

"Of course I do. I may be a patsy but I'm not disorganized," I said. Did he think I was a dilettante? Everything was online. "Yes, send the email. I'll send the documents."

"Thank . . ." But I hung up before he could get in the last word, even if it was a nice one.

"Victim," I said, standing up against the wall of the trailer, glad for its solid form because without it, I might have fallen over in a lump. What was my stress limit? Would there be a warning before I crumbled, or was the stressed-out the last to know?

I scanned the grounds as the crew wound cords and locked up. If I called security to unlock the wardrobe door, it would draw too much attention to everything about me. In the evenings I needed to be as invisible as the man I saw, sleeping in the median on my way into town. During the day I had to be the competent lady, solving problems and getting paid—getting more gigs.

I slid my back against the door, sat on the stairs, and noticed a small bag of dog food and two aluminum bowls, one filled with water. The mother-in-law must have realized Kevin needed to be fed. That put Cruella, the woman who handed off her dog to a stranger, above Emilie in the consideration department.

I unwound the sling, which felt suddenly too tight. I took a deep breath as I released the elastic from both of us.

"Victims," I said again, and visualized a gazelle chased by a cheetah. That was the wrong imagery for Dawna and me. I had been a rooted aquatic plant and Dawna a slow-moving sea potato. And this seagrass never saw the lumpy schemer coming.

"We really don't smell great, Kevin," I said, and he rolled his bulgy eyes and looked at me. I put him on his legs expecting those pins to fold for lack of use. Instead, he stretched one leg, then the other, then performed a perfect hot yoga, Los Angeles–proud downward dog.

"Though he be but little, he be flexible," I said, filling his bowl with kibble.

Kevin took a petite nibble. Sipped some water and gazed at me. I watched as he took another delicate bite, and I saw the reason for his careful noshing. He had to work around his unorganized tongue. Every other niblet flipped out of his mouth and landed between us.

"Buddy, we'll find you some soft food." I scratched his back and he rolled over for a tummy rub. That's when I realized Kevin the Dog was a girl.

I heard footsteps shuffle toward me. Before looking to see who it was, I needed a reason for not rushing home like the rest of the crew.

For why I was feeding this dog clutching what looked like a baby sling and my phone.

"Muh-wok-key, what are you still doing here?" The Teamster from earlier in the day stood near, an unlit cigarette in his hand.

Relief. Friendly fire.

"I could ask the same of you. Do you always do twelve-hour shifts?" Deliberately putting the attention squarely on the man and not myself.

"Nah. I went home after I saw you. Had to fill in an afternoon shift for one of the guys. I'm heading out."

"Me too!" I stood, scooped Kevin up with one arm, and a nugget of dog food hit my Teamster. "Long day. Hey, can I use the Honey Wagon one last time?" I didn't have to go, but I'd better empty my bladder because who knew what the night would bring.

"They're open. Cleaning truck coming in forty-five. Just don't lock it when you leave, okay. They don't have keys."

"I won't. Thanks. Have a good night . . ."

"Travis," he said, filling in the blank for me. He bent, picked up a Sharpie and a couple of manila garment tags that fell out of my back pocket. "Get some sleep. You're going to burn out. I see it all the time."

"Good tip," I said and waved, too tired to say anything more, and we walked in opposite directions.

I shifted Kevin to my left arm and hip and stood in front of the Honey Wagon. I'd never seen anything like it before yesterday—a long semitruck with a series of steps that led to doors. It was an ingenious setup, portable toilets driven to whatever location was needed for a shoot.

Instead of going to the same toilet I always used, I pulled one of the side doors open. To my astonishment, I'd found a small room with a sink, couch, and most importantly, a lock on the door. In a large mirror to my left I saw myself. I'd gotten some color on my cheeks and nose, and my hair had a tousled appearance. Kevin looked disorganized as usual but also happy in the way dogs do.

I flipped the switch on the wall, and the room illuminated a long closet rung that ran the length of the space. It was a dressing room, I guessed for the bit players. Never the stars. Maybe a spot for people to rest between takes.

I'd seen staff come and go and thought they were all using the toilets.

"Kevin. I think we can afford this place."

CHAPTER FOURTEEN
HOW THE MEDIOCRE HAVE FALLEN

At the sink in our tiny Honey Wagon home, I promptly gave Kevin a bath, drying her with large towels I found in a cabinet. Soaking-wet Kevin looked worse, if that was possible. Her skin was visible between her thinning coat, and she had age spots on her back. I tried to re-fluff Kevin, return her to her pre-bathing glory, but she needed a lavender spa weekend, not a scrub in a stainless-steel basin with no-name liquid soap. So did I, and after washing Kevin I gave myself a bird bath as well.

My phone lit up on the counter.

Three: I'm on set. I bet I missed you.

He was here. Finally. I needed to talk to him. I typed as quickly as possible. He appeared to jet in and out so quickly, I didn't think I could spare a second or an auto correct. I dropped my phone twice but was able to write.

Poppy: I'm still here.

Three: !!! Where?

The enthusiasm was comforting.

Poppy: Base camp. By the trailer.

I typed these new vocabulary words like I'd been using them for more than two days. It was a short walk, I'd be there quickly. I'd ask to stay in his basement, or whatever.

Three: Be right there.

Any makeup I'd put on in the morning was long gone, and the
humidity of Kevin's sink bath had curled the edges of my hair. At least
it was dark out; Three wouldn't notice if I had tired rings under my eyes,
the rumpled look of my clothing.

I pulled a Sharpie from my back pocket and wrote boldly on the
garment tag. *Hinge broken. Do not open. Maintenance notified.* I couldn't
lose this space to anyone with keys, workers who would tidy the space
and lock the door.

Kevin had a look in her eye that said, *This is where you leave me,
isn't it?*

I scoffed. "You're coming with me." I couldn't leave Kevin behind.
She was a preternaturally quiet dog. Yet if she barked while I was away,
they'd open the door and confiscate her. I tucked her under my arm and
noticed a flutter in my chest as I walked back to the wardrobe trailer.
I was nervous to see Three, and my heart whispered, *I thought we were
done with all of this.*

I eased through the door and tried to act casual—wet shirt, wet
dog, nervous pulse. I glanced at the time on my phone. Eight thirty in
the evening meant it was ten thirty in Wisconsin. Last week at this time
I was falling asleep with my accounting sheets, not hiding from security
and on my way to see a man after dark. I headed toward the trailer and
a cart rounded the corner with Three behind the wheel. Seeing his smile
was like seeing a treasured memory come to life. I waved my hand, as
if he might miss me.

"There you are," he said, utterly beaming. He pulled up in front of
me, the golf cart idling quietly.

"Here I am. I mean, here we are. This is Kevin."

"Oh, no way. You got Kevin. Well, that tracks, doesn't it?"

"Kevin needs a better agent." I silently congratulated myself for the
show business humor.

"Get in, you two." I climbed in and he said, "Long days, right? You'll
get used to it. Muriel is a ballbuster. My day hasn't really ended either."

"Long days but interesting ones. So many characters." I stepped into the cart, holding Kevin in my arm closest to Three, and she coughed twice and gagged. "Kevin?" This was the most I'd ever heard from her. I repositioned, put her chin on my other shoulder, and she settled.

I didn't want to let our Honey Wagon home slash bathroom out of sight, but like an astronaut stepping away from her rocket into the void of space, I said, "Where are we going?"

"What do you have keys to?" He threw me a mischievous grin and hit the accelerator.

"Only the wardrobe trailer. I'm kind of low on the totem pole for any other keys. I even locked myself out of the wardrobe trailer tonight."

"Some night we'll go to the costume vault. It's a great place for a field trip," he said, blowing past my last comment about being locked out of the trailer. I'd hoped the hint would have him opening it for me without asking directly. No luck. Clearly, he had a lot on his mind.

He continued, "Costumes from all the great roles are housed in there. Tippi Hedren's green suit from *The Birds* and Shirley MacLaine's iconic little black dress from *Sweet Charity*. I hear Cleopatra's emerald gown is on loan from Paramount."

"Elizabeth Taylor, right?" I said as we motored through the western town, taking a corner tightly.

"Yep. They're worth a lot of money."

That statement had echoes of my conversation with Emilie. I thought to mention the necklace, but Three said, "The studio keeps everything. You never know when you will need something for a movie. But there are collectors who will do anything to get their hands on an iconic suit or gown."

"Like that year Kim Kardashian wore Marilyn's gown to the Met Gala?"

"That's right. That gown is priceless, though a studio might loan it to a museum but never sell it."

"This is so far out of my experience. I sold a broken bike on Facebook Marketplace for fifty bucks. I can really wheel and deal," I joked and hugged Kevin close as we took another sharpish turn.

"That's why you're perfect for this job. You're a real person who does what it takes. They're self-important here. Out of touch, the people who work in film. They think they're curing cancer and that being broke is being unable to buy another beach house." He shrugged. "You know firsthand what it's like to have money problems."

I wasn't ready for a casual mention of my failures, the offhanded loss of everything summed up in a throwaway line. "Unfortunately," I said, and I must have sounded ashamed.

"Oh crap. I'm sorry." He took the hand that rested on my leg, folded it in his. "All the best people have money troubles. If you don't, you're not really living."

There was a familiarity to holding his hand, like my body remembered him but couldn't quite recall the context. *Poor thing,* I thought. So little touch to compare it to.

"You know you're in the movie business, right?" I squeezed his fingers, he squeezed back and let go. My hand went suddenly cool. He chuckled and I pictured the bones in my ears vibrating with the familiar sound of his laugh. With how his voice used to make me feel. Sexy. Adored. Energized.

"I wanted to see how you're faring. I hear good things."

"You do? Who could possibly say anything good? I don't know anything."

He shook his head. "Always so modest."

I noticed he'd gained a little weight; it softened his jaw. He was larger than I remembered from all those years ago or even more recently at the airport. My perception was off as I tried to see him as he was today rather than through the lens of the past.

His phone rang and he answered it. "Three here." He listened and said, "I'll be right there." He clicked off and said, "The party's over, I'm afraid."

"That was a fast party, even by my standards and bedtime."

He reached into the back of the golf cart, handed me a plastic bag, and said, "Someday we'll have a picnic at the *Psycho* house."

"I saw the *Psycho* house, but I haven't had a meal there yet. I bet it's scary good," I said, trying for a very low-bar horror movie joke.

"Sounds like I'm needed in the writer's room. For now, here's a sandwich on me."

The cart jerked forward. He knew his way around the lot, called out amicably to a security guy as we buzzed by. I clutched Kevin, hung on to the small handrail on the golf cart, the soft summer air breezing through my short hair.

"You haven't changed," he said, gazing at me longer than I was comfortable with both for safety and otherwise. I knew how I'd changed. And scrutiny of this kind needed discouragement.

"Oh yes I have," I said as if I wanted to win that argument. I tugged at the ends of my hair, brushed my bangs to the right.

"You haven't. I'm right and you know it." He gave me the side-eye, and something liquefied inside of me.

He stopped the cart, and the sudden loss of movement was disorienting. I opened my mouth to say something, and he cradled my face with that big, soft paw of his and said, "You're beautiful."

Kevin coughed once. Twice. A third time.

"No, you're beautiful," I said, and with Kevin wriggling more than usual.

I was off balance. No one had called me beautiful in such a long time, it was like eating a pie after being on a punishing diet. He put the cart in park and moved like he was going to step out.

"We'll argue about this when we go on our picnic. I have to go. Do you like red or white wine?"

"Both. Either. Each."

His face filled with mirth, as if he knew what he was doing to me but also maybe not. "It's decided. I'll bring one of each, then."

We were back at the costume trailer. Before I could stop myself I said, "You're exactly like you were all those years ago. Swooping in, dashing off." I wanted him to hear that I knew him too. "Three. I . . ." I said, thinking I'd do a quick ask, someplace to stay, and unbidden I heard my father's voice. *Who cares what you want. The rest of it followed: Always so much trouble. Who would want her around?* "I want you to get some rest. You work too hard."

"That's one of the reasons I wanted you here. You always did take care of me," he said, and hit the gas. I watched him motor away looking like a big brown bear in a tiny toy car.

Before going back to the Honey Wagon, Kevin and I went straight to my unlocked van. I knew enough never to lock the car if I wasn't inside it. I had spent enough time with me, keys, and locks to know I couldn't be trusted. Score one for knowing thyself.

I rummaged in my van, tsked at the flat tire, and hauled Dawna Klump's file folder out of the fire safe. I would have to check how many steps I did a day, I thought as walked back to the Honey Wagon. I needed a bright side.

I looked for any files I didn't have online, found none, and forwarded what I had, sick that I was helping the IRS in any way.

There were voices outside the trailer. I clutched Kevin and the sandwiches as the cleaning people rattled the door handle. Unjustifiably peevish, I thought, *Read the note, people. Do not open!* Cowering with Kevin and hoping she remained my weirdly mute dog slash roommate, I put her head against my cheek.

We didn't move until the cleaning crew left, and my shoulders hurt from crouching.

I knew this situation was untenable—a fifty-year-old stowaway on a movie set in the middle of Los Angeles. This would be the last night; I'd call a tow truck in the morning, when I got a minute—in a bathroom or hiding behind a tree. I'd get the tire fixed, find a place to park the van, move into it. The doors locked. I'd be fine. It was time for some frugal camping.

I opened a text to Robyn thinking a return to the mother role might stabilize my energies. Remind me why this was all so important despite the risks.

Poppy: Hi bestie.

I waited and said to Kevin, "She really is my bestie. Chelsea next. And now you." I scratched her chest, and she sighed.

Robyn: Mom. Hayden got hit in the mouth at tennis. Mom. It bled everywhere. I almost passed out.

Robyn: We got her cleaned up but mom. It was so wet. I had to lay down.

I texted the beginning of a joke about sharing a lack of genetics for ball sports. Something we always laughed about when either of us got hit in the face after tossing keys or a pen. I thought better of it and wrote:

Poppy: How are you feeling?

Robyn: Nervous. The Nurses laughed. Put me on a stretcher.

Poppy: I'm sure they did the same thing at the beginning of their careers.

I'd intended to ease Robyn into a bit of information about what was happening. Not the whole story—just enough.

When I realized my father was the problem in our household—mean, rigid, and terrible with money—I stopped sleeping through the night. He griped about the cost of having a kid. I helped my dad with the business. My grades suffered. Got in trouble for dozing off in class. I wouldn't put Robyn through any of this until it was absolutely necessary.

Robyn: I'm worried about the blood, mom.

Poppy: I hear you. I think it's something you get used to.

Robyn: What if I don't.

Poppy: You don't have to do anything you don't want to do.

Robyn: I gotta go. I hear the kids. Love you.

Like the vapor of dry ice, silence filled the room after Robyn signed off. I continued to look at my phone as if my daughter might rise from it and we could hug. Parenting was a teeter-totter of how much to tell a child about basically anything. I wondered if this blood thing was about blood or something else.

I stared at the walls of the Honey Wagon, then searched Craigslist for possible rooms to rent. Two thousand for a shared room an hour away. Nothing month to month, and every room required a damage deposit and first month's rent. I ate a sandwich.

To get out of my head, I opened YouTube on my phone and found *Everybody's Best Friend* starring Allen Carol. The show played on the idea that men didn't have best friends like women did. Allen's character, Bud, envious of his wife's book club, tried to form something similar. Instead, it became a kind of group therapy that Bud called the Crying Man Group—because inevitably, in the end, somebody cried.

After a few episodes, where I teared up, laughed, and examined Allen, I pulled a dry towel over Kevin and fell asleep.

———

I woke early with a crick in my neck, Kevin curled behind my knees, and a jolting awareness of a steady beeping sound of a truck backing up. People working nearby. I grabbed my phone and squinted at the time. Five a.m.

Kevin yawned. I found my glasses next to her sling and our blanket-towel that covered no part of us. With my finger to my lips, I lifted Kevin and when I didn't hear the beeping, I cracked open the door.

The grounds looked deserted, and we cautiously stepped onto the asphalt. I put Kevin on her feet, and she shook from top to tail, moved to a patch of grass, and relieved herself. "Attagirl. See, camping is fun. You can pee anywhere." Out of the corner of my eye I saw a man jog toward the back lot. I couldn't make out who it was. I should have slid into a shadow, behind the big fake moon, a prop from another show being filmed on the set. Instead, I watched, he nodded an acknowledgment, and I recognized him. Allen.

I imagined we had the twin thought—what are they doing here? I waved like I belonged. *No worries. I work here. Cheerio!* Silently using one of Chelsea's accents.

"How the mediocre have fallen, Kevin," I said, and we walked. Kevin kept close to my heels as we traveled the short distance to the wardrobe trailer. She sipped from her water dish and tried hard to flip a morsel of food into her mouth while I checked my phone and stretched my neck.

I'd missed a text from Robyn sometime in the night.

Robyn: Mom. I miss you. Maybe I could come home early.

She'd sent the text at 12:30 a.m. My sleepy kid who could barely get up in the morning for school if she went to bed at ten. I eased myself to the ground, sat cross-legged next to Kevin. I typed, I miss you too. Give it a few more days.

Bold statement from a woman who'd slept next to a potty the night before. I pushed "Send" and clicked on my email. There was a note from DPTaylor@UniversalSt.com, which I almost deleted before stopping myself. Instead, I clicked on it and, lo and behold, good news. The call sheet. Despite how much I'd irritated everyone, I had not been erased. It was ridiculous how money made you feel. Like hope, and sunshine. I forwarded it to Chelsea.

"Hey." I recognized Travis the Teamster's voice.

I smiled, but as soon as I realized what he had in his hand, my smile died on the vine. The note I'd written and hung on the doorknob, the one that said Maintenance was on the way. I'd forgotten it after seeing Allen. He knew. I'm sure he knew.

I'm such a third-rate criminal. I'm like one of those people you see on YouTube who rip off a convenience store with a green water pistol because they're color blind. The nausea came on immediately, and I swallowed to give myself time to think up something to say.

In second grade I was sent to the principal's office because I called Debbie Purvis a turtle head at recess. By the time I stopped crying, school was over, and my mom came to pick me up. "If you can't do the time, honey, don't do the crime." A phrase I didn't understand until the fourth grade did *Twelve Angry Men* with six pissy little boys in oversize suits. The drama teacher had said it to the kids to make a point.

I knew I was about to get yelled at. I stood, and preemptively I said, "I needed a place to sleep. I got locked out of my car last night. I usually sleep here," and I pointed very reasonably to the wardrobe trailer. "That's not the right thing to do either, but I don't have a place to live. I can't get fired. I just can't." My explanations came out fast at first, and then like my words were a ball meeting an incline, I puttered out a few more before rolling to a stop. "Dawna Klump. Lost everything. Need a shower."

Travis stood in front of me. Brow furrowed. "Wait. What?"

I looked at his hand holding the tag. He followed my gaze, surveyed my appearance. "You slept in the Honey Wagon dressing room?"

CHAPTER FIFTEEN
I DON'T BELIEVE A WORD
YOU'RE SAYING

Here I was, at the beginning of day three, only my second night on set, busted and confessing. "I slept in the Honey Wagon dressing room," I said. "I wasn't taking advantage of your niceness. I . . ." I searched for a sentence that might make it okay. "I've fallen on hard times," I blurted, feeling tears coming and knowing I couldn't stop them.

The stunned look on Travis's face seemed to say *keep talking*, and so I did. "I know that sounds very Scarlett O'Hara, but this person isn't me. I sleep in beds usually. Not usually. Like always." I gulped, tried to keep from crying. "And I have a daughter who I did not force to come to California with me because I make good choices."

Travis dropped the manila tag with my handwriting on it. It fluttered in the still air like a helicopter seed landing inches from my foot. I looked at it long and hard, my hands shaking as I picked it up. "I thought there was housing for people. I'm so . . . Look, I'll leave," I said. Tears of fatigue and hopelessness pricked my eyes. I could feel my face reddening. I was sure I looked like a large perspiring radish.

Travis dropped his head to the side and said, "Go on now, stop the tears."

"I can't go back home. There isn't one."

"Look, I'm not going to tell anyone here. Your secrets are safe with me," he said.

"I only have the one secret," I said. I didn't want him to think I had multiples and he might have to gather them like a thistle bouquet and hand them to whoever has the big call-sheet eraser.

"Hang on to that tag in case you need it again. I haven't punched in yet, so this is Travis talking, not Travis Universal Studios Employee. You think you're the only person who's spent a night on a movie set? The movie fanatics will sleep anywhere. Not that you're a fanatic, Muh-wok-key. You remind me so much of my little sister."

I opened my eyes and felt Kevin nuzzle up to my ankle. I stooped to pick her up.

"If you're going to do this, you have to do it right. It's early. I'll show you how to get a shower. Who to ask if you get locked out again. Some other hacks the regulars know."

"There are hacks?" I pulled my shirt out of my waistband and wiped my face, so grateful for this kindness. Wanting to offer him something in return, having only empty pockets.

"How long before you get a place to live? You know what? Don't tell me. I don't wanna know. Just let me know when you do."

"I rarely cry, but in the last two weeks I've been crying when I don't want to and dry as the desert when I'd like a good sob."

He gave me a heavy pat on the back, like I imagined he did when his sister fell apart. Travis led me over to Studio 37. "These enormous doors are elephant doors. For bringing in actual elephants back in the day. We'll be using this smaller door. See that light. If it's red, it means they're shooting. Never go in when they're shooting."

We stepped into a cavernous space that would dwarf the biggest Wisconsin barn ever built. "Geez," I said, unable to stop my hickish exclamations of wonder. "This is amazing." There was a wild and organized grid overhead, and I could see someone moving with confidence over what looked like narrow walkways.

"Catwalks." Travis followed my gaze with a serious look on his face. "Those are your perms. Permanent structures. Lighting, scenes, everything gets hung and strung. It's very dangerous up there. Never go up there." He stopped walking and repeated, "Never."

A few more paces and he opened a door where there was a full-size refrigerator with food inside it.

"This is the greenroom," he said. "The actors wait for their scenes here, the crew puts their lunches here, so it stays unlocked. It's kind of a catch-all place. There's a shower to the left and towels. I have a lot of keys, but not to the wardrobe trailer. Security does, and some of them have a chip on their shoulders. Best not to ask them for help."

"Could you get in trouble for this?" I looked up at him with a look that I hoped conveyed how utterly kind I knew he was being. He could get into trouble, and no part of him was doing this for himself. I'd run a 5K ages ago, and when a couple on the trail clapped in support of me, I cried. That was how I felt now. Exactly like that.

"I've been here so long, they wouldn't dare. I know the difference between someone who is having a hard time and someone who is going to burn me."

"I have not learned that, Travis. Most of my recent imbalances have to do with trusting the wrong person to do a job. Do you have a hack for telling the difference?"

"Don't take this the wrong way, but it's obvious with you. You are carrying around someone else's dog. You might need more than a tip or two." He looked at his watch, an old, simple silver-rimmed thing with a ribbon band, and said, "I gotta go. Stay out of trouble."

I showered quickly, listening carefully for the sound of the crew outside the doors. Kevin waited, primly looking away. I dressed quickly and found a coffee maker in the greenroom, made a huge pot as a sort of thank-you note. I poured myself a cup and faced the reality that this place was an instable gamble. I took a hot sip and instead of wanting to escape, Travis's trust made me feel stronger.

A man hauling an extension cord walked in the room, glanced around, said nothing, and left. I walked onto a set, dressed as a mock-up of the inside of a greasy spoon restaurant. I had the eerie feeling a waitress with strong calves would stroll in and take my order.

A bald man, with black glasses, in a navy T-shirt, joined another, bigger man and walked past me. The big guy said, "Hey, Ryan, get me a coffee, would ya?"

"Yup," Ryan said and added, "Did you see Travis was here last night?"

"Poor dude. Just can't give it up."

"I heard he's sleeping in the catwalks again."

"Yeah, but to be fair, everybody hides out up there."

"Only if they work here," said Ryan, sipping his coffee while scratching the bridge of his nose under his glasses.

I frowned and listened for more, but they'd gone on to talking about work and people I didn't know. But the news about Travis, my Travis? Sleeping in the catwalks? Was that how he knew all the hacks? He was using them himself? The men didn't sound outraged; they were pitying Travis.

The one person I trusted, confided in, accepted help from, was as much an outsider as I was. A renegade. Or a sad sack. The person that had been so kind needed kindness himself, and the sadness I felt for him, for all of us who needed to catch a break, it pinched. I put my hand on Kevin's little head, felt the warm, reassuring living warmth of her.

Kevin must have noticed my mood dump and licked my hand just as the man named Ryan emerged from the greenroom. He paused and said, "Hi, Kevin," and chucked her under her little doggie chin.

"She's cute, isn't she," I said, like a performer with a microphone—testing, testing. Can you hear me?

"Very cute. I don't know why they're always handing her off."

"I know. I guess it's one way to show hierarchy on the set," I said.

He laughed. "I guess so."

"Hey, can I ask you about Travis? He's been so great to me. Is he in trouble?"

The man hesitated. "You're the producer's friend, right? Work in wardrobe?" Ryan looked me in the eye. We'd never been introduced, but he knew who I was. I nodded and he said, "You should probably talk to Travis." He gave Kevin one more pat and without another word walked away.

People didn't trust me here; that would explain Emilie's hostility and the lack of niceties from others. They thought I'd tattle to my old friend, which was ironic because I was terrified someone would expose me for my digressions. I was in no place to tattle.

It was a catch-22, having this friendship with Three where people also saw me as a potential snitch. Like Travis, I'd have to win them over one person at a time. I walked a few steps and saw Emilie, head in her phone. I slowed my pace, curious about her expression. She wiped her face with the back of her hand. Her lip trembled while she texted and quickly wiped another tear before it slid too far and dropped onto her phone. Emilie's quiet cry pierced me. She was young to cry like an adult—noiselessly, head bowed, hiding her face—whatever it was that had us apologizing to bystanders when we sobbed legitimate tears for legitimate reasons.

"Emilie?"

She snapped her head up, a tear waiting to be brushed away on her lower lashes. "Shut up," she said.

"Can I help?"

She dragged her eyes to Kevin and back to mine and said, "You?" then scoffed and turned away.

"I talked to Muriel about the necklace. She thinks it will turn up. She didn't seem that worried." I knew the girl wasn't broken up about what Muriel thought of me, but the missing necklace was the only thing we had in common.

She shook her head like I couldn't possibly understand her problems, and my plan to win people over one by one folded.

———

At the costume trailer, Muriel had her hand on the door as I approached. She sighed, seemingly disappointed when she eyed Kevin and me. "Don't you have a life?"

I didn't, but she didn't know that. *Rude, Muriel.* I can take that from a teen, their frontal lobes aren't closed, but not an adult who had no reason to be rude to me.

"I do have a life," I said. And put my hand on Kevin's back as if she were proof, even though Kevin supported her question. "You're here just as early as I am."

Muriel reached into the side pocket of a pair of lightweight cargo pants and pulled out her lanyard. "This is my career. Sixteen-hour days are my life." The beaded string of her glasses holder got tangled in her lanyard, and I lifted it free, which seemed to exasperate her and she dodged my hand. "No one expects you to be here at the crack of dawn. An hour before call."

"To be early is to be on time. To be on time is to be late," I said. "I had a band teacher who said that, and I guess I believed it."

Muriel swung the door wide, and I saw my kit right where I'd left it, tucked into the corner by the dry-cleaning bag. Muriel followed my gaze; then she eyed my shirt, the same one I'd worn yesterday. I grabbed the clear plastic kit and my canvas tote and said, "Whew, I went home without this last night. So glad to see them here." Muriel watched me as I picked up my things.

Her expression said, *I don't believe a word you're saying. Something about you isn't adding up.*

"I carry my life in here." I stayed calm and plunged my hand into the STAY TRUE TO YOUR SHELF bag that continued to mock me. "My toothbrush. Thank God," I said like I'd just found my lost toddler at a shopping mall. I went back in. "My gum!" I took a step away from Muriel, who looked like she was just about to ask me something I wouldn't be able to answer. "I'm going to drop my bag at my car." I turned, felt around in my kit, and with great relief, touched the cool metal of the Wardrobe keys. I called back, "Can I get you a coffee or something?"

"I don't need you to get me something. Take care of yourself," she said, and in not a nice way.

CHAPTER SIXTEEN
LIKE A MELTING PIECE OF CHOCOLATE

I remembered a *New Yorker* cartoon, two angels tossing a lightning bolt from the clouds, the caption reading, *Pretty good, but I bet you can't hit him again.* I wanted to tell those angels, the Universe, or whatever dark cloud of fate that stalked me to knock-it-the-heavens off.

I knew coming here would be hard because I was so inexperienced, but I did not think everyone would hate me. I had no history as an adult with overt animosity; people liked me. I was likable. I could feel Muriel glowering around the trailer, finding me missing and being annoyed that I was gone but also coming back.

I tried for the attitude of a person who didn't care what others thought, like Emilie. *I'll get there when I get there, Muriel,* and the mere thought of that sass had me walking faster. It was like that old joke about people like me, people who cared knowing they shouldn't: *I'm going to give up people pleasing if that's okay with everyone.*

At my car I quickly changed shirts, choosing a light-blue oxford button-down made of linen that was in shockingly good shape. I rewrapped Kevin to me but warned her, "Today you're going to get some exercise, Kevin. You are becoming codependent."

I evaluated the chance of changing the tire, alone and without gossip and ridicule, and instead dialed my insurance plan that included road service. After a complicated menu of hitting buttons and being put on hold, a recording came on: "Please call back during normal business hours."

"Drop dead." *Take that.*

At the costume trailer, Muriel had her headset on and notebook out. Emilie was nowhere in sight. I didn't recognize everyone, but I smiled at a woman and said, "Have we met?"

The woman returned a close-lipped smile. "Poppy, right?" she said.

I brightened. "Yes. Poppy!" My heart lifted with something like hope.

"I heard about you. Kevin the Dog, huh? You lost big."

Infamy. That's how she knew my name. The stupid rando who got the dog.

"She's a doll. Really excellent at continuity." Trying for a movie lingo joke. "Steals underwear like a bandit," I said.

"I heard," she said and moved on.

There, I had my confirmation that I was the subject of conversations, not as a capable person but the woman left holding on to what no one else wanted. Hired by a friend who held a position of power. Basically an untrustworthy doormat—someone disposable, justifiably and easily let go.

"Poppy!" Muriel's voice from the back of the trailer.

"Yes." My right hand shot up. So eager. Kevin licked my other hand. *Be cool, Poppy, good God.* The costumes hanging on racks brushed my head and shoulders, and I threaded my way to Muriel.

"Lots of dogs on set today. So many extras for the busy mall scene. Trainers everywhere. My team is going to be in the middle of the chaos. You have to babysit Allen."

I figured for sure Allen was another dog, because surely Allen Carol, superstar, did not need a sitter. "You know I already have Kevin."

No one had a more annoyed expression than Muriel did when something nonsensical was said.

"Kevin does not inhibit your ability to help Allen Carol. Don't ask me why, but he called for you specifically. Bring this costume to his trailer. Drop it off. Come back here. His call is in an hour, and you'll go back to help him dress."

There it was again, the feeling that I was being summoned by the principal. I heard his voice from yesterday: *She's a problem.* I longed for my past secure life when I felt one emotion at a time; today the capable-exasperated me competed with the novice-obedient me. I fiddled with Kevin's ear and she pulled away.

"Are you sure?"

"Am I sure what? That he asked for you? Yes. Why? Did something happen?"

I put my hands up as if defending myself. "No, I don't think so. I mean, isn't he super important?"

"Which is why you're going now and not questioning my orders. Look, I get that you're new, but this isn't uncommon. We often give the star extra help from someone who has limited skills. Bring this costume to the trailer. Have your radio on. I need to be able to get hold of you at all times."

I nodded and held the costume up so I didn't drag it across Kevin's tongue or the ground. There was a plaid shirt and jeans, a pair of loafers.

"I only have limited skills on a movie set. Otherwise, I am very skilled," I said.

"Aren't you going to ask where you can leave Kevin?" Muriel said.

Kevin's ears perked up when she heard her name. Hesitantly, I said, "Where should I put Kevin?"

Muriel turned. "Nowhere. You gotta hang on to him."

"Are you punking me?" I flinched, hoping that *punking* wasn't out of date and some other word for tricking was in.

"No. I wondered if you'd ever ask."

I liked Muriel the moment I saw her, but this whole exchange irritated me. I wanted to say something back, toss a zinger that said, *I'm not the doormat you think I am.* So I said, "Muriel, I'm not the doormat you think I am." I turned on my heel, caught my kit on one of the hooks by the door, and bumped my head on the frame going through it.

That'll show her, Kevin said telepathically.

I didn't understand how doing a job without complaint equated to a reputation for being a pushover or, worse, a snitch. This infuriated me as I walked through the back lot toward the actors' trailers. Did a person have to be an irreverent brat like Emilie or mean-ish like Muriel?

I marched along the landscape that populated exponentially as call times approached. Dogs of all shapes and sizes were accompanied by trainers holding their leashes. No one had their animal strapped to them in a kangaroo carrier. Some dogs wore their costumes, which amounted to a collar and necktie, or a sweater vest. I recognized the fashion from the '80s sprinkled in throughout. The terrible sweaters for the men, the tiny preppy shirts and cardigans for the women. I had yet to spot the dogs playing the leads—Hairy and Sweetie, Meg Ryan's and Billy Crystal's parts in the movie so many years ago.

Out of the corner of my eye, I thought I saw the mother-in-law swoop in and out of the set through the small man door. Calling after her would doubtlessly be met with impatience and zero recognition. I had a job to do and that was deposit a costume. If I had time after, I'd try to find her.

At Allen's trailer, I knocked and waited.

Nothing.

I knocked again and worried that he might be asleep or showering or I'd catch him doing something personal like clipping his toenails. My instructions were clear, even though I had no idea why me. I called out, "Hello," and pulled the door open. Tentatively I stepped inside. "Hello?"

Quiet. I breathed a sigh of relief. I could drop off the clothes and get back to the trailer. Help him dress later, reducing the amount of time I'd have to quote unquote "babysit" him, whatever that meant. I hung the hangers on the costume hook and glanced around the narrow but well-appointed room. It was weird to be in someone's personal space without them present. A framed photograph of a girl in a yellow gingham dress clutching Allen's neck was propped on a table. A pair of discarded orange running shorts lay in a heap around a pair of New Balance running shoes.

I took a step to leave when the door opened. I didn't want to startle him, and I felt like a kid caught with her hand in the cookie jar, like I shouldn't be in the trailer, so I said, "I'm here. Hi. Hello. It's Poppy."

Allen Carol stood in the doorway. I recognized him now. It was obvious even with the mustache. How had I missed it before?

"That's quite the greeting," he said, handing me one of two cups of coffee in his hands.

"I didn't want to startle you. I brought your costume for today. That's why I'm in here. We brought it. Kevin carried the underwear. Just kidding. I carried the underwear. I didn't touch it, though. It was in this bag, and I carried it."

"Thank goodness you didn't touch it. I do not wear touched underwear."

I blinked, considering this odd fact. Wondering if this was a Hollywood thing.

"I'm joking. That was a joke. Lots of people have touched my underwear and I soldier on." His serious face was incongruent with the friendly face on YouTube.

"Oh! Ha ha," I said, but I said it like *ha*, not like a real laugh. "I'm nervous," I said, and Kevin gave an impatient sigh.

"Maybe you don't need that coffee, then." Allen reached for my cup.

"Don't you dare." I readjusted my plastic fanny pack; it was pushing my jeans off my hips. I'd lost weight in the last week, and my usually hipless body was even more curve-free. I needed a belt before I'd be showing my own pair of no-name underwear, made of cotton with an extra-wide waistband for tummy control. "I'm awkward until someone goes in for my coffee. Then I am a ninja." He gave me a disbelieving look and I said, "One sip and I'm elegance in motion," and to prove my point I mimed a karate chop and a stream of hot liquid hit my arm. "I haven't taken a sip yet," I said, wiping my arm on my pants.

"Take a gulp and help me with my pants. I'm going to need that rubber band trick again—one jog isn't going to do it. Then you can go gracefully about your day."

"I'm with you all day, I guess."

His face darkened and he made a noise in the back of his throat. "I don't need a sitter. You can go back and tell them I'm fine."

"They told me you asked for me. I don't imagine they think you're not fine." I readjusted Kevin; one of her toenails was digging into my tummy.

"For help this morning. Not all day," he grumbled. "Oh yeah, you're new to all this." Palm up, he gestured to the world around us. "You haven't heard."

"Heard?"

He shook his head. "You have a little trouble once in your life and they send you a *mom*."

I took the hit deep in my belly; embarrassment bloomed as I saw myself through the eyes of a stranger. I was either unseeable, pitiable, or dismissed as "just a mom," the culture's most misogynist label of a supremely capable individual.

"I am a mom," I said with what I hoped was quiet dignity.

I turned away from him, pulled the dry-cleaning bag off his clothing. I worked to wipe whatever emotion played across my face. I wanted to stand up for mothers everywhere, but I couldn't jeopardize this paycheck even for that much maligned group.

"Dammit. I'm sorry. I didn't mean how that sounded." He sighed, as if he were so very tired of explaining himself. "I meant, I don't need a mom, not that I think moms are beneath me. I should be so lucky to have a mom." He said this last part as a throwaway.

"We all should be so lucky," I said. Thinking if you'd grown up without one, you'd hold the word in your mouth like a melting piece of chocolate and savor it. You wouldn't spit it out like it was an insult. I turned to face him, the shirt in my hands unbuttoned and ready to be worn. He shrugged off his robe and I helped him, one arm, then the next.

"How many children do you have?" he asked, his back to me.

I smoothed the neck of his shirt, pulled a tuft of hair free. "One," I said. I wasn't going to provide information about the thing that made me a mother, the very essence of my motherness.

"That's my daughter there." He pointed with his head as he buttoned his cuff.

"She's lovely," I said, and pulled the pants off the hanger. Brushed my hand over the back of his shirt to smooth out the wrinkles.

"Look. I'm sorry. I didn't mean to offend you," said Allen.

"It's fine. I'm sure you weren't thinking of me at all," I said. "It's not your job to think of me. It's my job to think of you."

I busied myself to get him dressed, fix the front buttonhole with a rubber band, help him step into his shoes. Dressing a stranger as if he were a mannequin but with fresh coffee breath had me perspiring from the forced intimacy.

There was a quick voice in my headset. "Emilie? Copy, Emilie?"

"I think you're ready," I said to Allen. I bent to pick up his running clothes, threw them in a laundry basket for him.

"Poppy." Muriel in my ear.

"Yes," I said, touching the button with my free hand.

"You can leave those," Allen said.

The clothes were light and damp. Kevin sniffed and I looked for a hamper.

"I need you at the costume shop. Pick up a dog collar. Bring to set. ASAP." Muriel sounded stressed.

"Just drop them," Allen said.

"I'm sorry," I said reflexively, and let the clothes drop to my feet.

Allen made another irritated noise, something I was becoming familiar with.

"What is so maddening about me?" I said. I had Muriel, irritated, in my ear and Allen tsk-tsking. "Don't tell me. I can't take it. I have to go." And I rushed out of the trailer as if a swarm of bees were gaining speed toward me. Before I let the door slap shut, I said, "I'll be back soon to not be your mom."

CHAPTER SEVENTEEN
FLIPPER-OFFERS, CUSSER-OUTERS

I racewalked, the beginnings of a blister forming on my instep, past the Honey Wagon, across the pavement to the main building. I took the stairs two at a time while stabilizing Kevin. She bounced as if she were on a spring. But she bore it like a champ and was sound asleep. I could hear her wheezy snore despite my shortness of breath.

A woman I didn't recognize held a hanger with a tiny collar and necktie in her outstretched hand, and I said, "For the set?"

"I thought Emilie was collecting it?" the woman said.

"I think I'm supposed to get it to them."

"That girl better figure out who she's working for," she said.

I grabbed the costume, held the handrail as I raced to make my way toward the stage. I was about to turn the corner by a row of parked vehicles when I thought I saw the back of Emilie's head resting against the window in the back seat of a car. The girl always had a thick, black plastic pair of sunglasses perched on her nose or on her head; it was those glasses that I saw first.

I skidded to a stop and approached the car door. She wasn't examining her phone; she was asleep. I rapped sharply on the window. Emilie jolted upright, her glasses falling onto her nose, and stared unseeing at me. Then she focused and her blank stare turned from aggravation to anger. Her electric window opened an inch.

"What? What do you want?"

"Get up." I pulled the door open and stepped closer to her. As hard as I was working and as much as this girl was undermining me at every turn, I was not going to let her sleep undisturbed.

"God, can't you just leave me alone?" she whined, but she straightened and carefully rubbed a heavily mascaraed eye.

"Take this to the set right away. The more you irritate Muriel the more she picks on me. And you're going to get yourself fired."

"What do you care?" Both feet were out of the car and on the pavement.

I searched for an answer. Why did I care if this insolent, privileged girl got fired from this job? "Because . . . I don't know why I care," I said, sounding unhinged, as if I'd shouted a truism and reasonable answer to her perfectly reasonable question. I yanked her forearm until she stood. I forced her hand around the hanger.

"Okay. Okay. Don't come at me."

The same phrase Robyn used with me if I jumped to a conclusion or had more energy than a situation merited.

"I am coming at you. Move it," I said with a no-nonsense fierceness that I used all the time when Robyn was a kid and didn't want to go to school. That seemed to be a phrase Emilie responded to, and she kicked her speed up a notch. "Don't open the stage door if the red light is on."

Over her shoulder she said, "Duh." But then she took off running.

With a hand on Kevin's back I went to shut Emilie's car door. Her kit lay on the floor next to candy wrappers, empty, filthy Starbucks cups, wads of discarded clothing, and two hairbrushes filled with hair. Although the vehicle was a mess, it was a gorgeous BMW SUV. I grabbed her clear plastic kit bag, identical to mine, reasoning that I'd give it to Emilie outside the stage door, after I used the Honey Wagon. I clipped the waist strap and hitched it over my shoulder like I'd seen people on the set haul around extension cords.

My phone buzzed.

Robyn: I'm at the doctor's with the twins. Vaccinations. Feeling really woozy again.

I slammed the back door of Emilie's car and leaned against the warm metal.

Me: Put your head between your legs.

Robyn: I did. Have to get through both twins. Lizzie looks pissed.

Me: Drink some water. Keep your head low. It'll clear.

I wanted to talk to Robyn in a quiet place. She didn't love getting shots of any kind, but I'd never seen her react in this way. Toddlers were hard, their heads so heavy, toppling into every corner of every coffee table, but as a mother you could pick them up and move them out of harm's way. Teens, across the country, you still had the responsibility and stress of keeping their heads unharmed, but no parent had long enough arms for the adult hazards of the world. I headed toward the Honey Wagon, which was becoming my office, my refuge, my very untrendy tiny home.

Three dots bumped along, disappeared, and reappeared as I walked through people pushing carts, talking into their headsets. A trio of pale bearded men in variations of a slim blue suit and sneakers walked by with phones. Masters of the universe, unstressed, their children nowhere in sight. No golf carts asked them if they'd lost the tour bus; not one of them glanced my way.

I entered the Honey Wagon and waited for Robyn to reply. Kevin woke, stretched her dry tongue. I made my hand into a cup and let her have a drink. She gave me an adoring look.

There was a text from Chelsea on my phone.

Chelsea: Update?

If we were together, we'd dissect every conversation, diagnose each personality, choose the perfect words for each comeback. There wasn't time to let off that kind of steam. My frustration valve was screwed tight, and I could feel the pressure building.

Poppy: I'm alive.

It was all I could manage. She couldn't help me. I had to help me.

I opened the door and stepped into the bright Los Angeles sunshine, and there was Muriel on her way to the bathroom. "Poppy. What are you doing?"

"On my way back to babysit Allen. Right now. I had to use the potty."

"No. I mean helping that girl. She would step over your dead body without lifting an eyelash."

I blinked, thinking at first she meant my daughter, Robyn, and then I realized she knew I'd wrangled Emilie somehow. Maybe she'd talked to Costumes on her headset, or possibly she'd just put the pieces together. Either way, Muriel wasn't conflict averse, and I had some explaining to do.

"She's just a kid."

"Exactly, and she's not going to grow up anytime soon if you save her." Muriel skipped up the steps of the Honey Wagon. "Stand up to her, would you? I don't know what's going on between you two, but figure it out."

Muriel slammed the bathroom door as if that were her final word on the subject. I did not expect that. Emilie was the problem in this situation. She had all the power. I had . . . what? What did I have? I had a lot of people's irritation, and for what? For doing what was asked of me when it was asked.

I made my way back toward Allen's trailer amid the traffic of the crew, caterers, and racks of props, costumes, and lumber, working on what I would say to Emilie—to even the playing field between us.

That's when I remembered Kristi's note that rested in the bottom of my fanny pack. It seemed to wake up, stretch, and whisper, *Remember me? The button is in Emilie's kit. Call me when you find it.* "And guess what?" I said to Kevin. "I have Emilie's kit." And I'm not embarrassed to report I felt glee. I thought it was possible that Emilie had a hand in Kristi leaving. Kristi was the only person off set who knew Emilie, and maybe she'd talk to me. I had no idea what the button was about and I didn't care—that was Muriel's jurisdiction as far as I was concerned.

At Allen's trailer I did my usual knocking, calling out, warning that I was on my way in. The trailer was empty, so I unzipped Emilie's fanny pack and peered inside. Most of the bag was clear plastic, like mine, but there was a black bottom and sides that obscured some of its contents. Like my kit it was filled with sewing notions, scissors, patches, and a lint brush that had bobby pins and Velcro bits stuck to it. On the bottom, nestled against a pack of fluted nipple covers, was a button, made from a cluster of rhinestones that looked like diamonds. It was no bigger than a quarter, but was distinctive, heavy, and definitely vintage. And Kristi's phone number, the very thing I needed, sat in my kit.

I noticed something else at the bottom. It was the delicate strand of pearls with a charm. The necklace that went missing after I tidied up the costume trailer. Discovery turned to epic relief, the kind of deliverance from anxiety that came when you found your house keys and credit cards behind the couch and no longer had to cancel everything everywhere.

This relief turned to a low-key Dawna Klump fury. "Dammit, Emilie." That sealed it. I had to talk to Kristi. It was clear Emilie was going to get me fired—that she wasn't a confused kid trying to make it in a cold world. She was part of the ice.

I slipped the necklace into a side zippered pocket in my own pack. Before zipping up Emilie's pack, I took the button as well. It was connected to Kristi's note; maybe it would garner some kind of favor with Muriel, but mostly I was being petty. See, I can steal too—even though I would never.

Next, I would find that girl, haul her butt to the wardrobe trailer, and present the necklace to Muriel with Emilie's head on a platter. Okay, no. That's too much drama even for me, but, and I whispered this to Kevin, "No more mister nice guy," and she licked my hand as if to say, *I'll believe it when I see it.*

I heard footsteps on the trailer's stairs. Moved to open the door for Allen.

"Hello," I said, and spotted Emilie emerging from the trailer next door. The one I'd seen her leave the other morning. I grabbed Emilie's kit, brushed past Allen, hit the top step, said, "I'll be right back."

I skipped a few paces to catch up to Emilie and had to dodge a man carrying a flat of the top of the Empire State Building. She caught sight of me over her shoulder and dodged behind a tree. I ran right up to her and said, "I've had it with you, Emilie."

The girl ignored me, as if I were nothing, beneath consideration. And in as stern a voice as I could manage without causing a scene I said, "Emilie."

"Kiss my ass," she said, her hand on the tree, keeping it between us.

Robyn and I had close to a peer relationship that veered into a parent-child relationship when it was needed. I didn't call her names, shout, or even punish her. We talked it out. There were times when we were both furious, but we'd never lashed out. This was brand-new territory for me with someone Robyn's age. We were not flipper-offers. Cusser-outers. We were talker-outers, not low-blowers.

"I found the necklace in your pack. Why are you doing this?"

Emilie put both hands on the tree trunk. It was a small aspen, innocent, and only partially hiding the girl. "Ask your pal Three. He knows everything. Where's my bag?" She said this with a quiet, hissing fury.

I was ready to run a foot race with her back to the wardrobe trailer—holding her kit over my head while she punched the air trying to get it from me. "What does Three have to do with you, me, and a stupid piece of jewelry?"

"Lower your voice," she hissed.

I thrust her kit at her and dropped my voice. "I don't know what's going on. No idea. And maybe you could explain it to me instead of pissing Muriel off and turning her on me. I took the necklace out of your bag. And FYI, I'm not the only person sick of your shenanigans."

Why can't I hurl even one insult without sounding like a ninety-year-old with a vaudeville history?

Emilie narrowed her eyes at me and said, "FYI, nobody gives a shit about me. I'm the director's niece."

I should have wanted to fire back something harsh, an *I'm telling Muriel* threat. But there was something about the phrasing. She didn't say, *Nobody gives a shit about* you, *I'm the director's niece.* Her eyes challenged me. As if saying, *Tell me I'm wrong. Tell me someone gives a shit about me.*

I was out of breath from the exertion, Kevin the Dog's hot little body warming me, my adrenal glands acting like they were at a rave grinding out adrenaline. Instead of fighting or fleeing I said, "Emilie. You clearly hate me for reasons I can't fathom. But I'm too old for this. I genuinely need this job. I have to hang on for as long as I can. Not that I need to explain this to you, but my daughter and I are out of money and she wants to go to college. Can you stop being such a little dick for five minutes?"

She trained her eyes on mine. "The necklace was never about you. Can you just shut up about it?" She widened her eyes and said, "Please." Then she snapped her head around like a trained dancer doing a pirouette.

"No, I cannot shut up about it," I said, but she was gone, and I realized I must have looked like I was fighting with the tree.

I touched my headset to let Muriel know the necklace had been found. It would be so easy. *Muriel, I found the necklace in Emilie's kit. She had it all along.* Instead, I found that I wanted to hand it to Muriel, see the expression on her face, feel the satisfaction, the win without the petty tattletale. Without the vindictiveness. Once again miscalculating the speed at which this place moved.

CHAPTER EIGHTEEN
ALLEN HAS LEFT THE CHAT

"I'm back," I called out as I knocked on Allen's door. "Sorry about that." I tried to look like I'd come in from a healthy stroll and not a throwdown with a Gen Z or whatever letter we were at now. I wiped perspiration off my upper lip.

"Yup," he said. "That was really something." Once I stepped inside the trailer, he said, "Would you take that damn dog off for five minutes and breathe?"

I felt bad for Kevin; she was the least of the people—okay, mammals—that I'd met on this movie set that deserved the damn-anything label. I was glad to untie the sling, though, give myself some freedom. I'd sweated through my shirt as I shook the sling out. Allen poured a bowl of water for Kevin and handed my cup of coffee back to me. "Drink it," he said.

This job and its people were so topsy-turvy from what I expected. I'd have thought that this man would have been a diva and the other workers more like a team. It touched me, his gentle offers of coffee, even if he did it in a gruff and grumbly way.

I took a sip of the now lukewarm drink, but it was still heaven for the severely undercaffeinated woman I was. I rooted in my bag for an allergy pill, just in case, and after swallowing it, I'd be fine if I could stop sweating.

"That girl is a problem," he said. "She's always a problem on every set."

It dawned on me then that it was Emilie he'd been calling a problem when I'd overheard him talking on the phone. Not me. I'd assumed it was me. Why, why did I do that? No wonder Muriel was annoyed at me—I was annoyed at me.

He glanced at the photo of his own daughter and said, "Divorce is hard on kids. Doubly hard here in Tinseltown." He handed me a washcloth, indicated I should wipe my face with it.

"It's hard in Wisconsin too. But we have higher body fat, so the paparazzi doesn't care."

He laughed, to my credit, and said, "That girl had it particularly hard. Big media circus. Emilie's mother ran off with a group that tours with the rapper Nipsey Hussle."

"Nipsey Russell is a rapper?"

"No, Nipsey Russell is dead. Is Wisconsin in this solar system?"

"No. It has its own, and Hollywood isn't the sun."

"Fair enough. The mom came back, but a kid, just out of high school, no supervision with lots of money . . . it wasn't good."

One of my parental fears laid right out in front of me. Robyn, on her own, in NYC, out of her financial league, trying to stay true to herself. Too much money, too little money—the way that spectrum colored people's realities was different but equally messy.

"Where was the dad?"

"Divorce is hard on them too." He said this as if I'd suggested it wasn't. "This town remembers everything even though the news cycle travels fast. Everybody wants to see the rich and famous do poorly. It's the price they think we should pay for being rich and famous. As if that isn't cost enough."

He finished his coffee, put the cup in the sink, and said, "I know I'm privileged, but people don't divorce in context."

"What do you mean?"

"Just because I have more stuff, whatever, privilege, it doesn't mean I feel less when I lose something important. People think since we have a nice house we don't suffer."

"We?"

"Me. Celebrities. There's no compassion for us. I'm not whining; it's true." He stood, his back to me, washing his hands at the sink, his head turned toward the picture of his daughter. "Google it. You'll see."

He looked at his watch and said, "I'm headed to makeup. I'll get dressed when I get back. Don't go anywhere."

"Yeah, I know not to go anywhere. It's my job. I get it."

"No. I mean, it's good you're here," he said, then shut the door and spoke through the screen. "You're helpful."

I should have felt wonderful, hearing those words from this handsome, well-liked icon, but at this point, I didn't know who was sincere and who wasn't. Emilie obviously couldn't be trusted—how many people were like that girl on this set?

I had a memory of the first time I really understood that adults didn't say what they meant. After my mom left, a neighbor, I can't recall her name, dropped off a casserole at our house. I came to the door with my dad and heard her say, "I adored Gemini," and after the woman was out of earshot my father said, "She despised your mother."

That night, my dad told me to heat up the dish if I was hungry, and he headed downstairs to his office.

The white square dish with painted greens and onions on the side sat in our fridge for weeks. I didn't trust it wouldn't make me sick with its two-faced delivery.

I sat next to Kevin the Dog and opened my phone and googled "Emilie Director's Niece Los Angeles" and a photo of a younger Emilie materialized. Same black nails, rings on every finger, face slightly rounder, but her upper arms thinner and dyed black hair looking frayed.

The headlines were as Allen had said. Emilie left behind. Father living with girlfriend—a grainy color picture of two people leaving Nobu. There was a photo of Nipsey Hussle, a red circle around a group of people at a concert. Another of presumably Emilie's mother dancing, looking adoringly at a stage. The caption read, Fiji getaway. Hotel room trashed. I scrolled down the page. "Kevin, this looks exhausting."

I put in a few more searches. Examined startling photos of Emilie with blank eyes and a huge smile. My indignation at the girl dulled looking at the photos of her—younger, motherless. "Nobody gives a shit about me," she'd said as if everyone knew this but me.

I gazed out the side window of the trailer, looked back at my phone, and typed, "Allen Carol Divorce."

Faster than I was ready, a photo of a thinner Allen with blurry eyes and a stain on the front of his pants came into focus. Nighttime, under the lights of a hotel marquee. A black limo nearby. A caption read, Everyone's best friend Allen Carol enters rehab after divorce. I continued reading: Sources say wife has filed. "Please respect our privacy." The mother holding the daughter's hand in the photo. The girl about the same size and age of the girl in the photo. Another photo of the mother holding the hand of a man who wasn't Allen. Producer. Longtime affair. Allen has been released from contract at Sony Pictures, replaced with . . . and the story went on.

So this was why any sign of babysitting galled him. I hoped that he asked for me because in the realm of annoying sitters, I was the least of them. Even given that clearly not everyone felt that way.

You'd think that with all the *People* magazines I read at the dentist office I'd have heard about this—but I'd missed it along with the news that there was a train tunnel under the English Channel that had been dug thirty years ago. Sometimes the news cycle hurricanes past while you're trying to keep fruit in the house.

The trailer door reopened, Allen entered. "They don't need me just yet," and he paused. I must have appeared pained.

"What?" he said, closing the door behind him.

I couldn't wipe my expression clear without looking like I was hiding this new insight on him. I held up my phone. "Emilie. It's so hard."

"Don't let her ruin things for you," he said. His eyes fell on where Kevin had burrowed into a blanket at the foot of his bed. "Caring is dangerous. This is a job like any other. No different from working as the person who stacks the potato chips on the shelves in a gas station. If you don't want the job, there is a long line of people who do."

"You're the Best Friend, though," I said to acknowledge that I knew he wasn't dispensable, replaceable. That he and I were not the same. Also that I knew who he was now—the famous, award-winning sitcom slash movie star.

"Don't kid yourself. No one is safe." He coughed as a transition and said, "I don't suppose you've ever been on set, watching the magic?"

"Hardly. I was briefly in charge of holding a cloud during my daughter's rendition of *High School Musical* that they called *Fourth Grade Musical.*"

"It's the same," he said without a smile. His wry humor apparent. "Come on."

I followed him out of the trailer and over to Studio 37. The crew stayed out of his way; someone with a headset and a sturdy build held the door for him. He smiled broadly, thanked people, walked like a movie star. It was pretty fascinating to be in his wake; there was a little adulation that splashed on me. I could see it in a couple of the faces of the crew.

I must admit, I was enthralled with the set. Lights, camera, action was exactly what happened for several hours as they shot and reshot the same scene over and over again. In my headset, Muriel said she had to make a trip to Western Costume. Would return tomorrow. I touched my kit, the necklace safely stowed until I saw her.

I made sure Allen's collar sat right, that he didn't roll up his sleeves higher in one scene than the other, that his pants held their shape. Showed no bagging at the knees. Makeup artists dipped in and out. The director consulted with people and microphones were held. Allen delivered his lines, the dogs behaved, occasionally people laughed. The rest of the day, I babysat, or worked together quietly, with Allen. Kevin was back napping on the bed in the trailer, and I had to admit I missed the little joey, but also, everything was easier without a dog stuck to my middle.

It was dark when we emerged from shooting, and Allen didn't look the least bit tired until we got back into his trailer. There his shoulders dropped, his face relaxed, and he pulled off his costume. "What did you think?"

"It's a lot different from my cloud holding, I can tell you that right now."

My phone buzzed and without thinking I looked, hoping to hear from Robyn even though it was so late in New York City.

Three: See you tonight, beautiful?

While this text usually had a smile-producing, knee-weakening reaction from me, today was different. Emilie's words, the obvious mistrust from the crew. I wondered if it was all fear of my having the ear of the producer. Something else? If I asked Three about the necklace, would he know what I was talking about? Would there be fallout for Emilie, leading to more dislike from the crew—more sabotage?

"You look confused," Allen said, busying himself with the cuffs on his shirt. "I've seen you mortified, irked, and helpful. What's this?" His tone was flat, not the voice he used for the adoring crew, the director, the makeup pros.

"Oh, I got a message from Three. We've been friends for years. Been trying to connect." I pressed my lips together. I'd not mentioned this to Allen before. Wasn't sure what the reaction would be.

"Ahhhh, yes. That's how you ended up here. I'd heard that somewhere."

"Nobody misses a thing around here but me. I miss a lot, but I'm excellent at steaming clothing. Buttoning your shirts. I thought that was the job." My phone buzzed, but I didn't look at it. "Why does everyone care so much about how I showed up here? Doesn't everyone know someone or answer an ad? Are they afraid I'll smear reputations or something? Because I don't have that kind of clout. I rarely see him."

Allen looked exhausted. "Nothing. He's famous for filling positions with random people. Then randomly letting them go."

"Ouch," I said. "That was mean, Allen."

"Obviously I don't mean you, Poppy."

It was the first time he'd said my name. The intimacy of it stopped me. "You know what? I'll get Kevin and get out of your hair."

"I'm sorry," he said, his voice softer, sincere.

With my back to Allen, I moved to scoop up the little dog and she flopped onto her back, loose as a bag of cooked noodles, refusing to help me collect her disorganized body. "You little traitor. You cannot stay here. Come on."

"Damn, you normals are sensitive. I'm sorry. Really."

I heard him but I couldn't unpack every flickering emotion. Keeping this job, that was my focus. I gathered the sling in my arms and Kevin's floppy limbs and when I turned, Allen was nowhere in sight. I was getting the picture that film people did not run on the same social conventions that people who didn't have someone to put their socks on did.

"Kevin. Allen has left the chat."

CHAPTER NINETEEN
PEOPLE HAVE IMAGINATIONS

In the Honey Wagon, the only place I could remotely call my own on this set, I dialed Chelsea. When she answered I said, "I found the necklace. The director's niece had it in her kit."

"Oh, thank goodness. I was about to come out there with a metal detector," she said. "What did Muriel say?"

"She left for the day before I could give it to her. I'm keeping it safe until I can hand it right to her."

"So the director's niece had it?"

"She hates me. Or Three. I can't tell if there's a reason or not. Other people seem to be okay with me. I've never had such mixed reviews."

"Can you try not to worry if people like you or not?"

We both burst out laughing at that one. "That is not my brand, Chels," I said. "The girl that had the necklace. She doesn't have that problem. I want to kill her and take notes."

"Does she want your job or something?"

"She has my job. We're the same, except her uncle is the director. I'm way below her. It has something to do with Three, I think."

"Are you going to ask him?"

"I keep thinking that if I work hard, that will speak for itself. I'll stay as long as they need me. Maybe get another show, keep working.

If I make a big deal of anything, why keep me? They can fill this spot with anyone. I already stick out like an outsider."

"Don't underestimate your value, Poppy."

"I am enough," I said sarcastically, remembering the affirmation. "I'm enough to be Allen Carol's babysitter. So there's that."

"That's an important person to take care of, right? They wouldn't give him to just anyone."

"I couldn't tell you. It's weird, though. I'm the most comfortable with him and like this Teamster guy. Everyone else—I can't read anybody."

"Ask Three what's going on—pay attention to what he doesn't say."

I wanted to change the subject—I couldn't ask Three or anybody else. I did not understand the politics of this place, and the stakes were too high. It was more than that, though. I wanted him to see me as I'd been my whole life—capable with a home.

"Check in with Robyn if you get the chance. She's kind of all over the place," I said. "Text her. You know how the kids are about talking on the phone. It's like they're afraid the cell lines will take their soul if they pick up."

"Will do. I have to work a double tomorrow. Brad made soup for me," she said, and signed off.

Before I could put my phone back into my kit, I got a message from Three.

Three: Can we try tonight? So far, evening open.

Me: Definitely!

When we dated all those years ago, we were guileless, enthusiastic, sincere. I'd loved him, we broke up, and I thought about him for years. Yet here we were again. There were stories in magazines about this very thing. Lovers uniting after years apart, quotes bolded with the subheading, "I always knew we'd be together."

In his presence everything shone a little brighter. I was prettier, funnier, brilliant. The rush I felt was better than chocolate-covered toffee, which I pretty much think is close to God. In his presence I was the young, line-free woman he remembered, and he was the darling man who had made me feel that romance wasn't over because I'd given birth.

Three: 9 PM Meet you at the Psycho house?

I sent him a thumbs-up and searched in my kit for a Band-Aid for the sore beginning on my foot. I was about to dump everything out of my canvas bag and put Kevin inside it for our field trip slash date with Three when a knock on the door made both of us jump. I put my finger to my lips and Kevin attempted to pull her tongue into her mouth as if that were the noisiest part of her.

I hadn't heard footsteps, and if it was Travis, wouldn't he announce himself? If it was the cleaning crew, we could rush out and apologize, make an excuse for being late. The critical time for a casual callout of *Occupied!* ticked away.

"Poppy," said a stern whispered voice. It was Allen. Kevin rolled her eyes up to meet mine, panting. I covered her mouth, trying not to shift my weight even a fraction of an inch.

"I know you're in there. For God's sake open the door," he said. I considered silence as a response, but the consequences were so wide and varied that I flipped the tiny lock and inched the door open.

Allen Carol, the movie star, stood on the bottom step of our hideaway, hands on his hips looking like an aggrieved parent.

"Exactly what are you still doing there?"

Years ago, I hit black ice on the highway in the winter. Robyn was strapped in her car seat in the back singing about a manatee. *Barbara Manatee, you are the one for me.* The rear of my car slid, right, then left, then a full three sixty, stopping only as we slid backward into the snowy ditch. The whole Jesus Take the Wheel moment lasted seconds, but my thoughts spun faster than the wheels beneath us. I saw in my mind's eye the shovel in the trunk and AAA's number. I heard a voice reminding me not to pump the brakes, to countersteer, to, if possible, relax. I'd never thought of death, but the moment we'd stopped moving, ass deep in a snowbank, I cried.

My fragile plans spun out of control, this was my ditch, and tears pricked my nose. I tried to stop them, bit my lower lip, took a long, slow breath through my nose, but when I wheezed out a shuddering exhale, I couldn't hide it. I was only able to say, "We live here."

He closed his eyes as if he'd spent his entire career rousting intruders from various locations around movie sets and he was entirely sick of it. He said, "No you don't."

"I do." I nodded rapidly and said, "I actually do." The thought of explaining had my throat closing and my eyes watering.

"Please. For the love of God. Stop, get your stuff, and get out of there." He took a step and said, "Give me Kevin."

Kevin grumbled as I obediently handed her over. I dropped my Band-Aid, picked it up, and gathered my paltry belongings. I followed Allen out. "My car has a flat tire. Tax evasion. But I'm not an evader. I didn't evade. My daughter is in New York. I can't get fired."

"Nope. No." He put his hand up. "None of my business." With Kevin in his arms, appearing smaller than ever, Allen paced in a circle, finishing in front of me. "I've got to get home. Go to my trailer. Sleep there. We'll talk tomorrow."

"What? No." That felt worse than sleeping in a toilet or in the belfry of the iconic *Psycho* house, for that matter. "I don't think I can do that," I said.

He glanced at the Honey Wagon, then back at me, and said, "Oh, I think we both know very well you can and you will."

Allen off-loaded Kevin into my arms, and I smelled peppermint and sweat. His or mine, I wasn't sure. Then he crossed his arms and walked toward the parking lot. I walked the familiar trek to Allen's trailer, and inside, I clutched Kevin and waited for the next lightning bolt from above. Kevin wriggled in my arms when she spotted the soft dove-gray blanket from earlier in the day. I placed her in the center, and she walked in perfect circles before lying down. I washed my hands, gave myself a quick overall check of my sorry appearance, and the gurgle in my stomach said nerves, not hunger.

Robyn and I'd run a 10K for diabetes once. I'd trained up to about 8K believing what others said about running—the adrenaline would take you over the finish line. They didn't say how crappy it felt to have adrenaline fueling the last hill. Just before the finish I got stung by a bee, and that just did me in. I walked over the line and announced to the man with the microphone calling out the runners' numbers, "Never again."

Right into the mic for all to hear, the emcee said, "Poppy Lively. Not so lively after all." I had thought I'd get a minute to recharge before the next indignity, the next hard discovery, and I wasn't up for Allen to discover me living in a toilet. Not up for it at all.

The place smelled sweetly like Allen's soap, a hint of cologne, the big bed with blankets.

My phone said fifteen minutes and Three would be at the *Psycho* house.

Before pushing the door open, I peered through a side window, hoping for a clear path away from the line of trailers and onto the back lot. Fingers on the door handle, I paused when the neighboring trailer's door moved. I recognized a stealth exit, having become newly proficient at looking before leaving—anything.

It was the bald man with black glasses, the one I'd talked to about Travis. He emerged, stopped to speak to someone inside, then moved soundlessly into the shadows.

I pushed out the door in the same sneaky way I'd just observed and lightly stepped into the shadow of the trailer. The liquidity of the night air moved me to the back lot, the *Psycho* house in sight, a golf cart parked in the back.

I spied Three sitting on the steps of the ancient house with its steep sloped roof and dormers. His profile so much the same as his younger self.

We'd met in a restaurant where he was a waiter. He'd stood, grinning that magical grin and taking an order. We made eye contact as I walked in the door, and Three didn't look away until someone at the table cleared their throat.

Three placed me in his section and he flirted all night, asked for my number. When I told him I had a daughter, he said, "I'd like to meet her." I couldn't believe my luck. Not unlike the feeling when he'd offered me this job.

"Three," I said, approaching the *Psycho* house. I loved the iconic after-hour spaces on the back lot. No tour buses motoring by threatening to scoop me up and deposit me at the theme park. The grips having gone, the ghosts of movies past floating in and out, unseen but somehow present.

"You're here. It's so good to see you." He didn't stand. Instead, he moved over an inch, and I took two steps up and sat next to him. "Would you have believed me if I'd said all those years ago that we would be sitting inside Universal Studios working on a movie together?"

I slid in next to him and felt the warmth of his body, even without us touching. His lashes, still long, a faint shadow of whiskers. "No, I wouldn't have."

His eyes found mine and held them while he spoke. "You probably haven't had a chance to see much, but there's Amblin, Spielberg's offices, and that costume archive. It's the holy grail for movie and fashion geeks. You'll love it. Oh, Poppy." Three said it like he'd just discovered a new word. "You have no idea how wonderful it is to have someone near who knew me when. Who doesn't want to be in a movie, or show me a script, or be introduced to a director. To talk shop every minute of every day." He let out a heavy sigh and said, "Who doesn't want a thing from me except to sit here, on these steps of this iconic house, and reminisce."

It wasn't true. I did want things from him. I wanted more work. To know who to trust at this place. To interpret his behavior without asking outright. I knew from my childhood that asking questions came with answers you didn't necessarily want. I'd learned over the many years that keeping your questions close was a way to self-protect. I knew it was one of the reasons I didn't question Dawna when she took over my taxes, frowned when I said I had time to review them. Sometimes you wanted to float along without hearing the no.

Tonight I didn't want a no, a judgment, a rejection. I wanted to lean in and kiss him. Where was the harm in that? Letting myself fully dream for a minute in a way I hadn't in years.

"Was it hard to make connections being from Wisconsin?" I asked. I'd been so focused on my failing and fears since I'd arrived that I hadn't asked Three about his life. I'd been filling in blanks with the Three I used to know. It was time to discover him as he was today.

"Not really. You know me. All bootstraps and hard-work midwestern values. I met a few people but—you know, you make your own luck."

"Or you know the producer," I said, referring to how I'd been hired, how I happened to be sitting next to him on this step.

I thought he'd laugh, but his expression flashed annoyance. "I knew James, yeah, but I had to take a lot of risks to get in front of him."

I nudged him. "I meant me, silly."

"Oh." And he laughed his easy laugh then. "People always questioning your right to be anywhere. Get a slice of the pie." He pushed a pebble off the wooden step. "I've been meaning to ask. How's the director's niece to work with?"

"She's young. Smart. Impulsive. Can you imagine your old self in this job? You'd have charmed everyone and kept all the golf carts for yourself—returning late with apology candy."

"That's right. That old car of yours. I don't even remember where I went with it." He narrowed his eyes with the memory. "James is trying to give her an opportunity. His sister's kid, you know. He loves them both, but they're cut from the same cloth, rebellious. Don't let that girl tell you any stories."

"What kind of stories?" I asked, gazing at the view from the front steps of the old horror story of a house, down the hill and into the Bates Motel. This place where thousands of kisses were shared, dramas had unfolded in front of and behind rolling cameras.

He took a beat. The darkness made it difficult to read him.

"Oh, you know, the usual things. Work gossip that doesn't exist. Talk about who's richer than who. What's happening behind the scenes. Like, I once heard that someone thought I was selling tickets to watch us shoot *Fire in the Meadow*, dressing people up as crew and allowing them on set."

"That's ridiculous. As if you would ever do something like that. You're a producer!"

"You always were my champion. Knew I had something in me."

It felt like a win to sit on these steps, ease his mind, chat like we were the same, not Producer and Must Hire but man and woman, speaking in confidence and support.

My foot itched. I held the Band-Aid in my hot little hand and uncrumpled the package, peeling the paper back.

"Oh no," he said, concern in his voice. "Allow me." Three gestured for me to lift my foot onto his lap. He took off my shoe, slipping it off my heel, and the night air licked my arch.

This moment of caring was a surprise. I watched from above, as if I were not center stage in this moment. I was often the mouse in the corner in my own life, spying rather than experiencing. Experiencing was for people who were secure. I saw him examine the arch of my foot by the light of the moon. He ran his thumb over a rough patch, and I flinched. Not from pain but from hypersensitivity.

"Does it hurt?" he asked.

"When I'm walking it rubs. Sitting here on the stairs, my foot in your lap? No, it doesn't hurt." I did feel something, that was for sure, and it wasn't pain, but it did have a real need attached to it.

I heard the crinkle of the wrapper as he pulled the bandage apart, felt him rotate my foot an inch. He carefully placed the adhesive over the abrasion, pressed it in place. His long lashes, a boy, a man covering a wound. It was exquisite to be touched with such care, and I felt every part of his hand and fingers. I knew exactly where they were on my foot.

"There," he said and stroked the arch of my foot, and I did not pull back reflexively. I arched my foot.

Three removed my foot from his lap, stood, and held his hand out for me to stand. Put his arms out to hug me. A vision materialized. Not a match to a sparkler as it had been in the past, but more—Three a well-worn catcher's mitt and Poppy a softball rolling into home plate. Chelsea popping to mind, always protective, asking questions to keep me safe.

"Did you marry?" I asked.

"No, I never married."

"That can't be right. All these years?"

We were no longer hugging but close enough for our proximity to look private if anyone was watching.

"I had a long-term partner. We never married," he said. "It didn't end well."

A breeze kicked up, the perfect temperature for a movie moment, where a magical portal opens, time freezes in place, a wizard appears. Where the Universe seemed to be back in play setting a scene for us.

I looked up at him. He touched my chin with one finger, tilted my head, looked in my eyes, and kissed me.

CHAPTER TWENTY
THE VANITIES

It was the kind of kiss that if we were at a baseball game, the announcer would shout into a microphone, *And the crowd went wild!* Three's lips were as I remembered—warm, soft, confident—and his breath smelled of cinnamon. When our tongues touched, I considered moving inside his mouth to live for the rest of my life.

I wished I'd pulled away, but I'm sorry to report it was Three and once we separated, I said, "Holy cow," and he laughed.

"I remember you," he said, and touched my nose with his thumb. Before I could throw myself at him again or wax poetic and add a *gee whiz* to that *holy cow*, he said, "I brought you a sandwich."

"That's exactly what a girl wants to hear after an epic kiss." Organic desire was like drinking one too many fruity alcoholic beverages way too fast. Or, in Wisconsin language, chugging a beer bong in college, though at fifty years old, it was more of a hot toddy.

"You're just the same."

To my credit I did not point out my dry skin, gray hairs, or loss of confidence. No, instead I said, originally, "So are you. Should we kiss more or eat?"

"I was thinking, if it's not too forward to ask you, Would you like to come and see where I live?"

"Yes. Yes I would," I said, and like a bat did a quick echolocation of my body hair, underwear, and abdominal tone.

He gave me a slow smile that wrinkled into crow's-feet and he took my hand. "Come on." When his phone rang, I had moved on in my mind to my dry elbows and Kevin, wondering what to do about each one.

"Okay. Yes. Okay." We made eye contact. The moment was gone; I saw it in his eyes. He clicked off his phone. "I'm sorry, Poppy. This is how it is producing. The ground is constantly shifting."

"No more kissing?" I said, and disappointment fluttered along with a tinge of honest relief. I should have listened to that Kegel podcast, and Kevin would be glad to see me.

He shook his head, amused. "Not today."

"Another day?"

He nodded and as he climbed into the golf cart and started the engine, he said, "Absolutely another day. Maybe next time we can visit that costume archive. Do you think you might be able to get the keys?"

"Maybe," I said, not wanting to let him down. "I can look."

"Oh, hey, there's a new project being green-lit. Witherspoon and Kidman are attached. I can put in a good word with Wanda and Muriel if you like. If you still need money."

"I'd love to be considered for another job." Maybe Three and I could be a team, a success story finding happiness on movie sets, the seeds planted decades ago finally blooming.

"They're highly competitive. It's good to have an in," he said and grasped my hand, giving me a smoky look.

My heart packed her extra beats away, my nervous system patted itself down, and my upper lip considered stiffening as I watched him motor off.

I sat on the steps of the house a long time, opened the white bag, and unwrapped the cellophane from one of the best-tasting egg salad sandwiches I'd ever eaten in my life. Someone—Three?—had packed doubles of Orangina, chocolate chip cookies, and two snack-size bags of salt-and-vinegar chips. Was this the start of more? An actual visit to his home, dinner somewhere, a new idea of life?

I stood, stretched, kicked off my shoes, and walked barefoot across the pavement as if I belonged on this back lot, my Band-Aid be damned. I noticed the toes on my right foot turning in slightly—saying in their quiet, consistent way, *Stay alert*, and I said to myself, *I've never been more awake in my life.*

———

Inside Allen's trailer, Kevin glanced at me from her warm, cozy circle. There was a bowl with the remains of what looked like dog food and a half-chewed rawhide, a muffin tin with water in two of the circles.

Allen had been back? Kevin was not talking. I sat and scratched the space between her narrow shoulders, right where she liked it.

I texted Robyn:

Poppy: How are you feeling?

Robyn: Better. Mom. They charge a thousand dollars a week in Starbucks deliveries. They have someone who does their laundry, puts it away, and packs for them when they go away for the weekend.

I hit the FaceTime button and waited. Robyn didn't accept the call. I texted her.

Poppy: Can you talk?

Robyn: I'm in the kids' room.

Poppy: Aren't they asleep yet?

Robyn: Yes, they are. I'm staying in here. Lizzie's mom is visiting and staying in the other apartment.

Poppy: Your apartment?

Robyn: It's not mine, mom. I'm staying in the kids' room until her mom leaves.

Poppy: If you're paying with your time for room and board and you're sleeping full time with the kids they have to pay you for that.

Robyn: It's not like that. I'll explain tomorrow.

Poppy: Do you need me to call Lizzie?

Robyn: No. NO.

I knew better than to insist or call, in spite of her. She had to figure it out. Just like her mother did so many miles away.

———

The next morning, I didn't notice the door had opened and someone was in the trailer until I heard, "For God's sake." Allen's voice, irritated.

I bolted upright, spotted Kevin still comfortably snuggled into the bed, tried to gauge the hour. "What?" I sat, startled. "You told me to come here, didn't you? You did. I remember." I swung my feet off the couch, straightened my shirt. "Or didn't you mean it. I'm so confused. What is happening?"

"Why didn't you use the bed?" Allen wore the same orange shorts that had lain on his trailer floor the day before. He was winded, sweaty, and mopping his forehead with a lavender-colored microfiber towel.

I shook my head, possibly as exasperated as he was. "What is it with this place? I'm either sound asleep or in a panic. There is no middle ground. I am from the Midwest. We are by definition middle-ground people." I stood and found my canvas bag and said, "It's your bed. It didn't feel right sleeping in your bed."

"You're weird about sleeping on someone's else's sheets but not averse to sleeping in essentially a bathroom," he said, draping the towel around his neck and moving toward the coffee maker.

"I slept on a shower curtain in a place that looked like a kill room a couple of nights ago, so no, I'm not weird. I'm respectful. Considerate. Hygienic." I moved to where Kevin lay, unperturbed, sure someone would care for her. "Come here, Kevin," I said, and Kevin did not move. "It's time to go."

"Just wait. I'm making coffee. You need some."

I didn't like that he thought he knew what I needed. That two days together and he had my number: A mom who needed rescuing. A weakling. A wuss. "Okay. Yes. I need coffee, but you need a person to help you get dressed."

He stiffened. I saw it in his shoulders.

"Oh, I see how it is. You can dish it out but you can't take it," I said.

He turned, handed me a cup of coffee with the words BEST FRIEND on it. He drank from a cup with a scrawled I LOVE DADDY in pink crayon. He took a sip and said, "I thought for just a moment you were going to fight me." He smiled a one-sided smile that went all the way up to his eyebrows.

"I gave birth after thirty-six hours of labor without an epidural. If we duked it out, I would win. My uterus would win anyway. It's a beast."

I took a sip of coffee. He took a sip. A stalemate if there ever was one.

"I have to go to the bathroom and I'm not using yours, not because I'm weird but because I have a shy bladder."

"So much physiology so early," he said, and closed his eyes.

"Kevin. Time for the potty."

We stepped outside into the early-morning peace. Kevin squatted, relieved herself discreetly, and I motioned for her to follow me. "You need to use your legs." We walked to the Honey Wagon.

Before I stepped up onto the stairs, I saw familiar boots on the other side of the enormous wheels of the cab. I recognized Travis's heavy footwear and considered telling him what I'd overheard the day before. When I rounded the vehicle I stopped—it was a personal act, watching someone put the corner of a towel into their ear, squeegee it dry. His glasses were hooked to the neck of his shirt. There was a blob of shaving cream under his nose. It felt wrong to see him like this, when the motion must have caught his eye.

"Well, hello there, Poppy!" He said this with warmth and welcome in his voice. "You and that little guy have become quite the little campers, haven't you?" An inside joke between new friends.

"Thanks." I wanted to ask him if it was true. That he was as much of a stowaway as I was. More important, I thought he should know that people knew and maybe he wasn't as untouchable as he thought. Would this news be welcome, or would he bristle and remove the friendly tone from his greetings?

"Travis?" I said. He'd been such a help to me—it must have been nice to discover someone more in need than he was. I didn't want to trade places with him, make him feel small. I thought fast and said, "What would they do if I was discovered sleeping here?"

"Depends on who found you."

"What if it was the crew? You know, the guys who hang things from the rafters."

"I doubt they'd discover you. You'd have to be sleeping up in the perms. They're dangerous, and you'd get fired for sure."

"I overheard them say someone is sleeping in the catwalks. Can't stay away, they said."

Travis peered at me. "Is that right? It's confirmed?" He tried to act only partially interested; I saw it in the way he continued to wipe his face with the towel.

Kevin the Dog sniffed near Travis's steel-toed boots, and I bent to pick her up, hug her close.

"Sounds like it," I said. "Thought you'd like to know. Help that person like you helped me." I turned away even though I wanted to see if his expression would change from incurious to nervous. "See you around, Travis," I said. "Kevin and I have got to get our act together today."

"Poppy," he said, raising his voice just enough for me to hear it. "Keep your head down." But what I heard was, *Thanks.*

Outside Allen's trailer, I recognized Muriel's voice and had a thought to hide. The trailer door opened and Muriel stood in the doorway holding the stolen necklace by the clasp. "Poppy. Would you like to tell me about this?"

Allen stood over Muriel's shoulder, interested. I felt the urge to flip him off.

"That's the missing necklace," I said, because obviously. "I was going to bring it to you today!" I wanted to die right there.

"Yes. Do you want to tell me how it got into your kit?" Muriel said as she moved down the stairs.

"I put it there." Not a lie. If I told the story, pointed the blame to Emilie, Muriel would believe me. There was no doubt she already knew; the challenge in her eyes was one of a prison warden. *Will she snitch or not?* Nobody trusted a narc, but truth and loyalty were important.

"It was safe in my kit. I was going to return it to you today," I repeated.

"If this necklace hadn't turned up . . . Do you know how bad this makes Wardrobe look? We're already considered"—and here she lifted her hands to create air quotes—"'the Vanities,' as if we are playing dress-up, not adding dimensions to the character with clothes. We run our asses off to get a modicum of respect. Wardrobe can't be the department that screws up."

"I'm aware. That's why I've been looking for it like mad," I said. I knew I could point my accusing finger at Emilie, but it was so snively. Like immature sibling rivalry. And there was obviously hierarchy here. Point to the director's niece, blame her, and expect to keep my job? No way.

Muriel dropped her arms in frustration and said, "I don't have time for any of this. If I have to go to the director, I will." I followed Muriel's eyes as she glanced over her shoulder in the direction of Allen's trailer. "And for God's sake get rid of that dog."

Before I could stop myself, I said, "She's not hurting anyone," and that sentence seemed to baffle Muriel more than anything I'd done since our meeting just four days and three nights ago.

"You know, if you stood up for yourself like you do for everyone else, maybe I could respect you. You do good work. It's clear you're interested in this job, but you've got to focus on yourself." She took a step, stopped. "Get in there and help Allen, because for some reason only you can get him dressed," and that's when I realized Muriel and I were in the same confused boat, trying to get people dressed for work without drama.

Even so, Muriel's words were true. *You know, if you stood up for yourself like you do for everyone else, maybe I could respect you.* I did put others first. I'd long known that if you focus on other people, you don't have to figure out what you want. If you never ask anything for yourself, you'll never discover who cares or, for that matter, doesn't care. I'd done it for years, and it had always worked for me. Why wasn't it working anymore, though? That was the real question, and I didn't want to know the answer. My heart beat hard and my mouth went dry, as if my body were drawing attention to this crucial moment and I shouldn't miss it.

This was the first time that doing my best for others annoyed those others. The system I'd used my whole life was failing. I'd thought I was a woman of the world, but in fact I was a woman of my world, my *tiny* world that I had made work by wanting as little as possible. I tried to take a deep breath, but I couldn't fill my lungs.

Was I supposed to become someone who would take others down for my own needs? Like Dawna? Or tattle instead of manage my own battles? Or sabotage others to keep this job so I could pay my debts? Hurt people the way they had hurt me? And if I didn't, then I'd be out, scrounging for a way out of my crushing debt, far away from Three, having done everything wrong again. Losing him again.

Kevin started to pant, and I felt her trembling in the same way I was.

CHAPTER
TWENTY-ONE
TUGBOAT

Kevin was quivering so hard that if she had a regular set of teeth, they would be chattering. I placed my whole hand over her face, and shakes became pulses with calm moments in between until she settled and calmed me too. I had to change my approach if I wasn't going to go home broke, go to prison penniless, be unable to help Robyn do what she wanted. I needed to be a badass.

Muriel had set Allen's clothing for the day's filming, and I wasn't sure what to do. How does one transition to badassery when their job is to straighten another person's collar before heading out for the day? I could practice on Allen, say, *Do it yourself, bestie,* but he had a *don't talk to me* look on his face and I didn't want to bug him. Immediately wrong, Poppy Lively—a badass bugs people. I'd go in slow.

I put Kevin in front of her bowl to eat. "Did you drop this food off last night?"

"What food?" Allen said, glaring at his iPad.

I poured some kibble into the bowl in response, and the pellets made a plunking noise as if to say, *This food. Good, Poppy, that was passive-aggressive. Keep going,* I cheered myself on. I eyed his shoulders, one higher than the other, a stress-tell I knew from working with him. He was mad about something. I'd been ordered into this trailer last night by Allen, and appointed as his personal dresser, so why did I feel like I was the last thing he wanted around at this moment?

I knew enough not to chatter, to find something to do, so I pulled the dry-cleaning bags off the hangers and checked the shoes for scuff marks. The call sheet for the day's scenes were clipped to the hanger, and I examined the times, set a couple of alarms on my phone. Kevin sniffed the corners of the kitchen while I turned the water on to rinse a coffee mug.

"Leave it," he said, and Kevin sat—maybe that was a command she knew.

But the direction was meant for me. I'd had enough of being treated like a kid who'd left their math homework for the last minute. A kid that hadn't read directions.

"You have an hour before makeup and two before rehearsal. I'm going to go get breakfast." I scooped Kevin off the floor.

"Leave her here," he said, and I thought about tucking her into my kit, taking her to breakfast in spite of his command. A tiny bit of badass theater. A *you're not the boss of me* resistance.

But, remembering Muriel's last command telling me to get rid of Kevin, I chose the less damaging thing. I placed Kevin on what I now considered her blanket and saw, out the side window, one of the wardrobe staff, the only man, carry hangers up the steps of the trailer next door. The door opened, the items were handed off, and the transaction was completed.

"Who's in that trailer next door?"

"He's too young for you," Allen said.

His expression hadn't changed, his gaze on the screen in front of him. Was he joking?

I tried a laugh. "Noted," I said not good-naturedly.

"You go for the younger guys, I hear. Women hate the May-December romance unless it's their dalliance."

"Dalliance. That's quite a delicate word for an indelicate thing to say." I tried to say that with an edge. I added a disgusted tsk as a punctuation.

"It's true, isn't it?" He met my gaze. "People tell me everything. Haven't you heard? I'm everybody's best friend."

"Are you referring to Three?" I said. "And also, do I look like someone who's trolling for . . . honestly anything?" I tried to control my interest, that others had noticed a connection between us.

The fact that I was only visible for admonishment or speculation around Three and me, or to be made fun of as Kevin's keeper, irritated and fascinated me. Did these people whose days were spent in the most glamorous profession in the world not have enough to gab about? I expected that from my hometown, where excitement hit an all-time high when rumors hinted at the coming of a Shake Shack. Here among the spectacularly divorced and poorly behaved there was no shortage of interesting fodder that didn't include me.

"Yes, I dated him many years ago. Yes, he was younger than me then and is, indeed, younger than me still. He hired me. I came here to dress people, not to undress them on or off set." I saw myself intrigued by the idea that Three and I were seen as . . . something. At the same time that I was downplaying Three to Allen. Sure, there were lots of possible reasons for this, but I knew the real one and it had to do with how Allen smelled when I buttoned his shirt.

I wiped my hands on a dishcloth, imagined what people were saying, how they referred to me. The one with a scarlet letter of a dog, the letter being *d* for *doormat*. The unstylish oldie, bullied by the director's niece who was a third her age. The must hire who got the job because of ancient networking or—gasp—sex acts, and somehow was on thin ice with the star. Were there bets to see when I might be erased from the call sheets?

The whispering halls of grade school reared in my memory. The kids having heard from their parents that Gemini Lively had left her little girl behind. The teachers' pitying looks. And certainly some people knew about Dawna Klump and the Livelys.

"How long ago did it end?" Allen asked, surly at noticing my uncertainty and gaining fuel from it. "How many years ago?"

His tone sounded challenging, not questioning; the implication that he knew something about Three and me. Had someone seen us last night? Emilie? I'd dealt with bullies since fourth grade, and back then, when they made fun of my clothes, I'd ask, *What do you care?* Here, now I wanted to say, *What do you care if Three and I are whatever? You wouldn't want me. What's it to you?*

"It must be a shockingly slow news day on planet Hollywood if you've all reverted to talking about me." I tried a true Wisconsin accent to underscore the foolishness of the conversation.

"What could be more interesting than a stowaway must hire who's babysitting the hero?"

I frowned. There are benefits to being the girl who observes. The one voted best personality in high school, the one whose foot turns in when she's tired. The one who wasn't invited to prom so she managed the punch table instead. The one whose father was charming to some and dismissive to others.

The rewards of that kind of life reside in a bat-like ability to hear personal pain deeper than the initial broadcast. While his derision appeared to be for me, he was mocking himself. Babysitting. The. Hero. All said with halting disdain. But, while he ridiculed himself, I was being hauled along as camouflage.

I'd gone through a lot to get here. I was doing my best under difficult circumstances. I could feel my right foot making the turn inward from the stress of this face-off. I stretched my toes, moved my foot, and said in the voice of queen babysitter, "This conversation is beneath you, Allen. Before I get back, put your own damn pants on. It's time for the hero to help himself."

I moved across the threshold, over the steps, and tried to slam the door behind me. The effort threw me slightly off balance, so I decided that if I was going to keep standing while I stood up for myself, I'd have to give up any door slamming.

Outside I wiped my palms, damp from anxiety, on my pants. I did it. I stood up for myself, and I felt the coffee in my stomach turn to acid and travel up. I checked for an audience, waited for fallout, every hair on my arms vigilant. The world did not stop spinning, but I had the feeling I'd gone too far, picked the wrong person to assert myself with. Why Allen? Why would I push back with Muriel and Allen but not Three? Was I that much of a simp, that if I had a crush on someone, specifically Three, I couldn't be myself?

On top of all this, there was the constant reminder that you were dispensable. Where did anyone get the courage to say anything? The trailer next door opened and out walked the neighbor, the one I'd asked Allen about moments before. Robyn would call the man a Short King if she were here. He couldn't have been much taller than five foot six, but he had a strong jaw and a thick head of black, curly hair. He was good-looking but not better looking than many of the kids Robyn went to high school with.

He didn't glance my way before turning in the same direction of breakfast. He walked with confidence, as if he were entering an award ceremony or, I imagined, one of those huge post-Oscar parties. Was this swagger of his an act? Did he kvetch in his trailer to his dresser Emilie only to walk like a king later? Was everyone living a double life but me?

Members of the crew glanced, waved, called out to him; meanwhile not a soul spoke my name. Not a single acknowledgment that I walked the same ground as this young star. Not until a man with a carpet and a lamp tried to get around me.

"Watch it," the man said. "Coming through."

I rejoined the path to the food table a few steps behind the little prince, the name I would have given him if I had any friends to eat breakfast with. I surveyed the pastries, looking for a bit of protein for my blood sugar, waffling from stress and coffee. With a paper plate in hand, I chose cheese cubes for me and pea pods for Kevin and looked for something to stuff in a fridge for later in the night.

"I'm Jeffery," the young man said, and offered his hand.

"Poppy," I said, trying to hide my surprise.

He looked into my eyes. His warm handshake, stronger than I would have thought, held mine. "I know we haven't met."

I shook my head. "No, we haven't."

"What do you do here?" He let go of my hand. Picked up a plate and dropped a bagel onto it. Then met my eyes again.

"Wardrobe." I'd forgotten about my blood sugar. Such dark brown eyes, I couldn't look away.

"Are you the designer or a set costumer, or do you work in the trailer? I know there are a lot of moving parts in building out our characters through clothes."

"I'm . . ." I stopped myself from saying *a must hire*. I was tired of the demeaning title. "I go wherever they need me."

"A jack of all trades, then." He dropped his voice and tilted his head toward me as if we were part of a conspiracy, a squad. "It's good to have versatility in this business, that's for sure." He dropped a danish onto his plate. "Good chatting with you," he said, and touched my upper arm, and I smiled the smile of a teammate. A colleague.

I had the feeling that more time had passed than a few seconds. The belonging that momentarily engulfed me with our interaction faded as he moved on, touching another back here, giving a fist bump there.

I selected a croissant, took a bite, let the butter and flaky pastry pull my senses back to familiar territory. I felt like I'd been charisma'd. This must be why Emilie was spending time with Jeffery, in whatever way she was. He was compelling for a young man. His pull was similar to Three's and Allen's—a type of personality heroin.

I looked for someone to share my observations with and moved to the coffee cart, where two women stood. Maybe I'd strike up a conversation. *That Jeffery, am I right? Whew!*

As I approached, I heard one of them say, "Hot. Covered in tattoos."

"So dumb, though," the other said.

I followed their line of sight. The guy who I'd heard talking about Travis sleeping up in the catwalks, who'd been in Jeffery's trailer last night, stepped into view. He wore a ball cap, and a water jug dangled from his thumb.

"Perfect to make my husband jealous."

"Married. So he's safe."

The man noticed the woman who had the husband, and she licked the top of her coffee cup with the tip of her tongue. He stopped walking. Someone called, "Ryan!" He looked confused. "Ryan." The same voice. His bewilderment changed to understanding and he flushed. The friend moved next to him and hit him on the shoulder; they laughed. Ryan glanced back to the women.

"Checkmate," the woman who wanted a jealous husband said, and her friend hid her smile.

I visualized the wife of Ryan at her job—maybe she was a surgeon, maybe an accountant, running the numbers, unaware of a plot twist coming her way. This was the man who, because of my association with Three, didn't trust me. The one who petted Kevin after I showered for the first time in the greenroom. Both of us pawns, trying to do a job while it appeared others schemed and plotted. I moved the few steps to his side.

"Hi, Ryan. That woman with the tongue? She wants to use you to make her husband jealous. If you're into it she's all yours. But FYI, she thinks you're dumb. I'd want to know the whole story if it were me."

I didn't wait for a response. I was a new woman. Someone who would stand up for herself and not knock others down in the process. This would be the compromise between doormat and badass. I would be the rising tide that lifted all boats. I took another bite of my now cold croissant, but my stomach wasn't ready for pastry and biblical convictions. I spit out the crust and tossed the rest in the trash. Maybe I could be a tugboat and not the whole moon, tide, and ocean all together.

My phone vibrated. Chelsea.

Chelsea: Hey did you know Allen Carol's wife is getting married today. Big media circus. Daughter a bridesmaid. Many interviews dredging up Allen's pre-rehab pictures.

Poppy: No wonder he's so crabby today.

Allen emerged from his trailer and walked across the pavement as if he had not a care in the world. His wife marrying. His daughter experiencing it all firsthand. Yet there he was laughing, shaking hands, ready to work like a professional.

Then I realized that he'd put his pants on without me, and I said in what I now knew was a stage whisper, "Hey, Allen."

When he looked my way, I said, "Nice pants."

He showed me the top button, clasped together with a hair tie, and the acid in my tummy settled for a second.

CHAPTER
TWENTY-TWO
WHEN AWKWARD MET HOLLYWOOD

Before walking onto the set, I entered Allen's trailer to collect my kit of supplies. Was it my imagination or was it slightly lighter without the stolen, misplaced, recovered necklace? I should have raced the necklace back to the wardrobe trailer the moment I found it, put it somewhere safe where only Muriel would find it. Drawn a treasure map using coded letters to its whereabouts. I'd trusted that the safest place for the jewelry was with me until I personally handed it to Muriel. It didn't matter what I thought, though. It was what others thought of you that kept your business aloft, your finances safe.

Moving slowly for the early morning, already beaten down, I clipped the kit around my middle, and Kevin stood, stretched, and lifted one of her front paws.

"I wish I could sleep forever like you, Kev. You're going on thirty hours right now." Taking her tiny, toasty body into my arms, I said, "Don't worry. I'm not getting rid of you until Cruella returns or I get erased." I tried to hustle, to feel energy for the day, but it seemed that whatever I did wasn't quite what everyone else had in mind.

On the set, the stand-ins were dressed in clothing in the same colors as the actors would wear in filming. The director of photography checked lighting on the various stand-ins, and I marveled at the way the stars were babied. As if this necessary task was too exhausting for the celebs. The grips had to be grippy all day long, but the pampered actors could rest until they had to deliver lines someone else wrote.

I watched and listened while the crew worked and people stood in the light, and I thought about all the podcasts on sewing I'd listened to and considered how much I'd learned in only a couple of days. I'd thought working in costumes slash wardrobe would be about sewing, matching ties with shirts to an era, calling up personalities with clothing. It wasn't these things for the people who worked less in creative and more in logistics. It was detailed, physical work.

This is what I liked about this job. The care and keeping of costumes, transport, dressing, continuity. It was fast moving and organized and resourceful, with everyone working toward a larger goal. I wondered how these people found their way to a career here—one I'd never heard of.

I'd never been able to dream past taking on the family business. Since I was good at it, I didn't question my father while he was alive or after he'd died. When I had Robyn, I dug into making a living and being the best parent I could be.

Watching the crew build a diner out of an empty space, an actor gamely put on a costume and say lines a writer had written—this was the epitome of dreaming big. It towed a person along, spoke as you watched, said, *C'mon. Join in.*

I could easily see why, against all odds, actors pursued a career in movies. I could see me doing this, wanting this, now that coupons were in my past. Thinking past today into the future, being part of this troupe—this family. It was exhilarating watching it come together.

There was a pause in the action.

"Who are we missing?" the DP called, his voice impatient.

Allen sat in a chair with his last name, CAROL, printed on the back. A makeup person hovered near. By the slant of his head, I could tell he was tolerating the fussing, the brush that swept across his jaw.

Muriel stood at the director of photography's shoulder, her reading glasses on her nose. She flicked her gaze at me—the first she noticed was Kevin, and she began to shake her head. I wanted to frantically point to the director and say, *Ask him! I have to! This is my job too!*

She'd been so angry at me at Allen's—was she about to pull the director's arm, point to me, and like the Red Queen in *Alice in Wonderland* say, *Off with her head!* Her eyes moved to my clothing and I thought, *Oh God, what now?* Muriel's expression changed from disapproval to urgency, and she pointed toward the set.

I put my hand protectively on Kevin thinking she wanted me to get rid of her, and I shook my head like a catcher refusing a pitch behind home plate at a baseball game. Who was in charge: Muriel, the director, or Cruella? I tried to find someone with answers, my body a watershed of perspiration.

Muriel pointed again and this time mouthed *Go* with big eyes and a head nod to the stage. She plucked at her own shirt, pointed to the lights, and added a baffling circling with her finger.

Allen dropped his arm over the canvas of his director-style chair and with a grin said, "You, with the yellow shirt. Get in the light."

The yellow shirt indeed—he if anyone on the set knew my name. Also, Allen wore the same solid pastel-colored shirt I wore. They wanted to check the lighting against my yellow shirt for Allen. I would have made a face if the director of photography and the gaffer hadn't zeroed in on me with a *what are you waiting for?* expression.

I wiped the sweat from under my nose and walked onto the set that was dressed as a living room. The crew worked to light the scene in *When Harry Met Sally*, or now *When Hairy Met Sweetie*, where the characters play Pictionary at their costar's New York apartment. Soon dogs and people would occupy the carpet and couches, but for now, it was Kevin and Poppy starring in *When Awkward Met Hollywood*—an unlikely rom-com that would never see theaters.

The harsh lighting stung my eyes, and I shielded Kevin's bulbous peepers. Illumination changed; mumbled conversations were had. Notes were scribbled into iPads and notebooks. The director appeared, watched for a few seconds, then said, "Is that Kevin?"

Startled, I stood up straight, nodded. "Yes, sir. It's Kevin, sir," I said, as if I were Oliver the orphan. Muriel closed her eyes, and I heard Allen puff a muted laugh. I could only imagine the sight of me, illuminated in front of all these people accustomed to shiny, polished celebrity. Red carpet beauties. The kind of people for whom harsh lighting brought up their charming quirks, not their inexpensive haircut, eye bags, and the disorganized washcloth of a dog wrapped to their body.

"Has it been a hassle?" the director said.

"No. I want to watch it . . . her. I don't mind a bit."

I cringed. I'd said I *wanted* to. Under the harsh lights trained on my makeup-free face. I waited for the laughter. The scoffing. Muriel to say something about this.

I *did* want to take care of the calming Kevin. But I also wanted to point out that I was doing my job. I was standing up for myself and doing my job. *You could do both,* I wanted to shout. When does working hard turn into too much pleasing, and when is it just doing your job? I wanted an answer, but I hadn't had a mother for these things. I was the person to answer these gray areas, and I didn't know.

An errant memory from high school slid into my thoughts. I was the junior class treasurer, ironically given the Dawna Klump fiasco, and there was a class meeting. We were voting for a destination for our senior skip day—tubing the Wisconsin River or going to the Six Flags Great America amusement park. The vote was tied, and I had yet to raise my hand. The class secretary said, "Which one do you want, Poppy?"

And I, feeling pressured, blurted, "How should I know?"

Some jackass replied, "If you don't, who does?" and everyone laughed.

Growing up I wasn't asked my preferences on anything—my want muscle was as flaccid as the skin on our music teacher's underarm. In my house I did what I was told, and my father did the telling. He worked that way with everyone, as if his plans were the best, and his smile often sold it—but those smiles were never for me.

"Thank you for helping us," the director said.

That small phrase of appreciation . . . it felt like butter smoothing burned toast in the morning—if that was a feeling.

"It's helpful for the family. My mother-in-law is . . . ill. Kevin will have a cameo. I'll call for him when he's needed," he added.

"Sounds good," I said.

I tried to decipher Muriel's expression. This feeling of always being in trouble, being disapproved of coupled with waiting to be fired at any moment, had me holding my breath. My father hated this tic of mine. I'd release one breath with a wheeze and gulp another breath as if any moment the air in the room might get cut off. *Poppy, for the love of God,* he would say. *Go to your room if you're going to pant your way through dinner.* I tried to be silent, but he'd glare at me—I couldn't stop. He'd make me leave the table, and my mother would bring food up to me later. The breathing made me dizzy and upset my stomach, and I often didn't eat until the middle of the night.

I held my breath, looking between Muriel and then Allen. He looked at me with soft eyes, something I hadn't seen from him before. I knew his wife was getting married today; he couldn't be feeling great either.

When the director clapped his hands, Muriel looked away, rehearsal restarted, and I exhaled very slowly through my nose. I watched, on red alert for my next error but also fascinated by the conversations with the actors, the crew, and the dog trainers. *Blocking*, I learned, was the term for how the actors moved around the set. The amount of people that had to reposition for a shot was something I'd never considered before.

The cameras, lighting, and boom microphones were choreographed. Lines were repeated, dogs were led, trainers tried to stay out of shots. It did look tiring for the actors, I had to admit, yet they patiently and professionally complied with the director's multiple iterations of the same scene.

Minutes before the filming started again, I felt the vibration of my phone in my pocket. I did a quick check.

Three: Any chance you can get your hands on keys to the archive? Love to try that field trip.

The director called, "Places," and a dog relieved himself on one of the actors' shoes.

Muriel bolted from behind the camera. The trainer apologized and quickly mopped up the urine. A new pair of shoes and socks appeared. I got rid of the rags, all the while visualizing what a trip to a costume archive would be like, alone, inside somewhere with Three. Away from eyes and rumors. Feeling his lips again, his arms around me.

Poppy: I don't know where I'd get those keys.

Three: Muriel?

I would never ask Muriel for keys to a costume archive. If I had it my way, I'd never ask her for anything. I had the wardrobe trailer keys in case there was very late or early work to do, and that felt extravagant.

Poppy: I can look in the trailer?

I texted this half-heartedly, because the thought of it made my stomach dark and heavy. I wished he would drop this. His lips, being held—the memory sent a rush of feel-good into my brain. I'd do a lot for another moment like that one, but nothing that would jeopardize my relationship with Muriel.

Allen moved back onto the set and into the light. I pushed thoughts of Three's requests out of my mind. Muriel was here; now was my chance to show her I was more asset than liability. I took notes in my phone to show how hard I was trying.

Second button on his shirt undone.

Sleeves rolled twice up to mid-arm.

Belt buckle in the center of his pants.

Both shoes tied with a small bow.

Wedding ring? That was new. He hadn't worn it the day before. His character in the movie was not married. Before the cameras rolled I moved as unobtrusively to his side as possible.

"You weren't wearing that ring yesterday," I said.

He turned his hand, and as if the ring had magically appeared, he frowned in confusion. I held out my hand. "I'll keep it."

"It's fine," he said.

"I don't think it is. You weren't wearing it yesterday. Continuity," I said with one word explaining my job.

"Continuity. Uninterrupted connection. So like and unlike marriage," Allen said more to himself than to me. He tilted his hand, and the band caught the light; then he attempted to remove it but it did not slide easily off. He changed his grip. "Fat. I got fat," he said, yanking on his now red finger.

"Stop," I said, taking his hand in mine and placing it on top of Kevin's head for the purpose of holding it aloft to reduce the swelling from his finger being yanked. I found a small disposable Windex Wipe the size of an alcohol pad in my kit, tore it open with my teeth, and swabbed his finger. In seconds I was able to twist the gold band off his ring finger. I glanced over my shoulder at Muriel and there she was, her dark eyes watching me.

"Discontinuity," he said, then shook out his hand and with a jovial grin said, "Well done!"

"Are you okay?" I asked under my breath. He looked fine, but his energy had a manic edge to it.

"My babysitter wants to know if I'm okay," he said too loudly to sound composed. I had the urge to clap my hand over his mouth, tell him to stop drawing attention to me. I backed away out of the stage lighting and eased his ring onto my thumb to keep it safe. "I'm all good," he said. "Let's do this." It was a phrase I'd heard him utter before, but this time it lacked his cheerful tone. Other crew members noticed

179

a change, looked away, continued to work. Kevin snuggled deeper into the sling.

As the day progressed, Allen focused on acting and I watched his costume. He rolled a shirtsleeve three times, I rolled it one time. He fiddled with a shirt button, I counted the inches of his T-shirt exposed and unbuttoned or buttoned the collar as needed. I helped other actors too. A missing earring here, a bracelet removed and replaced on the wrong wrist there. There was no shortage of fiddling with what actors wore in the name of characterization—a whole new way to read people. *See how good I am at this?* I said with my diligence. *Look at how hard I'm working to learn.*

Jeffery strolled onto the set and over the course of several shots messed with the tails of his shirt, tucking and untucking them repeatedly. At one point, while the set costumer responsible for the star straightened Jeffery's Pomeranian's bow tie, I noticed his shirt was newly untucked. Before the director uttered commands to begin filming, I moved to Jeffery's side and said, "Your shirt is untucked again."

He zeroed in on me and said, "Poppy, right?"

"Yes. Let me get you tucked in."

"Good to see you. Thanks. Yeah. Can you scratch a spot on my back? I can't reach it."

"Will it stop you from untucking your shirt?" I said, quickly raking my fingers roughly on his back.

"It's driving me crazy. In the center."

I moved my fingers to the middle of his back, scratched between his shoulder blades. Watched to make sure I wasn't holding anything up, butting in on someone else's territory.

"Under my shirt," he said.

"What?"

"Go under my shirt. Can you just . . ." he said like a boy cringing under the tyranny of an itchy thread.

I lifted his shirt, ran my fingernails from the base of his neck to the center of his back in a quick scrubbing. I felt the goose bumps rise on his skin as I removed my hand and he shuddered. The noise he made in the back of his throat was filled with pleasure and satisfaction. I tucked his shirt in like an impatient nanny, maybe a nun trying to get her charge to church on time.

Jeffery's eyes met mine and communicated both gratefulness and apology. The gaze communicated none of the earlier charisma. It left me feeling forlorn for the boy he was only a few years clear of. An adolescent cub whose talent and looks swept him into a lion's den.

I glanced at Allen, who had one eyebrow raised as if to repeat, *Too young for you.* I felt myself go hot and red under Allen's suspicious and teasing stare. I was not interested in Jeffery, the boy, and wanted Allen to know that because . . . because . . . I was too anxious to unravel something so complicated under the hot rigged overhead lighting.

Jeffery took a step toward me and said, "I really appreciated that. I was so uncomfortable. Thanks for not making me feel angsty about it."

That was it, that was precisely how I felt about everything today. Angsty with a capital ANGSTY.

CHAPTER
TWENTY-THREE
PEOPLE DO WHAT THEY WANT

I itched for the director to call, "That's a wrap!" I wanted this workday finished. I couldn't concentrate on anything until I spoke to Muriel. If she was going to tell the director to fire me or erase me herself, I had to know. The anticipation was giving me gut rot. It made sense that she didn't fire me on the spot; she needed staffing for the day's shooting. What if she'd already given the order to let me go, but not until they had a replacement for me? Did they have must hires lined up? Or a waiting list of young people at home, full kits strapped to their middles willing to be called in?

My brain went to the finance math again. If I left this place, drove back home, searched and applied for jobs, it would be weeks before I started the payback plan. I'd have to confess everything to Robyn, sell and empty the house, and, and, and, this freight train of thoughts rocketed into a future. The woman under the highway, her hollow eyes met my mind's eye saying, *You're next.*

When the director called the day finished, I looked as alive as I could. I rolled working racks back to base camp and made the rounds of actors' trailers to collect costumes for washing, cataloging, and storing all while thinking about where I'd be tonight so I could talk to Robyn. Begin easing information her way, finishing with my being fired.

As I obsessed and worked, I noticed that the acknowledgment I'd received from the director had changed the atmosphere on set. It lifted one edge of the invisibility cloak I'd been shrouded in for the last three days. Actors handed off shoes meeting my eyes for a second. Some gave Kevin a little pat on her head. One lovely second-tier "star" offered Kevin a sip of water from a water bottle lid. At Jeffery's trailer I knocked and said, "Wardrobe."

"Come in," he called.

I pushed open the door and the first thing I saw was a naked butt, then a perfectly sculpted back and blemish-free skin. "Gah! I'm sorry!" I had costumes in my arms, lifted them to cover my face, and backed out the way I came.

"It's fine. I'm used to it," he said.

"I am not used to it! I'll wait out here. Just chuck your costume out."

I could hear his good-natured laughter, not at all mean-spirited, and I turned to face the road.

"I'm covered up," he said. "You can come back."

"It's fine. If you have your clothes, I'll take them. Maybe we can fix whatever was itchy."

At the door, he handed his shoes to me. "You're pretty when you're embarrassed."

"You don't have to flirt with me."

A montage of hurt, doubt, and suspicion flickered across his expressive face, but he recovered and finished with a curated amused look.

"You don't have to work so hard for me. I know how tiring it is."

Jeffery's amused expression changed to something I could only guess at. Exhaustion? Relief? Something akin to what I imagine a sex worker feels when her john wants only to talk? I thought about bringing up Emilie. What was she really like? Did he know why she hated me? What did it matter anymore? Who was pleasing who? What Emilie,

Allen, or even Three or anyone thought of me. If today was my last day, I'd never know a future with any of them.

I bundled his clothing, took his shoes from him. Without a hint of jokiness he said, "Next time I'll be dressed."

I offered him my mother smile, which was not so much maternal as it was made of sincerity without agenda—the kind of thing I hoped people could see when they looked at me. "We both probably need more boundaries. You have more time to practice. And more power. Don't forget that. It's something I didn't learn at your age." If I didn't see him again, at least I'd said something with substance we both needed to hear.

On my way to Allen's, I wondered if all famous people had to bribe the public with affected sex appeal and friendliness on steroids. One tweet about a rude interaction could go viral these days, and the cancel culture could ruin careers. It was bad enough to be decimated on a private scale; the public shaming had to be all that much worse.

At Allen's trailer, his clothes hung from a hanger on his doorknob. His socks, shoes, and boxers sat carefully folded on the front metal step. A pair of black-rimmed prop glasses were shoved into a shoe; one of the lenses rattled loosely. I lifted each item carefully, tucking the lens into the folds of Kevin's sling so I wouldn't break it. I hesitated outside Allen's door. "All okay in there?" I called and waited. Listened. I thought I heard a cupboard shutting. "Allen?"

I had his wedding ring—would that allow me one more moment with him, to tell him thanks for the memories? To say goodbye? Would he care if I didn't return, if a new sitter appeared the next day? Would he ask about me? I considered leaving his ring somewhere but instead slipped it into my pocket. I'd give it to Muriel to keep safe, to make sure he got it after I was gone.

What about Three? What would I tell him? Could I ask him to intervene? Would he let them fire me? Did he have sway on the back end like he did on the hiring side? What would he think of me then? Amazing? Hardly.

I knew it was time to face Muriel. I dragged myself back to the trailer, being extra careful not to trip. The usual ruckus of getting the laundry loaded, the dry-cleaning bags filled and sent, the signing out was happening inside the trailer. I pitched in and helped with the costume inventory books for the principals and extras. I tried to memorize this feeling of being part of a team where the outside world didn't wander in and insert itself. Would there be a community like this for me in the future? Out of nowhere, a voice I didn't recognize said, *Not if you don't ask for it, you won't.*

Muriel let the staff go one by one, until it was Emilie and me fidgeting with opposite energy. Hers durably defiant, and mine in deference.

There is an imaginary animal in the *Harry Potter* books and movies. The half eagle, half horse called the hippogriff. Before you speak or request anything from the legendary creature, you must bow to it to show you are well intentioned. That is how I felt about the fearsome Muriel. I wanted to offer an explanation that didn't insult her intelligence and firmly placed me in the position of part of the team. The whole squad, not just the members that suited me during crisis. That I wouldn't point out or deflect blame. That I had self-respect, and it didn't cost me anything to be a grown-up. I rifled through my brain for a mature explanation as the clock ticked down.

Muriel finished writing in her ledger, turned her chair to us, and said, "Spill it."

"We misplaced it. Then we found it," I said, and I felt my brain shrug, *That's all I got, bestie.* I waited for the admonishment.

With an impassive expression Muriel said, "Is that what happened, Emilie?"

Emilie tugged a piece of her bangs and said, "I mean. Like, yeah."

Brilliant. That girl should have been an expert witness in a murder trial. Noncommittal. Limiting details. The perfect un-lie.

I held my breath as Muriel's gaze darted between us. She rubbed her eyes under her readers, and they dropped to her chest suspended by their beaded tether. She didn't look at us when she said, "Emilie, you're on notice. If anything like this happens again, I'll talk to your uncle and have you moved out of Wardrobe."

Emilie nodded, more docile than I'd ever seen her.

"Go fold what's in the dryer. Then you're done for the day."

I exhaled as slowly and silently as I could. I didn't have an uncle here that cared about my outcome. I'd email the Realtor, initiate the payback plan with whatever I'd made at this job so far. I wondered if security escorted a person off the lot, would they help me fix my tire? I pictured myself waiting for a tow truck while making small talk with the security guard. *I was framed*, I'd say, like an old-time jailbird.

"Allen has an early call tomorrow with lots of changes. Make sure you're here to make absolute sure he's ready. He can be a pain in the ass sometimes, but he seems to listen to you."

"You're not firing me?"

"No, Poppy. I have no plans of letting you go."

I exhaled and Kevin's hair ruffled, and she flinched at the force of it. "Thank God. I don't want to leave. I'm getting the hang of it. I know I'm not your favorite, but I'm trying."

"You don't need to be my favorite to work here. You need to be meticulous."

I nodded, sat heavily on one of the benches, felt the hanging clothes against the top of my head pat down my panic. I could be meticulous. I *was* meticulous. "Allen needs a little extra give in the waist of his pants. He said he gained weight. I've been using a hair tie to ease it up a little."

Muriel made a note and said, "We'll measure him tomorrow." She placed the pencil behind her ear and said, "You have a daughter, right?"

I nodded, my heart still racing trying to catch up with my relief.

"This is a hard job for a woman. Too much travel, extremely long days, inflexible schedule. It's hard to even be married. Most successful costumers are some kind of unmarried. Divorced mostly, some never having taken the leap."

"I never married. My daughter graduated from high school last month. I'm working on getting her to college."

I touched the bench I'd slept on that first night on the Universal lot. Could it only be three nights ago? It seemed like weeks had gone by.

"You need to decide what you want."

"I know what I want. I want this job."

"That's not what you really want."

"You have no idea," I said and clamped my mouth shut in anger. How dare she? I drove across the country for this job. Left Chelsea, my community, Robyn, everything comfortable to come out here to do this. I was pivoting, doing what's necessary, *becoming* like Michelle Obama couldn't stop talking about.

Before I could get my outrage into a coherent defense, Muriel said, "People *do* what they want and from what I see, you want something. But you think you have to take care of everyone to feel okay about it."

"No," I said. "I mean, yes." I put my hand on Kevin's back, stalling to give me a chance to work out what I was trying to say. "Maybe the way I'm different is not because I'm from the Midwest but because I want to do a job but not at the expense of everyone around me." I kept my tone even, but it was anger that fueled my response.

"Sure, you can tell yourself that. But I think you like this job but for some reason you feel guilty about it, so you're sabotaging it. You pay careful attention. Do what is asked without complaint. You seem to enjoy it, are curious about what we do here. Yet when pushed you won't push back."

"That's ridiculous," I said, though an unsettled feeling rolled through me. I'd seen my own behavior. Had quite literally had this thought earlier in the day.

"Is it?" Muriel dropped a pile of clothing into a basket. Kicked it under one of the benches. "I know because you remind me of myself, early on. I was self-effacing, intimidated by . . . everything. The difference between us is that I had to feel okay about something I didn't want."

"And that was?" Through my irritation was the realization that Muriel was talking to me as a peer. I didn't feel like a child or an underling.

"Kids. You think it's hard to balance being a woman and a mother in this culture? You should try being a woman who doesn't want children. Once I figured this all out, I was so mad at myself for feeling bad about anything. For bowing to the culture—I had to work harder because I didn't have kids. I didn't have to pick kids up after school or leave early if they were sick. I had to cover.

"Women always have to work harder, kids or no. Seeing you struggle reminds me of my insecurity; watching you is like going through it myself again. I think that's why you irritate me so much."

I couldn't help but laugh at that frank statement. The honesty. Also the intimacy of her sharing her own journey from newbie to being in charge. In a flash I saw that Muriel was doing something here I'd never experienced before. She was mentoring me.

Muriel's phone rang and she answered it. From the tone of her voice, it was clearly a work call. I watched her speak without hesitation. Give commands. Ask for things. I tried to picture Muriel new, learning to stand her ground, thought about the value of learning that whatever the age—where did that strength come from when you were the lowest of the low?

After a minute Muriel spoke into the phone, "Talk later," and she hung up.

"How do you stand up for yourself when you don't have any power?" I asked.

"That's not the question you need an answer to. You need to know what you want first. Then what you need is dignity and integrity. That's how you do this job going forward, and from what I see, you might want that."

I considered protesting. *No, I'm going home as soon as I make some money for college. My house, my daughter. They need me. My life is in Wisconsin.* I kept silent, because I didn't want to convince this woman that I didn't want this job. Because what if I did? What if I wanted to stay for more reasons than a bank account? For the dignity and integrity of it?

"The washer's probably free if you want to throw in that sling. It must be getting grungy. Emilie, is the washer empty?"

"Yes, it is," she said, moving toward us.

"There are a few leftover underthings you can toss in with it. Unless you are ready to get out of here." She found her purse, the binder with script details she never strayed far from, her car keys. There was no doubt in my mind that she knew I wasn't hurrying anywhere. That I was alone here, no one waiting for me at whatever home I was going to. "Lock up when you're finished."

Emilie pulled her phone forward, tapped the screen, and followed Muriel out of the trailer.

"Just a minute," I said, and I rushed to catch up with Emilie. Kevin sat up as though she might be called to action. "Emilie. Wait," I said. The sun had dropped, and it was that late-evening time just before darkness settled in. "Can you stop?"

I'd been up since 5:00 a.m. trying not to get fired. I hadn't slept well on Allen's couch, and my body had a way of reminding me that fatigue was not my friend. My foot turned in, I caught the rubber toe of my sneaker, and I tripped. Because my hands were on Kevin, I hit the ground like a penguin, face first, then shoulder, then hip. If I'd really had some speed, I might have somersaulted on the pavement instead of stopping my roll with my chin.

Kevin yelped. I made a sound like, "Oof." It took a second to get my arms out from under my body and push myself to a sitting position. "I'm okay," I volunteered before anyone asked.

The toes of Emilie's tennis shoes appeared at my side as I checked Kevin. "You okay, buddy?" I said.

"Is she okay?" Emilie asked.

I tugged Kevin out of the sling and set her on her feet. She turned, put her tiny paw on my shoulder, and licked where I'd hit the ground. It stung, but it was sweet to be cared for. "Looks like she's fine," I said.

"Okay," Emilie said and turned to leave. I saw her phone light up as I imagined she texted this hilarious thing that had happened with this annoying woman on set. Then she stopped, turned, and said, "Here," and offered her hand. "Are you okay?"

I brushed my palm off and stood without her help. Touched my chin.

"No, Emilie. I'm not okay. This necklace stunt almost got both of us fired. Next time I'm not going to cover for you. I only did it this time because I have a daughter your age and, don't be shocked, I was your age once. You must feel powerless to come after me, the lowest person on the set."

Her lips twitched. She shook her head, and I knew she wanted to say something to me, but she walked off. I didn't try to stop her.

"I won't cover for you again, Emilie," I said, but the girl didn't hear me. I hadn't said it for her. I'd said it for me.

I brushed bits of dirt and gravel off my hands and went back in the wardrobe trailer, Kevin on her feet, at my heel. I needed to talk to my daughter. I needed to see Robyn's face and be reminded what I was fighting for besides my own dignity and integrity.

CHAPTER TWENTY-FOUR

YOU MINX

When Robyn's FaceTime rang at exactly 8:00 p.m. PDT, 11:00 EDT, I sat up and hit the red join button.

"Hi, sweetie. It's late. Are you in your apartment?"

"No. Lizzie's mom is still in there. I'm in Hollis's bathroom. The kids are in bed. I'm tired. I'm with them all the time. I broke a glass. And I've been thinking maybe I'm not ready to be a nurse." She inhaled. "Hollis is whiny, and I'm not allowed to put her in her room alone if she hits Hayden. I have to get them to ballet and playdates and sometimes pick up groceries. It's a lot. Nurses do a lot more than that."

It wasn't that unusual for Robyn to package all her worries in one sentence. To dump them out like pick-up sticks.

"That's a lot to think about so late at night. Can we work on one of these right now and deal with the rest later?"

Robyn's eyes held mine and she nodded. "The blood and needles. Lizzie said I'd have to get over my queasiness if I wanted to be a nurse."

I could have said a lot of things to reassure Robyn in this moment, pointed out that it would be convenient for Lizzie if Robyn stuck around instead of going to nursing school in the fall. Gotten Chelsea, an actual nurse, involved in this conversation, but my job here was to listen even if this revelation had me worrying. Nursing was the kind of degree that always came with a job. The world would never evolve out of sick people like it did coupons. Even if there was an apocalypse, a global warming meltdown, even underground preppers would want a nurse.

"Okay, I hear you. Is there more?"

"I don't sleep very well in the girls' room. There is a lot going on all the time."

I knew what it was like to be moving so fast you almost didn't have time to think. And then when you did, the problem had morphed into a new, more immediate one, and the treadmill had begun again. I hadn't had a parent to guide me, but I was here for Robyn. Maybe I didn't know exactly how to do it myself, but I always found a way for Robyn.

"Tomorrow, do you think you could say this to Lizzie: 'I'm restless sleeping in the girls' room, and I'm afraid I'll wake them. Is there another option for me? We'll all be at our best if we get enough sleep.'"

I saw Robyn visualize herself saying this to Lizzie. She nodded. "Will you text that to me? I'll put it in my words."

I heard a child's voice and Robyn looked away. "I'll be right there," she said to one of the children. "We don't watch people in the bathroom, Hollis," she said.

"Do we have to decide today about nursing school?" I said, smiling at my stunning child, the love of my life. Hoping that my calm countenance would show Robyn there was no emergency.

She shook her head instead of speaking, a sure sign tears were at the ready. The protective parent in me wanted to send her a plane ticket out of there. Take on her momentary growing pains. But the last thing Robyn needed was her mother seeming to agree with her fears, that she couldn't do the job. "You've babysat a lot more kids than two with less money and activities than the twins." Robyn nodded again, this time with more certainty. "Get some sleep, honey. Then you can figure out what you want," I said.

"I'm just a kid. How could I know what I want? How can anyone know?"

How indeed? I didn't add it doesn't get any easier, but I did say, "I think it takes trial and error and practice. Nothing is a forever decision. Nothing can't be undone."

Even an IRS debt, I thought. Prison, though. I bet it was hard to get out of prison. But I was a better mother than to say that sentence out loud and out of context.

The light in the bathroom room changed as the door creaked open and a little blonde head bobbled into view. The phone got knocked sideways and Robyn said, "Gah! Hollis. Bye, Mom."

I thought about Robyn, off in that enormous city by herself, feeling much like I did. Without bargaining power. Having to make decisions. I was proud of her taking this leap; it was bound to be overwhelming. I texted the script I'd suggested, but I added a sentence for my girl's eyes only: Just because it's hard doesn't mean it's wrong.

And then, Just because it's easy doesn't make it right. This one was for me. I'd slid into so many roles because of duty and ease. It was much harder to make strong choices, forge a new way forward. To figure out what you want to do, go for it, fail, and try again. I'd never done that in my life and when I did, I always said it was for Robyn and no one ever questioned me.

I sat heavily on the bench seat, Kevin rolled her bug eyes up, and I said, "I know what you're thinking. I need to take my own advice. You're right. I do."

I made sure Kevin had water and kibble, grabbed my phone and van keys, and slithered out the door, stuck to the shadows, half jogged, half walked to the parking lot. At my car I grabbed my striped and stuffed bag out of the back and noticed something different. There was no listing to the side, no noticeable tilt. The flat tire had been inflated or changed. I circled, kicked the inflated rubber, and felt for any softness. I had the rogue thought, *Does a tire reinflate if ignored?* It had to be

Three. No one else would have done this for me. Had he seen the car, the Wisconsin license plate?

Poppy: Did you fix my tire?

Three: We aim to please here at Universal Studios.

After the day I'd had, oh, to be cared for. By someone from my past, someone I cared so deeply for. Would he be that person for me, someone that recommended me for a job, fixed a tire, fed me food when I was tired? Someone to count on after all these years between us, all the years I'd been alone and in charge? I wanted to rest my chin on his shoulder right now. Tell him about my close call with Muriel, have him say, *I've got you.*

Poppy: How did you do it?

Three: We have ways

I pushed against the tire again, ran my hand around feeling for a patch.

Poppy: When can I see you?

Three: Soon.

I heard muttering, the sound of sprinkling water, and a shuffling. I stopped, listened closely, clutched my laundry to my chest, moved deeper into a shadow, closer to a fence. I opened my eyes wide in the dark.

There, in my path, I spotted the back of a man, white shirt lit in the moonlight. He wobbled right, then left, swore, and hit the pavement, his profile suddenly apparent.

"Allen," I whispered, moving to his side. "What the hell?"

He waved his arm over his head as if flagging a rescue plane. I smelled alcohol, and something nauseatingly spicy. Allen rolled onto his back, holding his head at an awkward angle, and pointed past me to the sky and said, "Pretty."

I placed my laundry bag under his head; he relaxed his neck. "Nice," he said, and closed his eyes.

As his sitter, was this part of my job? I did not want this to be my job. If I called security and they posted a photo of him, would Muriel open *People* magazine and say, *Where was Poppy?* Surely not. Maybe? What would I tell Robyn to do in this situation? Like if one of her New York kids was drunk on Pixy Stix, I would tell her to take care of them and have a conversation.

"Ugh. Allen!" I jammed my hands in my pockets and felt his wedding ring.

Poor guy—rich, famous, brokenhearted, and drunk. I was none of those, but I could imagine it must have felt terrible to watch your daughter dressed up for a ceremony bringing in another father figure. I stood over him, hands on my hips, and heard him emit a guttural snore.

"Oh, no. No sleeping, Allen. Let's get you to your trailer." I pushed an eyelid open and got in his line of sight. He tried to close it, blinked theatrically.

"Get up," I said in the voice I used to get Robyn out of bed in the final weeks of her senior year of high school. Allen sat so abruptly his unshaven face hit the scrape on my chin.

"Ow. Dammit," I said too loudly. I scanned the parking lot for anyone who might help. Surely this wasn't in my job description as a must hire in costume, but as a babysitter, it one hundred percent was. If an infant filled their pants under a sitter's care, it was their job to make it right. Even after they'd put them down for the night.

"Stay right there. Don't fall asleep," I said and bolted to where a small number of golf carts were charging for the night. Wardrobe's cart was decorated in pink leopard print on the dashboard and marabou feathers around the seats to keep other departments from stealing it.

I unplugged the vehicle and cringed at the sounds of the motor and the squeal the steering made when I cranked it into a tight turn. "Please, God, let him still be there."

I hit the accelerator and spotted Allen, waddling off with the gait of a toddler heading in the direction of the Universal Studios exit. One summer of working at a golf course to make "connections" for our coupon business in high school paid off as I maneuvered the cart just feet in front of him. Comically, Allen lifted his leg higher than needed and, by rote memory, hauled himself into the passenger seat without hurting either of us. I grabbed the elastic of his boxer shorts and tugged him closer.

"You minx," he said.

"Get over yourself," I said and placed his hand in the cup holder. "Hold on. You're a mess."

I retrieved my laundry bag and marveled once again at the freedom of not having a dog strapped to my middle. Allen for his part teetered along with the cart across the uneven pavement. I killed the engine and coasted to within steps of his trailer. I set the brake and as I got out, Allen fell across the bench seat of the cart, drew his knees up, and cuddled one hand under his chin. I'd lifted a lot of heavy things in my life, but never the deadweight of an intoxicated full-grown man slash movie star in his underpants. I was contemplating a kind of pulley system using straps I'd seen the grips using to move sets around when I spotted Travis, on his way to Studio 37, probably heading for his refuge in the perms.

"Travis," I whispered as loudly as I dared. He stopped, froze in place. "Over here! It's Poppy." I darted from the shadow of the cart and waved. "Hey," I said, and his shoulders dropped.

"What's up, Poppy?" he said jovially, and did the old man, arms pumping, half jog across the blackness to me.

"It's Allen. Can you help me get him into his trailer? He's . . . sick."

If I said the truth, another person would say it and so on and so on and so on until the paparazzi put a megaphone to it.

Travis the seasoned pro took the situation in and, as if this were an everyday thing, said, "Okay, buddy, up we go." The ease at which Travis lifted the loose-limbed mass that was Allen was a testament to the man's years of hauling sets and equipment. I held the door; Travis bumped no heads and Allen was in bed before I could do anything but let out my breath.

"I'm sorry to see this," Travis said. Silently, we took in this megastar in his plaid boxers and loafers. His yellow golf shirt was stained with perspiration and hopefully ketchup, not blood. An empty glass and a partially empty bottle of whiskey lay on its side on the counter next to an empty tray of sushi. Hollywood drinkers, so bourgeoisie compared to the brat-and-beer drunks of Wisconsin.

"Can you stay with him while I put the cart back? I have to get Kevin and my stuff out of the wardrobe trailer. I don't think Allen should be alone."

We both stared at Allen Carol and he snuffled. "I'll try to get a clean shirt on him," said Travis.

I eased the trailer door open, a light went off next to us, and once again I was reminded that the nights on set were almost as active as the daytimes. *Please let there be no audience,* I thought. There was so little dignity in what was happening, and if it were to get out, there would a dredging up of those old photos of Allen on the way to rehab. He'd been good to me, if annoying. I knew what it felt like to have your life tumble around you. I'd give him a hand, and I knew Muriel would approve.

CHAPTER TWENTY-FIVE

DIGNITY AND INTEGRITY

On the way back to Allen's I wondered if the solar system had kicked up some celestial seasoning causing an uptick in spicy adult behavior everywhere. Or was it just here in a back lot that should have been empty of drama save for Universal's night-shift security crew—which come to think of it was pretty spotty. Feedback I might provide if ever I secured a place to live.

The good girl in me thought, *Someone should tell someone more important than me about Allen.* The newly curated sneaky girl reminded me with impatience, *You only know this because you are one of the adults behaving badly.*

I'd talked my sane self into believing that sleeping in my clothes on a job site was defensible. It harmed no one that I could see, had measurable organizational benefits to the wardrobe trailer, and as for doing my part in combating climate change, well, I was unparalleled. Who had a smaller footprint than me? No one.

Kevin maybe. I patted her head and picked up my pace.

At the screen of Allen's trailer I said, "How's our patient," and let myself in.

"Quiet."

Travis hadn't moved since I left, and it was clear how uncomfortable he was watching over Allen.

"You go on. I've got him."

Travis nodded and, with a meaty palm, wordlessly patted Kevin on her head.

"Please . . ." I almost said *be safe*, but instead I said, "Get home safely." If he was driving or climbing up into the rafters, it covered both situations. He shut the door but through the screen said, "Look. Don't take this the wrong way. You might not have what it takes to do this job."

"Yeah, I'm sure you're right." I smiled, thinking he was joking.

"Seriously. You're not mean enough," he said.

"You're not the first to imply that. I assure you, I am not as soft-hearted as I appear. Can I ask you a question, Travis?" I didn't wait for him to answer for fear he might shake his head and disappear. I took a leap. "Why are you here? I know you're not working. I know you're sleeping in the perms. What's going on?"

There was no surprise in his expression, only deep fatigue and dark lines that etched a path from his eyes to his jaw.

"You might as well know. What difference does it make? Most people around here do."

He rubbed a spot on the palm of his hand. Maybe there was a stain I couldn't see, maybe a lifeline of pain. "I'm on leave. Supposed to be on leave. Bereavement. My son was a grip. Fell from a catwalk. I thought he was sober or I'd never have brought him in on the job." His eyes were dry when he added, "I couldn't get to him."

I couldn't get to him. I didn't just hear that phrase; it pushed into me and stuck there. Unable to be present for a child who was dying, it would be too much. "Oh, Travis," I said to this bear of a man standing pixelated through the screen. I wouldn't say the usual platitudes—*I'm so sorry. That must have been so hard for you.* Instead, I said, "You should stay up in the rafters as long as you need. I won't say a thing."

"You'll keep this between us?" He hesitated here. "What about your friend? The producer."

"It's none of my business. When someone loses a child, they get all the grace they need." I crossed my heart, because this phrase needed a hope-to-die pact.

He put his hands in his pockets and said, "Lock the door."

"Good night, Travis. Thank you," I said, and pulled my phone out to text Robyn an *I love you*. Maybe something else that said, *Be safe, you are everything.*

Kevin had settled herself on the couch as far away as possible from Allen the stinky star, who hiccuped. The sound tickled the hairs on my neck, because I knew what was coming but couldn't get there fast enough.

"Uh-oh," he said, then vomited into a plastic to-go container that Travis must have found and positioned nearby, predicting this might happen.

I grabbed a dishcloth. "Here!" I said with the kind of intensity with which a firefighter might call for a hose. I swung around and rifled through the cupboards until I found a large red plastic salad bowl.

Allen was in no shape to respond with a coordinated movement of limbs, which meant I was going to have to get closer to the sickly-sweet smell of whiskey vomit laced with raw fish and wasabi. Under the best of conditions—for example, a barfing child, Robyn—I was an adequate caregiver. In this situation I wanted to prop Allen up with a chopstick and put a Hefty Cinch Sak under his chin. I wasn't a monster, so I gagged my way through positioning the bowl and wiping his chin with a nearby take-out napkin.

"Get it out," I said, eyeing Kevin on the other side of the room. She stood, executed a perfect circle one and a half times, and curled up, her head turned distastefully away.

As inelegant as Allen had been lumbering in the parking lot, he made up for it with his bull's-eye vomiting. There was always a throaty warning followed by close to silent gastric emptying. Robyn barfed without precision or stoic silence. She'd start with an "Oh God!" Then scream "Mama!" If I was downstairs, I'd hear the thundering of her footsteps down the hall. "I'm gonna" was followed by a gagging watershed sound so ghastly that I often thought, as I ran up the stairs, *I'm not going in there.* By the time I'd arrived, Robyn had removed every item of clothing and had herself draped unflatteringly over the commode. I would have laughed if I hadn't been so grossed out.

It was after one of these episodes that Robyn had looked me in the eye, her bangs wet with perspiration, and said, "I want to be a nurse so I can put a washcloth on people's necks to make them feel better when they're sick, like you do for me."

Even at eight, so filled with empathy. We talked about nurses and nursing as her future after that ER visit.

Was it odd that I was barf-reminiscing about my daughter while watching this superstar lose his lunch? I guessed if I were a self-serving social media influencer wannabe, I'd film him. Use it to pay Robyn's tuition by selling it to *Us* magazine. Stars, they're just like us. They vomit. I'd never do that, nor would I have ever left him, even though I considered calling security while he lay on his back. He was a kind person going through a hard time. Sometimes you made decisions outside of what you wanted, and you did it with integrity.

I wiped his mouth with a washcloth, touched a towel to his forehead. Allen looked younger asleep. His forehead relaxed, and his mouth dropped its sly smile. I pulled a light blanket over his shoulder and brushed a bit of hair off his forehead.

In between emesis episodes I'd empty the salad bowl into the toilet, wet a washcloth, wipe his mouth. As Allen got more comfortable, I dozed off. When I heard the petite skip of air, I patted his back and said, "It's okay, hon." I corrected myself: "Allen." So glad he hadn't heard that slip. He was a bit of a sweetheart, mourning his ex-wife, loving his daughter. *Poor little rich boy,* I thought, but with warmth.

Around 3:00 a.m. I loaded clothes and towels into the washer, fed Kevin, aired out the trailer with a well-placed fan, and forced Allen to take ice chips from the fridge. He pushed my hand away and slurred, "Lauren."

I handed him a dry washcloth, which he dropped, then took my hand and placed it on his hip. "I lub you," he said. "Lub. Lub," trying to get the word right as if he were taking on water like a fast-sinking ship. "Lub," he said one more time, finishing with a soggy snore.

I knew from the internet that Lauren was Allen's ex-wife, now another man's spouse. I wondered if she'd heard these words enough from him in their marriage. Or had it taken alcohol and her wedding to eke it out of him?

I'd never heard my father tell my mother he loved her—and he certainly didn't offer those words up to me. I hadn't loved Liam and rarely thought of him unless I was wondering where Robyn got her spelling ability. Three and I never said *I love you*. Well, that's not right. I said it to him and he responded, *You know how I feel*. Or another time, *You have the keys to me*. It had bothered me then. I didn't know why he wouldn't speak the words. Had he changed in that way? Would he ever say them to me?

Allen coughed but this time didn't fill his salad bowl. Had he learned anything from acting as the helpful, affable, loyal, and funny main character slash best friend that had turned him into a star? Or did he shrug a nice-guy disguise on and off, camouflaging his true crabby adulterer nature as easily as all the other actors in Hollywood?

I moved to pull my hand away, but Allen closed his grip tenderly. If not for his clammy palm, I'd have enjoyed having my hand held in the dark by this man. This famous person who felt solidly real, the star here on Earth with the rest of us. I rubbed the back of his hand with my thumb and hummed a tuneless song, for the first time today, calm. When his breathing deepened, and with my free hand, I found his wedding ring in my pocket and placed it on the headboard.

———

The next morning, Allen groaned, the bed jiggled, and my right arm had fallen asleep. A slant of sun through the blinds said, *Get out while you can.* I'd never been the person who slunk away from an impromptu sleepover in wrinkled jeans, but if you live long enough, turns out you can be anything you never wanted to be. Ha ha.

If I inched my way off the bed, got clear of the trailer before Allen woke, maybe he'd never know I'd been there. I didn't want to embarrass him, and I saw another thing—I didn't want him to be disappointed that the person who had been there for him last night was not the woman he loved. I didn't want to see the letdown in his eyes. Something had shifted in my thoughts about him, and I needed to get myself on track.

I'd drooled a small pond on his expensive bedspread, but Allen was in no position to label wet spots on the bed as belonging to anyone but him. The room was a crime scene of scents, and it wouldn't take a detective to put the pieces of last night together.

I shook the pins and needles out of my arm and, with my other one, shoved my phone's power cord into my kit, slung my laundry bag over my shoulder, and tried not to drop Kevin as I scooped her from the couch. I unlocked the door. The morning air smelled fresh, and as I stepped off the last step, I heard a small click.

Emilie. In the doorway of Jeffery's trailer, only her head visible. Then she disappeared.

Muriel had been right. If I wanted to keep working, it was time to do it with dignity, integrity. Instead of reacting to everything, I had to do what I'd advised Robyn to do: advocate, and speak up. I was going to start asking real questions about Emilie's motives. Figure out if this was the end of our battle or the beginning.

CHAPTER
TWENTY-SIX
SUDDENLY SEEN

The wardrobe trailer was abuzz. The early call times for a large scene with several actors and extras meant everyone from costume supervisors to set costumers had to be on hand. I moved to Muriel's side wondering if I should have a word with only her about Allen. Would he be ill today and not make it to the set? Was it my job to tell Muriel or keep it utterly to myself?

"Hi, Poppy. What's up?"

I hesitated. I decided to say nothing about Allen. Every action on set had a subtext I didn't understand. And if I was being utterly truthful as I talked myself through these next seconds, I was feeling protective of Allen. He was suddenly in my eyes the Velveteen Rabbit; last night's messy vulnerability made him more real.

"Should I grab Allen's clothing. Head his way?"

"He's got a few changes today. Do you have your call sheet?"

The trailer quieted as if the worker bees and the runners wanted to hear my answer. I nodded. The sides came in the email with the call times. "I keep them in my notes app; I take notes there," I said and the trailer stilled even more.

A woman I'd seen helping the dog trainers didn't meet my eyes.

I know I heard someone say, "There she is," and I glanced to the front of the trailer expecting to see a star entering, possibly Hollywood Royalty by the way the noise in the trailer hushed.

Muriel leveled her gaze at me and said, "Long day today. You ready for it?"

This reminded me of the old *Mission: Impossible* television show that replayed on late-night channels occasionally. *Your mission. If you choose to accept it . . .*

Muriel handed several hangers of clothing to me and I said quietly, "What's going on? It feels weird in here."

"Does it?" Muriel said.

"Poppy. You free for lunch?" said a tall redhead who I'd seen all week. Who had gone out of their way to step around me when I dropped a basket of shoes rather than help me pick up the stray ones.

I shook my head, not meaning to refuse a lunch invitation but because I was thinking, *Why? You don't like me.*

I returned my attention to Muriel, who said, "I warned you, Madame Butterfly."

Another theater reference lost on me; if it wasn't *Willy Wonka* or *The King and I*, the coded language of the arts offered little understanding for me. Wanda Merinchowski swanned into the room, and Muriel moved to her side with no chance for clarification. I held the hangers in front of my face, hiding the scrape on my chin, wondering if my fall had anything to do with the sudden overt interest. Emilie had been there; it made sense. Kids were so speedy with their phones—had she shared a photo of me on the ground?

Outside, I walked with purpose. It was the oddest sensation, and not a good one, to be suddenly seen. It wasn't as if people stopped and stared as they might have if, say, Julia Roberts strode between sets, with her stunning choppers and glorious nostrils. It was more subtle. Yesterday, I could carry costumes, roll carts, and rummage through my kit for a safety pin never once thinking anyone was watching. Now, I had the feeling if I hitched a step or pivoted, someone would take note, whisper behind their hands.

I spoke into my phone: "Siri, who is Madame Butterfly?" The caterpillar of a tourist bus blew past me without stopping to ask if I needed a ride, and I knew somebody had seen something last night or this morning and spread the word. I just don't know which words were whispered. What was I being seen as?

Outside Allen's trailer, I knocked and waited. I could hear him in the kitchen, a rattle of a spoon, the clink of a ceramic cup. I knocked again.

"Just come in," he said, annoyed. "We don't have to stand on ceremony, do we? After last night?"

I looked left, then right, opened the door, and said, "Can you keep your voice down."

"Why? Everyone knows we're lovers now," he said, using his public Best Friend voice as if delivering a line written by a prize-winning showrunner. Here it was, the magnetism of his leading-man wattage. I touched my chin wound, the gawky, older, short-haired woman's version of a flirty hair flip. I'd seen him at his worst last night—why was I suddenly warm, an electric tingle zinging through me?

"If what we did last night is what lovers do, then I'm as out of touch as my daughter says," I said, joking like I did when I was uncomfortable. The reference to being lovers was enough to rewind the night for me, our hands together, watching him breathe. I knew this was silly, there'd been no real intimacy—his mind hadn't even been in the room. He'd been with Lauren.

Allen had showered and wore a crisp white robe. His black hair was glossy with water, and his face had been scrubbed and shaved clean. He appeared better than I'd ever seen him since we first met. Given his last several hours, I couldn't figure how this could be true. Still, Allen seemed to respond to barfing all night as if it were a high-end spa vacation.

"How do you look so . . . so . . . good? So shiny?"

"Sexy time always puts a spring in my step. Can't say the same for you. What's on your face?"

I ignored the question, hung the costumes on the hook by the bathroom, and pulled Kevin out of the sling. Handed her to Allen. I didn't know where to look—the closeness last night, the stark light of the day. Suddenly, I was a wallflower. A shy daisy. I cleared my throat. "It was Emilie, wasn't it? She saw me leave this morning. I thought I was making some progress with her. If I tell her you were ill, maybe she'll—"

"Denials are futile in Hollywood. A denial is a confession. Here's what you do—you give everyone a *Mona Lisa* smile until somebody more unlikely than you sleeps with, say, Jeffery."

If he noticed the insult he'd dished out, he didn't let on. He casually scratched Kevin behind the ears with his smug hands and flippant attitude. I felt the hit, like a ghostly punch that, instead of knocking me over, went straight through me.

Translation: this gossip was fascinating, not for the presence of an on-set supposed affair but that the affair was between a god and a less-than mortal. An older woman, a must hire, a stray, an actual nobody.

"Oh, I get it. The lowest of the on-set lows, the new must hire door-mat spends the night with last year's *People* magazine sexiest man alive." If I'd had more of a runway, I'd have snatched Kevin from his snooty grasp. The trailer was so narrow where we stood, all I could muster was a dart and a grab. Allen flinched and let Kevin go. "You don't deserve her. Or me, you jackass." I stared past his horn-rimmed cheaters and right in his stupid brown eyes and said, "You think it's funny. Just another day in the life in the movies. I'm trying to do a job. And you think it's hilarious that we might be considered lovers. My world has been turned upside down . . . and what. They'll fire me for 'hooking up' because I was warned. No hooking up. And I didn't. I wouldn't!"

I paced in a circle like Kevin did when she was trying to get com-fortable, sort out her feelings about bedtime. "Don't think it's lost on me what this rumor does for you. It gets you off the hook—hell, you were getting laid, not drinking yourself into a coma because poor you, your ex-wife is happy." I screwed my fist over my right eye and made a crying face. "Boo baby hoo," I said, feeling out of control and mean. "You think I wanted to wipe your mouth all night? Empty that disgusting bowl? Hold your hand while you tried to tell Lauren that you loved her but were too drunk to get out anything but 'lub'?"

He wasn't expecting that. *Direct hit,* I thought and instead of feeling satisfaction, I felt as if I'd taken the slap myself. I was such a stupid, bumbling Labradoodle, running in to say hi, to show my affection, and getting a swat on the nose with a newspaper. "Fine," I said, slowing my circle and coming to a full stop in front of him. "Fine, I'll go along with the charade on one condition. When you tell everyone, you make sure you say it right. Last night we were lubbers. Got it? Lubbers." And with that last word, I'd worked up way too much saliva to handle that many *b*'s and I sprayed spit onto his glasses. I wiped my mouth with the back of my hand and said, "Last year's sexiest man alive, my ass."

Allen blinked. Removed his glasses and with the terry cloth collar of his robe wiped the lenses free of my spittle. He replaced his spectacles with care and said, "When was the last time you told somebody off? Lubbers? I mean, we can work with that but, like next time, say it don't spray it."

I wanted so badly not to laugh or cry, to sit in my indignation, to score one or maybe a strong half point for a partial, outrageous tell-off. I bit the inside of my cheek, but his comic timing, the tone of his voice, the half lift of just the one eyebrow. It was what he got paid millions for. I felt my lips twitch. A stuttery exhale through my nostrils, then a wheezy laugh straight from my windpipe. A giggle escaped from the back of my throat that turned into another silent wheeze, and then only I knew that I wasn't laughing anymore. I was doing the laugh cry. The ingenious way to hide true emotions, disguise sadness for hilarity. I added an "oh my God" to sell it.

Allen put his finger to his lips.

"Shhhh, they'll know we're at it again," he said, and huffed a laugh.

"Here," I said between gasps. "Take. Kevin." I needed a towel to hide my face so I could pull myself together. Merge my reaction into one, into the more appropriate laughter to hide my hurt. I was there to help him last night. Where was my thank-you? Where was my soft look?

Allen was past chuckling and deep into breathless laughter. He shook his head and sat on the couch, both hands on his knees, laughing, and now I was laughing too. At myself, foolish girl. And the situation.

Kevin sneezed twice, which cracked me up even more. I lowered myself onto a small bench-like chair and covered my eyes, my shoulders hitching, my tears wrapping around my laughter like a strand of DNA.

My phone buzzed and I pulled it forward.

"Is that *Entertainment Tonight*?" he gasped. "Tell them I'm the best you've ever had. I promise I'll say the same when they call me."

I rolled my eyes and got myself under control enough to say, "It's Siri. I asked a question before. She seems annoyed that I haven't read her response."

"What's she got for you?" Allen said while wiping his eyes.

I read the text. "*Madama Butterfly* is an opera basically about a naive young geisha who dismisses warnings of ulterior motives because she's smitten with an American officer. Muriel called me Madame Butterfly and I didn't get the reference."

"And you do now?"

"She's been warning me about Emilie. The girl has been complicating everything I do here."

"Are you smitten with her?"

I put Kevin on the ground, and she drank and bathed at the same time with her crooked tongue trying its very best to get at least one of those jobs done.

"No more than I am with you," I said, leveling my gaze. A mean challenge. Would he dispute anything, try for something less guarded? Then I ruined it by saying, "No offense." Because I'm not *that* mean. He didn't react. It wasn't much of an insult—who cares if I was or wasn't attracted to him? Not Mr. Sexy of the Year, that was for sure.

Even though of course I felt something for him. As did so many other women across the nation. That's what made these people compelling on-screen. They could convince you, from thousands of miles away and through a screen, that they were into you when in fact they were just being themselves and they didn't know you existed.

"Who are you smitten with?" he said, all of a sudden standing so close that I could smell his cologne.

"Not Jeffery, if that's what you're getting at," I said quietly and tried not to look at his lips because, what was happening?

"I'm not 'getting at' anything." His eyes flicked over my shoulder. "By the way, your producer friend is talking to Emilie right now. That's what's so great about this trailer. It's in the perfect spot for spying."

I flipped around and peered through the blinds. Sure enough, a rare sighting of Three, looking himself. Tall, focused, dressed in a blazer. Emilie had his full attention. Was she telling him that the new must hire was shacking up with the troubled hero?

"Should I go out there? Make sure he knows we're not . . ."

"What do you want to do, Poppy?" Allen said.

"Why all of a sudden is everyone asking me that? I need this job to get my family back on our feet. Why else does anyone work?"

"Why else?" Allen said.

I peered at the two outside Allen's trailer. The older version of Three and this girl that reminded me of Robyn. "Emilie doesn't look like she's gossiping. She looks . . . unsure." I glanced over my shoulder. "She never looks like that."

Three shielded the sun from his eyes as he peered at Allen's trailer. I shrank back. Emilie shifted her weight onto her back leg. I didn't touch the blinds, held my breath, hoped there was no shadow of my head in the window.

"I can't see what they're saying."

I pulled out my phone and texted Three.

Poppy: Do you have a minute today?

I watched him lift his phone, read from it. He returned his attention to Emilie. Touched her on her shoulder. I knew exactly what that felt like.

He put a finger up for Emilie to wait. Texted into his phone. Emilie touched her headset and said something. Moved a step. I heard her say, "Thank you so much," but not with sarcasm like she spoke to me.

My phone vibrated.

Three: Where are you now?

I thought quickly. Where should I say I was that would give me enough lead time to get there and wasn't in Allen's trailer just a few feet from him?

Poppy: Wardrobe Trailer.

This would give me a minute to figure out what to say. See if he had heard the rumors.

Three: I'm not on set at all today. I'm in Pasadena.

CHAPTER TWENTY-SEVEN

A JOB, A KISS, AND A LIE

"He just lied to me," I said, eyes wide, watching Three drop his phone into his pocket and get into a golf cart, driven by someone with a lanyard name tag. A below-the-line person.

"Welcome to the party, baby," Allen said, pouring coffee into two mugs. "I had them bring some half-and-half if you want it."

"So that's how it is around here? Your longtime friend lies and you sip your coffee and look for the cream?" I couldn't tear my eyes away from Three, outside, steps away, denying his location. To me. Of all people. I touched my lips, remembering his.

"He's not *my* longtime friend. What did he say?" His amused attitude rankled.

"He says he's in Pasadena but he's right there," I said, pointing to his back as the knifelike sun lit the asphalt as his golf cart drove away.

"He could be on his way to Pasadena."

"Do you think that's what he meant? Like he was on his way to Pasadena, and he wouldn't be back?" Maybe this wasn't a lie but a timing thing? I grasped at explanations.

Early as it was, the morning activity ramped up for the shoot. Tables and chairs were being hauled inside the elephant doors. A large truck backed up, beeping, making ready to place or take away set pieces as I stared at the spot Three had stood.

"Awwww, look at you. So hopeful. Honestly, you and your sunflower ways are heartbreaking. Such a purehearted soul." Allen handed me the coffee in what I now recognized as my cup; I'd used it several times before, had washed it while he slept. I swallowed the black liquid, the heat stark on my throat.

"I think you're just jealous that your shirt buttoner is thinking about anyone other than you every minute of every day," I said, hoping to toss something back that sounded cavalier. Like I didn't care about anyone but myself like everyone else around here.

"Not me," he said.

It came out sounding like *Maybe*, and I peered at him.

"I'm only as happy as my dresser is happy. I'm only thinking of you," he said.

"Don't act so innocent. You don't care. You're not running out there and clearing my name." Did Three's text have anything to do with rumors of Allen and me? Was I making a huge thing out of nothing? Three's lie wasn't egregious. But he could have said something like *I'm here now but leaving for the day*. Why the tiny untruth to me, his longtime person?

Allen leaned against the counter in a Hugh Hefner pose, one hand in his robe pocket, his weight on his hip. The terry cloth robe did not rob him of any sex appeal, and he knew it and so did I. With Three behind me and Allen in front of me, I couldn't untangle who I was outraged at and who I was attracted to.

"You really do think it looks poorly to have people think you're sleeping with the star." Maybe it was the way he talked about himself in a subtle third person. The star. As if it wasn't him. He was just a guy, in a robe, making sense of a situation he didn't understand. "It would make you happy to disavow our love? Is that what you want me to do?" he said.

"Yes. Anything that doesn't appropriately represent me as a person is not good for me. I'm not a chameleon who changes with every rock."

"Aren't you?"

"No, I'm not. I'm working. To make a living." I thought about that. I was adapting, sure. But I was trying to stay out of trouble. Yes, I'd become incredibly sneaky, but not for nefarious reasons. For survival. For pay. To save money to send my daughter to school. To create a future out of nothing. The only muddied place in this scenario was my heart-shaped feelings about Three. The present-day version of Three who I now wondered about. Had there been other small untruths in his messages to me?

"So you're happy, then? You're happy to get people dressed and take notes. Stay behind the scenes, below the line," said Allen.

"Yes, Allen. I'm happy doing this job. Hooking up gets you fired."

"Hooking up with anyone or just me?" Allen said this like an elementary school teacher trying to force their student to make a connection.

"Anyone," I said, wanting him to know I got his point. And to confirm that I wasn't sleeping with anyone. For honesty's sake but also because I didn't want him to know I had a heartbreakingly obvious crush on Three because . . . what? Poppy? Because it was pathetic? Risky. And what would Allen think about that? And why did I care? My right brain shouted to my left brain. *Why did I care* what Allen thought about my romantic notions? I didn't like all this analysis. This hot focus on my motivations. I could feel my defensiveness rising like a heat rash. Like an unorganized spray of boxing gloves unsure where to hit back first.

"You're not so unaffected by all of this." I gestured at the trailer, the robe, the creamer he had somebody bring. "Don't think I didn't learn a few things about you last night."

He crossed his arms. "Oh yeah? What'd you learn?"

"That a few tweets about your ex-wife getting married again and you erase all your hard work of getting sober. That you need caring for, just like the rest of us. And, just like the rest of us, when we feel desperate, we want to hold somebody's hand in the night. We'll pretend we didn't need it. It was all a mistake of identity. The star's needs are the same as all of us peons. *Us* magazine has it right. Stars, they're sad. Just like us."

"I held your hand?" he said and looked like he was trying hard to recall doing anything like that.

I nodded. "But why would you remember when someone below the line does anything. We're just tools to make you shine. We're props in your show."

"And then we became lubbers," he said seriously without putting his jaunty mask back on, his vulnerability on display.

"Except we didn't become lubbers, Allen."

The cranking sound of a door opening, a golf cart motoring by, but I didn't look to see what was happening outside. I watched Allen's expression sort itself out, turn mischievous.

"We're having a tiff," he said, teasing the joker back. Biting his cheek and trying not to laugh. He was so very appealing. I gave my head a tiny shake. I was falling under a spell that he cast knowingly or unknowingly on women everywhere. I was a fish in a communal net.

I had to get ahold of myself. The Universal set was not a dating app. It was high time to get very stinkin' clear on why I was here and what each person I worked with meant to me. It meant paying the IRS. Nothing else. At least the IRS was a straight talker. *Pay up, lady.* No mixed messages there.

This moment had a stretched rubber band about to break quality to it. So little sleep. Too much change.

"Every conversation on this set feels like a chess move on a slippery, tilted board," I said, sounding angrier than the unsteady confusion I was actually feeling.

He moved. Placed his coffee cup down by the sink.

"You're not mad at me. You're mad at yourself. Don't drag me into it."

"Aren't you pissed at yourself? Don't you have to go to rehab again now?"

"Siri is good at her job." He took ahold of one of the hangers with a costume on it. "I'm not an alcoholic. I just played one for the media. I drink too much about once every few years." He eyed me. "My PR team told me to lean into the rehab story. People like a guy who's trying to get better."

Last night I thought I was helping a guy who'd made an epically bad life decision, not someone who'd had a few too many beers and made himself sick.

"Don't look so sad that I'm not a drunk. That's good news."

"That's what an alcoholic would say," I said, wanting to be the hero for once instead of the person who cleaned up after an overindulgent bender.

"I can assure you, I am not an alcoholic. I am a product of Hollywood."

"I don't think I'd want to be a product of Hollywood," I said. Kevin had an interested look on her spiky little sea urchin face. "Is anything real around here? Anything?" I said, squatting to pet her. Let her dry tongue lick my palm. "You're the real thing, aren't you, Kevin?"

Allen handed me the shirt for his first shot, gestured at the button, and said, "This button is real, baby."

I stood. "I think I habe you now," I said and concentrated on unbuttoning the top button on his shirt. Hate would be good, or dis-interest would be better. I was going to cultivate detachment all around and keep my clear-eyed gaze directly where it should be: on my daughter's future.

"I habe you too," he said. "See, we've had a whole Hollywood love affair—I mean, ours was longer than most, but we did it. From love to hate in just a few hours. That's Hollywood—everything is done on warp speed, on shifting ground, and between two people who don't understand each other."

Kevin whined, one of the only sounds she ever made. She had a whine if she needed attention of some sort, sneezed if she got excited, and I'd heard a gag once. No growls, yips, or yowls. She was attentive to her surroundings and heard the barking before Allen or I did. The day was starting. Ready or not.

"Allen, all kidding aside. I need you to be clear that I only button you up. There has been no unbuttoning. Okay? For the sake of my job."

"I will do the right thing where you are concerned," he said seriously.

Outside in front of the trailers, dogs of all shapes and sizes paraded through the elephant doors. Trainers shouted commands, fed treats, and tried to keep the butt sniffing and humping to a minimum.

"It's the Katz's Deli scene with all the extras today," Allen said. "This is going to be the longest shoot of our lives."

He paled, and I said, "You okay? You didn't get much sleep."

"I'm fine. I'm a pro," he said, shrugging off his robe and reaching for his shirt and slipping it on.

"You're buttoning it wrong. Let go." I swatted his hands away and lined up his collar. I smoothed the fabric at the center of his chest, maneuvered the button into the casing. Worked my way up to his neck. His breath smelled of coffee and peppermint, and I detected no trace of alcohol there. "Lift your chin," I said. I leaned in, tried to get that last button done, but it was a stubborn one, the shirt new and unused to being flexible. I was close, his breath on my cheek, and I was doing my best to ignore anything but the job of slipping a button through an opening.

"You know what I notice?" he said in a low voice. "You are very careful with everyone on set, but you bust my balls every chance you get. What's that about?"

"Maybe you take it from here," I said and stepped back, feeling caught without an answer.

"Hey, how did you get me inside this trailer last night? I weigh at least a buck seventy-five." He rolled a cuff. "You're a brute to be sure . . . but even with your outrage I don't think you can lift this Fiat of a body."

"Travis the Teamster helped me get you inside. You know. He's everywhere. Manages a bunch of stuff," I said, happy to have something other than the feeling in my pants to focus on.

"No way. That guy hates me."

"Travis isn't a hater. He's just scary looking. He's a doll. Super sad. But I couldn't have gotten you inside without him."

He didn't move to button his shirt. His skin had a waxy sheen, and Allen looked like he might be sick again.

"What's going on? Do you feel sick?"

"I was drinking with his son the night he died. He wanted to be an actor. I didn't know he had a drinking problem. It never occurred to me he'd climb into the perms."

"Ohhhhh buddy. I'm sorry." I touched his shoulder, imagining Travis, his son, and Allen all at once. "He doesn't blame you. At least that's not what he said. He blames himself."

He finished buttoning his shirt, all cocky joviality gone, and he said, "Don't worry, Poppy. I'll tell Muriel what happened last night. And thank you." He dropped his arms to his sides, let his eyes wander to Kevin. "Thank you."

"You're welcome, Allen." In that instant I wanted to hug him. Not just for offering to clear the air for me but because, deep down, he was a good guy. Maybe that was part of his allure in front of the camera. Sure, he was handsome, charismatic, funny, but there was an aura of honesty that radiated through his lines. He wasn't acting.

It was new to feel for something outside of being a mother to a teen, of saving a home, paying for college. It wasn't desire in this moment, although I couldn't deny that feeling, try as I might. Allen's breath on my cheek moments ago had been lovely. I'd felt interest on set, eagle-eyed for continuity. And focus while in the wardrobe trailer organizing, and watching Muriel talk to the staff with authority and respect.

This time it was desire for myself, and I hadn't felt that since I'd . . . good God, I had no idea. And as a gift to myself, I didn't make myself figure it out.

CHAPTER TWENTY-EIGHT

THE GIRL HE USED TO LOVE

I started the day replacing an ugly sweater for the dog playing Hairy before the shooting could begin again. The two tiny knitted sweaters they'd created for the Katz's Deli scene had been decimated by two Pomapoo extras who were mad about something. The movie required a 1980s-patterned sweater that could be reshaped for a dog that was the Billy Crystal look-alike springer spaniel.

On set, the cameras waiting, Muriel signaled for me to go for it. I hesitated and said to Allen, "You good?"

"I'm fine," he said. "Go get the hound his outfit. I won't do anything untoward to myself while you're gone." I glanced at Muriel, and she gestured with both hands—shoo! Now!

As I moved around the chairs, cameras, boom operators, yes, I heard the talk. It couldn't be helped. Everyone was mic'd, and if they weren't talking into their microphones they were chatting in between takes.

Is it true? The woman who carries around that dog? She's so old. Is everyone sure? Who is she again?

Maybe with me off the set for a minute, Allen would clear up any rumors, make sure Muriel knew I hadn't broken the cardinal rule. Then the rumor network could play their game of telephone and when I came back, they'd be talking about anything but me.

In the costume department, while I waited for a woman to finish sewing up a side seam, I texted Three.

Poppy: People are talking about things that aren't true.

Three: Yup. All in a day's work. All Good 😌.

Should I ask if he'd heard anything? Tell him Allen had been sick? Ask about the weather in Pasadena or if he'd talked to Emilie? Suddenly Three felt like a stranger to me. I longed for the straightforward interactions of a bake sale when you offered to bring cupcakes and you brought cupcakes.

"Here you go," the woman said, handing me two identical sweaters that looked like they would fit a very narrow-chested toddler. "There's a bit of give in the neck. I put in some Velcro insets. Don't let the trainers get ahold of it."

"Got it. I won't." Oh, to be trusted to deliver such an important piece for the day's filming. To focus on the needed tasks. This was what I liked about this job. Get this, bring this there, put this in a bag, watch the actors.

The chatter in my headset indicated that the director and the director of photography were debating the best illumination for the apricot fur of Sweetie, Hairy's love interest. I exited the Edith Head building and, with my hand on the white metal railing, eased myself down the concrete steps.

On the loading dock, amid fake tree props and benches, I noticed one shapely leg, jiggling. I'd recognize that flawless skin anywhere. Emilie. She was on the phone. Talking. She had to be speaking to someone older. Robyn never spoke on the phone to anyone but Chelsea and me. Was Three texting me and talking to Emilie?

"I don't have it anymore." She paused. "Yes, I know what it looks like. Biggish blue button. Vintage. Rhinestones. I used to have it but it disappeared."

I knew she was talking about the button in my kit, and Emilie knew I had it.

"I know you need it. I know."

I peered through the fake leaves of the prop tree. Emilie's voice had a rare pleading quality—as if talking to someone asking too much from her.

I took one step back. Emilie snapped her head up seconds before I could turn away. We made eye contact. "Sorry!" I said instinctively, those words seemingly always ready on my tongue.

"I'll get it." And she hung up.

"I need the button you took," she said. Her hand out flat, her black nail polish chipped.

"Why? Who were you talking to?"

I must have looked reasonably baffled, because the disappointment in her expression was filled with disdain and an *OMG, are you kidding me right now?*

"If you're not going to give it to him, let me. I want to get this over with," said Emilie.

"Who wants the button, Emilie? And why? Are you in trouble somehow?" Emilie wore no makeup today. No thick mascara that typically made her eyes bigger; no red lips highlighted her teenage pout. She had a small spray of freckles on one side of her face. So young. So defenseless.

"One of us is out, you know," she said. "It's either you or me. If you think you're safe because you're friends with him, think again. Kristi thought that too."

"Who? With Allen?" I said at exactly the same time that she said, "Three. Your boyfriend."

"Three isn't my boyfriend." As if this were the important part of this conversation. This was another conversation I couldn't get a grip on. Like I'd walked into a party of strangers.

"Like, I don't get why everyone protects him. Like why people believe his bullshit. My uncle. And you. Jeffery and I thought you were in on things with him—that's why people don't trust you."

"Emilie, what in God's name are you talking about?" I said. "You are making zero sense and stressing me out. I literally . . ." I let out a loud puff of air because I *literally* didn't know what to say. Three? Bullshit? Trust? "You're the one who is making my life miserable, Emilie. Every interaction with you is a jigsaw puzzle."

Emilie stopped and looked at me. "You really don't know, do you? Oh my God. You and Kristi." She shook her head.

Muriel's voice came through both of our headsets. "Emilie. We need you to shop. Stat. Poppy, where are the sweaters? We need them now."

"Go ahead. Give that button to Three and watch all of us lose our jobs. I could give a rat's ass anymore," said Emilie.

I watched her go and slipped my hand into my kit. The button, like a cowering mouse, lay on the bottom. Give the button to Three? Why would I do that? Was Emilie being her scheming self, sending me on some trust exercise? Give the button to Three. See what happens?

I jogged to the set and dressed the springer spaniel sitting across from Sweetie, who would soon fake a doggie orgasm while working hard not to eat the pastrami on rye in front of her.

Allen nodded to me while I rejected Hairy's repeated attempts to shake instead of putting his arm through the sleeve. The trainer gave several commands until I accepted the shake and eased him into the sweater, saying, "Who's a good Hairy? You are," in a low voice.

The director said, "Voilà! The Dog Whisperer," and the shooting resumed.

The rest of the day was filled with the usual rushing, waiting, sweating. Dog treats, barking, cleanup. In between takes I asked myself where Emilie was right now. Was Three really in Pasadena? There had been more texts from him but nothing helpful.

Three: Let's get together.

Three: Everything okay on set? At home? Financially? Better?

I couldn't respond. There was too much going on. And what would I say anyway? *No, nothing is okay. There are rumors, I need them cleared up. I don't understand Emilie. What is it with you two? Maybe we shouldn't get together until this movie is over. It seems like everyone is mad at me. Not everyone. Ugh.*

I hated this feeling and found that I didn't want to see Three. I wanted to sit in the wardrobe trailer and fold clothing. Or watch the filming and roll up cuffs. That's what I wanted to do. I wanted to do what I was doing. Listen to actors say their lines. Follow commands.

When the director eventually called, "That's a wrap," I should have been relieved, but it was in between the tasks of this job that I found impossible. That I felt the sharks circling.

Three: Let's talk when you get a chance. I think I have a way to help.

These texts had a different tone to them. These were not flirty. They were businesslike. Or was I reading into everything, misunderstanding the smallest interactions as Emilie seemed to think. My mother hadn't doled out much wisdom before she left, or maybe she did but I was too young to remember. But there was something she'd said about travel that opened doors in my brain that had been closed while living in the same old house, same old life.

It was as if all my stored-away life experiences were tumbling out this open door and falling in front of my now open eyes. And it was my job to sort them like unnumbered index cards and try to make sense of the old and the new. Three was complicated, changeable. Emilie was not Robyn. Allen was a wild card. And something was happening on this set that I legitimately didn't understand, and it wasn't just because I didn't speak the language of movies. It was because I didn't have all the information.

———

At the wardrobe trailer I held several costumes collected from all over the set. "I think this is it. The dog trainers leave this stuff everywhere." I was afraid to look Muriel in the eye for fear of seeing anything that wasn't trusting and positive.

"I noticed," said Muriel, pointing to the spot in front of the washing machine where I'd dropped the sorted and dirty items. "You can go; I'll take it from here. Good work today."

"Really?" I hated how my voice sounded as if I needed more. I was embarrassed by my insecurity, the want that fueled it, something I'd never allowed myself to have before. I touched my chin, a strawberry scab of healing replacing the pain.

"Allen cleared a few things up for me. He says that you catch on fast."

If Emilie were present, she'd scoff so loudly she'd toss a tonsil at us. I appreciated Muriel's compliment—I knew they didn't come easily; she wasn't effusive. She wouldn't say, *Don't worry, you're doing great. Your job is solid. Everyone loves you.* I celebrated the win by flattening the urge to rush and hug Muriel. Instead I said, "Thank you. That means a lot to me. I like working here."

I let myself breathe as I walked among the finishing crew back to Allen's trailer. Inside, Kevin uncurled herself and wagged her little bum in a way I'd never seen before. Her teensy mouth dropped open into a smile, and she wag-walked over to where I stood, greeting me like Robyn used to when I picked her up from grade school. I scooped her into my arms. Let her dry tongue touch my chin. "She said I did a good job, Kev," I said.

Allen entered, already dressed in his street clothes but not looking as fresh as he had in the morning.

"Stay here tonight. I'll make a lot of noise when I leave so everyone knows I'm off set." He flashed a wry smile despite his sallow complexion.

"Thank you. I don't know what you said to Muriel, but she praised me instead of firing me."

"Muriel is my favorite wardrobe person. She runs a tight ship, takes no nonsense, but knows a good, hard worker when she sees one."

"I think you're complimenting me too. And if you aren't, please don't ruin this for me."

He rubbed his eyes. Yawned.

"Hold still. You have foundation, or whatever you guys call it, on your ear." I wet the corner of a towel and scrubbed.

"Thank you," he said and not in a smart-ass way.

"You're being so nice. What's gotten into you? Rough night?" I said, then followed up with "LOL."

He cleared his throat and said, "I shouldn't have lost control last night. I'm sorry there was fallout for you. I was very clear with Muriel that we weren't . . ." He paused. "Intimate."

I re-wet the cloth. He tilted his head to the other side, accommodating, used to the ministrations of others. I touched his chin tenderly, feeling protective after seeing him so sick the night before—even if it had been his doing. A man losing it over a woman, the tough master of the universe showing his soft belly—it was hard to resist.

"I've forgotten what it's like to interact with non–movie people. We get so few here—everybody is related to somebody either by blood or projects."

"You need to get out more, see the world." I gave him half a smile so he knew I was teasing.

"Most people are scared of the star," he said. "Just a movie note to keep in mind."

"You know what they say about picturing people in their underwear—I've seen you in your underwear. It takes the bite out of all interactions."

I felt Allen's eyes on me as I wiped his forehead. This close, every line on my face must have been showing. The chicken pox mark on my forehead, the abrasion on my chin. The pull was strong to meet his close gaze. To drop my eyes a fraction of an inch and stay there, to see if he was feeling what I was. What if I did that and he stepped back, looked away, laughed at how easy I was to seduce?

I concentrated on the now invisible line of makeup at his hairline. "There. All pretty. Go get 'em, tiger."

He lingered before grabbing his keys. At the door he touched the handle, paused. "It's dusk. Stay out of trouble. You are good at this job," he said.

"That's very fatherly of you, Allen." I was testing him, I knew. Wanting to see if he was being a mentor or something else.

"You don't need a father, Poppy," he said, delivering the line like a pro.

Now that he was across the small room from me, I could breathe without blowing a come-hither pheromone into his face that he would likely fan away.

"Can I ask you something?" I asked, wiping something nonexistent off my hands.

He nodded.

"It's about Three. Do you know him very well?"

He could razz me about our friendship, about how I'd come to be here, working alongside stars with so little experience. I could see he was too tired to kibbitz.

"He's one of several producers, like all big films these days. He's an associate producer. Basically introduces the dealmakers to money," he said. He didn't turn to leave.

"What?"

"Are you going to jump down my throat if I say something you don't like?" he said.

"Ha. That's fair. No. I promise."

"He's James's friend. No real power. Acts like every call is an emergency. After you're in the business for a while, you can pick these people out. Sure, if you really cross him, you can get yourself in trouble, but he's a nobody. We all kind of put up with him because of James. He scares the shit out of the below-the-line people, though, which I hate."

He was right—I did feel a ton of mixed emotions with that negative assessment of Three.

I moved to the sink to wash my hands, avert my eyes. I'd held Three tightly, metaphorically, to me for years. If not with love, then definitely with infatuation. I'd seen him as an old, sparkling soul who I compared all other men to. Men that wouldn't measure up. I'd told myself we would have been together if not for our stages of life; it made me feel okay about being alone. I'd met my man, but he was too young.

Had he always been full of hubris that I'd chalked up as a young man's dreams for himself? There was a pinch of longing in the center of my chest, for that man and for my loss standing here at this sink, washing makeup off my fingertips.

"You don't need him to do well here," Allen added. His voice was closer to me, just over my shoulder.

"What do I need, do you think?" I wiped my hands on a hand towel near the coffeepot.

"That's your job, isn't it?" I heard him turn and open the door.

"I just thought, you know, from an outside, nonbiased observer."

The steps creaked with Allen's weight. "Oh, Poppy, I'm not unbiased," he said as he moved away from the trailer.

"Oof," I said. Feeling those words in my belly, where they warmed and slid down my legs, making me feel rubbery. "Kevin, do these people know how to deliver a line or what?" I sat on the bench and considered putting my fingers on my pulse and putting a number to Allen's increasing effect on me.

I sat for a long time without moving. Replaying Allen's words, both flirtatious and informative. I got up as the evening turned dark, moved into the small bathroom, and turned the shower on. With the hot spray of water washing over me came embarrassment for my big, moony beliefs. For Three's shiny representation of himself. Maybe he knew what others thought of him. Maybe not. The balloon that popped in this moment was a reality I'd never needed in my Three fantasy before. It was tied to real consequences in my life. If I was going to stay at this job I needed to know who Three really was and what was going on with him and Emilie.

It was Friday night. This would be my fifth night on set, even though my first night felt like a month ago. In Allen's trailer, amid his scents, belongings, running clothes, I found myself staring at his king-size bed thinking two things: (1) how extravagant to require a bed that big in temporary housing that he rarely stays in, and (2) I wish I had that bed in my house. The next thought came in Muriel's imperious voice. *Why don't you?*

My phone buzzed and a text from Three lit up my screen.

Three: Hey want to meet?

Unbidden I thought, *No, I don't.* What would I say to this man that I'd built in my head? In his presence I seemed to slip into the past, take up the old torch instead of discovering who he'd become. I didn't touch my phone. I didn't want to accidentally indicate in some unknown way that I'd read his text and didn't reply. I wanted to calculate how much I'd made this week. I wanted to go through all my emails and catch up on my tax woes, prison threats, and thoughts of the housing market in the Madison, Wisconsin, area.

That seemed less threatening than deciphering Three and his mixed messages or estimating the value of a button in my kit that held the key to staying employed. I didn't want to talk to Emilie, Robyn, or Chelsea. I wanted to go to sleep.

———

The next morning, after a twitchy night of dreams where I was late to prom and wearing boxer shorts, I sat up feeling only partially rested, grit under my eyelids, my jaw tight from clenching. I'd woken around 3:00 a.m. dreaming of Three, coming in for a kiss, and turning in the last second to nothing. It had to be early; the buzzing, beeping, and bustling of the crew was missing. Kevin snored next to my head.

I opened my email to check out call times before going to my car to get fresh clothing. Maybe I'd call Robyn if there was time to check in. I scrolled on, looking for DPTaylor@UniversalSt.com, the person who always sent the call sheet. For the past week it had been the first email in my box. Nothing. I scrolled up, touched the junk mail folder. Nothing.

"Where is it? Erased?" I said. "Oh my God." I thought Allen had cleared everything up. This was how they'd said it would happen. You just didn't get the email. I stood, jostled Kevin, peered out of the blinds, and spotted Emilie sprinting across the asphalt from Jeffery's trailer past me. I wanted to grab her, say, *You got your wish*, but my legs were weak with failure.

I wouldn't be checking in with Muriel, gathering clothes. Running all over the set, steaming, collecting costumes anymore. I'd have my parking pass revoked. I wouldn't see Travis. Allen. Muriel. They'd take my name tag. I touched my lanyard, as if it were a part of my body that would be snipped off. Would I even be able to say goodbye to Three? Look into his eyes? Find out what he'd had in mind for us or if I was stupid and naive?

Would someone come get Kevin?

I lifted my phone to check my email again. My fingers shook but before I could swipe the screen, I saw it. The time and date—6:00 a.m., Saturday, June 6.

I wasn't fired. It was Saturday. I never considered that movie people took weekends off. I reached for Kevin, sniffed her fur. She smelled like Allen's aftershave and my deodorant and Doritos.

I hadn't been deleted. I dropped my head back and laughed not at myself, not at my foolishness, but with joy. In that moment when I thought I'd been discussed by someone and deemed finished, I saw how badly I wanted to stay. Not to save Robyn, or our home, or pay off the IRS. Nope. For me.

I was fascinated by this creative, double-crossing, messy new world. I liked the clear tasks, how the workday ended when someone other than me said so. I felt alive and challenged in ways I hadn't felt for years—even if it seemed clear to many that I wasn't up to the task. Which also made me laugh, as if, *you turds*. As if.

I grabbed my kit and tipped it upside down, and every item that solved a costume problem tumbled onto the carpeted floor of Allen's trailer. Amid the two-sided tape and nail scissors, gum wrappers, and loose threads were the famous button and the note from Kristi. Emilie had killed Kristi's career; I bet she would talk to me. I bet she'd tell me anything I didn't know I needed to know.

I sent a text:

Poppy: Hi. I'm the person who inherited your kit. You left a note and your phone number. I wonder if you'd like to talk.

Instantly three dots emerged. I pushed my back against the bench on the floor and waited.

Kristi: Is this Poppy?

An incredulous noise popped right out of my throat. Kristi knew my name? "What the hell?" I should have expected this—everyone here was a football field ahead of me at every turn.

Poppy: Yes. This is Poppy.

Kristi: Jesus, it's about time.

CHAPTER TWENTY-NINE

ALWAYS A BIG SPENDER

Kristi: Call me.

To say that was surprising on every level was an understatement.

I dialed and after the first ring, I heard a woman's voice. "So, this is the famous Poppy."

I wasn't expecting the scorn in her voice. I thought I'd call and this Kristi-person would say, *Thank goodness, Emilie ruined me.* We'd talk about the button and what it meant to Emilie. She'd tell me that her friend Three had been a hero who had tried to help her, but Emilie the director's niece had made it impossible. He'd given me a job for no reason other than to help me. Had he done the same for Kristi? I wanted to know that Three, however flawed, might still be the man I had carried with me in my heart all these years.

"Hardly famous," I said. "Barely functional these days is more like it."

"We wondered if you would call."

"We?"

"Me and Emilie. Jeffery thought no way," Kristi said.

"I . . . Wait. You all talked about me? I don't follow. You are all friends? All in touch?" I fixed my posture, shoulders back, internal strength activated, and said, "I'm confused. I'm trying to understand what's going on. Why you left your number in your kit."

"Why do you want to know?"

"I thought since Emilie had something to do with you being let go . . ."

"Whoa, what?"

"Your note. And the button? I figured she had something to do with getting rid of you." I could hear myself, like a rookie cop, making an unsure case. I changed my apologetic tone to something more befitting my age. "I'm trying hard to understand why Emilie is screwing with me. What is going on, if anything, with her and my friend Three. And what any of it has to do with me and my job in Wardrobe. That's it. If you can clear anything up for me, that would be great."

"Em said it was hard to tell if you were clueless or, like, evil."

"I've obviously gotten this wrong. Forget it," I said, annoyed.

I moved to hang up when she said, "Nobody knows if they can trust you."

"That's . . . that's . . ." I shook my head as if we were in the same room. "That's ridiculous. I'm the most trustworthy person on this set, from what I can tell."

I heard rustling through the phone. The hinge on a door yawned, the hitch of a cigarette lighter sounded. "Why didn't you tell Muriel that Em took the necklace?"

"Yeah, I don't know anymore. She's a kid. I have a kid her age. Apparently, that's not a big enough reason out here."

Kristi inhaled and I pictured her blowing the smoke into the early-morning air. Her breakfast cigarette.

"Emilie didn't get me fired. She's been trying to help me."

This was a plot point that had no place in the story I had created where Emilie functioned as the bratty antagonist. "No, I don't think so," I said reasonably. "Wait, on second thought, that makes sense. I took your spot. If she gets rid of me, you can come back."

"If it were only that simple." A sigh. A beat. "We want to know whose side you're on."

This appeared to be a game of verbal chicken. Like Kristi wasn't going to say anything incriminating. Given she was already fired and was still talking to me, I didn't understand why she wasn't saying what she obviously wanted to say.

"Okay. Look, I'm a fifty-year-old lady who is doing a good job. That's it. I like this job. I really, really need the money. I want to pick up clothes, tie shoes, and make sure people are ready for their shots. That's it. The only side I'm on is Poppy's side." I cleared my throat and said, "I'm going to hang up."

"Wait," she said in a surprisingly young voice. Less jaded. More desperate. I glanced at Kevin, who was panting, the thing I noticed she did when my anxiety rose. "I'll tell you what happened. I've got nothing to lose, and Emilie and Jeffery have hit a wall. Emilie says Jeffery is kind of worthless."

"Okay. Fine. Go on, but I'm hanging up when I've heard enough, whether you're done or not."

I heard her laugh. "Em said you were nice but not that nice. That sometimes you could really get your shit together."

"Up until recently, my shit was always together," I said. I had to admit that it felt nice that Emilie had said something complimentary given how many hits I'd taken this week. "Fine. Go on."

"I went to design school. I've always wanted to be a designer for film. Your job was my big break."

"And you borrowed something and got erased," I said, wanting to move this story along.

"Nope. I didn't. I did not borrow anything. I would never. This job was my big chance. I had good relationships with everyone. I was living my dream."

"Kristi, no offense but what did you do wrong?"

"Ha!" Her laugh clapped across the airwaves. "Nobody trusts you, Poppy. What did you do wrong?" she shot back.

"Okay. That's fair," I said.

"We all heard there was a new project being green-lit. Witherspoon was attached. Possibly Kidman. A 1950s Hollywood remake. Wanda would design. I could work as a set costumer. Not lead or anything. That's the way these jobs work. People hire the workers they can depend on. You work your way up," she said.

I changed positions, got a glass of water, pressed the phone to my ear. Three had talked about this the night we kissed. Using the same words.

"This producer attached was an old guy. I liked him. He had dad vibes. Sometimes we ate together. Shot the shit. He knew I had school loans, a car payment, was barely making it. We talked, you know? One day at lunchtime he asked if I wanted to see the costumes they'd pulled in the historic archive for the tone for the project. Thought it might help when I talked to Wanda about working with her. He said it was the holy grail for movie geeks."

I put my water down even though my mouth went suddenly dry. "You're talking about Three."

"Yeah. Your friend." She lit another cigarette.

"He's not that old," I said, defensive, as if his age had anything to do with anything.

"Okaaay," she said, like, *Get yourself together, it gets worse.* "There's no real archive. It's just an office in Edith Head. Its weird costumes aren't prioritized like you'd think they would be. I guess us movie geeks are the only ones who care. I lifted a set of keys from Muriel's desk. We tried all of them."

"Keep going," I said. I tried to reserve judgment. Stay loyal. Why should I believe them? *Keys. Can you get keys?* Three had asked more than once. That's why.

"It was the middle of the day, lunch. I had my notebook ready to sketch, get ideas, take notes. I couldn't believe my luck." She took a drag and spoke while she exhaled. "I walk into the room. The whole place is filled with racks upon racks of clothing. He's pointing out all these famous outfits. Vivien Leigh's dresses in *Gone with the Wind*. Lauren Bacall's suits. He pulls this blue suit from a rack. Marilyn Monroe's from the movie *Niagara*. Some of them are on loan from Western Costume, some are to be returned to other studios. Anyway, I guess the original buttons on Marilyn's suit were changed out, and these fancier ones were put on so she could wear it to a dinner or something. Supposedly Marilyn was wearing the suit when she met JFK. It's that story that made it more valuable, that's what Three said."

I picked up the button. Held it up to the light. This historic thing had been tumbling around nipple covers and Super Glue. Not at all befitting a kind of royalty.

"We watched a YouTube clip—about iconic dresses. It had millions of views. Said there were so many dresses, getting eaten by moths, when they could go somewhere. Be taken care of. You know how he is—friendly, especially to the wardrobe people. He starts talking about my future as a designer. Maybe bringing back the classic suits. Starting my own line or whatever."

"Yeah, he is super. Full of ideas. Hard to resist," I said without the organic enthusiasm I'd had driving across the country. I wanted to hold on to that feeling—there was so much hope and Cinderella-like simplicity surrounding it, but my grasp on the fairy tale loosened as I listened.

"I said starting my own line would take some real money. I didn't say it as if I wanted to do it. I never wanted that. I've always wanted to work in film," Kristi said.

I knew what it was like to have Three's full attention on you, to listen to him make a compelling argument. How it could sway you if you weren't careful.

"That's when he got serious. Started in on this whole plan on selling the 'inventory' to his contacts. 'Nobody even knows what's up here,' he said. 'Could make a fortune.' I was like, 'Dude, no way. I'm not doing that.' He poured it on after that. Blew right past everything I said. We'd

make a great team, I was being too proud. I owed him. He was maaad."
She took another puff on her cigarette.

Those were the very words he used at the airport with me. Too
proud; I owed him.

I felt sick. The acid from my empty stomach climbed up into my
throat. I stood over the sink and spit yellow saliva into the stainless-steel
basin. I turned the water on, let it run cold onto my fingers.

"Hang on. I need a drink of water." I grabbed Allen's coffee mug,
the one his daughter had made, and filled it. Took a sip. I thought
of Three's concern for my finances. How he'd asked for the costume
archive keys. Emilie's mistrust of my presence from the beginning, and
suddenly cold, I grabbed Kevin's blanket and threw it around my shoulders and shivered. "Okay. Go on."

"Then he brought up my debt. Said he overspent too sometimes.
Needed help. Guilted me by saying, 'I thought we were friends.' It was
like he couldn't stop talking."

One of the things I always left out of the filmy love story that I
clung to over the years was this. There were times I paid a bill or two
of Three's, nothing too extravagant. A dinner here, maybe a textbook
there—he was always overdrawn. Not enough tips at the restaurant,
he'd explain. Then he'd come over wearing new, expensive shoes, a new
shirt. I never knew if he used my money for those purchases or needed
money because of them. I should have said something, but making
people happy is complicated.

My dad popped into my mind. He'd been the same with money.
Keeping him happy was imperative—I knew how to do that without
asking too many questions.

"Always a big spender," I said, and my meticulously curated blue
sky view of Three darkened.

"Yeah. Seems like it. Drives a Porsche SUV, the small-dick car of
the century. Anyway, they're all so loaded. But throw it away too." A
dog barked in the distance and Kevin's ear twitched. She looked relaxed,
as if she could finally rest now that I was getting all the information I

needed to survive. "Three said he couldn't do it without me. All I had to do was get a key made, get the inventory. As if we were collecting his things, not Universal's property," Kristi said.

How many times had Three said to me, *You're perfect for this job.* I'd thought it was a commentary on my competence. I was so low, I ate it up. That and the idea that there might be a lovey-dovey, take care of each other when we're old future for us. In reality, what Three thought of when he saw me was a con artist's mark.

In grade school we made rock candy once by boiling water and adding sugar until the pot was filled with gooey syrup. We dropped our individual sticks into the syrup and waited. Over the course of six days, minute crystals fused to the stick until we had a jagged column of rock sugar, unbendable and solid. Our teacher told us to be careful of our teeth.

As Kristy spoke, her sticky words provided the spine I needed to decipher what had been too good to be true. When I brought my treat home, my mother was still with us and made me throw mine out. *Just because it's sweet doesn't mean it's soft,* she said. Maybe it was a dental warning or maybe it was a life lesson.

"Tell me about the button."

"He took a photo of me holding the suit up to myself. One of the bejeweled buttons was loose, and I was fiddling with it. He snatched the jacket, and the button came off in my hand. No more dad vibes. Scared the crap out of me. I turned and got the hell out of there. I heard him yelling.

"I knew right away I was screwed. I had two choices. Say no and get fired. Steal costumes and eventually get caught and get fired. That's why Emilie is so pissed. She knows my story, and it's clear she's next, if you don't work out. Then Jeffery."

"Jeffery? He's a star. Why him?" This, the only loose end that didn't fit the story. My last hope for finding something that didn't add up.

I could almost feel the puff of air from Kristi's loud sigh having to explain every last detail to this stranger, and for what? "Jeffery's last two movies tanked. They were released in theaters at the beginning of the pandemic. Everyone knows he's got money troubles too—Three targets the vulnerable."

Vulnerable. I wanted to crack my tooth on that word, spit it into the ocean that I heard was close by but hadn't seen because WTF.

"Emilie and Jeffery are inseparable—where one goes, the other is there. Only children in Hollywood gravitate to each other. They could do worse. They've been trying to figure out a way to expose Three."

I'd thought they were a couple, that Emilie would get in trouble for hooking up. I'd seen everything through the eyes of a rule follower. A non–wave maker. Someone who lived her life guided by others' rules because how easy was that? You didn't have to think about the reasons for your actions at all.

"Anyway, whatever happens, you're eventually out as well," Kristi said.

"I can't be out, Kristi. I'll go to prison. I'm not kidding. I'm in tax debt. I need this job and if I can keep working . . ."

"Get in line. Nobody cares."

I blinked. That phrase again. That stupid, ruthless phrase.

"I care, Kristi," I said. I cared about Kristi because that's who I am. But I cared about me—finally. I would absolutely not default on whatever payback plan the IRS had because of another predator who didn't have the guts to go after bigger fish. It wasn't just the money, though, that motivated me. I cared about how I'd be seen, remembered, thought of. In this short time here, I saw that I cared a lot.

CHAPTER THIRTY

HARD CANDY

"I've been in therapy," Kristi said. "I've been so depressed. I read up on narcissists and grooming. I'd never been groomed before. It starts slowly. They can read you better than you know yourself."

Three. He knew me when. He knew I'd been dumped again and again. That he could get whatever he wanted from me by shining his adoring light in my direction. I slept with him, fed him, did his laundry, paid bills. He even knew how to leave me without a ruckus, made it look like it was for me. I'd been his employee, just like I'd been for my father. Just like my mother had been before me.

In the airport, he saw immediately I hadn't changed, as he'd said. He knew a little flattery, a job, a kiss went a long way with me. Why wouldn't I go get the keys to the archive? Hell, I'd given him the keys to me. In the car on the way to California, I'd sung "Somewhere Over the Rainbow"—cried over the final words, a girl asking the question *Why, oh why can't I?* when faced with wanting only rainbows. The little girl without a mother, the older woman thinking her only value was to be pleasing. So many like us, just like us, misunderstanding the adoring looks, only to be tossed aside when asserting . . . anything real. Fired for a *no, I don't want to be a criminal.* A no to basically anything. Women learn to be pleasing—often their lives and livelihoods depend on it.

I could have cried. Possibly a younger version of me would have. But this Poppy Lively on the phone with Kristi. She was not close to tears. Three misjudged me. I had changed. I'd turned to hard candy when I had Robyn, and this man, well, he thought he was coming after me but in effect, he was coming after my daughter's future. That was where I put my foot down, and not the one that turned in and tripped me. The other one. The scary one.

"You there?"

"Yeah, I'm thinking." I touched Kevin's soft fur. She'd become a living talisman, something grounding. "Kristi, I need you to tell me everything. We're going to stop him."

"I mean, okay," she said, unconvinced. "After it happened, that day I couldn't work. Asked to go home. Emilie was at the dentist, and we weren't that close yet. I wanted to tell her, so when I found her kit, I dropped the button into it. Get this: I didn't want to be accused of stealing it or damaging the suit. Ironic, huh? The next day I wasn't on the call sheet. Security at the gate wouldn't let me in. I gave the guard my kit hoping someone would find my note and call me. Wardrobe career over." She took a sip of something, swallowed.

There had to be a plan somewhere in the details. I was a problem solver, I would figure this out. "Where is the suit?"

"Three called me once. Wanted to make me a deal if I gave him the button. I blocked him. I was sick of his shit. There's no way I was going to win no matter what he promised. Besides, I didn't have the button."

"So when did Emilie find all of this out?"

"At first she'd believed what people were saying. That I borrowed a costume and got caught. We barely knew each other—you know how busy it gets, and she doesn't trust people easily. Three had already approached her. She doesn't trust people; she knew he was up to something. Like, why all of a sudden was he talking to her, you know? When you arrived on set she found my number and called me."

"So people thought Three was shady and since he brought me in, I was shady by association."

Kristi inhaled deeply. I imagined the corrosive smoke entering her lungs, swirling through the tissue, and unfurling in her airways. She blew into the phone.

"Yeah. Hollywood is the worst place in the world for a decent person. Decency is a narcissist magnet. They feed to control. I learned that in therapy. And on TikTok."

"The necklace disappearing?"

"Emilie took it. To get you in trouble if you were working with Three. But then you were great about it. That's why I said if you called, I'd talk to you."

"Aren't you afraid I'll go to Three? Tell him Emilie is onto him?"

"No offense, but you're not the conniving type."

"That's a compliment in Wisconsin."

"Like where is that? Near Idaho?"

"No, it's not. So it seems like for you to be vindicated and Emilie and I to keep our jobs, we have to work together. I have the button, Three trusts me, we have history, and he underestimates me."

"How do you know that?"

"All arrogant men underestimate women. It's a thing. I heard the best Cleopatra podcast. She outsmarted the entire Roman army."

"I mean, what's the plan, though?" she said with real interest in her voice. More youthful, less hopeless.

"Has anyone besides you seen the suit? Where do you think it is?" I asked again.

"No idea. It's possible he sold it."

"Maybe, but not without that distinctive button. You can't sell a damaged suit for big money. If he has it, I think I can get him to show it to me. Hang on. Let me think. When you were erased, you couldn't get back on set?"

"Nope. I wanted to tell Muriel. She's a fair person. I admire her, and I didn't want her to think the worst of me. I didn't have any proof. Everybody's job is on the line all the time. It's not a very stable profession until you prove yourself."

"Text Emilie. She's on set with Jeffery, I think. I saw her this morning. Tell her to come to Allen Carol's trailer. That's where I am now. We're going to start proving ourselves."

"Oh yeah, she told me you were living there."

"Yeah, I am." The time for being coy about where I was sleeping was over. "For what I'm thinking to work, Three has to still have the suit. We've gotta make sure he didn't return the jacket to the archives somehow."

"Hey, Poppy. Thank you for listening. Even if nothing comes of it. Thank you."

"Keep your phone close. We might need you."

The moment I hung up I googled, "Marilyn Monroe's blue suit in the movie Niagara."

No sooner had I hit "Send" than Emilie knocked and let herself in in her usual fearless way.

"Kristi filled me in. She thinks you're okay. I'm not sure."

"Oh brother." I rolled my eyes like a kid who'd just graduated from high school when someone bought them a typewriter and they wanted an iPad. "I'm your only hope here. You need me more than I need you."

"How do you figure that?" she said.

"I have the button, Three trusts me, I'm waaay more under the radar than you, and I have connections with people you don't."

"Doubtful, but look, it's going to take some time to find this suit. You can't get tired and fall over," she said, her eyes skimming the scab on my chin.

"You can't sprint away when the going gets tough."

"Kevin stays here."

"Jeffery stays in the trailer. He's a doll, but we can't use him."

Emilie nodded and tapped into her phone. "He's no use to us. He's more terrified of getting fired than you are."

"The archive is upstairs in Edith Head, right?" I said.

"How do we get in there?"

I waved her words away and said, "Follow me. I know exactly who to see about this."

CHAPTER
THIRTY-ONE
HOW ABOUT "HELP"?

"Do you ever go home?" I asked Emilie.

"No. Rarely. It's complicated. My mom is clingy because she knows she f'd up with me. I'm trying to unlearn some stuff from her. It's kind of the same for Jeffery."

I launched right into thoughts of what Robyn needed to unlearn from me. Emilie gave me the side-eye and said, "At ease, Poppy. We'll figure out your daughter later."

I shoved her with my shoulder and said, "You don't know me," and we had our first laugh together.

Outside, Emilie and I walked into Studio 37, the safety lights dimly illuminating the enormous eerie space. I called out, "Travis, I need you," as if I were summoning a spirit from movies past. "It's Poppy. Emilie is with me. We're alone. Can you come?"

Emilie scoffed. "What's happening?"

"Travis. This is your opportunity to show these little idiots that people over forty are not to be scoffed at," I said.

There was a rustling and heavy movement overhead. "Saturday morning idiot management. My favorite," he said. Dust fell down from the perms while he carefully stepped to our level. "Listen, Muh-wok-key. I can't haul any bodies around today—my back is stiff from Thursday." He was a big man and moved as though his hips hurt and the extra weight around his middle stressed his knees. It couldn't have been fun for him—those stairs, sleeping on the unforgiving planks overhead.

I moved to his side, thinking of the loss of his son, squeezed his arm, and quietly said, "You okay?"

He nodded, and he did look more rested, I had to admit.

"No heavy lifting this time. Grab your keys. I'll fill you in. This is Emilie," I said and saw skepticism in his expression. "She's okay. We're working together."

I gave him an abbreviated version of Kristi's story. He knew bits and pieces, had heard the rumors of her here one day, gone the next story. "If we don't do something, I'm gone, and so is Emilie. You know how it is, Travis. There's kind people working on this set; we want to keep them."

He hiked up his pants and gave me a *I hope you know what you're doing* look. "Where to?"

"Edith Head. The archives. We're looking for a suit."

Pragmatic Emilie said, "You could get fired. So you know."

He exhaled loudly. "I'm on leave. It's probably time for me to pack it totally in. Let's go." He set off and we followed in his tailwind.

"What was he doing way up in the catwalks?" Emilie whispered, and I shook my head and mouthed, *Not now.* Instead of her usual middle-finger salute, she nodded.

As we moved up the outer stairs, Jeffery appeared from the prop area. He wore a bucket hat, glasses, and a pair of blue jeans that appeared at least a size too big for his small frame. He had his hand in front of his face as if hiding from a pack of paparazzi, and Emilie said, "Jeff. No one is here but us. Go back to the trailer."

"No. Fill me in. I want to help, Emilie." He put his long arm around Emilie's shoulders and rested his chin on her head.

Emilie waited for my okay. An actual nod that I was in charge of this caper.

"Fine," I said, wanting to keep moving. We introduced Travis, who unlocked our door. There was enough light to move through the halls, past racks of clothing, office doors, and upstairs. Photos of iconic stars lined the walls: Cary Grant, Gene Kelly, Julie Andrews. It was as if their eyes followed us saying, *You think it's bad now, you should have seen what it was like for us.*

At the end of a long hall, Travis jiggled his keys, looking for the right one. Jeffery pulled Emilie close, one arm around her middle, and I found the photo of Marilyn Monroe in my phone.

"Here's what we're looking for." The suit was a tight two-piece number with a shawl collar and three buttons. We had one of the three elaborate ones they'd used to make the suit fancier. Emilie held up her phone with another photograph of Marilyn Monroe, same suit, different position. "Kristi said we have the top button."

The door opened, Travis hit the lights, and before us was a deep and wide space filled with garments, garment bags, clothing racks, tall wooden armoires, and a library table with ledgers.

"This is the holding room until they get a climate-controlled space to preserve the more iconic pieces," said Emilie. "I heard Muriel and Wanda saying it was a surprise more costumes aren't stolen all the time."

"It's crazy that they haven't done this long ago. The Smithsonian has Dorothy's slippers and Harry Potter's robe, so they know how important these costumes are," said Jeffery.

"If they put them all in a museum and mark them historic, they can't rent or auction them off. No money? Nobody cares," Emilie said.

Jeffery unzipped a white cotton garment bag and peered inside. "This is overwhelming. The racks go on forever. How are we going to get through all of this?"

"There is some organization, it looks like. By star. By movie. But here's a rack with no labels and tons of unmarked clothing," said Travis.

"There's four of us. We'll split this in quarters and systematically go through every inch. Don't mess with the shoes and accessories. Forget about anything that is obviously menswear," said Emilie.

"Either way, if we do or don't find the suit, it doesn't prove anything," Jeffery said.

"It's going to make me more comfortable in phase two," I said.

"Do we have a phase two?" Travis asked, for the first time looking nervous.

"Yes, but it's all me. You guys are off the hook," I said, leaving out details I hadn't worked out myself yet.

After an hour of searching, Emilie helped pull a wooden desk away from a wardrobe so we could look inside. "This is Gregory Peck's suit from *To Kill a Mockingbird*," she said, reading a tag in her hand. "It's criminal that all these just sit up here unprotected."

"You like this, don't you? Movies, costumes, the people," I said. "You act like you hate everything."

"No, just you," she said, her smile a crooked emoji, and the sun peeked around a cloud in my mind. "It's just that there's so much bullshit. I want the adults to be like, you know, adults, in charge, trustworthy. They can be the worst, so I give people a lot of shit to see who they really are." Emilie lifted a dress out of the armoire and held it up to her. "G. K. Grace Kelly?" She performed a playful bow. "Like, I don't even know if I can trust you totally. You're Three's friend, so like, how nice of a person could you be? At least that's what I used to think. You were super classy about the necklace thing. I'm sorry about all of that."

I can't explain how accepted this made me feel. That this insolent girl, who'd been so hell-bent on getting rid of me, had opened her mind where I was concerned.

"Once you figured everything out, why didn't you talk to your uncle?"

"My mom, his sister. She drives him crazy. They're not close. He gave me this job, but you know, he'd want proof if I was telling him something this big. He and Three have been friends forever." She pushed past suits and dresses on a hanging rack. "It's frustrating," she said softly. "Nobody believes anything without some kind of evidence."

To my credit I did not try and hug her, but I wanted to, this young girl collecting wisdom the hard way. There were enough taxing things in life; for your mother to be one of them was terrible, I knew. While I didn't have to work around my mother, I had to figure out how to traverse the hole where she should have been.

I mentally added this to the list to talk to Robyn about. To move away barriers that might shut down our ability to communicate. The thought of what I'd taught my daughter because of my inability to ask for things, to push back, all out of fear. Was there still time to show Robyn a new way so when Lizzie, or anyone, pushed her she could respectfully create a boundary?

"You sick? You look a little gross."

"My daughter. She doesn't know why I'm here. And I'm trying to be a parent far away, listen to her. She learned some stuff from me she might have to unlearn."

Emilie pushed aside the last of the costumes in the cabinet. "I can talk to her. If you want. Maybe she doesn't know you are trying your best."

"I'm trying so hard, Emilie."

"I know."

So that I didn't clutch her to my breast in relief and understanding, I said, "I thought you and Jeffery were a thing. I misunderstood."

"Jeffery's gay. He's trustworthy. I tell him everything. I don't have a boyfriend. I think Travis is straight but might like a satin pair of boxers, the way I saw him touch a silk scarf to his cheek a half hour ago."

"Ugh. I miss everything."

"Yeah," Emilie said. "He and Ryan fixed your tire, you know. Ryan said you warned him off a woman from props. He wasn't into her but thought that was nice of you to do. So they patched your tire. Ryan fixes everything."

"How would he know it was my car?"

"You have a gigantic van with a *Harry Potter* Muggles sticker on the back. Who else would own that car?" Emilie said.

I thought of the night I thanked Three. He hadn't explicitly said he'd fixed the tire. *We aim to please* is what he said.

"Emilie always made sure Kevin had food," said Jeffery.

"It was your first day. Where were you going to get dog food? My grandma has dementia. I knew she didn't give you any. I like Kevin. I don't want to carry her around, but I didn't want her to starve."

"Why not give it straight to me?"

"I hated you then, remember?"

Hated. Past tense.

———

What started out like an exciting safari through old Hollywood fashion became a silent slog. The room, filled with rack after rack of clothing, was deceptively large, and even with four of us working continuously it felt insurmountable.

"I'm hungry," Jeffery said, and sat on the floor.

"You guys," Emilie said. "Check it out. It's a Marilyn area."

The three of us made our way over. An unmarked rolling rack with garment bags sat up against the back wall. Each had a tag with MM and the name of a movie or event clipped to the zipper. Swatches of vibrant fabrics fashioned into dresses, capes, and jackets emerged as Emilie searched for the light-blue suit.

The sound of the hangers scraping along the metal rung grated, but I didn't look away. I willed the suit to be on this rack—I needed something concrete to look at, to match the button in my pocket to. Even if it screwed up the beginnings of a plan.

"It's not here," said Emilie. "At least, I don't see it."

She looked again, but by then I knew the plan I had was sketchy at best and would be a gamble. As a last-ditch effort, I said, "Do we absolutely know Kristi doesn't have the suit?"

Emilie closed her eyes. "What are the odds? Kristi got in here, stole a suit, yanked the button off, put it in my kit, put a note in her kit. Three discovered a suit was missing, tracked it to Kristi, and fired her for theft? Even in Oh My Gosh, Wisconsin, you'd have to admit that is less likely than Three luring her up here."

"Okay. Yeah. Let's get out of here."

Emilie and Jeffery did a quick check to make sure everything was as we'd found it. Travis riffled through his keys, getting ready to shut off the lights and lock the doors. We walked silently through the halls, past the movie star portraits, past the limp dresses and suits from every era—lifeless without their actors, waiting patiently for their next gig. Outside, we moved together, in the warm California afternoon amid the false reality of the Universal lot.

It was Jeffery who broke the silence outside Allen's trailer. "What's our plan?"

"Jeffery, no offense, but you're done," said Emilie. "You're in no immediate danger, so why step into this?"

"I can be sneaky and brave," he said, offended, chewing his thumbnail where there was nothing left to chew. He didn't see Emilie's expression that said, *No, you can't, honey.*

"This is where I go it alone." Each of the others protested, and I put my hand up to stop them. "I don't want to do this. I wasn't being dramatic when I said I need this job. I have to figure a way out of this debacle or no matter what I do, I eventually end up fired. I'm already going to lose my house, and this money may help my daughter be a nurse, but more likely it will keep me out of prison." Each of their faces looked appropriately shocked; only Travis probably knew what it was like to truly live on the edge. "Those helpful things you all did for me—I absorbed them. Some I attributed to Three to support my infatuation when I should have been falling in love with all of you."

"Yeah, so," Emilie said, uncomfortable. "I'm setting up a group text for us. If anyone needs anything, text the group."

"We need a safe word or an emergency phrase. Like 'Mayday' or 'SOS,'" I said, trying to lighten up my true-love energy.

Jeffery caught Emilie's eye, an absurd expression on his face. "How about 'help'?" he said.

"Okay. Yep. This isn't a movie. 'Help' works," I said.

CHAPTER THIRTY-TWO

DON'T TAKE DRUGS

In front of Allen's trailer, our little group shuffled their feet, kicked a pebble or two, and looked at their phones. This ragtag bunch of below the liners with the one, Jeffery, above the liner were like me. People with a job, who wanted to do their job, and for one reason or another were disposable to the powers that be.

"Can you at least tell us what your plans are?" said Travis.

"We can be your backup," said Jeffery, still hiding behind his hat and glasses.

"It's not that I am trying to be a hero here. I legitimately think this is something only I can do. I'm the one Three would least expect anything other than wide-eyed wonder from. I might get the truth from him."

"You won't, though," Emilie said. "So you better have something in mind other than running up to Three and asking why he's a douche or we're all screwed eventually."

This was a sharp reminder that we needed, if not proof, then evidence that Three had Kristi fired unfairly. Evidence that Three, my old boyfriend, my often-visited fantasy man, my employer, was a crook who preyed upon those without power. My Hubbell was not Robert Redford, the ultimate romantic loss. Three was Herman Blatterman, and nobody in the twenty-first century wanted to be a Herman Blatterman.

"I know what I look like to you—a woman barely worth notice—but I assure you, I am the best I've ever been with regards to knowledge, experience, and stealth." I let out a quick laugh. "'Stealth' might be going too far."

"You've been living on set for a week. Not everyone can manage that," Travis said. "Especially with a dog tied to you."

"I'll keep you posted and if I need you, I'll call."

We split up with unsatisfied energy—and for a minute I thought, I could walk away. Go home, sell everything we owned, postpone nursing school, find a job that didn't pay as well, and take years to pay off the IRS plan. Kids are like tiny hostages to their parents—I recalled that child on the backpack leash while I talked to Three. It galled me that Robyn's life would be handicapped because of me and mine would be because of Three.

It was time to tell Robyn what was going on. What was coming with the house and what she wanted in life. I couldn't do this with dignity and integrity until I did this for myself.

The first thing I did when I got into Allen's trailer, after greeting Kevin and letting her out to relieve herself, was to text my daughter.

Poppy: Can we talk soon?

Robyn: We're in the Hamptons all weekend. Monday?

I knew I'd have the whole story by then, so I sent her a thumbs-up, a heart, an emoji with heart eyes, and a letter sealed with a heart. A picture is worth a thousand words.

Time to start phase one of my two-phase plan. I did a quick pace around the trailer. Drank a glass of water, shook out my hands, and texted Three.

Poppy: Hey. Want to meet for a picnic tonight? I've scored some cold noodles and beer. I can come back on set if you're working. Our place?

The noodles and beer thing was a ruse. I wouldn't even look for them. If all went as planned, neither of us would want to eat. I hit "Send."

Three: Fantastic. Yes. Can't tonight. Tomorrow lunch. yes.

The suspense of waiting a day, how would I manage it? I wanted to get this over with, but he had to call the shots.

Poppy: Noon??? I deleted the additional question marks, then hit "Send." This was a casual question, not an inquisition.

Three: It's a date. I'll be there.

Poppy: Away from tour buses. Maybe by offices? Amblin?

He sent a thumbs-up.

For the first time since arriving on set, I hoped he would break this promise. I hoped he would text back soon, say that he wouldn't be able to come. What I was about to do could go a thousand ways, but it would probably go one of two: I'd burn all my bridges, get erased, and be blacklisted like Kristi, or I'd get enough information to talk to Muriel. I might get fired anyway, but I'd surely get fired if I did nothing.

I'd use the time to get ready for anything.

———

I spent the next few hours doing laundry, packing my car, and getting ready to leave if my plan backfired. I tried to tell myself how nice it would be to shower on the regular, not scrounge for food, stop lurking in shadows and waiting for the next double cross. I took Kevin everywhere with me because getting fired would mean no more furry, silent sidekick. No more tiny heart beating against my sternum. No more absent-minded hand to Kevin's tiny head as a way to calm my anxiety. Maybe there'd be less angst after all of this. I'd get a different job, move on.

Kevin and I unloaded and organized the van, checked the oil and the tires. I even re-parked so that the nose of the van was pointed toward the exit. I wanted no awkward three-point turns, no stilted-exit slowing of my escape. When, if, I was erased, I wanted to have my Stay True To Your SHELF bag already sitting shotgun pointing toward the exit. I'd accelerate through security, the Universal gates getting smaller in my rearview mirror.

Occasionally there was a group text from Jeffery or Emilie:

Everyone OK?

Is something happening?

Do you want to get together?

And each time I replied, Yes, Yes, and No. I'm still working out the details.

But I did ask for one thing, for no other reason than I had people now, people I could ask this of.

Poppy: Stay close. Just in case.

Hearts and thumbs-ups appeared as tiny e-supports.

In the wardrobe trailer I tidied like I'd done that first night. I said goodbye to the basket of shoes, took special care with the necklaces and bracelets to find spots for them in the plastic shoe hangers over Wanda's desk. I straightened tiny doggie shirts and skirts next to adult-size clothing for scenes yet to be filmed.

Muriel's pinched handwriting was everywhere, along with several pairs of readers that she wore interchangeably. I touched a black pair and thought of how much I admired her. Muriel seemed able to be straight, tough, and job focused without getting dragged into drama. I wished I'd have more time with her. I penned a quick note and fastened it to the clipboard Muriel always checked upon arrival. *It was an honor, Muriel. Thank you for your patience. –PL* I pulled it down and crumpled it up. Defeatist. That was what that was. I tossed it into the trash.

Evidence of the others on the Wardrobe team, people I hadn't gotten to know, had me wistful and wishing for more.

There was so much to learn, and it occurred to me that the largest life lesson of all had to be answering the question of how much to give, how much to keep. How much do you matter versus how much do others count when trying to be a mother, friend, or good person? My mother knew to take care of herself first, and I'd learned the opposite in reaction. I couldn't fault her anymore. I didn't agree with her, but I got it.

———

The sun had set during my long farewell. The ministrations in my van and the wardrobe trailer functioned to calm my nerves. I looked forward to confronting Three just to extinguish the unbearable anticipation.

I'd locked the wardrobe trailer and put Kevin onto her legs as we walked back to Allen's trailer. "You have to get stronger, girl. I'm not going to be here to carry you." Those words caught in my throat. Kevin stopped walking. "Come on, honey," I said, and I took a couple of steps away. She lifted her old-lady face, the faintest gray bristles on her chin, eyes not dry but not rheumy either. Teary. "Don't look at me like that. I'm trying." She sat, as if I'd given her a command. We looked at each other. I scooped her up and kissed her on the top of her head. She dry-licked my hand, and I said, "Let's get you some water. I think that's still allowed."

———

In Allen's trailer, after heating one of his diet meals and eating it, I cleaned the microwave. That led to wiping the stove top, sink, back-splash, and countertops. The dusty recessed lighting looked as if no one had run a cloth over them in ages, so I took a dish towel and went to work. The place where I'd drooled on the bedspread was dry but visible, and I tried to blot it out while remembering the feel of his hand. "I think I'll miss you the most, Scarecrow," I said and would have been annoyed by my sentimentality, but it was true. I was sweet on him, but my picker had a screw loose and needed tightening before I fell again for someone.

When I found Allen's candy stash, I popped a gumdrop in my mouth and took a rag to the inside of his bedside table. There I found a round tin with the words Camino. Cannabis-Infused Gummies printed on the top and a single sticky blue lump still inside, identical to the one I'd just chewed and swallowed.

"Crap."

I took to Google and tried not to panic. I tried pot once in college and became frantically suspicious that the blue Ford Taurus in my apartment parking lot was an unmarked cop car. I had binoculars from a bird-watching elective and peered at the empty vehicle until my roommate came home and took them from me. After much hydration and time, my paranoia subsided, but I vowed to stay away from the devil's lettuce forever.

My online queries became more focused as I searched for a way to head off any untoward effects of that innocent-looking clump of sugar.

Q: Is there any way not to get high?

A: Don't take drugs.

Q: Accidental edible ingestion????

A: Keep your edibles away from dogs and kids, but . . .

Q: I ate a gummy how do I counteract?

A: Consume lemon water, black pepper, pine nuts, and CBD.

Thirty minutes in and each suggestion sounded sillier than the next. When I came to the instruction that directed me to focus on something else and cuddle a pet, I put my phone away and thought about texting Chelsea, then promptly forgot why I wanted to text her.

The trailer door opened, and Allen walked in, and I said dreamily, "Is it really you?"

"Yes, it's really me," he said, giving me jazz hands, and it was possible his face was less jokester and more lubber but I was under the influence by then. An unreliable narrator.

"I ate one of your gummies. I thought it was candy. I've accidentally ingested an edible! Why don't you keep them in the appropriate container?"

He did not share my alarm. "I can never get the tin open when I want one. This is my trailer, and if I want to keep a bong at the ready, I should be able to. And of all the people that could use some"—and he mimed quotation marks—"'accidental ingestion,' it's you."

"I don't feel anything, so I think it's going to be fine." Then I stood and the trailer tipped on its side and I grabbed a dish towel to steady myself.

"Oh boy," he said, and with both hands on my shoulders, he sat me on the foot of his bed.

"I'm high," I said. "Too much weed." I mimed smoking a joint, my eyes squinty and my lips tight.

"I understand," he said with a half grin.

"The internet said to hug a pet."

"Okay, let's get you some water and we'll leave Kevin out of this. What usually happens when you use?"

"Usually," I said and snorted a laugh. "Oops." I snorted again and wiped my nose. "What are you doing here?"

"I left my gym locker key here and my best running shoes. I came to get them," he said but didn't open his closet or make a move for his shoes.

"Are you leaving? I don't want you to leave. Can you not leave? Can you run another time? Get me some pepper and pine nuts?"

At his bedside table, he found the last gummy and ate it.

"Oh no. Now we're both high."

"I usually need more than one."

"Do you think you are being watched in this trailer? You know, with a hidden camera?"

"Poppy, do you get paranoid when you use?"

"Did somebody tell you that?"

"No. This is legal in California." He fake-read from the container, "This strain of cannabis does not cause paranoia. You are not going to get in trouble."

"Yes, I am," I said. "Just not tonight."

"Let's go take a walk." Before I could agree or disagree, he had me out the door. "I'll give you a proper tour of the back lot. I'll show you Steven Spielberg Drive. The fresh air will do us good."

"How come you're not married?" I said. On some level I knew that I would never have asked him that if I weren't high. On another level, I wasn't really here, having this conversation. As we walked his shoulder functioned as a bumper, keeping me strolling along.

"Gun shy," he said. "How come you're not married?"

"I have a daughter," I said, as if that were the full answer to that question.

He pointed out Steven Spielberg Drive, the *War of the Worlds* set, *Jaws*, all things I'd seen on my first days while trying to decide where to sleep. "We know each other," I said, pointing to several of the storefronts in the western town. "Hi, saloon," I said. A breeze wafted past, and I stood, lifted my face to feel the air, and visualized animated clouds puffing past.

"I love it here," I said as we finished our walk back at Allen's trailer. "I love the hustle and bustle."

He guided me to the trailer and said, "Let's get you some more water."

I waited. He filled a glass with ice and water, and when I drank I felt a trail of cold down my throat all the way to my stomach. I picked up Kevin and said, "I love her."

"So, first paranoia and then you fall in love?"

"Yeah. That's how it goes. But I haven't been in love for a really long time."

"Why is that?"

"What?"

"Why haven't you been in love for a really long time?"

I sighed a deep sigh that felt so clean and clear, so calming. I closed my eyes and when I opened them, I said, "Wait, what was the question?"

"Let's get you to bed."

I nodded and crawled onto his bed, scooted right up to his pillow, and laid my head down. Kevin cuddled into my tummy. I held out my hand to Allen and said, "Can you lie with me? I know it's not right to ask. Like, I know it's not right to ask *you*. But it won't matter."

The bed shifted with his weight. He lay next to me and took my hand.

"Don't go anywhere, bestie. The world's best friend. My movie BFF."

"Okay."

"Don't leave. Just stay put for a change."

I felt him squeeze my hand.

CHAPTER THIRTY-THREE

THERE'S NO COMING BACK FROM THIS

I woke, mouth dry, on Sunday morning, Kevin stretching one, then two legs. Without lifting my head from the pillow, I peered around the space and with disappointment saw that I was alone. Had I dreamed that Allen had come back? No, I'd been high, high, high last night, but not so addled that I didn't know reality. A song from *Soundtrack of the Seventies* that my dad used to listen to popped into my mind.

"Alone Again (Naturally)." A terrible tune about a man who certainly had a depression diagnosis, and someone should have taken away his piano. I disliked how my brain returned to self-pity at times when I thought someone important to me was near and then they weren't. I sat up. It would be okay, though. I'd lost a lot and made it right through to the other side altered for the better in so many ways. Understanding that leavers leave because of them, not me.

I used the bathroom, made coffee, and tried to act like I wasn't looking for a note from Allen, maybe stuck to the coffeepot or the microwave, that said something supportive. I shook myself. Only in the movies. Those things only happen in the movies. I could leave him one, though. Instead of thinking how he would feel about that, I realized it would please me.

In Allen's shower I thought, *This is the last time I'll shower here. This is the last time I'll be in this trailer looking out the windows at Studio 37, Jeffery's trailer, see my first on-set apartment—the Honey Wagon.* I was like a high schooler graduating and writing sappy signatures in a yearbook. *Dear Universal, you're awesome, never change.*

With every melancholy thought, the pleaser part of my brain worked and reworked the loop where I tried to problem solve, talk myself out of moving forward with my plan. I could leave this place. Steal Kevin. Leave a note. Reason with Three. The IRS played defense and blocked every notion with the weight of my debt.

I'd woken too early to stop this maddening cycle. I needed something to do, so I considered a yoga pose, maybe a push-up, and even moved to the floor as if I were the kind of person who would try fitness instead of worry to feel better.

Then I got ahold of myself. I was Poppy Lively, and I was good at the pivot. I'd been saying it for years, and here I was hearing it for myself. I knew I was ready. I wanted to have this confrontation with Three. I wanted the opportunity to stay at this job or, if I had to leave, then I would have done it to myself. I'd stood up to the foe instead of cowering and letting the foe come to me and take me down.

At 11:00 a.m. I sent Three a text.

Poppy: Looking forward to seeing you.

Three: Me too!

Despite everything, those words after his name—"Me too!"—sent a shock of pleasure through me. An aftershock. The earthquake had come and gone, but there were tiny fault lines in my heart that hadn't gotten the memo. I patted my chest and whispered, "Remember, there is no good to be had with Three." I'd done so many harder things in life. Delivered an infant without the father holding my legs for support, buried my dad, and made it through graduations without a family celebration dinner.

My fingers did not shake as I texted back.

Poppy: By the way. There's a super fancy button in my kit. It looks old. Has a note attached to it. Return to the Costume Archive.

This last line an embellishment for the dramaturge. I sent a picture of the button in the palm of my hand.

Poppy: You mentioned an archive once. Should I give it to you?

I waited. He typed.

When I was in the delivery room with Robyn, the nurse asked if I had anyone that would be joining me. I said no, I was alone.

The nurse, possibly so used to frantic fathers and irritated mothers-to-be, said, "Sometimes I think it's better. You can focus only on yourself."

I'd smiled.

"You sure don't seem nervous."

"I'm not. I feel ready."

My phone vibrated.

Three: Yes! Amazing. If I bring something with me can you sew the button on it?

Confirmation. Three had the suit and it was missing a button. This button. If there had been any hope that he wasn't who Kristi and Emilie claimed him to be, it fizzled.

Poppy: I'll bring my kit.

I'd banked on something I'd learned over the years. That arrogance and an inability to assess risk go hand in hand. There was no end to stories of politicians having affairs in plain sight, millionaires drunk on their own control failing to factor in the little guy, the whistleblower. Three believed his own invulnerability and would carry that costume back on set, especially if someone was going to do something he wanted.

At a few minutes before noon, I didn't put any lipstick on, nor did I give my hair a final toss. I didn't have noodles or beer or strap Kevin to me with my sling. I clipped my kit around my middle and moved to the door.

A Post-it fluttered next to the metal frame right at eye level. If I'd gone outside before this, I'd have seen it right away.

See you Monday. Off to see my daughter. Your bestie, Allen

And I smiled. Not so alone after all.

———

Three sat on the steps of the *Psycho* house, waiting for me. It was a rare thing for Three to arrive early where I was concerned. Well, I told myself there were real stakes in the game he didn't realize he was playing with me. I stutter-stepped, realizing what this meant. In our history together—back sixteen years or on this day—I hadn't understood the game. I'd bring up his lateness, his ever-changing schedule.

He'd say, "I'm just naturally less ruled by the clock. But you understand me. We run on our own time. You know how I feel about you."

I bought it, but in the end the truth was that he didn't care what I wanted. Neither had my father. But others did. Most of all, I cared.

Today I approached the *Psycho* house and moved to the stairs that I no longer referred to in my mind as *our steps*.

"Three. Hi!"

Good ol' friendly Midwest Poppy, the girl who didn't know a thing. The puppy you could swat on the nose, but she'd come right back so you could swat her again.

"Poppy Lively." His warm, buttery expression, my name in the air between us.

He stood, and for a moment I thought he might hug me, but he held the suit in a tinted dry-cleaner bag. His hands were busy lifting the light plastic, presenting the suit to me. Not attempting to kiss his long-lost love, not desiring a physical connection. Wanting a task completed. And this was one below-the-line person who would do the job.

"It's amazing that you found the button. This suit is an important piece in my next picture."

"What are the odds?"

"What are the odds?" he repeated.

I rummaged in my bag and pulled out both the button and the needle and thread I'd already prepared for this moment. I did not want to be fumbling with fraying thread and a tiny eye of a needle in case my nerves got the best of me.

It was obvious he was eager to see the button, maybe even get his hands on it. He played it cool, caught a glimpse and handed me the short jacket, which looked impossibly small. I held the fabric in my hands, smoothed it in my lap as I took a seat one step away from Three.

I'd seen and read about the fragile, breathtaking beauty of Marilyn Monroe. She'd worn this suit, possibly under imperfect circumstances. Afraid to lose a job, misunderstanding a kindly invitation, only to understand too late that she was no more than a piece of cloth to certain men. An object that can be used and tossed. Something she thought about herself. Disposable, dispensable, invisible except as an object of sexual fantasies for millions of people she'd never be in a room with.

In some ways, it was her legacy that had the last laugh. Even the men who used her couldn't have known her impact, how her story would be told and retold forever. The many villains' names repeated, listed, accused, and recorded time and time again. How she hadn't been disposable but in fact long remembered by masses of people who yearned to help, understand, and prevent it from happening again. This better world was the one I wished for Robyn, Emilie, Kristi, and yes, myself.

The button slid into place as I punctured the fabric with precision. I pushed the needle through again and again, pulled the thread taut. Not too tight that it wouldn't release under pressure, in case another woman needed evidence in the future. The button clutched tightly in her hand for later.

"You're a lifesaver, Poppy. This is just terrific."

The needle pierced the suit material one last time, and I tied a knot with the thread.

With Three distracted by something on his phone, trusting me, I took a photo. One of the suit, the button, the needle, and thread. One just wide enough to get Three's face in it.

With a small pair of scissors, I cut the thread.

"Good as new," I said.

I fixed an innocent expression onto my face as my heart thundered, the tip of the needle in my hand keeping a subtle beat. I looked at Three.

"Now we can call Kristi and tell her the suit has been found and repaired."

"What?" He pulled his gaze from his phone and focused on me. I could see him trying to make sense of what I'd said.

"Kristi. She was fired for stealing this suit. But here it is. In fact, this is her kit. She left her phone number in it. I can call her right now."

I'd been holding her number in the palm of my hand while I sewed. I unfolded it and pulled my phone forward.

"Poppy, that is so you." He oozed warmth. "So kind to think of her. You have her position. There isn't an opening for her anymore." Ignoring the far more important part of the conversation—the alleged stolen costume.

"I'm sure you'll find a place for her. Kristi will be so relieved. You can give her the news yourself." Here I affected a *Mona Lisa* smile. Held him in my stare.

"Poppy. That girl was trouble. There's more to this suit story than you know."

"Is there?"

Unruffled, cool, not a wrinkle on his forehead when he patiently explained to this ragamuffin from Wisconsin, "She used me to get to the archive. To get this suit. A total manipulator."

I did not react to the audacity of that claim, that poor Three was the victim of a twentysomething bully.

Three. The lines of his face softer, but so familiar to me. I knew how those lips felt, how long it had been since I'd felt anyone's admiration, embrace, attention. But a switch had been tossed. I was over it.

He didn't notice that he'd lost me. Continued talking. "They're users. Anything to be in films. That's why when you got here it was such a relief."

I let my midwestern smile flood my expression and I said, "I wanted to thank you again for fixing my tire. How did you know it was my car? Was it the University of Wisconsin Badger sticker on the trunk or the fact that I still drive a Volkswagen that gave me away?"

"I know you," he said without confirming or denying. "Go Badgers," he laughed, clearly having no idea that I drove a Toyota van with a wizard sticker. The noncommittal slickness of his response. The sly insincerity. In a flash I saw something I'd never considered before.

My mother, Gemini, hadn't left because she was beleaguered by my needs. She left my intolerable, dismissive, probably abusive father. She didn't come and go out of guilt. Most of all, she didn't lie. That woman knew what was right for her, and she essentially said, *Peace out, people*. For the first time in my life, I saw something that I hadn't learned from her that would have been helpful. She'd been honest about what she needed. Granted, I wished she'd taken me with her so I could have seen her happy, off meds she maybe didn't need, building a life away from meanness.

The memory of my mother must have softened my expression, because Three saw an opening and took it.

"We have all day. Let's get reacquainted. You've always been my one that got away."

You'd think my heart would soar hearing those words, even if by bad habit. But the insincerity hit my tympanic membrane and bounced right out, landing who knows where. I was no longer looking for them.

"Great," I said. "I'm free. If you still want to after I text Kristi we found the suit."

"Poppy. Don't." The wounded expression on his face. Yes. I knew this face. Next, if I didn't capitulate, I predicted it would turn cold.

When he saw I was unmoved, the silence stretched between us. He refused to look away; he knew who was in charge. That he could hire me and fire me. Simple as that. That contacting Kristi meant nothing in the hallowed halls that protected those in power. And I knew I'd be okay anyway.

I lifted my phone.

"There's no coming back from this, Poppy." There it was, the flash of *how dare you*. Not betrayal or hurt. No *I'm innocent*. His reaction was like that of a king to a pawn. This was familiar too.

Chelsea had been right. Three was a lot like my father. I'd watch my father smile and persuade advertisers, parents, teachers, and if anyone didn't see things his way, he became furious. I hadn't put them together because I'd done everything for Three—there had been no reason for him to get angry.

My father's charisma and watching him manipulate had been my gateway drug to Three. His anger when I was a dependent child and my abandonment issues kept me quiet and complacent. My father had me convinced that whatever I wanted would draw conflict. So I stopped wanting, and Three was the beneficiary.

I locked eyes with Three and pulled my phone forward. He didn't move. Why would he? I stood, his eyes on me, took a step backward, and I hit the button to call Kristi. When she picked up I said, "Hi, Kristi. I found the suit."

Since I didn't trust myself to make a backward exit without falling over, I turned, faced the studio, and said into my phone, "I'll call you in a minute," and I ran without looking over my shoulder. I had one more ace up my sleeve, as they say. Something only Travis, Emilie, Jeffery, and Allen knew about me, not my old friend Three.

When I knew I was out of sight, I sent the photos of the repaired jacket top and the whole suit with Three to the group text and sped up. Rounding the corner by the Honey Wagon, I checked my toes. Neither had defaulted inward; both were pointed at the three people crowding the outside stairs to Allen's trailer.

"How did you get this photo?" Emilie looked joyous. That was the only way to describe her expression.

Jeffery wasted no time getting inside Allen's unlocked trailer. He was like a field mouse terrified of owls awakening and finding him unprotected. He waved us inside. "Get in. We can talk in here."

Travis was the last one in. He looked both ways and shut the door, pulled the blinds, and said, "The coast is clear."

I picked Kevin up from her favorite blanket at the foot of Allen's bed. I'd make a case, if I were still here in the morning, for Allen to care for Kevin until the mother-in-law returned. A tremor shot through me, and suddenly my legs felt jelly-like.

"Kristi wants to FaceTime," said Emilie.

Before anyone could answer, Emilie's phone rang and a woman's face appeared. "Where is she?" Emilie tilted her phone toward me. I waved.

"I'm Kristi," the clear-skinned, blue-eyed woman said. "Thank you for this."

"This is all we need, right? We can show Muriel or my uncle. It's proof," Emilie said.

Kristi's bright but sorrowful eyes showed she knew better. "It's amazing. The best thing I've ever seen. The suit is real. Three is holding the suit. I obviously don't have the suit. It's not proof. Three will say he retrieved it from me. Bought me out. Settled out of court. Something."

"Poppy will tell them. Right, Poppy?"

"I will. If I'm able. He didn't admit to anything. And I'm likely to get erased tonight. Which in some ways is more evidence for us—but it's circumstantial at best. He could say anything about me. For certain he can bring up Allen and my supposed affair."

Travis repositioned, his face pained, and said, "Poppy's right. There's no other proof. That's what makes this so hard. We all know it's happening. Abuse. Addiction. Risky behavior, but it's hard to provide evidence that doesn't blame the harmed. Even with my son"—he took a beat—"it was a lack of security that at least somewhat contributed to him being up in the perms after hours. He was rowdy. If there had been adequate on-set security, he might be alive now. It's his fault he drank, but the studio decided his death was a one-off. Why bother creating safer work areas for just one death."

Emilie's eyes widened, and Jeffery put his hand on the big man's shoulder. I shook my head and said, "Travis, I can't even imagine." From one parent to another, we honored his son in a silent second. Emilie stood, maybe understanding something about others and their woes that might outmatch hers.

"We don't need actual proof, it's not a court of law," said Emilie. "We need enough to show my uncle."

A knock at the door startled all of us except Jeffery. "It's Ryan. He wants to hear everything."

Travis let the man in, and I said, "Thank you so much for patching my tire."

"Thank you so much for giving me the heads-up. It's hard to tell who is friend or foe around here."

I'd found friends and foes here, but only after sticking my neck out. The younger generations took a lot of heat for being irreverent. Now, less reverent, less dutiful, more purposeful was where I was headed.

"Everyone, find a seat. Poppy, you have to tell us everything," said Emilie.

CHAPTER
THIRTY-FOUR
POPPY. POPPY LIVELY.

Emilie couldn't be dissuaded from her belief that my photograph would be enough. She'd bring it to her uncle privately. See if he would listen. Kristi offered something new. "Three took a photo of me holding the suit. I don't even know why. I'm sure he's deleted it by now, but it shows we were together."

"It doesn't matter. It's on Three's phone. We're theater nerds, not IT geeks. It's not like we can hack his phone," said Jeffery. "I can hear my dad saying, 'See, I told you, computers are the future. Why did you want to act?'"

That gave me some insight into Jeffery, that rising star, trying to make his parents happy. "The only thing we really have is a story with a couple of photos. It will be up to your uncle to listen or not."

Kristi had an exhausted look on her face and as our conversations slowed, she wanted to have a cigarette and go to sleep. Travis and Ryan decided to raid the greenroom refrigerator, and I needed to think through my next move.

I put my hand on Emilie's shoulder and said in her ear, "If you can wait to talk to your uncle until after tomorrow morning, I'd be grateful. I want to try one more thing."

"What are you thinking?"

"I can be erased, but I can't be locked out. Three doesn't know I've been sleeping on set. My old friend Three never once considered where I landed when I got here." I scoffed, hiding the hurt that I knew a careful listener would detect. "I think if I show up, in front of everyone, maybe it will take this secret out of the shadows. And I want Three to see that if I am fired, I'm still here. That you can't erase a woman, anyone, and walk away without blowback. And I have to give Kevin back."

"They might call security," said Emilie.

"I've lived too careful of a life. Maybe security needs to be called," I said, smiling.

Her eyes shone with hope, something so new and lovely I didn't have to hold back from hugging her. She initiated a quiet clasp around my neck and said, "Okay."

"We can't all sleep together," I said. "That's even too much closeness for me. Let's get back to our lives and see what happens next."

———

Alone in Allen's trailer, amid his ghostly presence, I needed something to do, so I scrolled through Instagram and other notifications on my phone. It was easy to see why Robyn and her friends mindlessly scrolled through their phones during any less-than-optimal experiences in life—boredom, shyness, jaw-clenching agitation. It was a great way to check out in plain sight from a place you couldn't leave—the confines of your thinking, history, or thoughts of the future.

Amid photos of dogs in swim goggles, summer vacations, and unappetizing meals, I noticed a missed call and a voice mail. I braced myself for whatever horror was to come, when I saw it was from the man I'd ignored time and time again until finally accidentally picking up his call. The person who'd asked about Dawna and requested scanned files. Brian. The forensic accountant who had me thinking of bloody autopsies, a roped-off crime scene.

"This is the IRS. There is a new notice posted in your account. Please confirm receipt. Reply with questions if appropriate."

I went straight to the IRS site, figuring a new message must contain a recalculation that would quote a higher debt. A number it would take even more years to come back from. Or maybe the man needed more information about the business, thinking I had an offshore account—whatever that was.

I'd done some hard things in the last hours. I could click and find out about the next plot point in my life. So I did. Miraculously I recalled my password on the first try and logged in.

I scanned the letter for numbers amid the text to see the new bill. The words see attached documents almost had me opening the attachment, but something else caught my eye: the words Preliminary investigations along with recovery of Dawna Klump. I slowed down. Started from the top. This is to notify. Resolution of debt likely. Law enforcement in concert with the IRS . . .

Resolution. The shock of that unexpected word rang through me like the rocketing bell on a strongman game. All funds sequestered but recovered. IRS interest dispute, pending. The words appeared to lift off the page, as if my email couldn't wait to make eye contact, see my relief.

I held my breath, afraid that this was an e-joke, a glitch that would evaporate if I breathed normally. I slowed, read it again. Hidden accounts, restitution, Klump signing over bank accounts, and the last words in the paragraph, Full recovery of all accounts.

> I'm out of pocket for the rest of the weekend. I'm sure you have questions. Please call Monday.

"Kevin!" I said, and she sat up so quickly she struggled to stay on the bench. It was the clean and clear voice of pure, solid relief and joy. Something that had been missing since we met that must have shocked her. The weighted blanket of despair dropped an inch off my neck, slid down to my shoulders, slid off my back. I breathed so deeply, I felt every capillary, every alveoli, fill with oxygen deep in my center. The guilt, relief, shame, and anxiety that had moved into my chest packed their bags with every gorgeous respiration.

You're Poppy Lively. Robyn's mom. No matter what happens now, you'll go home. Get a new job, watch Robyn go to football games, and listen to her complain about her college classes. You'll go to flea markets with Chelsea, and Robyn will . . . Robyn will finish college and move. Or maybe she'll stay in New York and put off college. Or possibly another opportunity will come her way, and I will encourage her to take it. Because I never had those opportunities. Because Robyn could have them.

The goal had always been to return home and resume life as I knew it. To go back to my childhood home where I came from.

Kevin sat alert, eyeing me, unused to this still person, pondering her next move instead of darting off to solve everyone's problems. I closed my eyes and visualized me, in the van, passing Vegas, reading signs to Denver, and some of the weighted feeling crept around my waist. Inched to my shoulders. I opened my eyes wide, shook my head. The money was back. I could do anything.

Anything at all. But today, I still had things to do.

I'd cleaned, packed up the last of my belongings, and now there was nothing but refreshing my emails while searching for Monday's call sheet, which I knew wouldn't come. At 4:00 a.m., when the call sheet didn't arrive, I took Kevin for one more furtive walk behind a couple of trees, then from Allen's perfect vantage point, I settled in to watch the activity outside of Studio 37.

Muriel and others from Wardrobe rushed by carrying costumes, holding coffee from breakfast, calling out instructions and greetings. Ryan carried what looked like a karaoke machine, and the director strode confidently inside the studio talking, white earbuds in view. Jeffery donned the posture of a movie star, so unlike the nail-biting boy who cautioned danger the night before. Three wasn't the last to arrive but close enough for my mouth to be dry as a desert and my heart rate dangerously high. I needed him present. With his typical self-assurance, hands in his pockets, Three amicably greeted crew members.

It was time.

I smoothed my shirt and touched Allen's door handle, his Post-it Note cheering me on. Three was right: there would be no coming back from this. Kevin yawned, her squeaky version that sometimes functioned as a bid for attention. One of her few repertoires of diminutive noises that I'd come to learn. "Not this time, sweetie." I couldn't bear to say goodbye to her. My plan included walking out of Allen's trailer, acting like I'd be right back.

I made the mistake of looking over my shoulder at her big black eyes, the wild scruff of her bristle-like hair. That tiny flap of a tongue, and in two steps I had her in my arms. In one more, I'd retrieved the sling and swung it in place around my body.

No one noticed me right away as I moved into the studio space. Emilie fussed over Jeffery's costume. Muriel was in consultation with the director, and Three stood nearby, listening. The whole tableau had a surreal quality to it, but I'll tell you this. Seeing Three unworried, not a wrinkle on his brow, his career and ego intact, made me lioness-with-hungry-pups furious.

Ryan saw me first and stopped working, and one by one, that signaled to others that something might be amiss. The noise level reduced. Someone dropped something metal.

Three noticed me, and his cool countenance flickered from surprise to displeasure. He shook his head, communicating *no* to me. As if he were a pitcher waving off the catcher squatting at the plate, waiting for approval for the ball game to continue. I made the call to keep moving. *I* did.

Three said, loudly, "How did you get back on the set?" It was the contempt in the word *you* that made the statement sound overly personal, out of character, and Muriel snapped her head up.

I stopped. As if I'd taken diction classes I said, "You never asked where I was staying, old friend."

"You." Three pointed at Ryan. "Call security."

Muriel watched, and I saw the look she reserved for workers who'd finally done what she wanted on time and in the right order. I imagined Travis up in the perms listening.

The director had an uncomfortable expression on his face, and I turned to him. "Sir, I want to thank you for allowing me to care for Kevin."

Three clapped his hands. "Okay, that's enough. Time is money, people."

"I was fired yesterday, sir. So I'll have to give her back to you." I had my hands protectively holding Kevin's back and my phone.

Three took a step toward us. "I removed her last night. Absolutely unacceptable," he sputtered without giving a reason.

Undeterred, and because the director seemed unmoved by Three's dismissal, I said, "I was fired because I discovered the truth behind Kristi Koski's removal. The woman who held my job before me was pressured by Three to steal and sell costumes from the Universal vault. We—excuse me, I—don't have proof, but I do have her side of the story and a couple of photographs that indicate she is telling the truth. Emilie said you're a fair person . . ."

I would have continued but Three bolted in my direction. I didn't move. It was Three; I wasn't afraid of him.

The next moments happened in syrupy slow motion. He reached for my phone, his face determined, angry. Our eyes made contact, and he remembered me, Poppy. His face shifted to a mix of emotions I couldn't begin to read.

In that hot second, Kevin reared up, snarled, and savagely bit Three's hand, piercing his skin. As quickly as she bit down, she released and gagged three times and vomited her breakfast.

"Three. Get back," said the director.

"Son of a bitch," Three shouted and dropped his phone into the dog's stomach contents.

Emilie, using her dancer moves, slid onto her knees and had the phone in her hand before Three could react. For my part, my mouth hung open unheroically. I had no idea I was packing a ninja around my middle this entire week. I had no idea who Three was.

"Uncle Jim, it's a studio phone. There's a photo in here too." Emilie wiped the phone of Kevin's sick with her T-shirt. "If you'll let me, I can explain what's been going on. I know I haven't been easy. This is why."

"This is ludicrous. I'm bleeding. Security! Give me that." Three couldn't seem to prioritize which thing to take care of first, which felt like poetic justice, even if no justice had been done quite yet. His gaze swung everywhere except to me.

"Get ahold of yourself," the director said to Three. Then more softly: "Three, cool off."

Three heard something in his old friend's voice and found himself.

With the quiet countenance of a woman who'd nursed a child through mastitis, drove herself to her own colonoscopy, and understood deeply that life was loss spelled incorrectly, I checked on Kevin, who was back to being basically a breathing washcloth.

To me the director said, "Are you all right?" Kindness. No recrimination or impatience.

I had confronted Three alone yesterday. I shivered. So grateful I was in the center of a crowd today. Protected. I nodded to the director. I was physically fine, but I would need a minute to get over this. All these years, My Three. The love I'd returned to as the gold standard because I thought he saw me, really saw me. And I'd been right. He saw a woman he could manipulate just by being nice. Until he couldn't, and then, like my father, turned into whatever he thought he deserved.

Three, clutching his injured hand, stepped next to the director and said, "Buddy, listen to me."

The director, without looking at Three, said, "Go to my office. I'll meet you there after we wrap."

Three, pleading, said, "James." And when the director stiffened, Three put his hands up and said, "All right. Okay." His voice sounded almost apologetic, but he did not look anything but entitled and insulted. Childish, the boy hadn't grown up—he was still the boy who wanted it all, but that ambition had become gluttony.

"Okay, everyone take a few minutes," said the director, and he pulled me aside. "There is much to talk about. I of course will need details of what you and others know." The director wore a ball cap with SWEETIE embroidered on the brim. I'd seen others with hats that said HAIRY. Merch for the crew, identifiers of those above and below the line.

"I understand. I'm happy to share what I know. If other people want to chat with you, I will let them seek you out."

"Have you seen what's on this phone?"

I shook my head. "I think it's part of this story. Maybe helps put a time line together? There are always time stamps on pics."

"Three and I have been friends for years," he said. "I understand that is true for you as well. He and I worked our way up together. This is such low-level stuff, costume thievery, et cetera. But it's the poor treatment of the team that erodes what we're building here." He rubbed his eyes as if he were home alone, in his bed, waking from a troublesome dream. "I'd hoped that bringing Emilie here to work would be good for her, not put her in harm's way. I don't know what the answer is." His eyes fell on the living room set, now mostly quiet, free of dogs, crew moving cords, lights, and set pieces. "Do you have kids?"

"I have a daughter, Emilie's age."

"I have a ten-year-old going on twenty," he said. Dropped his gaze to Kevin, now a small bundle of practically nothing. "Kevin has only ever bitten one person before in the history of her life. That person was the drummer Emilie's mother ran off with for that unhinged time." He turned his attention to me. "Remind me of your name again?"

"Poppy. Poppy Lively."

He took a beat. Digested my name.

I heard his phone buzz, and it moved him from reflective to business. Before he answered he said, "Your job is secure. We will need all the information you have."

"James," I said, using his name. "Emilie is . . . I know she's trying to be something more than her family history. She appreciates this job."

He nodded and said, "Why don't you find a seat. Take the day off."

I pictured myself going back to Allen's all hopped up on self-esteem and desire. I'd wear the carpet out, make Kevin dizzy with my energy. I wanted to celebrate by straightening a collar and watching for wedding rings.

"I'd like to keep working, if that's all right."

The director nodded. Called out for a huddle and moved away.

Muriel thumbed in the direction of the door, and I turned to see Allen, his unreadable movie star mantle around his shoulders. I nodded and headed his way. A few steps from him, my foot finally said, *Not so fast*, turned in, and I tripped but not enough to ruin this unlikely hero's journey from battle to resolution.

Allen steadied me easily with one hand on my shoulder. "When I saw him go for you . . ." he said, flushed and speaking quietly. "I haven't been in a fight since junior high."

"I kicked a girl once," I said. He patted my shoulder awkwardly for a man who I'd dressed repeatedly. "Plus, you know, there's Kevin, my petite bodyguard."

"From what I've seen here, you could take him by yourself. I was wondering when everyone else would get to see you irritated. I'm just glad this time it wasn't at me."

I had a moment where I thought I might laugh, but not in a happy way, more in a let-off-steam hysterical way, but it wafted through and left without causing embarrassment. I shook my arms out, and my knees started to shake.

"Can you do that trick with the elastic band on my pants? I got high with my friend the other night and ate my weight in Doritos."

I giggled. Literally giggled with glee. We had inside jokes. We had memories.

As if we hadn't just discovered what amounted to a poisonous black mold eating away at the magical fantasy of the story, the show went on, and I had this job for at least another day. It wasn't a typical day either. While I fixed collars, helped trainers wrangle dogs, and moved out of shots, people asked if I was okay. They nodded, acknowledged me. Said hello. Whispered thank you, so quietly it was as if they didn't trust this had happened. That their alliances had to be secret because you just never knew. And the love I felt for this place and these people didn't match the hours I had spent here. It was more than I could hold. Like the mother I would always be, I wondered if I could get everyone's address so I could send them a valentine in February.

It hadn't occurred to me that doing something you wanted for yourself would come with satisfaction and happiness. How had that not occurred to me?

After the director called it a wrap, he said one last thing to me. "Your job is secure. You can't sleep on set."

CHAPTER
THIRTY-FIVE
THE GETTING LOST GAME

In the wardrobe trailer, Muriel, with keys in hand, pointed to the washing machine and said, "The others have done the wash. We'll need to retag and store that grouping by the door. Get those back to costume eventually. Not you, Poppy. You're done for the night."

"Can I talk to you, Muriel?" Kevin shivered. Muriel stressed her out, but I rubbed her back and her trembling subsided.

"I knew you were living on set, if that's what you want to talk about. I've known since the first night. I spend more time in this trailer than my own house—a pencil gets moved and I make a note of it. Details are my addiction, but seriously, your first mistake was giving Emilie credit for cleaning. She would never."

"She may surprise you going forward. Over the last twenty-four hours, I've seen an altogether different Emilie."

Muriel moved a tennis shoe into a box on her way to the door.

"Why didn't you toss me out of here?" I asked.

"I probably should have. You're a likable person, Poppy. It's your strength and your downfall. None of us are perfect. My first movie, I camped until I could afford a place. Not on set, mind you. It takes desperation and balls for that move. It was the only thing you did early on that showed me who you were. A person who would do what it takes and cleans up after herself. That's at the heart of Wardrobe."

"I can't believe you knew. I thought I was being wicked sneaky."

"That's the most outrageous thing I've heard all day, and this has been a day for the books."

"You'll miss my nighttime nervous-guilt cleaning when I move off set," I said. "Did you know Three was shady?"

She gave me the old Muriel peeve. "Oh, sweetie. Everyone in this business is dodgy. Even me," she said. "So watch yourself." She kicked a closet shut. "I'm glad you're sticking around. If you do well, I'll recommend you for another job. If you want it."

"Thanks," I said, too quietly for her to hear me. I didn't want to overplay it, but eager-me shouted, "Thanks, Muriel!" And one of the guys hauling studio lights paused to assess this display of 911 gratitude. I waved and sat on the bench-bed I'd used that first night.

Robyn. I wanted to see my daughter's face, tell her we'd lost money but it had miraculously reappeared. I dialed.

Her face flitted onto the screen. "Hi, Mom," she said with a shy smile. Robyn sat against a white quilted chair or possibly it was a headboard, and the lights were on.

"You look like you're in your apartment." Her black hair against the white, like Snow White, but empowered having said no to the prince who didn't understand consent.

"I did what you said and Lizzie totally understood. Her mother-in-law moved upstairs!"

"Were you scared to ask her?"

"A little bit, but you gave me the words and so I felt more confident," she said, and my happiness curled around us as if we were in the same room.

"There's quite a lot to tell you, but first we should talk about nursing school—what you're thinking. What's right for you."

"No, Mom. It's not that I don't want to go," she said, her eyes soft. "I know we're having money troubles."

"We're not anymore! It's all over." A rushing wind of relief blew through me. I was right not to worry her. All was well, but had her trust in me been tarnished?

She gave me a skeptical look.

"It's such a long story. I'm sorry I didn't tell you. I thought I could fix everything, and you'd never have to know. Kids shouldn't know about their parents' money woes."

"I didn't know at first, but Mom, you are super easy to read. When you get stressed, everything goes bonkers."

"That's not true. Is that true?"

Robyn counted off her fingers. "You bump into everything. Start talking about selling weird things like, I don't know, the art cart in the back hallway, which is caked with Silly String and Goop." She cringed. "I don't want to tell you what else you do."

"Tell me. You have to." I closed one eye and watched my girl with the other.

"All of a sudden everything you say is a little bit louder than normal. Everything. Even when you're talking to yourself. Your Google history is insane. Embezzlement laws, side hustles, and don't get me started on your Pinterest '107 Ways to Cut Your Grocery Bill.' That big, long one on saving soap fragments. I mean, come on." Robyn was loving this a little.

"I thought I was holding it together, LOL."

"Mom. Don't say *LOL*," she said, teasing me. "I'm sure other people didn't notice. I know you too well. I think the day you found out was the night you had a glass of wine. We'd had that bottle on the counter for like five years."

We said nothing for a long moment. I tried to get used to the loss of my little girl's blind trust and, yes, innocence from the big financial realities of the world. It wasn't shame I felt, exactly; it was something more complicated. What would be the term for loss of a childhood but gaining an adult? A combination of grief and pride—surely this word could be found in a parenting dictionary somewhere.

"I knew you didn't want me to see you like that. I knew you'd fix things. You always do." Robyn, her brown eyes so kind and filled with an awareness, taking care of me. I'd done the same for my father after my mom left, but at a much younger age. The grocery lists, signing permission slips, doing laundry. I'd seen need and provided, and I passed that behavior on to my daughter. The difference was that Robyn knew I was a parent who you could count on and did her part by not compounding or solving the problems. She remained a kid.

"It's my job to take care of you. I tried to shield you from the chaos."

"It's okay. I only understood part of it. And we are Team Lively. I take care of you too."

Caring seems so simple. Someone needs help and you help them. It took me so long to understand what was healthy and what wasn't and why. I didn't know everything, but I knew this: I was going to choose who to help and how much using my own wants as a barometer for a change.

"This entire debacle could have been avoided if I'd learned tax law and healthy relationships in high school instead of the definition of *mitochondria*," I said.

"The powerhouse of the cell," said Robyn. She took a sip from a water bottle. "I didn't know how bad things were and now they're better. So that's good!"

"It feels like a month, not a week ago that I dropped you at the airport. Are you second-guessing nursing school in the fall?"

"Blood does make me woozy. Hollis barfed last night and I was okay, so I think I was homesick."

"I went to Girl Scout camp for two nights in eighth grade and cried in the latrine the whole time, then threw up. You have time to decide what you want. Money is no object." And with that overloud and ridiculous assertion we both laughed.

"It's a big object over here," she said, dropping her voice. "If I stay working at least a year, I can save a ton and then go to nursing school the next year."

Today, FaceTime was a beautiful thing. I saw my daughter's familiar expressions of impatience, love, and reason and enjoyed that there was no way I could interrupt her with a bone-crushing hug. I considered reexamining the traditional pathway of high school to college to job. Thought about how I'd drawn a career map and threw it away, how the best-laid plans of moms and daughters often go awry.

"You look a little tired, Mom."

"It's been a big day. Hey, are you trying to take care of me with this gap year idea? To deny yourself starting college like the rest of your friends?"

"What?" Robyn seemed genuinely surprised. "No. A lot of my friends are taking a gap year."

"Wobyn," came a voice from somewhere in the room.

"I'll be right there, Hollis," Robyn said, her eyes no longer on mine. Her face youthful, a familiar mole on the side of her nose apparent. "Shhhh, don't wake Hayden. We're playing the getting lost game. We're working on the rules if we get lost, right, Hollis?"

A cheeky blonde child's face appeared, and Robyn said, "Don't leave. Find a lady. Secret words. Phone number."

Hollis had some r's and l's trouble, so when she responded it sounded like, "Don't yeave, find a yady, secwet wood, phone numbo." Hollis repeated, "Find a yady," and examined my face as if to see if I understood the seriousness of the situation.

I'd created this game, taught it to my daughter, and she was doing the same for her little charges. I hadn't singularly modeled invisibility, after all. I'd given her tools for speaking up.

So that she didn't see me blinking hard against the sudden tears that sprang to my eyes, I quickly said our secret words, as I knew Hollis would say them. "Bawbwa Manatee."

And Robyn replied, "You are the one for me." She blew me a kiss and said, "Say bye to my mom, Hollis."

I saw the child's chubby finger move to the phone, and without a word, the screen went blank.

"Peace out, Hollis."

I wiped my eyes on Kevin's head, thinking that maybe Robyn had escaped the faulty parenting trap I'd set: Do everything. Ask for nothing. I kissed Kevin, silently apologizing for not introducing her.

I hit FaceTime for Chelsea next.

"You were right. Three is like my dad," I said. "And all our money has been recovered."

Her face turned instantly pink and she said, "Can I cry now?" I nodded and she did. In between wet eyes and sniffles she said, "The money is back."

I filled her in with what I knew and I watched her expression change. "It doesn't feel real."

Chelsea nodded and wiped her face with her hand. "Tell me the Three bit before you have to run and find a gown or something," she said.

"It's such a long story. I stood up to him like I never did with my dad. I could have walked away, Chels, but I didn't. You know why?"

She shook her head.

"Because I didn't want to. I wanted to decide if I work here or not. If I move home and live in the house or not. This place is not healthy by a long shot, but nobody likes a doormat, no matter how much it aims to please." After delivering this tiny, obvious tip that took me years to learn, I said, "Robyn still wants to be a nurse."

"Nursing is in her blood," she said. But she affected a Transylvanian accent and said, "Eeen her blood," as if she were Dracula. "Are you coming home?"

"I don't know what I'm doing. I'd like to stay here, see this out."

I heard a beeping sound coming through the phone line. "Where are you?"

"I'm in my patient's room, but he's in a coma. You can tell me all of your secrets. He might be listening, but I think it's fine. He doesn't talk much."

"This whole time you've been at work in a patient's room?"

The screen swooped out of view, and I heard Chelsea say, "X-ray? Sure. He's ready," and the phone went dead.

I knew our friendship had been unbalanced for the past few months, but it always leveled out—I never worried that Chelsea's friendship hinged on quid pro quo. I did think it was time to identify the people in my life who liked me for me, not for what I did for them.

My mother's words on the wall of my house had me thinking. Again.

Whatever all else comes and goes—memories, parents, houses, children—the truth I'm left with is this: I am mine. What if that was enough?

———

I had a little time before the laundry would be finished. Enough time to find a hotel for the night, maybe one that didn't look like a crime scene. I'd wake, open my email, and if I did indeed still have this job, I'd drive on set, park, and go straight to the wardrobe trailer. If not? Well, I would decide.

With zero fanfare, Emilie strolled into the trailer. "What the hell? We're all over at Allen's. Celebrating." She crouched in front of Kevin. "This little hero has a party waiting for her." Emilie plucked her out of my sling. "Come on."

Kevin's eyes said, *Come on!* I swear they did.

I followed Emilie and Kevin out of the trailer. "You can stay at my apartment until you get your own. I can help you look. There are areas in LA you do not want to be in." She said this like she hadn't hated me days before.

My middle felt cold without Kevin, but Emilie held her like she was burping her. Her wide eyes watched me to make sure I was keeping up.

"They don't allow dogs at my place, but this gal isn't a dog. She's a person." Then with baby talk she said, "Aren't you, girl? You saved the day." I caught up to her shoulder and she said, "Grandma had to go into memory care. Kevin is yours now."

"She did? She is? Oh my."

"Oh my," Emilie mocked me sweetly into Kevin's ear. "She's been off her nut for a while. Now she's super pissed. She can't smoke there and thinks my mom is Kevin. Yesterday Gram called her best friend Tessa Bunk to break her out, and it took my mom two hours to find them."

Suddenly it was fine not to have Kevin tied to my middle. I could let someone else carry her as long as I knew, in the end, she'd go home, wherever that might be, with me.

CHAPTER
THIRTY-SIX
THE BRAILLE OF ATTRACTION

Inside Allen's trailer, key players moved from cautious wonderment to giddy triumph.

I moved to Travis's side.

"You did good, Muh-wok-key," he said.

"I couldn't have done it without you. You let me stay for no good reason except that you are a softie wrapped in a mountain of a man."

"This mountain has a little erosion. I've gotta get some help. Some of the guys around here are talking about a support group. It's a stressful business. Hardly any time for an outside life. And when something goes wrong here, it takes over."

"Who's in on this?"

"Me, Jeffery, Ryan, even Allen. You know, keep communication lines open. Talk therapy without the therapy part."

"Just men?"

"For now."

"What are you going to call this new chatty group of yours?"

"We're thinking the Crying Man Group."

"Oh, Allen will love that." I glanced over my shoulder. Allen held up his portion of the wall, not completely comfortable, if I read him right. We made eye contact. I smiled. I turned and to Travis I said, "Are you coming back to work officially?"

"I have a few weeks off and then yes. Plus, the group will need my tears to get things started. I decided I'm not ready to retire."

"Want me to put in a good word with the director? We're pals now."

He laughed. Someone played music. Travis was pulled away.

Our little victory was having a party. Nothing had really changed, but there was no place on Earth that celebrated glorious triumphs without any real transformation like Hollywood. I saw it in the man's eyes. Travis was happy, but measuring a tick or two below the others, not enough to dampen the fun. He knew that little would actually change. There would always be a below and above the line. He knew that Three would most likely fall up. It didn't matter to me what happened to him. What mattered was that I stood up for myself.

Emilie found a bottle of rosé under Allen's sink and shouted, "Rosé all day," lifting her pinkie as if drinking from a teacup.

Allen shot back, "Do not gender my drink. Pink is for everyone."

Emilie said, "Cheers," but couldn't get the cap off to take a drink and had to ask Ryan for help. I watched Allen, and Emilie and Allen kept an eye on me. I was working my way to his side, trying to sidle up instead of rush him.

Jeffery, God bless him, tried to celebrate, but his show of delight didn't mask his underlying anxiety. He came off like a Dickens character—stiff and more comfortable shouting felicitations when everyone else howled, *F yeah.*

Ryan gazed at Emilie and Jeffery, his expression flickering with their animated relationship. As if he sat in front of a television screen, watching from the outside. They were fun to watch, those two. I didn't blame him.

Travis held Emilie's phone with Kristi on FaceTime, and she kept shouting, "You guys," trying to get everyone's attention, succeeding only to draw Kevin's eyes to her.

A woman from Edith Head who had been dressing one of the dogs when everything went down on set said to me, "That took guts. You walked in there like James isn't one of the most powerful directors in film. After everybody thought you were a goner."

"I don't have as much to lose as you all. At least not yet. I hope I get to stay until this job is over."

A shout broke out when someone tried to take Kevin from Emilie and she refused to give her up. I wandered over to Allen—enjoying the tension I'd created by waiting, keeping an eye on him.

"Kevin looks tired," he said.

"It's hard to be an icon, no?"

"I'll let you know when I become iconic."

"Modesty does not become you," I said. "You and Kev know who you are. Don't fight the glory."

"You're quite the minx yourself. I called it." Allen's energy had settled somewhere between charismatic Best Friend and normal guy. If I had to guess, this was probably who he was with the people who knew him best. Probably exactly what the casting director saw in him when he was discovered.

"You barely remember anything from that boozy night, but you remember calling me a minx?"

"Selective memory. I remember a few other things," he said, watching the group. "I thought Three had you under his spell."

"He did. I was trying to heal my relationship with my father through him." I shrugged. "Then I looked up the word 'narcissist.'"

"You don't like narcissists, then?"

"They aren't known for their likability."

"My ex-wife texted me an online narcissist quiz to take."

"What was your score?"

"I didn't take it. I texted back, 'Oh, Lauren, I don't think you're a narcissist.'"

"Allen, let that woman live her life," I said.

He puffed a laugh. Waited a beat. "You know, I wasn't as surprised as everyone else when you waltzed in with that look in your eye. You've been putting me in my place since I first saw you and you didn't recognize me." The music changed to a song I knew, Taylor Swift. Robyn listened to it on repeat. A dreamy romantic song about love, waiting, and dreams. "It took you being erased for the pain in the ass I know to show up," he said.

"I think you annoyed me right from the start. That gave me permission to annoy you right back," I said, feeling in charge and delicious. Not the least bit nervous.

"No polite honeymoon stage, just right into 'put your own damn pants on.'"

"I don't know why you didn't get rid of me, find a dresser who would twinkle in your starlight." I wanted to hear him confess how much he liked me. I could feel it, but I wanted to hear it from his lips.

"I think you underestimate the Poppy Effect. You aren't as glitter-free as you make yourself out to be." I heard his voice change when he said that. It dropped, quieted, and it had the effect of an ocean breeze stroking the inside my brain.

I watched Travis pat Ryan on the back, and Jeffery fixed his hair in the reflection of the microwave, then Emilie messed it up.

"I'm not allowed to sleep here anymore. Thank you for letting me stay."

"I'll restock my gummies."

I elbowed him, and his fingers grazed my arm. Goose bumps rose, turning my emotions physical. I wondered if he could read the braille of my attraction. Neither of us pulled away.

"I can still put your pants on in the morning," I said, because I was flirting. Actually freaking flirting. I took his hand, remembered how it felt when he was sick with sweat, and again when I needed an anchor to go to sleep. I drew him near to me, fast enough so I wouldn't change my mind but slow enough for him to resist. He looked at my lips, the sexiest thing a man can do in my mind, as I shifted past and spoke into his ear. The intoxication of acting on desire for someone swept me along, created its own current of longing.

"When you're not the hero and I'm not your babysitter, could we get a cup of coffee outside of this trailer?"

"Whatever you want," he said, his mouth brushing my ear.

"Whatever I want," I said. A statement, not a question.

And with the perfect timing of a professional comic, his mustache tickled my temple, and I giggled. He held me in place, whispered, "Why are your hands wet?"

"I'm nervous. Wanting makes me sweaty."

"I want things too." He exhaled these words as if he'd been holding them in for some time, waiting for the right moment.

"I'm going to needle a lot of help. Just sew you know."

And oh my gosh, did he laugh at that.

ACKNOWLEDGMENTS

Instead of a book launch, I will have a party for the people who talked me down, walked me through, educated me, and said, "Okay, Ann, that's enough for now. Go lie down."

Some of you won't come, and why would you? You must be as sick of me and my book as I am. Some of you will come because, dammit, you deserve a wine cooler and a fig or two. We did it. We wrote a book.

To Rachel Ekstrom, my agent, I so appreciate your calm approach and healthy responses when I call. I usually wait until I'm frantic about something, and I love that you don't join my drama. My acquisition editor, Christopher Werner, knows a lot more about me than he bargained for, but he is a Wisconsin native, and he doesn't seem to mind that I am ten parts TMI and ten parts enthusiasm. I promise I will not keep bugging you. He got me started at Lake Union, and I am incredibly grateful. My current editor, Melissa Valentine, is the kind of editor who lets me work quietly and steadily. Our relationship is a new one, and I'm hoping it will get to the TMI stage too.

Thank you to Tiffany Yates Martin, my developmental editor, whose on-point editing skills are a magical divining rod for a story. My first reader, Christine DeSmet, gave me early confidence in this character and story, and every writer needs a Christine in their life.

An enormous thank-you to Valerie Zielonka and her husband, Richard Kuhn, who spent days talking and touring me through studios and costume departments. The stories! The details! I could not have written this book without them, and that is not an exaggeration. Through them, I met Mitzi Haralson, Jordanna Fineberg, Lori Harris, and Ellen Lutter. These hardworking, generous professionals who dress the stars with so little acknowledgment were open and welcoming. I geeked out about their meticulous jobs, and they smiled indulgently. I pretended I was one of them, and they didn't scoff at me, even once.

I have the kinds of friends who never read any early pages but know everything there is to know about my books. They let me talk endlessly about my characters and story as if it were nonfiction. Linda Wick, Tammy Scerpella, Annie McCormick, Lisa Roe, Jacquelyn Mitchard, Carolyn Bach, Samantha Hoffman—really, there are no words. Not even for me, and I am rarely without them.

My brothers, Raymond and Jonathan Wertz, you help me understand love and kindness. I love you.

And thank you to Julie, Meghan, and John. You are my lifeboat on the high seas of life. I am so little without you.

ABOUT THE AUTHOR

Ann Garvin, PhD, is the *USA Today* bestselling author of five funny and sad novels about people who do too much, in a world that asks too much from them. Ann teaches in the low-residency master of fine arts program at Drexel University and lives in Wisconsin with her anxious and overly protective dog, Peanut. She is the founder of the Tall Poppy Writers and is dedicated to helping authors find readers and vice versa. For more information visit www.anngarvin.net.